DEVILS HOLE

DEVILS HOLE

Bill Branon

HarperCollins*Publishers*

HarperCollins books may be purchased for educational, business, or sales promotional use. For information, please write: Special Markets Department, HarperCollins Publishers, Inc., 10 East 53rd Street, New York, NY 10022.

FIRST EDITION

Designed by Alma Hochhauser Orenstein

Library of Congress Cataloging-in-Publication Data

Branon, Bill.
  Devils hole / Bill Branon. — 1st ed.
    p. cm.
  ISBN 0-06-017760-8
  I. Title.
PS3552.R3253D48 1995
813'.54—dc20   95-6260

95 96 97 98 99 ❖/HC 10 9 8 7 6 5 4 3 2 1

. . . for Lolly,
. . . my Melody.

This divided personality [is] a symptom of a general unconsciousness that is the undeniable common inheritance of all mankind. . . . This identity takes a variety of forms . . . contemporary man is blind to the fact that his gods and demons have not disappeared at all. . . . A man likes to believe that he is the master of his soul. But . . .

—DR. CARL G. JUNG, *MAN AND HIS SYMBOLS*

Prologue

The killing lance punched into the chest of the Kiowa madman. Setangya's thrust was efficient. He drove the blade forward on a horizontal plane until it sliced through red muscle that knit white ribs together, then he quarter-turned the shaft so the spear tip was locked inside the bony cage. He forced the prey onto its back. The wooden shaft shook and rattled the bunched muscles of Setangya's forearms. He squared his naked shoulders, pushed down, and twisted his weapon deeper into the man on the sand.

The feel of life thrashing toward death on the end of a skewer was familiar to him. He had felt it as a boy when his narrow fishing gig found its mark in the silver riverfish, felt it as a young man in the violent recoil of the buffalo when the killing lance finished the work of the arrows, and felt it as a man in the years when the people of the Red Hills had come through the mist to steal and kill. Warriors and hunters knew the fury of life ending on the lance. Such a feeling was never forgotten.

The jolting contractions died away, and Setangya felt only the deep, muted beat of the other's heart as its rubbery bulk pulsed against the side of the wooden shaft inside the chest, the last fluttering of life's retreat.

Setangya crouched in the hollow of a shallow cave low on the face of a redstone cliff. He built a small fire of mesquite branches and watched the smoke rise into the night. Spirit shapes flickered behind tongues of flame, human faces turned in the plume of smoke, a dead claw of mesquite rotated on the red coals and reached toward him as fire-shadows cut silent patterns on the stone wall at his back. In the black night a gray wolf howled.

From the war belt of the beast he had killed he took the dried scalps of the four young ones, the children, and cast them one by one into the fire. The parched skin and long black strands of hair crackled in the flame and passed into the other world to make the lost spirits of the small ones whole again.

He roasted and ate the heart of the other. The renegade Kiowa would take no more from his people.

He dreamed that night of two things. The first, a small memory from the time he was a boy, a dream where prairie dogs stood on hind legs in the morning sun and played "catch-the-laugh" . . . one hurling a chirp to another and that one to another and so on until the call had passed through all their sand-mound town. It was an unimportant dream. The second dream was one that came each time he hunted as he had hunted on this day. In the second dream, he heard once more the elder speak words across a yellow fire.

"Each child will have its warrior . . . "

And in his sleep, Setangya knew a lonely pride.

1

The Difficult Year

A t the beginning of the year 1944, Arthur Arthur was six years old. He lived in the town of Wethersfield, Connecticut. He had a younger brother named David and David was four. Arthur's mother was a nurse and his father built houses. Arthur owned a black dog of unknown heritage, and the dog's name was Bonny.

The three teenagers, high school seniors, were driving a green pickup truck. They steered the truck close to Arthur over the brown shale that sloped down to the edge of Wethersfield Cove, nosed the truck slightly toward the water's edge so that Arthur had to stop walking, pinned him and his dog into a small space between the truck and the still, brown water of the cove.

Arthur heard the brittle plates of shale crack like breaking tile beneath the wheels of the pickup as it came to a stop.

"Hey, Red. Where you live?" From the one by the passenger-side window.

Arthur didn't reply, surprised by the sudden appearance of the truck. He bent slightly and put a small hand into the fur on the dog's neck. The pup's tail wagged at the sight of the new humans, and Arthur didn't want her to jump up on the side of the truck and put marks there.

Two boys, lean and hard, stepped out of the truck's cab from each side, and when the door on the cove side of the cab opened Arthur could see a girl smiling at him from the middle of the front seat. Arthur gave a quick smile back to her. With his free hand he made a small, tentative wave. She didn't wave back. She looked like the girls who came to stay with him when his mother and father went to the movies. Friendly, warm, someone to trust. But he hadn't seen any of these people before.

"Where you live?" . . . that one towered close to Arthur, and Arthur heard the shale grate under the feet of the other, the driver, who came around the back end of the truck.

"On Burbank Road. By the river." Arthur was afraid. He didn't like the eyes.

The second one was now also standing close, threatening, staring down at him. "Where'd he say, Gorsky?"

"Said by the river," from the first.

Arthur looked between them at the girl in the truck, tried to understand. She looked back, impassive, inert.

"What are you doing here?"

"Walking. Going to Stanley's."

"Who's Stanley?"

"My friend."

"How old are you, boy?"

"Be seven in the summer."

Now the driver leaned against the truck, fingers meshed, elbow on the bed edge, watching.

The first one continued to talk. "I don't know, Slick, looks like he don't like us. You scared, kid?"

"No." Lying now. Holding onto his dog. Pup whining to greet the newcomers . . . pulling forward against Arthur's hand to lick and greet.

"I don't think you're supposed to be down here. You supposed to be down here?" Again from the one called Gorsky . . . squatting now, eyes on a level with Arthur's.

"I can be here."

"I'll say where you can be."

Arthur's eyes flicked over Gorsky's head, looked up at the girl in the front seat, looked for some kind of help. The girl had swung partly around so she was turned toward Arthur. She had moved her legs apart, one foot still on the cab floor, the other foot up on the seat, that knee bent and resting against the passenger-side seatback. Her blue skirt rode high on the raised knee and Arthur saw the white strip of panties that covered her between her legs. The one called Gorsky looked over his shoulder at the girl, then slowly back at Arthur. Gorsky was smiling, but Arthur saw it wasn't a good smile.

"What you looking at, boy?"

Arthur dissolved back into the snakelike eyes of the person crouching before him and didn't say anything, didn't know what they wanted him to say.

"You looking at her beaver, boy?" Half-turning back to the girl, eyes flicking from Arthur to her, then back to Arthur. "Hey, Janet! This here shit-boy is looking at your beaver."

At first, Arthur wasn't sure he knew what they were talking about. He was six years old, an average boy from an average family living in a typical small New England town. The boy, the family, the town . . . no more, no less sophisticated than the age demanded. But he made the connection. He had looked between the girl's legs, had seen her underwear, and somehow they had known he had seen her underwear. They said what he saw was a beaver. The animal image of a beaver on a riverbank log jumped into his mind, an image from the yellow zoo book his father had given him when he was learning words. But the word now meant something else. It meant two things. "Damn, boy! You know it ain't right to look at a girl's beaver? You know that?"

"I'm sorry."

"Sorry, boy? Sorry!?! What do you think, Slick?" Eyes still on Arthur. "You think we should tell the police about this shit-boy?"

The one called Slick looked serious, nodded his head.

Arthur looked back at the girl in confusion, hoping for a reason.

"There, boy! Goddamn it! You did it again!"

Arthur felt tears sting the lower edges of his eyes. He heard the girl giggle, but didn't dare look up again. He pulled the pup's head close against his leg.

The one called Gorsky stared at Arthur for a long moment. The eyes hardened. "Your daddy rich, boy?"

Arthur didn't know how to answer.

"You think we should call the police on you?"

Arthur shook his head. Then his eyes locked onto the muzzle of a single-barreled shotgun Slick casually lifted from the bed of the truck. The dark hole of the bore floated inches from Arthur's face, centered his attention, stopped his breathing.

Gorsky snickered maliciously. "Got any money, shit-boy?"

Arthur used his free hand to remove two quarters from the pocket of his shorts. He held the money out to Gorsky.

"What you gonna do with them?"

"For comic books. For Captain Marvel. Superman."

"They's ten cents, boy. You got too much money."

"For Stanley's mom. For sodas. Grape sodas." Eyes on the gun.

"Little rich shit." Gorsky took the quarters. "Little rich shits don't need more comics. This all you got?"

"Yes, sir."

The one called Slick reached again into the bed of the pickup and took out a length of rope, rope like Arthur's mother used to hang clothes on in the back yard. Slick flipped the rope to Gorsky. "Think that there dog needs some running."

Gorsky fingered the rope. Smiled. "I believe you're right. Dog needs some running."

Arthur watched as Gorsky roughly pulled the pup away, watched as the teenager tied a loop around the dog's neck. Slick trotted around the back of the truck and got behind the wheel. The one called Gorsky climbed into the cab, transferring the free end of the rope through the open window to his other hand as he closed the truck door. Arthur looked up at the mean face above him.

"We're going to get the police on you, boy. You hear that?"

Fear lifted a soft bile to the back of Arthur's throat. The truck started up.

Arthur ran after the truck, ran as fast as he could. The brown shale crunched and clicked beneath his feet. Slippery. Shifting. He said no words.

The truck moved away from him. The small dog, now off its feet, twisted around on the cruel shale, rolled over and over like some rag on a long tow line pulled behind a moving boat. Around and around. Legs folded and useless. Pieces of fur, then skin, dressed the sharp shale in a random paste. Arthur saw these bits of his dog on the mean slate through eyes going blind in a wash of hot, salty tears. As he ran, his mind flashed pictures at him, sparks of memory: of Bonny running at him after school; of her asleep on the end of his bed; of her glowing eyes at the bottom of the stairs on Christmas morning a few months ago, eyes that frightened him at first, froze him as he looked down where black fur blended into darkness at the base of the staircase . . . down where the dark made the eyes float.

Arthur ran and ran. He could not close the distance as the truck crackled over the shale, ever out of his reach. He ran after the thing tied to the rope, the thing that had taught him love.

He stumbled down, exhausted and crying with no sound. The truck stopped after he fell. When Arthur couldn't get up, couldn't move anymore except to gasp air and make tears that rolled on hard surfaces, the rope end was cast off.

The dog didn't move. It lay motionless in the filmy distance. Arthur tried to go to it, but the fatigue was total. He only put his head down onto the flats of rock and tried for air. As his face shuddered against gritty slabs of stone, he learned the taste of shale . . . and something more.

I I I

People who live in Texas say there is no heat like that of a West Texas August afternoon. Folks in middle Georgia speak of summer air so heavy with humidity and temperature that bugs walk on it. South Florida souls hunt words to describe how estival sun reflecting off white building fronts at noon can cook bone. In midday July, downtown New York cynics defile prose as skin meets vinyl in baked, black vehicles parked where shade doesn't go, where car windows wait closed up all the way against ugly possibilities, where steering wheels sauté fingertips.

But try central Connecticut during that three-day stretch in July every other year when air stops moving and rearview mirrors fall off the inside glass of windshields; when dogs lie on white cement in shadows, half-foot of tongue bathed in slather that ants drink; when fan blades push tepid currents across glistening, oily human flesh.

"I want to take my shoes off."

"Leave them on. You'll lose them."

"Mom!"

"Leave them on, Arthur."

"But Mom."

"They'll get lost under the bleachers, sweetheart. If they fall down there we can't get them."

"Jeeze."

"Show your brother the elephants. Here."

"Look at this one," Arthur said. Program page folded back.

"Yeah. Where's elephants?"

"Pretty soon. A whole bunch." Arthur pointed. "Right down there."

"Where?"

"Down there."

"It's hot," Arthur complained.

No reply.

"Mom, I'm hot."

"Look at the clowns."

"I want to take my shirt off."

"Give it here. Do you want to take your shirt off too, David?"

"Yeah. Here."

"Dave. Over there."

"Where?"

"Over there," Arthur said. "See? Tigers. In those things. Why are they doing that, Mom?"

"They're making a place for the tigers to come in. They put the cages like that so the tigers can come. Like a tunnel. To the big cage there. See the lady? The lady can make the tigers do tricks. Show your brother."

"Tigers do tricks, Dave. In there."

"Where?"

"That big round thing."

"Yeah."

"Look at the lady and the man, Arthur."

"Where?"

"Right here in front. That middle circle. Right there."

"Up that rope, Dave. Look how high she is!"

"She'll fall off!"

"They do tricks up there," Arthur said.

"Trapeze," their mother pointed out. "Those are the trapeze people."

"Trapeze. Look, Dave."

"Yeah."

"See the man?"

"Yeah."

SPECIAL TO A.P. DATELINE: HARTFORD, CONN. 6 JUL 1944

"Mom. Why is she doing that?"

"Oh my God!"

"Why is she screaming, Mom?"

"David! Get up!"

"Mom. She's jumping off!"

*BULLETIN * * * BULLETIN * * * BULLETIN SOURCE:* STAFF POOL HARTFORD COURANT HTFD. CONN.

TO: NATIONAL WIRE

COMT/RTE: SPECIAL BULLETIN ALL IMMEDIATE

"Don't let go! This hand, Arthur! This hand!"

"Mom!"

"Leave it there, David!"

"Arthur?"

"It's on fire, Dave. See up there?"

"God, NO!" their mother screamed. "Don't let go!"

"Why are they throwing things? . . . chairs?"

"Don't let go!"

HARTFORD CONN STOP FIRE SWEEPS RINGLING BROS MAIN TENT THIS P.M. STOP MASSIVE CASUALTIES FIRE/STAMPEDE STOP INFO. FATALS: HARTFORD HOSPITAL/ST. FRANCIS HOSPITAL/MCCOOK HOSPITAL HARTFORD CONN STOP ESTIMATE FATALS 100 PLUS STOP HOLD LINE OPEN STOP MORE STOP

"That man hit that lady!"

"Push, Arthur! Push them!" from their mother. "David! Get up! Don't let go!"

"Mommy!"

"GOD! David, don't fall down. I've got to hold David!"

"Hold him, Mom!"

"Arthur?" "ARTHUR!" "ARTHUR!"

HARTFORD CONN STOP NEED POOL AUGMENT ASAP STOP ALL SOURCE STOP

"Get out! Get out of the way, kid! MOVE!"

"Mister . . . "

Arthur took the full weight of the swinging fist on the left side of his face. The blow was so solid and ferocious that it knocked Arthur out of both his shoes. One of his low-cut sneakers twisted high into the air.

They were all under a bowl of flame. The canvas, a parabolic reflector in its shape, concentrated the radiation onto the boil of humanity jamming the tent floor where the three huge supporting poles centered the three circus rings. The crowd-brain saw only the two large exits at either end of the flaming tent, and in seconds the exists were packed.

A few souls, driven by desperation or intelligence, looked for an alternative and found it in the open riser faces on which the banks of chairs were set. These few rolled through that opening, dropped the many or few feet to the area under the grandstand and scrambled toward the skirt where the tent met the ground. Once beneath that, they were outside.

Arthur Arthur, senses refocused after the crushing blow to his face, did not realize he could escape through the risers. But he saw no chance in going down into the panic that surged on the tent floor. The instinct of a seven-year-old boy made him move away from the larger humans who struggled in terror under the flames. He ran back up the bleacher steps where only a few adults sat, some holding bewildered children, entranced, as though they were watching a movie. But the heat was ferocious, ever greater the higher he climbed.

At the top of the steps, where the tent top met the tent sidewall thirty-five feet above the earth, sat an enormous man. The image of that person would be forever etched on Arthur's brain. Small pig-eyes; sweat-soaked white shirt open at the collar; lavender necktie pulled almost apart and slewed to one side; tan pants plastered over three huge rolls of belly fat and pinched in at the top by a barely visible brown belt. White sleeves rolled up above the elbows. Tufts of light-colored hair splayed out from little round ears.

Arthur stopped next to the big man, who occupied the last seat next to the row of steps.

"How's it going, Red?" A gentle smile among the rivers of facial sweat.

Arthur slowly sat down on the topmost riser. He didn't say anything in reply, and his eyes moved from the man back to the maelstrom on the circus floor.

The flaming dome was almost completed. An edge of fire walked down the last of the roof canvas, almost upon them.

Arthur moved closer to the man and rested his elbow on the fat knee next to him.

"Here." The fat one leaned back, fished a pocketknife from his left pants pocket. Arthur watched him pry open the blade with a neat fingernail. The man turned and pushed the knife into the thick canvas. It was a sharp knife. The man sawed at the material and the fabric slowly parted in a long slit.

The flames were very close.

Using both hands, that quiet one spread the edges of the opening apart, then placed a foot on the lower border to make it wider.

"There you go."

Arthur stuck his head out of the opening. Sweet air, hot in fact, but cool in comparison, rushed into his lungs. Down below, where tent met grass, Arthur saw a line of servicemen, eight of them, navy whites, Dixie cup hats, in line and holding up the tent skirt so people who had dropped through the riser openings could crawl out. The raised tent skirt formed a curve that Arthur could jump into.

"Go on, kid."

Arthur pulled his head back inside and looked into the man's eyes. "You going to jump too?"

"Me?" The fat man snorted. "I'd break my damn neck."

Their eyes held.

"Go on, Red. Hit the air."

"No."

"No? All right. You first."

"Coming?"

"Sure."

Arthur moved out on the edge of the opening.

"Hey, Red."

Arthur saw a smile.

"Give 'em hell, kid."

And Arthur jumped.

"Jesus! Chief! Chief! Get this kid!"

Strong hands spun him around, shoved him.

"Run, kid. Get the hell out of here."

Arthur stumbled at the push, then regained his balance. He looked up and saw flames chewing up the peeling edges of the dark slit.

I   I   I

He was barefoot. No shirt. Only his blue shorts.

To get away from the tent he had to walk through a tangle of briars, then climb over a rusted barbed-wire fence, and he was cut on the bottoms of both feet. He'd walked across the roofs of five cars that were packed tightly in a grass parking lot, and he saw the red marks his feet left on the hot metal car tops. He went through the lot out to the sidewalk. Down the street to his left, he spied the big elm tree that marked the place where his mother had parked their car. He found the car in the lot. He expected to find his mother and David there. He waited by the vehicle.

He stood on the rise of roots beneath the big tree and looked back at the tent across the road. Shreds of black canvas flapped and disintegrated in what remained of the horrible firestorm. As he watched, the tall center pole of the circus carcass began to heel. The giant spar hung for a few, slow seconds in the falling, checked in its travel by some last, invisible restraint. Then it began to move again. Accelerating through a bursting swirl of black fragments, it crashed all the way down.

As the pole fell, Arthur heard the sound . . . the most striking memory he would take from that brutal day . . . a sound like that of a strong, sad wind moving across the mouth of a deep cave, a sound of such utter and overwhelming despair that it froze everything that moved between him and it. Everything and every person there seemed to stop in that eerie moment. At first Arthur didn't know what made that sound. Everyone should have been out.

Then it came to him.

That sound came from human beings, from people still inside, from people injured too badly to move but alive. People trampled. People broken. People staying with hurt-people . . . people still in there when the thing came down.

❙ ❙ ❙

Arthur heard his brother long before he saw him. They came around the corner of the first row of cars. They walked toward him.

David howled the whole length of the lot. Never seemed to inhale . . . a straight-ahead, high-pitched, steady, unwavering scream of pain. Their mother walked beside his brother. Bent over, black arms holding the boy up. Hair not there on her head, only a dust, like a soot-colored cap. A strange wrinkled coating seemed pasted on her back. The remnants of her rayon blouse.

And smoke, or was it some kind of steam, came up from her.

He saw that David's shirt wasn't blackened, did not look like his mother's back. Wondered for a second, then realized his mother must have bent over David all that while, shielded him. But one of his brother's shoulders had not been covered. The left one. And it was melted off, melted at a flat angle that took that shoulder's curve away. As they passed by him, Arthur looked into the burn and saw ripples and rough, curled things, saw a surface that looked much like the gnarled bark on the pine tree they climbed in their back yard.

They went right past Arthur. Right past the car. Where they were going he did not know. Neither seemed to even see him. He started to say something but they just kept walking away.

So he stayed by the tree in a city he did not live in.

❙ ❙ ❙

Trucks came. Dump trucks with dirt in them like the ones that rumbled back and forth along the riverbank by their house.

Arthur had watched all the people running and yelling and trying to do things for over an hour. He saw the ambulances with the red lights on top, some Army trucks, even two of the long, black cars that his mother once told him carried dead people to the cemetery. But he could see burned people still alive being put into one of those long cars when it stopped at the edge of the street that was near him.

URGENT/*REPEAT*/URGENT: ALL AVAILABLE TRANSPORT CODE 10 TO AREA SEVEN. *REPEAT*: MULTIPLE CODE 10 TO AREA SEVEN

A large dump truck came into the lot where Arthur was and, in the lane between the cars, dumped its load of black dirt onto the ground. The truck made jerking, backward stops that caused the open dump gate to clank against the raised-up bed so leftover dirt fell out. Arthur wondered where the truck was going because he had seen two others do the same thing in the lot across the road.

Arthur guessed that his mother and brother wouldn't be back soon, so he decided to follow the truck into the field where the wreckage of the tent smoldered.

For the next forty-five minutes Arthur wandered among ordered rows of burned humans, some still moving, some not; some with eyes open and fixed, some with eyes that would blink and roll; some with arms frozen and raised to the sky as they lay on their backs, some with arms in that same position but whose charred fingers moved a bit; some big bodies, some little bodies . . . all in a sensible pattern, lined up by someone in charge, lined up and part of that grisly horizontal fraternity waiting for a ride to the hospital in dump trucks because that was all that was left to take them.

Living would ride with dead because nobody in this field could tell them apart.

Arthur watched as the truck he had followed was loaded with victims, thirteen blackened forms carefully lifted and placed side by side down the center line of the bed. He could see that at least one of them was still alive, chest moving beneath a fissured, dark crust. The truck started up with a clattering roar and moved off. An image floated in Arthur's mind of those bodies being dumped out onto the ground somewhere so doctors could work on them . . . dumped out like the dirt.

HARTFORD CONN STOP RINGLING BROS. CIRCUS FIRE STOP APPROX 160 FATALS STOP APPROX 500 INJURED STOP CAUSE UNKNOWN STOP TENT

TREATED WITH PARAFFIN/OIL MIX TO WATERPROOF VS RAIN STOP 50%
RINGLING FIRE CREW IN BOSTON FOR RED SOX BASEBALL GAME STOP

Arthur turned around as the truck drove away and was surprised to find himself looking into the face of a clown who knelt on
the ground beside him staring after the truck. There was a bucket of
water on the grass beside the clown. A rag was draped over the edge
of the bucket, and a fly walked on a stain on the rag.

Arthur looked at the clown's face and saw real tears glitter on
painted tears.

I I I

He knew his address. Had known how to say it for the last four
years. That gave him confidence.

The sun was low on the tops of houses to the west when Arthur
left that place. A tall man with yellow papers on a blue pad had told
him to go away when he saw Arthur lean over one of the bodies to
see what the smoke coming up smelled like.

Many people still wandered in and around the area. New ones
came to look, others left. Some of those cried and wiped at their eyes
with soot-streaked handkerchiefs. Some sat on the ground and
stared. It appeared to Arthur that the fire had used up all the helpers
from the city. No one seemed to want to take charge of him. He liked
that part, but his feet were hurting and he wished that someone
could get him a pair of shoes. He had seen a pair of sneakers about
his size on the ground near a bloody sheet, but they were charred. He
knew those wouldn't be comfortable.

Arthur went back to the street. He crossed to the parking lot
again to see if his mother had come back to the car.

No.

He walked slowly on the warm sidewalks of the city. Barefoot.
No shirt. Red, curving scratches and black carbon smears patterned
his torso. After he had walked a mile, he came to a crossing where he
waited for the light to change. As he stood on the curb, a blue and
white city bus stopped in front of him. The door folded open with a
squeak and a puff of air. He looked up at the brown-skinned driver.
The man had short, gray-black, curly hair and wore a blue-gray uniform, a short-peaked bus driver's cap. Arthur could not tell how old

the driver was because he wasn't good at those things . . . he thought the driver not very old.

"Step up here, boy."

Arthur did as he was told and when he was standing in the bus he could see about twenty people sitting in the seats . . . looking at him. Arthur rested his hand self-consciously on the token machine.

"In the fire?"

"Yes, sir."

"Where your folks at?"

"Don't know."

"Where you live, son?"

Arthur gave the man his address. The house in Wethersfield was twelve miles out of Hartford by the river. Arthur watched two tears, one from each eye, curve down the dark brown skin at the same speed, one in pace with the other.

"Feet hurt?"

"Yeah." Looking down. "Lost my shoes."

He remembered how the crazy man had hit him in the face.

"Sit there, boy. You got neighbors can help you?"

Arthur nodded.

The man drove the bus out of the city, far off its assigned route. He took Arthur to the house by the river, took him right to the front door.

And no one said a thing. Except for one woman who came up and sat beside him and held him in her arms.

At eight o'clock in the evening, on the last day of August in that same year, a pickup truck parked beneath the overhang of a dark brown boathouse that belonged to the Wethersfield Cove Boat Club. The boathouse was the largest structure on the edge of the cove with the exception of a massive stone presence, that of the Connecticut State Prison brooding impassively on the south shore.

A brutal summer lightning storm tore sudden, violent holes in the black sky, thunder grumbled and banged, and the land flickered under random, stroboscopic bursts of mean, white flare. Thick walls of rain rattled over the shale and stalked across the waters of the cove. Tree limbs twisted, writhed in the confusion of wind.

In the truck cab, on the inside surface of the windshield, small beads of moisture formed and ran, condensed against glass that was colder than the smothering, humid air lifting from the flesh of the young couple sprawled across the front seat.

"That's it, baby . . . go for it, don't stop." His head pressing back against the driver side door. His legs apart. His naked back arching upward. Her head pumping with sultry, rhythmic insistence above his midsection.

"Oh, yeah, Janet. Harder, baby, harder."

She lengthened the travel of her sliding supplications, rolled her tongue against him inside her mouth, sealed her full lips more tightly around the pulsing flesh.

Rain swept across the metal hood of the truck, the only part of the vehicle unprotected by the overhang of the boathouse. The irregular tempo of the rain surges beating on the engine cover prodded and magnified the passions of the two within. The girl raised her right leg, moved it to the outside of his left leg, then lowered her heated sex parts to press against the hardness presented by his shin. She crushed and shoved herself against his lower leg, struggled with the disconcerting intensity of working his excitement and her own. She overtook and passed his passion, began her surrender to the giddy, charging, electric rush that boiled past her resolve and through her hips. She curved away from him, left his wet pleasure in cold air, her spine contracting in a feast of ecstacy, going upright onto her knees, arms straight, head raised and back.

"Slick . . . oh, Christ, Slick!" Husky, guttural sounds.

As Janet's fiery orgasm rode hard over her senses, in that fervid instant, the windshield exploded into the cab. Shards of thick glass flew and struck and cut at fabric and skin. Cold, wet outside air burst through the hole that gaped in the center of the glass, and a rock rumbled slowly off the hood of the truck. As she stared in shocked confusion through the opening, a brilliant flash of lightning froze the facing hillside. Through pupils yet dilated by fierce passion, her brain snapped a picture of the outside world. The dead-still mural painted by the lightning's blaze was etched in crisp relief. There on the hill, beneath a great oak whose thrashing branches splayed without motion in the white strobe of that great spark, was a human figure. A small boy. Arms at his side. Coat wet and dark. Looking down at the truck through the somber drops of rain.

The world went black again. Pitch black. And when the next hot flash of lightning blazed, the figure on the hill was gone.

2

Kid Stuff

Arthur Arthur turned the rented Chevrolet Caprice to the right and moved up the off-ramp. The rise of the road and what remained of his freeway momentum pushed him down in the seat as the car angled up. He sensed the tickle in his lower back muscles at the new pressure. Arthur registered the sensation and the thought came again that he'd like to try driving a familiar stretch of road like this completely blindfolded, picking his way along by the sound and feel of the drunk-bumps, the crunch of roadside sand, and the subtle lift of the freeway exit road. A persistent, gentle challenge. The thought teased him with its whispering danger. Like the siren feeling that came over him in high places.

He came to a full stop at the road sign, then turned left and went across the freeway overpass. The ramp access merged with a narrow blacktop ribbon that wound through oak, birch, and even a few surviving elm trees, genetic rebels that made it through the Dutch elm scourge. He drove past old but fresh-looking two-story houses. The New England architecture familiar from his early days in Connecticut triggered a bittersweet nostalgia. Behind those white-painted clapboard walls he could picture the layout of high-ceilinged rooms where children played and plotted and imagined and built. Pantries, old stoves. Rich, dark, silent, even scary interiors cut through by hallways of shiny, buckled, wide-planked pine. Kitchens where mothers bent down to look inside ovens, kitchens where burned-brown pot holders lifted deep-dish baked apples that floated plump raisins in juice hot enough to stop the hungriest kitchen pirate. Pastel Hummel prisoners incarcerated in glass-bellied cabinets along with old-generation photographs, amber images, not looked at . . . as much a part of the house as the front door, trinkets and ghosts sometimes more alive than the people who lived there. Rooms with real fireplaces that burned real wood almost every winter night, fireplaces that during the day exhaled pungent aromas that mingled with the diesel smell of ancient oil burners in cellars a person could stand up in . . . cellars where water seeped and mice ran and monsters stared from behind old boxes.

The town he was driving into was not his town, the town of his childhood, but in a real sense he was home.

Arthur looked around his room at Hodges' Bed and Breakfast. A wide bed. Neatly made up, soft pillows placed by a compulsive house artist. One window, small-paned, sash-weighted . . . paintbrush marks etched for eternity in the white horizontal of the sill. Flawless white gauze curtains. Quilted comforter. Darkwood dresser next to an oak table sporting a small television set whose antenna wires spaghettied onto the rug, out of place, unnatural in this pristine period piece. A bathroom you could take to the Home Show. Fat blue bar of soap. Fragrant. Logo focused. Unused.

"Will this do, Mr. Chandler?"

"It's very nice, Mrs. Hodges." Arthur set his suitcase on the floor. He was impressed. "You keep it nice."

"One week is all? Like you to stay longer. Not much trade 'til the summer people get here."

He hadn't heard the term "summer people" in a long time. Words from the past, his past. Words owned by the old families, natives, folks numbed by the sudden popularity of Southern New England shoreline towns. These old souls who, if not yet hardened and defensive and resentful, seemed genuinely and perpetually confused by it all.

Arthur removed his shoes and sat on the edge of the bed. He would stretch out on the thing but felt intimidated by the prim delicacy of his surroundings. Small, blue flecks of flower on white wallpaper loitered in sterile, stoic rows.

Instead, he put his suitcase across his lap, popped it open, and lifted out the contents. With the suitcase emptied, he slipped the edge of a nail file into the lining where it joined the sidewall and pried up a Velcro-sealed partition revealing a Glock 17 auto pistol nested next to its seventeen-shot magazine and two boxes of nine-millimeter Parabellum bullets. He snapped back the slide and checked the receiver chamber for dust and lint. The oil-sheened surface was clean. He replaced the pistol and resealed the Velcro. He arranged his clothing in the dresser and in a closet lined with cedar. He put his toilet articles in the bathroom on the sink shelf and grouped them in orderly fashion. He stripped off his clothes and looked at himself in the full-length mirror that was mounted on the inside of the bathroom door. Fifty-seven years of face looked back. Short-cropped sandy hair made the ears seem too prominent, made them appear to flare forward almost like canine ears, even to the subtle arch in their top turns. Sharply defined blue eyes glittered, eyes that didn't simply look at things but flickered and focused in the instant. They were alert eyes . . . haunting . . . etched in sharp relief by wrinkles that time insisted on . . . alive with something that, in a superficial moment, might be interpreted as fear, but which, in a next bit of time, showed as something unequivocally opposite. Hard neck muscles ran down in skin tunnels like silk-covered cables. The freckled forearms were dressed by a soft pelt of fine bronze hair curved like drawn filament in the glow of the electric light. The only suggestion of his years was the skin at each side of his waist; his stomach, though, was flat, cut firm in flesh more leather than cotton.

There were defects. A four-legged scar formed a star cross in his left cheek beneath the eye. The front center of his left thigh was cross-hatched as though it had been pressed by some great weight, and the flesh there was indelibly speckled black with minute particles, as from a gunpowder blast.

He had no smell. No lotion smell. No cigarette smell. No lingering aura of sweat.

A light stubble dressed his chin since it was late in the day and he'd driven through interminable traffic jams on the way from the airport north of Hartford, on a road torn up and being built for the last ten years.

He said his name at the mirror. "Arthur." The sound of his voice was low, deep, just a fraction above a rasp. It cracked when he spoke that single word.

He got into the shower. Hot water ran down his chest and swirled into a polished drain in the tiled floorpan, disappeared into a brass shine that spoke to the pride and perhaps to some homey guilt that spun soft webs in Mrs. Hodges. He closed his eyes in the steamy torrent and concentrated on the harsh, prickling sensation that plump, hot drops tattooed on his pale skin. The sound of rushing water pushed into his brain and he remembered the rains.

He heard again the hard staccato sound of a Mekong downpour on poncho-halves strung together in the treeline. Monsoon. A bashing, raucous, unremitting, smothering fall of water. Fat drops, hard drops. Big and chilling in the tepid, tropical heat. Heavy drops. Thickly persistent. Chunks of water that turned dust to soup, mud to quicksand, hope to despair. Drops that called up every kind of bloodsucking, skin-chewing, testicle-piercing crawdaddy from the black ooze. Drops that floated green vipers in the FNG's face and made that fucking new guy scream when no one else breathed. Bloated, obscene drops that brought sudden, palpable detestation.

Not always detested.

Not when you were pinioned by fear in Charlie's back yard. Not when the dogs were there and the nasty little man in black pajamas walked grid through the dark bush. Not when rancid stuff ran up from your stomach and bathed your back teeth in slippery acid. Not then. Then the rain was God.

Arthur drove to a seafood restaurant later that evening, a small, wooden-walled eatery down on the Saybrook docks where the wide line of river met the dark perpendicular of Long Island Sound. He ate his meal of crab salad and white chowder in a room half-full of softly speaking strangers. Along the inboard wall of that place was an old, neon-banked jukebox, a garish, real-time metaphor that harvested vertically stored memories from its cache of fifties sound.

Occasionally a diner, older or wanting to be older, got up and went over to the stolid machine, pushed down on the large, square, red-lit buttons. B-5. E-3. D-1. The selector mechanism would go into a stalking slide. Vibrate into position. Move to the code. Move with wire-trailing dignity to a place it had moved thousands of times before. Like a person remembering. It would pause on a ratchet tooth, remove a slice of that other decade. A decade of parades and malts. Of kids who slept with a baseball laced into the pocket of a neat's-foot-soaked mitt all pressed beneath a pillow and that itself beneath a dreaming head full of line-drive-ending leaps. A decade of two-handed set shots, of reel mowers shoved through thick, sweet grass, of teachers who attacked knuckles with rulers and whose opinion counted. A decade of heavy black Pontiacs, quick Fords, back seats and chaperones; of Saturday night stock car races with castor oil and burned rubber barging the senses. A decade of small, faded flowers pressed between the pages of velvet-covered dance books. Of girls who sock-danced with other girls in custard-smelling cafeterias while boys watched, shuffled, told stories, and grew self-conscious. A time when watches needed winding and ladies wore hats on Sunday and high school girls wriggled into garters trailing hard-rubber clips to keep stockings right under pleated dresses. A time when dogs were let out at night to trot and sniff and socialize and not return until dawn and no one thought it should be different. And cats were careful.

A time when mothers laughed and danced in kitchens with the baby on one arm, cooked biscuits, wrapped leftovers in wax paper, sealed summer things in winter jars ... then stole a bit of cooking sherry in the private corner of an afternoon.

And boys fought with fists. Girls with words. When the most feared gang in town wore Cub Scout blue and yellow.

Arthur Arthur sat alone by a window that jutted out into the night over the river's edge ... a window that carefully mimed every move of his hand, every empty look he directed toward the shifting surface of black, moving water. The old jukebox popped his brain without mercy. Memory ran up the heels of memory. Other diners murmured low sounds, laughed, chatted with the waitress. But the man in the window kept silent, moved with him, returned each glance, stared when he stared, kept hitting him in the face with the fact that this dining companion wasn't much into conversation.

Back in his room he removed a folded news clipping from his billfold. He flattened the paper by running it over the edge of the nightstand and looked at the face that centered the article. The face was unremarkable except for the hint of a cocky smirk drifting at one corner of the mouth. The newsprint summarized the history of Richard Alton Doubleton. Stolen car at age fifteen, given four years in a youth corrections center. Escaped thirteen months later, recaptured with a year tacked onto his sentence. Assaulted a guard in the federal prison camp at Boron. Transferred to the prison at Lompoc, California. Twenty-one days after his release, he sadistically beat an itinerant worker in a rented room in Compton, California. After pummeling the man for three hours, Doubleton sprayed lighter fluid on the victim and set him on fire. The man died two days later, but not before he identified his assailant. Doubleton did two years on a manslaughter charge. Six months after serving his time, Doubleton was recaptured after abducting, raping, and sodomizing a twelve-year-old girl west of Yuma. Unfortunately, the crime was committed on the California side of the state line. The crime drew national attention because Doubleton sliced off the girl's right breast, hacked off her right hand, and dumped her in the desert to die. She didn't die. Seven and one-half years later he was released on a technical appeal. Upon his release, the powers-that-be tried to establish him in a town in northern California, but word got out. In the face of rabid local pressure, he was moved to a location out of state. In Gainesville, Florida, ten months later, another child, this time an eight-year-old boy, was attacked in similar fashion. Doubleton, with no breast to sever, instead took off the victim's penis. The mutilated youngster survived. Doubleton was identified by the youngster's description and by fingerprints. Then Doubleton vanished.

But Mr. Doubleton had another problem. He was a good friend of heroin.

The article was written when a drug dealer by the name of Lurch Mukes was busted in Paterson, New Jersey, six months after the Gainesville mutilation. The news story recapped the adventures of Doubleton as filler to the incident of Mukes's arrest because Mr. Mukes, in typical dime-dropping desperation, had informed the New Jersey authorities that he thought one of his "customers" was Doubleton. The information made the news, but nothing came of it. Nothing came of it because nobody wanted to bargain. Sending a local dealer to the slammer was more "important" that week in Paterson than nailing an out-of-state pervert. It was vote-hunting season.

Arthur had been given the news article as part of a package passed to him by an intermediary contacted by the father of the Gainesville boy . . . a father willing to pay big for simple, final resolutions.

Arthur was a hunter. Independent. Skilled. Unfettered by convention. One who moved beyond legal delicacies.

Lurch Mukes had served in Vietnam, a Speedy-Four pushing paper in Saigon. A place, no doubt, where Mukes established a working knowledge of things injectable. Arthur had spent his share of time in Saigon on R & R breaks, or I & I to the bush-folk . . . I & I as in Intercourse and Intoxication. With this bit of common history, Arthur figured he could loosen up Mukes, if he could find him.

Finding was easy.

Mukes's military record had worked to secure an early parole. The man was still in Paterson . . . still in Paterson because he was hooked to a halfway house there . . . and because his heroin-dependent clientele needed tending.

Over white rum and sea stories Mukes was given to talk. He told Arthur something he hadn't told anyone else. Mukes possessed that eerie, street-bred sixth sense ever confounding to the best of narcs, the capacity to peg a man in seconds as non-fed. Some bills, some memories, some eye-to-eye, some more white rum. What he told Arthur was that Doubleton wanted to get connected up north, needed a name in the Connecticut River area on the Sound. Someone dependable. Someone who didn't ask questions. Someone who sold but didn't use. Users could roll when things got tight and the monkey howled.

Mukes gave Arthur a name. And a place.

In a small, red-painted tavern on the other side of the river, close by the great arching bridge, Arthur found Doubleton's new connection. Doubleton's dealer was tending bar.

Sitting at a table back from the light, Arthur watched the man build drinks for old clamdiggers, winter tourists, and college boys who came in from the sun with sideways looks and nervous feet.

Some of those, mostly the pale-skinned college boys, didn't even bother with the pretense of ordering drinks. They would talk to the man, pass money in a folded newspaper or bit of napkin, then with a quick and phony handshake take the pass. Arthur was depressed by the lack of cover. Try that in L.A. and they'd be in so deep they'd need sunlight pumped in.

Arthur played the winter beach drunk. A lost, dyspeptic soul, doer of crossword puzzles, in hiding from harpy wife. Five days he sat until he blended with the oars and wooden seagulls on the wall. Slowly sipping drinks, studying his pencil, twisting small, giraffelike creatures into existence from accumulated cocktail straws. Trying to make them stand. They would do that thing for a while, but then the legs would straighten and they would topple over into the small lakes of moisture that glistened on the black Formica tabletop. Once Arthur made four of them and bent their heads down around a flat of wet to make it look like they were drinking from a water hole on his plastic Serengeti.

Roy was the pusher's name. On a hook, back near the restroom, Roy hung an old field jacket. Bits of white thread, like anorexic worms, spiraled from the shoulder seams on both sides where old unit insignias were torn off. Arthur looked at the patch outlines closely when he went to use the urinal, which he did frequently, a drink-carrying exercise that gave him the chance to pour gin and tonic down the drain and put water in its place. He drank some gin and tonic, but not too much. Just enough to make himself look real. The faded tracings held no clue for him, no burned-in shape to tell where Roy did his time, if indeed the jacket was his own and not trade bait from a pogue ground-pounder.

On the afternoon of day five, he watched Doubleton come in. The man had grown a full beard and shaved back an already receding hairline. But two twisted upper front teeth betrayed the effort . . . those and the genetic smirk that twisted in the thick, mouth-side tendrils of beard.

This one was more careful. He sat and ordered beer and smoked a cigarette. Another beer and two more cigarettes. Once, with a quick, slippery turn, Doubleton looked at Arthur for long seconds. Assessing. Wondering. A guarded but hostile stare. And abruptly turned to finish the second beer. The man paid for the drinks. From where Arthur sat he couldn't see the bills cross the bar, but he figured Doubleton was being severely overcharged for the amount of beer consumed. Back came the change. Lumped-up bills. Tenting some small bit of tube. Doubleton took the change in one grasping cage of fingers. Into the side pocket. Not counting, not sorting the bills into his wallet. The giveaway.

Still riding the hawk.

Doubleton left the bar, went out into the sun, and Arthur heard no engine start. He went to the door. Unsteady. Dropped his pencil once. Doubleton walked along the road toward the cottages that faced the creek that flowed to the Sound. That way was no way out. That way led past the marsh to the beach and other cottages. So Arthur did not have to follow. Doubleton lived there. Arthur made a fart, returned to his table with a sly grin at the barman. "Couldn't let that bird fly in here."

"The house appreciates small favors." The pusher grinned back and shoved Doubleton's beer glass onto a turning sinkbrush. The brush made gurgle, gurgle, gurgle sounds as it spun inside the glass.

Arthur ordered another drink and settled back with his puzzle. In through the door came two men. Holding hands. They went to the inside end of the bar. Sat down. One hand patted the other backside.

"Can we get two margaritas?"

No reply.

"Today?" Shoulders touch.

Pause.

"On the rocks?" From the pusher.

"The other way."

"Salt?"

"No salt."

Pusher smiled. Two glasses in one hand. Scoops of shaved ice. Dropped high above the glasses. Some of the ice managed to get into the glasses. Tequila, Triple Sec, sweet-n-sour, wedge of lime, straws. Onto the bar.

"Five seventy-five."

"Five seventy-five? How's that? What's one cost?"

"One's three bucks. Twenty-five cents off you order two at a time."

The two customers looked at one another. Exaggerated mouth shapes. Out came a twenty.

"I've never heard of such a thing."

Change.

Arthur signaled for another G & T. Pusher put it together, started toward Arthur's table.

From the barstool, "What if we order ten?" Elbows rub. "What would that be?" Snickers.

Pusher sets the G & T next to Arthur's giraffes.

Under his breath to Arthur. "Say something else, asshole, I'll put your dick in the blender and cut it into a pile of lemon twists."

Arthur chuckled.

Roy corralled four animals, one empty glass, and headed back to the bar.

Arthur would return to the bar each afternoon for the next three days. But first he made Mrs. Hodges a present of two more weeks of model tenant. It had been his intention, once Doubleton was located, to leave the area, maybe head up the coast to Boston, change cars. Make the airline reservation for the return to the West Coast by way of Miami. Get set to roll after he did the man. When he first moved into the bed and breakfast, he thought the place would wear on him, get him antsy with all its starched-white perfections, but that hadn't been the case. He liked the place. No secrets. Silent nights. No questions.

He and Mrs. Hodges were the only two for breakfast on those cold mornings. Eggs and sausage one day. Pancakes the next. Then over again. Fat jelly donuts waited under a plastic dome on the table outside his door each morning for those days he had to miss sitting down with her at breakfast. Only two misses, though.

"You like your room?"

"Great room."

"Used to have a fireplace."

"Oh?"

"Lost too much heat. Blocked it up."

On the third day of his revisitation, Arthur watched Doubleton stroll into the tavern and take the same seat he had on the first pickup.

Came in almost at the same time, to the minute. As Mr. Doubleton settled in, Arthur left the place and went outside to his car. He drove toward the beach on the dead-end road that led to the cottages. Doubleton had held to the right side of the street when he left the bar after the earlier buy, so Arthur chose the cluster of fourteen cottages to the right. He went to a spot where the cottages fronted the beach, got out of his car, and walked out onto the sand toting a metal detector purchased from a store called the Cipher Shoppe. He pulled his floppy sun hat down on his head to keep the twenty-knot sea breeze from blowing it off and began to sweep the sparkling sand. The smell of rotting New England seaweed laced his nostrils. Three seagulls wheeled over his floppy hat. A blue-green fiddler crab badgered him in brassy fluster: Find another beach, big guy, or else.

Eighteen minutes later he watched as Doubleton came down the road and went into a bleached-gray, wood-shingled bungalow.

Arthur's coin-detecting buzzer went off. He squatted down and uncovered a quarter in the sand.

The cottage had a front porch on the road and a back porch facing the water. Sharp-edged sea grass grew on either side of a sand trail that led from the house to the beach. The chest-high stalks made hissing sounds as the blades rubbed in the wind. The cottage to the left of the one occupied by Doubleton was empty. A Jeep Wrangler was parked on the sand beside the right-hand cottage.

Arthur Arthur would run these images through his mind as he lay on the sweet-smelling sheets in his room. The winter days were pleasant, and he spent them in coiled repose. He moved around the trim little town only twice ... once to see a double feature at the brick moviehouse and once to buy a used bicycle from a man named Coulter who smoked green cigars and ran a secondhand shop stuffed with push mowers, black tools, and other bikes.

"Be needin' a rack?"

"Rack?"

"For the bike. For your car."

"Got one?"

"Got three."

"Need a rack."

"Thought so." A Yankee conversation.

*   *   *

Arthur waited for the weather. For five days he waited for the weather.

Mrs. Hodges pushed a delicate blue plate stacked with five pieces of toast at him.

"One thing about New England." She patted her thin lips with a pressed cloth napkin.

"What's that?"

"If you don't like the weather, just wait fifteen minutes."

"That's what they say." He moved a wedge of pancake through thick maple syrup streaked with yellow channels of melted butter.

"Yep. . . . Nor'easter. Any day now. Maybe tomorrow, next day, latest . . . looks to me." She moved the butter dish up next to the toast plate. The block of spread was precisely centered on its carrier. No maverick dabs of butter fouled the crystal edges of the dish. "Mackerel sky," she said and nodded at the window.

The storm boiled over the coast at two in the afternoon the next day. Trees bent, waves went white on their tops, and seagulls walked in compact gangs on brittle winter grass behind the high school. By four o'clock cars moved along the wet road with pale headlights shining in the swirling mist. Mrs. Hodges scurried through the house checking windows. She gave them all an extra hard downward shove.

"Going out in this?"

"I guess I'll drive down by the water. I'd like to watch the storm come in." He raised the rubber rain hood over his head.

Arthur crossed the great bridge to the other side of the river. The world was dark and wet and windy when he pulled his car into a deserted parking area at the head of the road leading down to the tavern and the cottages by the beach. In the gusty race of the storm he took the bicycle off the rack. The evening was black.

He walked the bike along the edge of the road, his hood pulled down over his upper face in the freshening gale. He passed the tavern where the pusher made drinks for a stalwart few, where the yellow light of the bar spilled out only to be swallowed up after venturing a few tentative yards into the shroud of the waterstorm. Arthur moved to the far side of the road, careful to keep out of the light and away from any curious eyes that might record the incongruity of a man pushing a bike in a rainstorm. Once, when a pair of headlights loomed out of the rain, he leaned the bicycle against a hedge and walked on without it—until the car passed him by; then he went back and retrieved it. The bicycle was more than a means of quick exit, more than that. It was intended to serve a critical, if brief, purpose. It would do that small thing only for a fraction of a second . . . move Doubleton's eyes.

Arthur walked past Doubleton's house. Lights burned at the back of the cottage where the kitchen would be. Of the other bungalows, only two showed lights. One of those was the one next to Doubleton's place.

Arthur felt his world tighten. His senses grew crisp, focused, hyperreactive. The confusion of the weather contrasted with the intensity that defined his sense of self and what he was doing.

Arthur continued past the cottage. He pushed the bike slowly through the rain and took care to remain on the blacktop out of the sand. His mind rolled back the years.

"Alfa Wolf. You got another Chuck to grease, boy. Up the creek in Fantasyland. Booked on a PRB. Got a Zippo to the halfway point. You leave at twenty-one-hundred tomorrow. Stay sober tonight, Wolfer."

Alfa Wolf. His call. Given to him by his spotter, a ranch boy from Montana who shot wolf for two dollars an ear on daddy's ranch. Montana wore a dried wolf's ear on a thong around his neck.

"Wolfer, you got those hairy eyes. I swear I can see you think. You ever sweat?"

Arthur didn't like the name. He didn't get off on the homey bush patches that showed skulls and lightning bolts, didn't like the implication of being someone who was inhuman. For longer than he cared to remember Arthur had been aware that somewhere, somewhere long ago, he'd lost a part of his heart.

He turned the bike and stopped. He put on thin black gloves.

"Oh, Wolfer. That was fuckin' beautiful! Three singles in a fuckin' row. Nothin' under five hundred meters. Fuckin' beautiful."

Then the fear rising in Montana's eyes. The run out. The real hump. Lungs burning. Fast and low. Get yourself and him away. Get to the slick, to the boat, to wherever or whatever it was that pulled your ass back to what passed for the real world.

He wished he *had* been afraid. Just a little bit afraid.

Arthur stopped about fifty yards from the cottage. He bent down and sprung the bicycle chain off the sprocket. He lifted the rear wheel off the ground to keep the chain from wrapping. He went to the front of the bungalow, then up the path, and carried the bike onto the porch.

Heart strong but steady. Everything slowing down. All color leaving the world. Black and white now. Details in sharp relief. Testicles doing the slow crawl, retracting.

Arthur rapped on the door. Softly at first. Then a bit harder when nothing moved in the house.

The curtain to his left moved slightly. Arthur bent down to the bicycle chain. Fussed with it.

Water drops fell from his black raincoat onto the pine deck of the porch.

The door opened with a swift motion.

"Yeah?"

Arthur looked up from the chain. Smiled.

"Sorry to bother you," Arthur said, standing slowly. "Chain came off. Could I get a screwdriver from you . . . something to pry it back on?"

Doubleton's eyes left Arthur's face for a second, flicked down at the bicycle chain.

In that speck of inattention, Arthur put the Glock pistol in front of Doubleton's chest. Not too close. Two feet away. Arthur let the bike go and carefully gave it a slight shove away from his position. It crashed against the porch rail. He squared his body and tensed. Planted. Ready. Doubleton made no move. The man's pupils were dilated slightly. Drug sign. Fatal.

"Back."

And Doubleton stepped backward into the room. Arthur followed.

Hands raised, palms out toward Arthur. "Hey, man. Easy. Easy."

Arthur closed the door.

"Bathroom."

The pair, Doubleton backing, moved down the half-lit hallway to the bathroom door. Arthur motioned with the pistol, angled his body so his free hand was well to the front. Doubleton stepped backward into the small room. Before Arthur stepped forward, Doubleton shifted his weight quickly and tried to kick the door closed in Arthur's face. Arthur caught the door with his free hand, then snapped his palm into Doubleton's chest, shoving the man backward. Doubleton's legs hit the edge of the high-sided tub and he crashed down into it, arms against the back wall to break his fall.

"Stay there!"

Doubleton settled back crosswise in the bathtub. Tension drained from the man's body.

Arthur watched Doubleton's eyes. They searched Arthur's face. Tried to find some reason. Tried to place the face he'd seen somewhere before.

"I only got a little left, man. You want it, you got it. In the kitchen. In the toaster."

"Get your clothes off."

"Swear it's all I got."

"Get 'em off. Slow."

"Christ."

Doubleton removed his clothes. Awkward in his position, he dropped the articles of clothing on the floor beside the tub in the place Arthur motioned with the Glock.

The man was naked. Skin pale. No fat. Veins cut against skin as fear overrode the drug. Penis small and getting smaller in the cold. Tattoos on both forearms . . . uncompromising blue dragons covering compromised blue capillaries.

"On your stomach."

"Oh, man."

Doubleton rolled facedown in the tub.

"Hands."

Doubleton put his hands behind his back. Arthur, eyes locked on the man, pistol deathly steady, pulled a bath towel from the rack and dropped it in the sink. He ran water from the crusty spigot until the material was saturated.

Arthur moved next to the tub. "Look down the drain."

Doubleton began to shiver. Arthur, with his free hand, wrapped the dripping towel around the Glock pistol. Two black inches of muzzle extended from the wet cloth.

Arthur bent forward and seized the man's crossed wrists with a sudden placement of his free hand. He shoved the pinioned wrists upward between Doubleton's shoulder blades, robbing the man of power and leverage.

Doubleton continued to shake. Pressed onto the cold enamel surface of the bathtub and filled with a building terror, his arms pinned and racked, the naked man started to urinate.

Arthur moved the barrel close to the man's anus. Doubleton flinched as an edge of cold fabric touched the back of his thighs.

"Yuma." Arthur let five seconds pass. "Gainesville." Five more seconds.

Arthur rammed the muzzle hard up into Doubleton's anus and fired the weapon once.

Doubleton's spine bowed in a violent backward arch. Arthur held the weapon hard into the man, but Doubleton's contortion was so severe that the grip on the crossed wrists came apart. Arthur smoothly grabbed the back of the man's neck and forced the head down again toward the drain. The spasm died. Doubleton died.

"Jesus, Wolfer. One fuckin' shot."

"Jesus, Wolfer."

"Jesus."

Arthur rolled the body over in the tub, reversed its position so it rested against the tub back like it was bathing. He closed the drain and filled the tub partway with water, then drained away that water, replugged the drain, and refilled the tub to bath level. Arthur stood and looked at Doubleton. The man's face was somewhat twisted and Arthur thought to manipulate the muscles around to give the man a more peaceful appearance. He decided against that, however, and went to the kitchen where a small radio twanged a country piece on the counter. Willie Nelson sang of troubled waters.

Arthur unplugged the radio and carried it back to the bathroom and dropped it into the water next to Doubleton. He squeezed the towel to remove most of the wet, then folded it and put it in the pocket of his raincoat. After a bit of tidying, he plugged the cord into the wall socket and waited for the lights to sputter out.

Back on the front porch, Arthur fed the bicycle chain back onto its sprocket, portaged the bike out to the road, and, in the driving rain, rode it back over the macadam surface of the lane that led past the quiet bar to the place where his car was parked.

When Arthur finished remounting the bike on the car rack, he got into the front seat and lit a cigarette. He smoked slowly, relaxed in the steady resonance of falling rain. He retraced the events of the evening, went over every detail. The fire of the kill spun down and a calmness took his mind. The business with Doubleton left him with a sense of well-being, a rich feeling that he'd done a thing of value.

He finished the cigarette. He pinched the smoking ember between his fingers, put out the glow, then carefully wrapped the stub in a bit of paper and stuffed it into his pocket.

In the quiet of the car, he reached up and wrote his name in the film of moisture on the inside of the windshield glass.

Arthur Arthur.

Before recrossing the bridge to the Saybrook side of the river, he pulled off into a rest stop at the foot of the bridge. In the dark rain he got out of the car and removed the bike from the carrier rack. From the edge of the overlook he heaved the bicycle into the black waters below. He unbolted the rack and threw it, along with the towel from his raincoat pocket, into the depths. Then removed the wrapped cigarette butt, wetted it on the rain-soaked guardrail to give it weight, and flicked it over the edge into the swirling river.

And he drove back to the world of Mrs. Hodges.

On the cool, pressed sheets, Arthur dreamed that night of the time he saw the hawk. He was ten years old. The predator had ravaged the nest of a sparrow. Arthur watched the large bird rip apart the nestlings, then carry the last one up into the sky. The hawk flew east away from Arthur with its still-living capture. That dark shape had moved two hundred yards from the spot where Arthur stood transfixed. He had watched the killing, hypnotized by the savage, violent endings, the helplessness, the rarity of the circumstance of being witness to the act.

Arthur had snapped out of his disabling trance, raised his single-shot .22 rifle to his cheek. Kept his eye on the hawk. He didn't remember aiming.

He fired. The creature buckled in the air. Arthur saw the small form of the last nestling fall from the talons. The hawk dropped fifteen feet and tried to recover. It turned in awkward circles, but still flew. Arthur chambered another round. He fired again at the turning outline. Nothing. A third round went into the breech and Arthur closed the bolt. Lined up. Fired. The hawk jerked against the gray sky. Feathers came out. And the thing plunged down in a straight line and crashed into the marsh.

In later years Arthur would run the sequence through his brain many times. He would come to appreciate, more than most, what the odds were of hitting that target in those parameters. Not so much the first shot. The third shot. That was the wonder. The first shot might be called luck. Even by him. But the third one. That was the wonder.

3

Goes Around, Comes Around

Arthur didn't check out of his room at the bed and breakfast. The discovery of Doubleton's body would precipitate a detailed check of area motels. He wanted to keep his alias off the resulting list of people who left town immediately after the incident. Running was a guaranteed attention-getter.

Knowing how the authorities would conduct their investigation, he would return to the bar run by the pusher, would maintain his position, hold to his cover, not do the expected. Despite the real possibility that he might be questioned as an incidental witness, there was a greater danger in not continuing the cover, a danger that someone might remember his presence as an everyday fixture and notice his sudden absence.

The system worked by the book. And Arthur had read the book.

On his second revisitation three days later, as he sat at his usual table under the wooden seagulls flying among crossed oars, as he drank gin and tonic, did crossword puzzles, and bent cocktail straws into animal shapes, Arthur made a discovery. In the late afternoon quiet of the place, he watched two men enter the bar, the same two he'd seen days earlier holding hands and twitting the barkeep about the price of margaritas. Arthur was not surprised that nothing seemed to be happening. Apparently no one had discovered or missed Double-ton . . . not unusual . . . the man was a loner, perhaps showed himself infrequently. And the bathwater would suppress the smell of decomposition. Because he'd taken out Doubleton with the old Mafia technique of a self-silencing tail shot, Arthur knew that even when the body was discovered, the coroner might miss the cause of death for some days. Then the forensic investigators would surmise that the killer was a pro who used the tail shot method to gain time for his getaway, to disappear before things got hot. The locals would be called off. The time of death would be established . . . the bugs would see to that.

What Arthur Arthur discovered as he observed the gay couple was exciting. The men took their position again on the inside barstools. They ordered the usual. Then one of the men got up and went outside. From his spot against the back wall, Arthur could see the one outside standing next to the front window. The man was positioned out of the line of sight of the bartender. Arthur watched the man take a handheld radio from his belt and begin to speak into it. His expression and the way he carried his body exuded professionalism. He completed his transmission and came back into the bar, but held position near the door. Through the window Arthur saw three cars pull up in front of the bar, stop bumper to bumper, and disgorge men in blue jackets. More handheld radios, weapons. The dust in the parking lot swirled up in the wake of the sudden activity of men and vehicles.

As one, the two men in the bar drew down on the bartender.

"Hands on the bar, Roy."

In a few seconds the pusher was in handcuffs and spread-legged on the deck. The activity outside increased. Too much activity, too many cars for a simple sidewalk-server bust.

Squatting inches from Roy's face, one of the agents began a rough, no-nonsense interrogation.

"Your buyer, Roy." Some photographs shoved in front of Roy's face. "Is he carrying?"

"I don't know, man, I don't know. Maybe. Never seen no piece."

Arthur sipped his drink. He had taken out Doubleton right under their noses. The small hairs on the back of his neck started to tickle.

An elderly couple occupied a table one up from Arthur. The inside agent, handgun raised toward the ceiling, looked at Arthur and the other couple.

"Federal agents, folks. Nothing to worry about. Please stay seated."

Roy was pulled to his feet, hustled out the front door, and put into one of the cars. The agent who had spoken to them stayed inside.

"Won't keep you long." And the agent took a position at the front of the bar.

No special attention directed toward Arthur. No suspicion in that instruction. No threat. No intensity.

Safe.

The three cars outside were being flanked by more vehicles. Dust drifted through the open front door, settled on the dark tables by the entrance. More radios. Squawking sounds cut through the air. Reedy voices rode the ether, professional, abrupt.

The cars began to move away from the bar. Quiet engines reverberated in their number.

"What's going on?"

"Looks like some kind of raid," Arthur replied to the lady at the other table.

"Drugs, you think?"

"Could be," said Arthur.

"Oh my, Harry."

Arthur watched the agent by the door. Sidearm back in its belt sheath.

Safe.

Twenty minutes later an ambulance passed by the bar heading toward the beach cottages. No flashing lights on the overhead bar.

Arthur tried to imagine the scene in the bungalow, tried to construct the conversations taking place in the bathroom over the bloated body of Doubleton. And because he knew the agents' minds, he knew their surprise would yield to chagrin, then to wonder. And then, in some of those minds, to satisfaction, satisfaction born of the realization that Doubleton wasn't going to beat this one.

As he sat nursing the last of his drink, the last one Roy would mix for the next few years, Arthur thought back to the time north of Souy Dai when he hung a VC cadre leader in the cross-hairs. The setup had been classic. Three days of waiting. Wind, sun, angle, cover, stalk . . . all perfect. The target standing in front of a grass hootch, full front, stationary. As he began to squeeze off, the scope picture erupted in a riot of dirt, flame, and debris. A random mortar round, friendly or hostile, no way of knowing, landing practically on the target's head. Arthur remembered the conflicting wash of emotions. Yes, he knew what the agents were feeling. He also knew he'd pulled off the Doubleton business without one hell of a lot of room to spare.

❙ ❙ ❙

There wasn't much in the papers about Doubleton. His body had been found in the bathtub at the beach house. Cause of death yet to be determined. Probably electrocuted when the radio fell into the tub. The remains were badly decomposed. The local medical examiner needed more time.

"Can you finish these pancakes? Go to waste."

"Trying to kill me with all this food?"

"You don't show much weight."

Arthur succumbed. Wouldn't get maple syrup like this again.

"Speak of killing. You see that about the fellow over to Black Point? The one cut up them kids?"

"I did." Without looking up at Mrs. Hodges.

"Goes around, comes around."

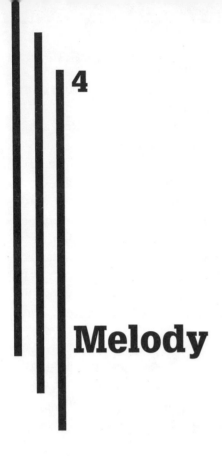

Melody

Melody Poppins threw her one and only Hummel at the wall. The rosy-cheeked figurine bounced off the black-velvet fabric of the Tijuana oil painting and rebounded onto the wood floor. The ceramic didn't even chip, a testament to Teutonic engineering and, in that same moment, an infuriating reinforcement of a flickering suspicion that, no matter how hard she tried, she seemed to have very little effect on the real world. The trite, soulful eyes of a black-hatted matador gazed back at her from the cheap painting. The serene face of the bullfighter looked suspiciously like Elvis Presley.

In a surge of frustration Melody went across the room and stomped down on the little fellow with the green umbrella who smiled up at her from the floor. She turned her ankle. The Hummel squirted away and slid under the TV stand.

Melody limped over to the couch, eased herself down between the population of cardboard boxes, and began to cry.

A sharp rap on the door.

"Come in, Karla."

"What the hell is wrong now?"

"I turned my ankle, damn it all to hell."

"Jesus, you're having a bad month. Got any ice?"

"No. Defrosting."

"Then have a cigarette."

"Karla . . . !"

"Melody . . . !" in a mimicking falsetto. "Here, go back to quitting tomorrow."

Melody took a cigarette from the pack Karla waved in front of her face. She snatched the butane cigarette lighter from Karla's hand, lit the cigarette, then threw the lighter across the room where it ricocheted off the doorjamb and disappeared into the kitchen. The thing finally stopped bouncing around the floor of the other room.

"Nice," from Karla.

Melody inhaled and stopped crying. Karla went off to retrieve the wayward lighter; she returned and sat down on a number-three cardboard box.

"Not there. My lampshades!"

"Fuck the lampshades. They're ugly." But she moved anyway and sat on the other end of the couch after pushing two small cartons onto the floor.

"Why don't you just set fire to my place?"

"Wouldn't help. Garbage doesn't burn. Besides, it's not your place anymore."

Melody rested her head against the back of the couch and closed her eyes. The rush of nicotine made her dizzy after three weeks of not having a cigarette in her mouth. It looked like that wasn't going to work out either. "Oh, God."

"There ain't no God, Mel. If there was, Craig would be nailed upside-down by his prick to some cactus in Arizona."

The image danced into Melody's mind. It was vivid. Karla had the knack of speed-painting her brain, one of those delightfully distracting characteristics of real friendship. Despite herself, Melody smiled. "With a rusty spike," she said.

"You got it! With a rusty, hot spike. And honey on his face. And red ants coming up the cactus. And a fishhook in his balls tied to a piece of roast beef on the ground and two hungry coyotes dapping down the desert."

"Dapping?" from Melody.

"Whatever. And a tarantula trapped between the cactus and his ass cheeks."

"Right. And no sunglasses."

"Sunglasses?" She looked at Melody.

"Yeah. They fall off. On the sand."

"Gee."

I   I   I

Craig had split three days ago. He was a lawyer—a young, obnoxious lawyer. Melody and the wannabe Darrow had lived together for the past two years, sharing a condo on the periphery of the La Costa Resort in Carlsbad. Craig's choice. So he could leverage the La Costa address and mystique. A big thing to him.

The couple divided the rent and utility payments down the middle. While he crawled around the senior partner's desk doing his gofer things, she waited tables, swept up stale nachos, and hustled fruity drinks for equally fruity tourists at the new "Old Mexican Restaurant." Like clockwork each month, there was at least one carefully unpublicized assault on the charming brown tiles among the darling begonia plants beneath the cutesy adobe arches.

Her sweet Craig had astonished Melody one afternoon when he suggested that she show Mr. Yoshitsu Kasuga a "good time." Kasuga was a heavyweight client of Craig's San Diego law firm, Crabbes, Reese, and McCabe. The big-chip industrialist was having trouble settling into Western ways; his penchant for young boys and girls, easily sated in the dirt-poor slums of Manila and Bangkok, was meeting some difficulty in the sunlit environs of Southern California. Not that such diversions were unknown in San Diego . . . it was more that Mr. Crabbes et al. were a bit edgy and out of synch with the local pedophile scene.

Craig to the rescue. His plan was for Melody to dress up in a six-year-old's bloomers and blouse. Sporting a big red ribbon and a lollipop or two and pedaling a tricycle around the condo to the tune of "I Know What Boys Want" should do the trick. He got the idea for the props while accompanying Mr. Reese and Mr. Kasuga to a seedy bistro called Body Parts, a local fixture near the Naval Training Center that served nonalcoholic drinks and therefore was granted the right by the Powers That Be to exhibit totally nude females. Mr. Big-Yen was in the process of making a bid to buy the western side of Southern California with some of his exchange-bolstered currency, and Crabbes and Company dearly wanted to land the finder's fee.

"If we land this one, there's a nice piece of change in it for you, " Craig said, his eyes alive with assumptions.

"What?"

"This one gets Melody into the big time. Whaddaya say?"

Melody just stared at him. Craig could tell by the kryptonite look he was getting that he and she were on vastly different wavelengths.

His lawyer mind raced. He'd promised boss-Crabbes there wouldn't be a problem. "Should be a piece of cake, Mel. Mr. Kasuga is a great guy, sort of short and real gentle. Your making him happy would strictly be a business thing. I mean, it wouldn't bother me, your getting it on with him."

Melody split Craig's face open with a can of Ultra Slim-Fast.

The next day, at Karla's urging, she called the offices of Mr. Crabbes. Talked to him personally. In a sweet voice tinged with disappointment—and showing none of the anger and sarcasm she really felt—she told him that she appreciated the offer, but that her religion prevented her from seizing this kind of opportunity. She did suggest that Craig had expressed a willingness to stand in for her, but was too bashful to bring up the possibility for fear of offending. Melody told Mr. Crabbes that she was taking the initiative in revealing Craig's feelings because she knew how much Craig wanted to do the right thing. She told Mr. Crabbes that Craig had a cute Little Lord Fauntleroy outfit and a pair of woolly Dr. Denton's that were sure to create the effect the client was looking for. And she knew where a tricycle could be found. She hoped Mr. Crabbes would take Craig's offer in the spirit in which it was intended. After all, it wasn't like Craig hadn't done something like this before. "He's just so shy—he needs some assurance and a little prodding. I hope you'll give him a chance, and . . . well, it's been sure nice talking to you."

I I I

With Karla's help, she loaded the U-Haul attached to a bumper hitch behind her Colt Vista van. When all her things, which didn't amount to much, were loaded, she cheated and smoked a thin black cigarillo produced by Karla to celebrate the heady occasion of her leaving Southern California. Karla had bought two of the little cigars to get around Melody's New Age resolve not to start with the cigarettes again. Karla also produced and opened two cold cans of beer, light beer, as a budget toast to their parting. It seemed an auspicious moment. As the two girls sipped and smoked and made small talk, the U-Haul mysteriously lifted off the hitchball and crunched at a backward angle into the ground.

"Darn," said Melody.

Karla studied the situation. The beer she held in her hand was not her first of the day. "I think we have to put more weight in the front. To keep the damn thing down."

"I think we didn't snap the grabber-thing right."

"The grabber-thing?"

"Yes. The thing that goes over the ball-thing."

"Better it comes off here than on the highway."

"Sure is."

They moved the contents of the trailer around and pushed more of the stuff forward. While Karla balanced on the hitch, Melody hammered the ball-grabber-thing into place with a rock.

"What about these wires?"

"I think they work the lights." Melody had borrowed the U-Haul from a hairy young man named Luciano who lived down the row of condos. She intercepted him two days ago because she wanted to find out where she could rent one. He said she could take it, said she could leave the thing in Vegas when she got there. Gave her his brother's number. The brother would pick it up since it had come from Vegas in the first place. "No big," he said. His brother owned the gas station that rented the things. "Won't cost nothing. Had to take it back sometime, anyway." Luciano snorted up a lunker and spat it on the trailer tire. He tugged at his testicles from the outside of his Levis.

"Thanks," said Melody. For a second, she thought she was going to throw up. So much for La Costa class.

"No prob, dude," from Luciano. "Saves me dragging the fucker back." Melody wondered what this man did for companionship.

Because of the strong probability that Luciano would launch

another phlegm construction onto the trailer wheel, Melody didn't question him about how to hook up the wires. "Take it whenever. I sleep days. Just don't wake me up." As she walked away, leaving him there still trying to arrange his genitals, she was assaulted by the image of herself attempting to wake Luciano from a deep sleep. Twenty feet farther down the concrete drive she heard the man pass a raucous belch. "Why me, God?" she said aloud as she accelerated away.

Karla chugged the last of her beer. "So, what about lights?"

"I'm not going to be driving at night."

"Yeah. You shouldn't need them."

"That's what I figure."

"If a cop stops you, act dumb."

"That shouldn't be a problem."

I I I

Ambrosiae is the name given to a group of plants in the sunflower family. Most sunflowers display beautiful springtime colors. Yellow blossoms dominate the class, and creams and whites are frequently seen. As the days pass, many of these initial colors deepen into brilliant orange, then blue, purple, and lavender. Sunflowers grace most of the continental United States with a lush, vibrant beauty. But not the ambrosiae. These plants—also called western ragweed—populate the sprawling southwestern flatlands of the Mojave, the Sonoran, and the Great Basin deserts. On harsh land where beauty is too fleeting, too undependable, ambrosiae have chosen to roll the dice. Their weapon of propagation is not the seductive color that attracts pollen-carrying insects, but rather a sheer abundance of pollen. All energy is channeled into practical preparation. Then they wait. Wait for the wind.

Melody drove through the Big Empty, the gentle twisting of Interstate 15 yielding its hypnotic desert secrets of space and time in graceful, sweeping turns. As the white sun vaulted over, then behind her van and late afternoon shadow began to cut sharp patterns behind black rock, her memories drifted up. She carried her thirty-seven years with dignified and delicate resolve. She looked into the rearview mirror, saw shoulder-length dark hair framing strong, high cheekbones, hazel eyes, and movie-star teeth. Eyes back on the road, she inventoried. She knew she had a smile that worked wonders when she cared about working wonders. And a hard, lean body that insisted on four-mile runs every morning with peremptory addiction. Hers was a body and a soul given hopefully, sincerely, but given too many times in good faith to jerks. She trusted but was beginning to question trusting. Her efficient good looks had tricked her into believing that life was a matter of association and faith rather than of preparation and discipline. She'd been sucker-punched by the California dream.

Now she was alone with eighteen hundred dollars in a six-year-old van pulling a U-Haul down a desert highway. She didn't know what she hoped to find in that mirage called Las Vegas, but she would look. Look in a place where dreams crashed and soared, a place where pretense thrived until the chips disappeared, a place without clocks, and a place where make-believe worked only to the point of empty-pocket reality. But she would look.

Karla's father had leased an apartment for her. He'd gotten her a casino job running drinks on the graveyard shift. A start. A paycheck.

She would work hard. She would relearn the odds. Not the table odds, but the survival odds. She would prepare again, this time with her eyes open. She would make herself ready for chance when chance chose to come.

Then wait for the wind.

I   I   I

The formidable climb from Baker to Halloran Summit, then up to Mountain Pass, was forcing the van's temperature gauge into new territory. Though it was late in the day, the air pouring out of Death Valley was testing fan belts and radiators all along the highway. Vehicles sat on the roadside, hoods raised, looking about to chomp down on frazzled drivers who peered at engines that ticked and contracted under the broiling challenge of the Mojave's version of a wok.

Melody coaxed her straining charge up the last mile to the crest of the pass, one eye on the traffic, one on the gauge. Teeth clenched, thigh muscles bunched, fists hard on the wheel . . . fifty miles per hour, forty-five, forty, thirty-five, thirty . . . transmission frantically hunting for answers . . . then thirty-five, forty-five, and back to speed as the road leveled and the engine gulped cooler air. Melody relaxed her parts one by one. Twenty miles to the state line, all downhill.

She and those around her rolled down the mountain in a frisky, reckless rush. In the aftermath of the uphill struggle, everyone seemed determined to get back at gravity, using it like a judo fighter uses the momentum of a stronger opponent to gain back the advantage. Even those few rusted clunkers that had somehow crested the high ridge careened and swayed in the heady continuum of the downward romp. Melody turned on the radio. She'd turned it off when she began the climb on the other side of the mountain. She figured that leaving the radio off would conserve energy.

At seventy miles an hour and nearing the Nipton cutoff, a car full of goofball guys came up on her left side. They looked to be in their mid-twenties, a real nerd posse. All of them, even the driver, were making faces and waving at her. *It never ends*, she thought, . . . *even out here in the middle of nowhere they try to hit on you. Like a pack of coyotes in heat.* In spite of herself and in the glow of the downhill, she sent a little smile back at them. It didn't work. They only made stranger faces, pointed, and waved more. She thought of flipping them off. Karla would probably moon them.

She was startled by a movement on her right. She couldn't believe it. Some idiot was trying to pass her on the shoulder . . . at seventy-five miles an hour. What a dumbo! Talk about being in a hurry to lose your money! Then she took a real look. Big black letters on an orange background. U-Haul.

It took the Highway Patrol only twenty minutes to get there, which surprised her since the state line was so close. There wasn't much she or the cop could do. The U-Haul had decided to ignore the sweeping left bias of the road and had elected to take a shot at flying. It did that thing without grace and impacted a vertical slab of plutonic igneous granite at considerable speed after completing a series of hypnotic, slow-motion somersaults.

"Looks like the hitch let go, ma'am."

"Do I have to get someone to clean this up, Officer?"

"The state will cart it off. Anything you want?"

Melody stared at the mess. "No." She was too depressed to cry.

She climbed back to the car. He called after her, "Ma'am?"

She waited. He came up the slope to where she stood. "Not a total loss, ma'am." He handed over the Hummel. Not a scratch.

5

Come Again?

Arthur forced the wooden deck chair back on its rear legs, balanced it against the rough log wall of the narrow porch in a comfortable equilibrium that satisfied the requirements of body, chair, and gravity. He put his feet up on the pine railing in front of him and looked out across the small sand beach at the choppy waters of Lake Tahoe. In the twilight-gray distance, the lights of the casino hotels on the far shore to the east twinkled red and green and yellow, lending gaudy definition to the faint line where the lake ended and the mountains of the Sierra began to rise massively toward the snow clouds. He had chosen the western side of the lake to avoid the bustle of the tourists, to distance himself from the noise and smell of the traffic that clogged the single road that circled the lake, to put some space between himself and the seamy greed that swelled beneath the tall trees.

The air was colder than he had expected, and he zipped the front of his windbreaker up to his neck. The silence was total. It settled over him like a liquid weight pouring down from the great mountains at his back. He felt satisfied with the Doubleton hit.

He sat for a long time. Almost an hour. He ate one apple and drank a can of grape juice and watched the night come to the lake. The solitude was deep. No bird sang, no wave splashed, and no sound ranged across the ten miles of water that separated him from the sparkling tourist tumor nesting on the far shore.

As he sat alone on the small porch, Arthur wondered if the old dreams would come that night. When he finished a job, when the challenge and excitement had drained away, when he stepped into that strange, hanging void of inaction, then his mind seemed reluctant to let go. A hunting took place, a chasing down of past moments, of impressions, an almost random search for connections, details, particulars of technique, for items missed. For memories.

But not for guilt. And not for second guesses. When Arthur threw the switch, the switch stayed thrown.

He had decided many years ago that the strange, aimless introspection that followed each hit was an attempt by his conscious mind to find an explanation for the dreams, dreams of places and faces he had never seen before. At times it seemed his body was shared by someone else.

Two more things perplexed him. First, he didn't understand why he seemed to be the only one hunting. He thought there should be others. Second, he never felt certain that his punishment fit their transgression, whether he had adequately balanced the spectral scale that weighed evil in the left pan, retribution in the right. Occasionally he felt he hadn't done enough, had been too easy. The thought nagged him, but he usually ended up accepting the doubt as a peculiar, protective compulsion, an asset in his line of work.

There were also times when he had to admit that he'd done more than enough, usually due to some personal monkey on his back that wouldn't go away without an extra shove. Like in '75. Twenty years ago. After the war.

Hell, no one was perfect.

"You get anything you want, long as it don't break bones or draw blood," Janet said. She winked and drained the last dollop of vodka from her glass. She looked him in the eye. "Long as you got the cash." A hint of firmness. A bargain about to be struck.

Arthur lowered his gaze, fiddled with the corner of a soggy cocktail napkin. "I could never break your bones. You're too pretty." He paused and scratched the side of his nose, a childlike motion, fingers together, eyes still down, chin tucked in. "I hope you don't think I'm too much of a nutcase."

She laughed, reached across the small table, her elbow sliding through small water rings left by the succession of vodka twists. "I think you're sweet." Pinching his forearm. Tugging playfully at his skin. "Hey, nice guys like you don't come by every day. I like to play games, too. Nothing wrong with having a little fun."

She leaned back and signaled the waitress for another drink.

"I don't know a lot of girls."

"I don't believe it. Not with them looks. Not after two tours over there chasing bargirls. Or have you been jerking my chain?"

He ignored the question. "Do I have to pay someone else?"

"You mean does Janet work alone? Do I have a pimp?"

He averted his eyes. Shy. Awkward.

"I work solo. On my own, kiddo."

"Sorry. I didn't mean to . . . "

"That's all right, sweetie." She laughed. "I used to have an arrangement, a manager, if you want to call it that."

"You broke up? . . . I mean, did you . . . ?"

"Yeah. It wasn't pretty. Ol' Slick was a scumbag, anyway."

"What happened?" Concern and sympathy.

"I guess one of his butthead deals went sour. Drugs, maybe. He got himself roped to the back of a train one night. Got dragged from Westerly to New London. Least his arm did. That's all they found when the train got to New London. The rest of him was stuck all over the tracks. I saw him do something like that to a kid's dog once."

"I'm sorry . . . "

"Sorry, shit. I'm sure he had it coming."

The drinks arrived. He paid with a ten-dollar bill and waved off the change. A TV mounted on the wall over the bar showed grainy pictures of a helicopter picking marines off a rooftop somewhere in Saigon.

"All right. Let's see if I got this straight. I go to the room. You want me to put those ropes on my ankles, hitch them to the end of the bed so's my legs are spread apart?"

"Not tight. I just want to see you that way." Awkward again.

She tossed her head back and laughed easily. The skin on her throat tightened and stretched flat the corrugations of forty-plus years. "My hands? You want them tied?"

"I'd like to do that. When I come in . . . if that's okay."

"You want me bareass? On top of the covers?"

He looked around the darkened room. A guilty glance. Furtive. Discomfited. "Yes . . . if that's all right." Eyes down again. "Could you maybe roll the covers up? So they're sort of bunched up on your chest. Like you can't see me? So I can see you and you can't see me?"

"Two hundred gets you all the 'see' you want, handsome."

He was gentle. The way he touched her, so shyly, so tenderly, that touch dissolving away the small, instinctive stab of fear she felt when he had snapped handcuffs onto her wrists, then had attached the cuffs to the headboard. She felt him nip and lick at her thighs, his hard hands pressing, kneading, drifting lightly over the soft flesh of her belly and hips. It had been a long time, months she guessed, since she had experienced the slow moisture that was building inside her. The vodka and his practiced ministrations worked her brain, pushed her to a dreamy, sensual place. She began to grind her backside slowly on the sheets, a sweet losing of control, a deep, delicious recall of passion rising. Erotic shivers rode into her flesh, gained intensity in the faceless positioning of her and him. The bedclothes, rolled in soft partition between them, parlayed the strength of the moment, let her concentrate only on the building sea of luxurious dissipation now loose upon her. And then he touched her there. Finally. Deliciously. She bucked involuntarily at the fiery jolt of pleasure, snapped her hips upward seeking more.

He stood, left her flesh, his face visible above the folds of blanket. He fashioned a knot in a piece of cloth and tied it around her head so the knot of fabric filled her mouth. Passion fought with vodka, and both of those with confusion . . . control an ended thing.

He was back on her flesh. Volley after volley, electric waves of pleasure, this time stronger than before, these cracked across her skin, burned her composure, all sensation magnified by the restraints.

She heard a scratching sound. Vaguely familiar. Brittle. Like a styrofoam cooler top coming up.

Her body boiled anew. He was everywhere upon her. With a joint-popping spasm, she surrendered to a fierce and shattering orgasm, her legs taut and twisting in the ropes. Then, incredibly, another as he probed her heat, expert fingers going deep. She strained and rolled and came again. Then a fourth time.

Exhausted, faint, defenseless, spent, disabled by pleasure and alcohol, she slept.

An hour later, prodded from her slumber by a deep muscle cramp in her left thigh, she awoke. Eyes still shut, she felt again the tingle and sensuous weight of the touching. She was cold, the confusion of blanket and sheets gone from her chest. With her tongue, she tried to push the gag out of her mouth, but couldn't do that thing.

She became more aware, looked down at the pale vista of her body stretching away toward the ankle ropes. Looked for her lover.

Arthur drove through the night. He hoped the maid who came to make up the motel beds in the morning had a strong heart. He had left a generous tip to put things right.

He came to a small bridge, stopped, and got out of the car. He shook the open cooler over the black water. Of the twenty-two leeches, three were left. There hadn't been enough room for them all. Not after he had set seventeen of them to feeding on her hips and thighs. Not even after putting two inside her. The three stragglers, *Macrobdella decora*, each about six inches long, ambitious north-lake seekers of man, cattle, frogs, and fish, tumbled through the damp air into the small river.

6

School Days

How about a twist in this little ol' drink, girlie?"

Melody stared at the greaseball. Even in the gray light of the lounge, she could make out every repulsive detail of the man's puffy, ticklike upper body. His exophthalmic eyes, red and bulging from vulvalike folds of flesh riding heavy skull sockets, three chins dressed in sweat despite the dry air of the casino, top four shirt buttons open at the collar framing a gross mat of hair that tangled and curled as though seeded from his doubtless malevolent crotch, pudgy fingers sporting chewed fingernail beds lined with small streaks of black grease that looked possibly prenatal in origin. His slimy, brown-toothed grin. His methane smell.

She gritted her teeth, clenched her jaw muscles with awesome intensity . . . an act that lent classic, soaring definition to her high cheekbones. "Lime or lemon, sir?"

"Ooooo. Don't get your panties in a bunch, girlie." The tick elbowed his dank, sleepy-eyed male companion in the ribs. The thin, semicomatose male in the adjoining chair received the elbow jolt with numb indifference. "Make it lime, sugar."

Melody stalked to the bar station. She slammed a saucer onto her tray and scooped three lime slices from the stainless steel condiment container. She stalked back toward the table. *Keep cool, Melody.*

As she lifted the saucer with its cargo of citrus sections to place it on the table, the slug unexpectedly reached out, and his stubby fingers blundered into the side of the small dish. The lime wedges went flying. One landed on the man's lap. The others spun off into the darkness.

"I'm sorry, sir." Instinctive words, not reasoned.

"Clumsy bitch!"

Melody grabbed a paper cocktail napkin from the tray and made a reflexive move to go after the piece of lime that nestled in the polyester folds of the man's fly. She pinched the wayward fruit between the napkin's edges but snagged some of the fabric in the process. As she pulled her hand up, her motion was arrested by the fact she had hold of his trousers. She froze.

"Jesus, Frank," from the tick. "I think the twat's in love!" A leering grin split its way through facial fat.

Instantly, she released the cocktail napkin and its small load. The juice of the troublesome lime slice welded fly and paper together in a small, obscene wad. The man stared at the gooey construction as Melody recoiled with an awkward backstep.

In her confusion she could think of nothing to say and bent, straight-legged, her backside turned slightly in the direction of the table, to pick up the other lime pieces that were camped on the carpet beside her foot.

With unexpected and deft execution, the grotesque customer yanked the crotch fabric of Melody's satin cocktail shorts and panties to one side and stuffed the lime and napkin into her private area. With an evil giggle he let the shorts snap back into position.

Melody jolted upright, the cold, acidic shock of the lime chunk raising havoc with her sensory system.

"Hee, hee," from behind her.

Melody stared hard at the far wall of the lounge where a wall-mounted TV showed a bunch of horses sprinting toward the finish line at Santa Anita. She slowly turned around.

The sharp clank of the cocktail tray impacting on the man's bald head was heard all the way across the casino floor to the dice pits.

▮ ▮ ▮

"All right, people, listen up. You got any sense you'll stack these checks every goddamn minute you're not sleeping. When you're watching the TV, when you're eating your Wheaties, when you're using the phone, when you're on the goddamn can. The faster you get your sticky little fingers breaking down stacks instead of picking your nose, the faster you get your goddamn ticket . . . the faster we get the other half of your five hundred bucks . . . the faster you frigging losers get out of my frigging face."

"You mean the chips?" A tentative male voice from somebody in the group of nervous students. Melody glanced sideways at the only other female dealer-trainee, a breasty girl of twenty-five with a vacant face and full lips. The two stood slightly away from the ten males who made up the rest of the class.

"Jesus Christ! Yes, bugface! You refer to these little fuckers as checks! Not chips! Checks, asshole!" The instructor's cold eyes stared up at the dirty ceiling, impatience and irritation riding the air.

"The first thing you're going to learn if you want to deal twenty-one in this town is how to shuffle. My way. Not like your papa showed you, not like your buddy showed you, not like you learned when you were playing Old Maid. My way. On that table behind you are some decks. Go get one. Come back here and watch me."

The dealer school was as seedy inside as it looked from the outside. Two high-railed craps tables stood against the far wall, and around these a few students hunkered down over stacks of checks. A roulette table, empty, perched on a narrow riser back in the shadows. Ten blackjack tables filled the rest of the space. Half the tables had chairs, and these were being used by small groups of students who took turns pitching cards to one another and making ersatz payoffs. Other than a large, battered metal desk that served as the instructor's repository for faded, mimeographed payoff charts and girly magazines, the place was bare. On the floor along the wall by the front door were jackets and coats, a knapsack, and two motorcycle helmets belonging to the students. Two large plate-glass windows streaked with dirt fronted the street. Banks of flickering fluorescent lights fed a harsh glare through the perpetual cloud of smoke that hung in the air.

"My name's Tammy."

"Mine's Melody."

"First time?"

"First time." Melody watched as Tammy attempted to shuffle the worn deck. About twenty cards flipped out and fluttered to the floor.

"Darn!" from Tammy.

"Have you been through this before?" Melody watched as Tammy bent to retrieve the escaped cards. She couldn't suppress a smile as her buxom tablemate leaned forward and a pair of mega-mammaries made a silicon-inspired roll toward freedom. Melody noticed how Tammy's posturing brought the action at three nearby tables to a soundless halt.

Cards back where they belonged, Tammy tried again and managed to carry off a passable shuffle. "Yeah. This is my third shot. I can't seem to keep the cards straight. I get it, then it goes away." Two cards squirted out of Tammy's deck and hit Melody in the stomach. "Darn!"

"Do you have to pay full each time you come back?"

"Well," with a shifty glance to each side, "Sammy gave me a break last time. This time, too. Half-price. Don't tell anyone."

Melody nodded. Shuffled.

"Sammy is all right. Nice guy." Tammy paused. "Know what? He's got a thing in his penis."

Melody looked up.

"Yeah. Like a tube. He has this pump thing in his, you know, his balls? He presses on his balls a few times and the tube gets all stiff. Ever see anything like that?"

"No."

Melody practiced with her faded, dog-eared cards every night for four nights. After the third day, she had blisters on two fingers. She practiced and practiced. She put off decorating her two-room flat on Flamingo. She put off buying a vacuum cleaner, her old one somewhere out in the desert next to I-15 transitioning into a scorpion condo. She put off the dreaded trip to the U-Haul gas station; she didn't need that right now. She abandoned her morning jog. Lost six pounds anyway. She ate cheeseburgers and drank diet sodas. Raisin Bran and skim milk each morning. She found a thrift shop on

Charleston and bought five pairs of black slacks and six used long-sleeved dealer shirts. Four yellow, two white. One afternoon she went crazy in Dillard's, a real white-out . . . silk undies, bras, bedsheets and pillowcases. Lost it. But lost it on purpose. She had to put at least a thin layer of class between her and reality.

"We can't guarantee you're going to walk out of here and into Caesar's, people. But this is where they come for table meat when the time comes. They want a dealer, they ask us. If you make the grade, we'll give you a recommendation. Don't expect nothing else. This ain't a miracle shop."

"This is the drop cut, dummies." A stack of checks, maybe twenty, in Sammy's right hand. The hand flashed toward the felt. "Five and five." The big stack touched the table lightly, rose, kissed the table again, then up. In its wake, solid on the green surface, two perfect towers of five checks each.

"Four, two, four." More neat little piles. Instantly. Without looking.

"Also known as the thumb-cut. You use it on any table in the house. Craps, twenty-one, poker, even roulette. Everywhere. Without it, you're downtown for the rest of your dealing life . . . which won't be long. With it, you get to work the highway. Toke city. The black check store. Learn, little people, learn."

Melody went home with a purse fat with checks . . . glad to give her blisters a chance to heal. Tammy kept trying, still mired in the shuffle, still ejecting cards through the smoky air into ashtrays and off foreheads. Ever cheerful. Lit by some inner confidence. Buttons straining. An optimistic smile in the hard, stale air—air punctuated like clockwork by "Darn!"

Karla called. She asked if her dad had set things up all right. Melody responded in the affirmative. "He even left the phone hooked up. Put it in my name, six months . . . his treat till I get going. He's so sweet."

"How's the cocktail job?"

"I'm going to dealers' school, Karla. Going to deal twenty-one if it kills me. God! My fingers look like I catch rocks for a living."

"Still hauling drinks to pay the rent? Pops says that place is crawling with big spenders."

"Right. Crawling."

"Nice thing about serving booze in a town filled with heavy hitters, you get to squirrel some tips, maybe meet Mr. Right." Pause. Voice lower. Conspiracy in Melody's ear. "You met anyone? Bet you got a few trying to get into your skivvies. Tell Sister Karla."

"One guy."

"Serious?"

"Not really."

"Damn, Mel! You sound great. I ought to haul my ass out there. Six months and we'd own the town."

"I need a few months to bag this twenty-one job . . . I don't have time to sneeze these days. But I'm getting there."

"Give my best to Pops."

"I will, Karla."

"What happens if you get a counter?" asked a male student.

"Call your floorman," replied Sammy.

"What'll he do?"

"Probably make you break the deck, Charlie. Shuffle. Most places make that clear up front. You see someone triple his bet, you break. If he wants to press, that's kosher. Anytime else, you break. It depends on the joint. Ask. And watch for a customer walking up cold and dropping big stuff right off. Especially if he's been standing around watching."

"How do we get the floorman? Walk away from the table?"

"Christ, give me strength. Never leave the table, dickhead. You call 'Checks play.' Then you wait until the floor boss comes to watch. Never leave the table. Not even if the fucking house is burning down!"

"What if you get an invite from a customer to have a drink on your break?"

"You do that, you start looking for another job."

"Do the casinos ever close?"

"Never. Not in this town. Check that. Stopped three hours for Kennedy's funeral. For an hour or two when King got shot. Not likely you'll see that happen, dearie."

"Can we chat it up with the customers?"

"You get paid to deal, stupid. Don't forget it. And don't get antsy. Scratch your ass, rub your nose, adjust your tits" . . . with a quick smile at Tammy . . . "you get a shitload of heat coming your way. The floorman looks for signals. If he thinks you're telling the player you got to hit your hand, you better put on those tap dance shoes. Talk your way out of that and you might as well be a god-damn lawyer . . . it pays better."

"Can players cheat? Seems like it'd be tough to cheat twenty-one."

"There's cappers, dildo. Someone who adds checks to a good hand or slips a few off his bet when things ain't going right. You look for a player drifting over his bet, picking up his checks and setting 'em back down. Moves like that, you get to your floorman, not so the world can hear, but get him. Tell him there's a capper on third if that's where the bastard is sitting. Then you give the chiseler room to move, look away, play dumb, give security a chance to nail the son of a bitch."

Melody had no trouble remembering these things. She would simply conjure up some gem from her past, some crudball who'd taken advantage of her trust back in that scam capital of the universe, San Diego. Then she'd assign that face to the concept of chiseler, counter, or cheater . . . Craig made a great capper. Easy. If there was any benefit to being a bit older than the rest of her fellow students, that was it. She knew chiselers.

Melody got her dealer ticket in three weeks.

And Tammy kept firing cards into the ether. "Darn."

❚ ❚ ❚

"You from the dealers' school?"

"Yes, sir." Melody mustered as much confidence as she could despite the fact that she was staring into the coldest set of slate-gray eyes she'd ever seen.

"Ever deal the wheel?"

"Just twenty-one."

"Christ. I could use some wheel dealers."

Melody didn't offer.

"All right, honey. Do what you're told. Don't screw up. We eat break-ins for breakfast here." The eyes flickered away, locked onto a portly dealer at a dead table. "Lou! Take this break-in to number seven. See what she can do."

Lou smiled, crooked a stubby finger in Melody's direction.

"Break-in, Jimbo." Lou had stopped behind a table at the far end of the twenty-one section after waddling through the pit with Melody in tow, after passing the small podium where the pit phones and player bios were kept. A young couple sat at the table playing silver dollar tokens, small-time action.

Jimbo dusted off his hands, clapped them together once in the ritual of dealers being taken off a game. Jimbo stepped back and Lou nodded to Melody to take the table. The player couple looked up, a concerned, wary expression on both faces. It was a look frequently directed at relief dealers, a guarded hostility that showed the players had been winning and didn't appreciate any alteration of circumstance, any change in the parameters of what had been a good situation.

Melody tried to ignore the wooden feeling that perfused her fingers as she shuffled the single deck. At least she wasn't faced with the suddenly imposing threat of having to shuffle up a four-deck shoe. Dealing from the plastic shoe was regarded by longtime dealers as insulting—"something a trained monkey could do," according to her dealer-school instructor. And the single deck felt bulky enough; she thanked God for small favors.

She dealt six games to the couple. The cards felt stiff, cold in her shaking hands. She realized her palms were beginning to sweat. The slate-gray eyes had come across the pit to watch. Nothing existed in the moment except the pitch and slide of the cards, the clank of silver dollars that had taken on the character of manhole covers.

She didn't feel the first tap on her shoulder. She jumped at the second tap.

She dusted her hands together, clapped, stumbled back two steps, and stepped on Lou's foot.

"Can you work graveyard? Tomorrow? Three to eleven?" from the shift boss. Steel eyes still threatening . . . but resigned.

Lou hopped around on one foot. He said a swearword.

"I can." Her voice wavering, high-pitched, someone else's.

"Take this to the pay office. They'll tell you what you need. Be in the dealer's lounge at two-thirty. Be at your table five minutes early. Roster is posted in the lounge."

"Thank you, sir."

No reply. Only the back of a pinstriped jacket moving away.

In the pay office she filled out forms, got a work slip with instructions to take it to the police department to pick up her police card. Then back to the casino cage where a nametag was stamped with her first name. A dealer apron was passed to her across the marble counter.

Piece of cake. Right.

Melody sat on the outside steps that fronted the entrance to her walk-up apartment. Next to her right foot and poking tentative green buds above the hard-packed soil was a small plant. She knew the plant wouldn't survive in that location close to the stairs.

She took her car keys out of her pocket. She bent and gently pried into the dirt around the tiny flower. The plant, liberated from its precarious site and nesting in a dark, root-laced ball of earth, rested in her palm. She went to a spot close by the wall of the building where an outside faucet dripped water. Melody knelt and prepared the ground to receive her charge.

As she worked, the dark soil cool and damp to her touch, she thought of the times she'd planted seeds with her father when she was small, how he loved to work with his hands in the earth, how he would smile and show her the secrets of growing things, show her the way shoots and bulbs should be placed in the ground so they could have a chance at the sun. He'd gone away, left them when she was nine. She never knew why he'd gone away, and her mother never gave reasons. But those days with him . . . sweet, warm, gentle days . . . soft spring days. The smell of his cigarette, of his shaving lotion, of his brown woolen jacket, of the turned earth. He said to her once—and it made her feel afraid at the time—that when he died he wanted to be buried in the earth. Not in a box, not pumped full of chemicals, but buried so all the things of the ground could make his body a part of theirs, so he could live in the plants, the grasses, the worms, and the hard little bugs that trundled through the summer weeds. He told her he wanted to be put down with all those small ones that were simple and clean and part of forever.

Every time she reached into the soil, anywhere, even now, especially now, she thought of him, thought of those private minutes they shared, minutes stolen from the others. He was ever as one and mixed with this clay . . . for her to touch . . . for her to remember.

Melody wondered—wondered often—if he'd known what he'd given her when he said those things.

❙ ❙ ❙

Lou poked at his salad and looked at Melody. "You got a super George on four, don't you?"

"He's putting the dealer up every fifth hand, Lou."

George . . . a tipper in casino parlance. Melody was doing the one thing she needed to do to make her a genuine hero in the eyes of her fellow dealers. She was pulling tokes, the tips that made the difference between minimum wage and the good life. The Silver Lode Casino worked on a shift-for-shift basis, all the tokes going into a communal kitty that was split between all dealers working that particular shift. The real pros, the lifers, the black-tie dealers who worked the dice pits in the rich Strip casinos—they preferred table-for-table toke splits. A sharp crew skilled in the art of getting customers to place a bet "for the boys" during a game with heavy action and working table-for-table on a big weekend could keep what they took in, not have to share the tokes with the dead-timers. If a crew was big league, table-for-table was the way to fly. But for break-in dealers, and Melody was a break-in dealer, the Silver Lode policy of splitting tokes shift-for-shift provided a visible and meaningful entry into that oppressed fraternity of folks trying to earn a living "behind the tables." To be a team player in that community was important. It was the key to moving up, to being told of job openings that got you to the Big Show, to making those connections—"juice" in dealer talk—that translated into serious take-home coin.

"How you doing?" Melody bit into a rubbery stick of carrot, tried to estimate how long it had been adrift on the salad bar.

Lou herded a tomato wedge through a mire of Russian dressing.

He shook his head. "How am I doing? You want turkeys, Mel? I got turkeys. One damn stiff after another. Stiff, stiff, stiff. It's a frigging parade. Must be a full moon."

"It'll pick up."

"Pick up? Last three go-rounds all I get is a dollar sleeper. Giggler from Turkey Flats so drunk she sets her glass on a piece of silver. Didn't realize it she's so wasted. She gets dragged off the table by some pussy farmer from Bone City. Before I can lock it up, the waitress comes by on a drink run and scoops it. Pick up? Yeah, it'll pick up. Next year."

Lou jabbed his fork with its cargo of dressing-smeared tomato in the direction of the pit. A greasy dollop of sauce flew through the air and landed on Melody's shirt.

"Lou!"

"Sorry about that."

7

Sailing, Sailing

Montana sat next to Arthur at the bar. Usually, Arthur would be noticed first because of the way he moved—*and* because of his lighter skin and the way his blue eyes seemed to dissect things. Too, his physique showed a level of strength that belied his years. Montana, also in his fifties, was less physically imposing. Still, his expression conveyed a certain power that caused men in dimly lit rooms to look twice. There was something in his pockmarked, grainy skin that hinted of black powder and hard times, and gave warning to those who might consider his slight build an invitation to confrontation. Though differing in color of hair, eye, and skin, when seen together, Montana appeared in some unnatural way to be Arthur's shadow. And Arthur his.

"Got one for you in Vegas," Montana said quietly.

The dark-haired Mexican girl tending the horseshoe-shaped bar at the Crazy Burro delivered two more vodka tonics to them. Arthur centered his drink on his cocktail napkin. "Who?" he asked.

"Casino."

They stopped talking while the girl brought the change. She moved away and went to fill a restaurant order for one of the table waitresses standing at the pickup station. Montana stared after her and watched as she bent to fill the glasses. He studied her compact, well-formed backside, her strong runner's legs, her long dark hair. At fifty-six, he was still at it.

"Casino?" Arthur did not look at the girl.

"They got some kind of problem with a scammer. He's beating the shit out of them. Sports bettor."

"How did you make the connection?"

"Sitting on my ass in the Sands."

"They found you?"

"That they did."

"How do you figure they made you?"

Montana turned to look at Arthur. Paused. "Don't have the foggiest." Montana turned back to watch the barkeep deliver her concoctions onto the tray of the waitress. "How the hell does *anyone* find out about you? Fucking mystery to me."

Arthur didn't reply.

"Funny when it happens this way. Make you jumpy, Wolfer?"

"No."

"Gives *me* something to think about. Bingo . . . right between the running lights. You're not putting ads in the paper, are you?"

"Not this week."

They drank in unison, arms coming up at the same time.

The idea nibbled at Arthur's composure, but he didn't let it show. Montana was the one who trolled the twilight world of potential contacts; who reconnoitered the frustrated families of victims eaten by social predators; who hovered around courtrooms and talked softly with bystanders, with off-duty law officers, with anyone who couldn't stomach the sight of slimy monsters unleashed by plea-bargaining lawyers to prey again. He was able to find those people who were willing to risk that dark, extra step . . . and could pay the freight.

Montana was still doing the spotting. Just like in Nam. Only this time it was different. Killing like this took a special brand of commitment, needed more conviction than killing for country where causes flew on flags. Killing for country was dangerous, but killing this way required something extra. This needed scars.

■ ■ ■

"And now this from the South Bay."

The image of a female newscaster flickered off the TV screen and was replaced by that of a young male reporter standing on a south San Diego sidewalk that fronted a narrow alley running between shabby, two-story brick buildings.

"Officer Mariann Gonzales"—picture of Gonzales talking to an off-camera mike, no sound—"was responding to a 415 suspicious person report last night at eleven-thirty. As she came down this street, here, at the opening to this alley"—picture of alley—"Officer Gonzales saw a small dog engulfed in flames run into the street. Using her leather jacket, she managed to cover the dog and keep it down while she smothered the flames."

Cut to a still photo of the dog, its entire left side charred and denuded of hair and skin, lying down, apparently unconscious.

"Leaving the burned animal, Gonzales proceeded down the alley, where she discovered the badly beaten body of this man"—head-and-shoulders shot of a gaunt male—"who authorities have today identified as John Guidry, age twenty-three, of Imperial Beach. Guidry, an AIDS patient living at Care House, a hospice for AIDS-afflicted young men, was still alive despite a severely fractured skull and other serious injuries."

Cut back to the male reporter.

"The victim was taken to County General, where he is reported in critical condition."

Close-up on the reporter.

"Witnesses say two young men and a young woman were seen running from the alley."

The reporter's eyes moved to the sheet of paper he held in his free hand.

"Dr. Michael Young of County General gave a guarded prognosis for Guidry. According to Young, the victim, before going into surgery late this morning, said the three had accosted him on the street, calling him 'faggot' and forcing him into the alley where the assault allegedly took place. Guidry gave a partial description of his attackers, but was more interested in the condition of his pet dog." Eyes back to the camera. "Officials at Bay Veterinary Clinic say the dog, despite extensive burns, is expected to live." Pause.

"Back to you, Carol."

Arthur hit the mute button as the local newscast continued. Now-silent video scenes flashed and flickered and illuminated the ceiling of the room. He could feel his heart beating beneath his black T-shirt, could see how his pulse caused a tremble in the shirtfront material over his chest. He detected a faint ringing in his ears as the flesh on his face began to acquire a discernible patina of moisture.

His mind perched on the edge of the moment, then dropped away from the confines of the place where he lay on the bed. Perception drifted in dark, breathless spins, hesitated, selected bits of memory, then moved past that and stopped in another place. Pain.

The pain began to change. Not melt away, not dissipate.

It reshaped and became another thing.

▌ ▌ ▌

"Since when do we do charity work?"

"This is my charity." Arthur looked straight at Montana.

Montana shrugged and looked away. "All right. That's cool. Hope you don't fuck up the business."

"I won't." Eyes back to the notes Montana had put together. "I don't get this La Jolla address. They play in South Bay, live in La Jolla? That's a switch."

"That's also why you ain't going to see this one solved. Lots of big green fences to climb."

"How did you break it down?"

"The 911 caller heard names. Two of the three were chatting it up big-time while they worked over the victim. The witness got a good look at them. Didn't tell the cops, though. South Bay ethics. If you drop the dime there, you better have a relative in Maine."

"These three hang together?"

"All the time. Tennis. Sailboats. Roll queers. BMWs. The beach at the Cove. Top-leaf weed merchants. Cocaine. You name it, if it sparkles, they do it. It'd be tougher to tail the Amtrak than it is to follow these three."

"Sailboat?"

"Quivira Basin. A twenty-five-foot Cal-Jensen. White. Hangs a ten-horse Johnson on a transom bracket."

Arthur folded the notepaper, put it in his shirt pocket.

"So what's up, Wolf? Thought you were going to goof off, kick back till we start the Vegas thing next month. You can't handle some vacation time?"

"I can handle it."

"Right."

"I think I'll go sailing. I haven't been sailing since we cleaned those Special Service squids in Subic Bay."

"Christ."

"Get me a boat. Charter it for a week. A twenty-five or a twenty-seven. Find me some sail tape so I can switch sail numbers. I'll need mastic to jimmy the hull number. And drop some sugar in their outboard tank."

"Lovely. Enjoy yourself."

He waited until their boat cleared the jetty at Medanos Point, watched as it proceeded straight out to sea, then fell in behind. They could sail. Main full and drawing well. Jib slot stable. Telltale strips pressed flat against white dacron. Papa paid top dollar for those lessons.

The Catalina 27 that Montana had rented for him was clean—worn gel coat, powdery from summer sun, but clean. He drew comfort from the extra two feet of hull that gave him the edge in boat speed if the wind picked up.

Arthur smiled as the Cal beat steadily seaward ahead of him, heeling steeply as it undulated over the long ocean swell rolling in from the northwest.

They were doing the day-trip bit. The high-seas special. Grass and blow on the way out in the morning, booze and shrooms coming home in the afternoon. No destination other than some good chemicals, a little deep-sea sex, lots of killer rays. The California saltwater shoot-'em-up.

As the two boats moved away from land, the shoreline faded to a low-lying smudge of brown haze in the east. Ten miles. Fifteen. The two white hulls, always a mile apart, moved in slow lockstep. When the Cal tacked, the Catalina tacked . . . a dreamy, delicate, spinster waltz. Arthur kept his sailboat precisely between the other boat and the land, covered from behind like an ocean racer. But this situation was the reverse of the standard racing situation, where the boat in front protected her lead by keeping the trailing boat on her hip. This was different.

This was a lot different.

At 1:35 in the afternoon, Arthur sailed over a floating beer bottle. Corona. Another eight hundred meters and he sailed past two more. He put on his shirt and folded closed the half-eaten bag of potato chips on the seat by his side, put a clip on the bag. He repacked his Louis L'Amour western. He put his 7 X 50 binoculars back into an imitation leather case, removed a Steyr A.U.G. rifle from his duffle, drained the last of a can of Diet Pepsi, cleaned his sunglasses, snapped a transparent thirty-shot .223 magazine into the Steyr, and turned off the Padres baseball game. The Padres were behind 6-2. Summertime.

Arthur watched the other boat jibe around and begin to close the gap, sails poled out and running as it headed toward him.

Arthur freed up the mainsail, allowing it to spill its wind. The sail smacked and luffed violently in the fresh breeze, then quieted and only popped and rippled as the boat's momentum wore off. Arthur moved smoothly about the slowing hull. With a short piece of line, he fastened the tiller to a leeward cleat, then hauled hard on the windward jib sheet. The jib foot crossed the foredeck, expertly backed and locked to windward, where it balanced the turned rudder. The boat hove to, anchored without anchor, hobbled and stopped on the surface of the sea. Arthur could have jumped overboard and gone for a swim. The boat would hold station.

But Arthur didn't jump overboard. And he didn't go for a swim.

Instead, he watched through the 1.5X scope of the A.U.G. as the other boat came at him.

At three hundred meters, Arthur blew apart the top of a small, peaking wave ten feet from the left elbow of the young, tanned, chemically compromised La Jollan who manned the helm of the charging Cal.

Nothing happened. Then Arthur saw a head poke over the side of the other boat beneath the poled-out jib. The head was looking back at the spot in the water where the bullet had splattered the wave. A hand gestured toward the spot.

Despite the fact that Arthur's boat was nicely hove to, he had to battle the jogging motion of the hull. Shooting long on moving water was proving to be a task of consummate concentration. He worked on assimilating the wave rhythm, tried to anticipate that momentary pause when his craft reversed its rise at the top of a swell. In that microsecond, when his own world stopped moving, that other world, his target, was almost always shifting.

Arthur smiled. He was as focused as he had ever been; he swam in the delicious technical intricacy of what he tried, found himself immersed in the moment, immersed so completely that he didn't think to compare himself, not this time, with yesterday's Arthur, with yesterday's steadiness, yesterday's eyes, muscles, timing, and stamina.

And Montana had implied he couldn't enjoy himself!

As the second shot blew a six-foot saltwater column skyward, this time three feet from the hull, Arthur saw two beer bottles cartwheel through the air. The other boat heeled sharply and laid completely down on its port rail as it executed a flying jibe that broke its metal whisker pole in half. The Cal snap-rolled onto a new course, bow once again to seaward, sheets braced to the centerline, desperate to get away.

Arthur guessed they had finally heard the sound of the rifle, had put it all together despite the effects of whatever it was they were mixing with reality. The Cal had been directly upwind as he fired the rounds, and the blast of the first shot was likely lost in the wave noise and in the rattling resonance of the running gear. Arthur freed up the restraints on his tiller and jib, sheeted home both sails, and resumed the austere two-step toward China.

He rummaged around in his duffle and found his Louis L'Amour. He settled back and opened the book to his marker. He popped the top on another can of soda and began to read as he trailed after the seaward boat without having to look up, matching it step for step, tack for tack, always between it and the shore . . . a shore now only a memory.

At dusk Arthur put a shot into the space beneath the boom and above the cockpit coaming of the Cal in order to set the right mood for the evening sail. Before he fired, he slotted the nose of the .223 bullet with his pocket knife. Enough to make it howl like a banshee as it traversed the narrow area above the three heads peeking over the larboard rail.

He was pleased with his La Jolla–based Outward Bound program.

As night settled around the boats, now alone and far at sea, Arthur took sail tape and wrapped every loose metal fitting tightly, wrapped each one so the sailing would be soundless save for the chuckle of his bow wave and the flutter of a stalled-out luff. There was a twenty-minute blind spot around eight o'clock during which Arthur lost sight of the Cal, but a crescent moon rose out of the eastern haze and there she was, right where she was supposed to be . . . still heading out.

With no light to read by, Arthur settled back against the cockpit coaming and contemplated the easy motion of the boat as it caressed the dark face of the Pacific. The gentle night water of the ocean glittered in the roll of the bow curl, and his boat cut a luminous trail of blue and yellow phosphorescence as swarming mobs of plankton fired their tiny charges of nervous light in response to the passing of hull and rudder. The sea air wove a subtle fragrance into the night, a scent that whispered of salt, of wandering kelp, of wood smoke adrift on some mysterious chance of atmosphere. Wetness rode on silent currents and formed silver beads on flat outside surfaces.

Arthur found a memory from long ago, from the time his uncle paid thirty dollars to send him to a summer camp. He hadn't been much into games and stories and campfire songs, hadn't garnered one of the brass and wood trophies each member of the baseball team received when they beat the camp across the lake. But he learned to sail there. He shot arrows, carved things out of sticky pine, and always was the first to close the heels of the camp counselors when they played the game called Hare and Hounds. No trophies for that. But it was the sailing that made those days special. The one time he got in trouble that summer was when the camp director had to phone his father with a warning. Arthur had gone down to the lake, rigged a boat, and sailed all through the night alone. It was a magic adventure full of freedom and motion and learning in the push and pull of natural things, of moving in a prideful envelope of his own decisions, decisions culled from wind and water and sail and mind.

That summer his father died.

A fish broke the surface near his arm and splashed back into the sea, and the memory went away. He looked up and located the other boat, found it not by the sight of white sail and hull but by the progression of lost and reappearing stars that hovered low above the water to the west.

At midnight the sea breeze started to drop off as the inland deserts cooled and the warm surface of the Pacific caused sea air to rise and reverse the daytime onshore pattern.

Arthur began to walk up the Cal's wake. In the minimal light his sharp senses, trained and uncompromised by substance as in the seaward boat, took the measure of the other. He felt the soft wind on his face, on the hairs of his neck, could feel the gentle heel of the hull as it found the slot, as it suckled at the timid breeze. Once, he saw on the sail of the Cal a quick, weak beam of light as someone tried to pick out the lay of the telltales up near the spreader, an effort that belied the ability of the helmsman to feel his boat.

Arthur heard them try to start their outboard motor, but that effort failed, as he knew it would. He visualized the black gum that plugged the venturi throats, the residue of the sugar Montana had put into the tank—sugar ingested by the engine when the Cal had motored out of the channel that morning.

He closed to within two hundred meters, closed quickly and silently despite the sleepy breeze. He sat to leeward in the cockpit, his weight heeling the boat so that whatever small energy remaining in the wind was not lost in shaping the sails. A thing learned long ago.

No wind-driven wavelets kissed the hull, and the night water was ink black and heaved like oil.

He pushed quietly away from the side of his boat. With her sails furled, the Catalina floated motionless and silent tethered to the canvas sea anchor he'd put deep into the sea, down where tan shrimp clicked and darted and ate and were eaten.

Black knit watch cap. Black cotton long-sleeved shirt. Face smeared with bush grease. Black swim fins. No watch. No ring. No buckle or button to reflect starlight. Dark-colored sweat pants tucked into black socks in the fin straps. Black-handled knife, black sheath, greased blade.

White eyes.

The other boat sat motionless, defeated by the light, shifting air. That hull rolled gently on the breast of a languid northwest swell, its rigging slapping and fittings clacking. The swimmer moved through the water propelled by slow, vertical sweeps of his legs. Occasionally he used a breaststroke, but soundless, arms always beneath the surface.

One person in the cockpit, starboard side, head bent, chin on his chest. Eyes closed. Exhausted, drug-beat, scared, and likely not asleep. And maybe falsely confident . . . lulled by the absence of wind into thinking that their distant pursuer was also, finally, stopped back there.

Arthur crossed fifty yards ahead of the Cal, then turned directly toward it. He ghosted through dark water. He touched the stem of the pale hull. He moved along the port side. He stopped at the forward edge of the cockpit coaming, reached slowly up and held the rub rail lightly, only enough to keep position there, not enough to heel the boat.

Shrimp cracked. Plankton flickered. Shackles rattled. Loose halyards clanked against the aluminum mainmast, making more noise than when the boat was under way and running gear was taut.

From beneath his shirt, Arthur removed a sealed plastic bag. Inside the bag, dry and mealy and potent . . . white powder. Pure and deadly strong. Only a trace of talc. No gray motes, no bits of twig, no moisture-glued lumps.

Imperceptibly lifted up, a shadow hanging, water droplets smoothed away from the plastic, the bag of drug moved inboard of the coaming rail . . . slid softly onto the cockpit cushion.

Dawn dressed out in gaudy sheets of orange. The Pacific went from black to gray to brilliant blue. Small waves began to march, to spill white peaks before the shouldering breeze. Three white-bellied herring gulls in tight formation powered straight and true to the west on their way to somewhere. Silent. Fast. All business. Not fishing now.

Eighty miles away, under the spreading light, small towns began to stir, the city to murmur.

Arthur ate Cheerios from a yellow box. Then an apple. Then an orange. He watched the other boat pitch and slat one thousand meters to the west. He'd moved back during the night, moved as far away as when they'd last seen him yesterday.

He shot at them to get them going. One shot. Then he chased them all day long. Not so much chased as herded. He turned off his radio transceiver. There was no further need to monitor the call frequency. The Cal showed no mast-top antenna, and the possibility of them having a handheld was moot . . . both boats were too far out, well past line-of-sight range.

One hour before dusk he watched the Cal screw awkwardly, her bow to wind, sheets flailing, sails luffing. The tiller had been let go, and no helmsman reached to steady it. Then the jib was backed by an unseen hand, the bow fell off the wind, and the boat got under way again. Still beating westward.

Arthur worried them into the folds of an evil night, then he turned his boat and headed for home. He piled on sail and rode the rising gale. He urged his craft, cheered aloud as she began to surf the lifting faces of waves that rushed her from behind. He and she together on a sleigh ride. The bow wave rumbled and spit. White sails swelled like pregnant silk. The laminated tiller vibrated and thrummed a hand-tickling moan as it knifed through water at speeds strange and new.

Arthur was a boy again. Alive and eager. Racing through sweet and privileged between-places. Between sky and sea. Between design and disaster. Between the mean past and a future that waited with yellow eyes.

He thought no more of those on the other boat. Their fate was their own to chart. What they had become would decide what they would be.

8

Montana

Reminds me of the ocean." Montana slowed to the speed limit. "How so?" Arthur looked up from the road map.

Montana flipped his cigarette butt out of the window and shifted his position in the driver's seat. "All this space. Those sand dunes. Like waves. Nothing out here."

The Taurus swayed as a gust of dry cross-wind spawned by a nearby dust devil buffeted the car. The spinning vortex danced on the hot sand, sucked up pieces of loose sage, wrestled with a stunted stand of creosote bushes, then twisted across the empty road behind them. Montana rolled up the window. Dry, cool air from the air conditioner began to displace the dry, hot air of the outside.

Arthur rubbed the corner of one eye, pushed at the irritation caused by the smoke and dryness. He didn't harp at his companion about the annoying habit. Another time, another place, back when it counted—maybe. Not here. Cigarettes were a low-percentage luxury. They killed your sense of smell, important in the bush; sabotaged a shooter's night vision—thirty percent if you were a pack-a-day junkie; gave you the shakes when withdrawal was the only option; and, night or day, gave the bad guys a great visual. But they both knew that. Knew it as well as they knew each other. Arthur went back to his map.

"Ever see air like this, Wolfer? Clear as gin, ain't it?"

"Nice stuff to shoot through." Arthur spoke without looking up.

"Damn, the visibility is forty miles out here."

They drove north on the road from Baker. They would turn east where Route 127 intersected 178 into Pahrump and stay in that small, wind-scrubbed desert town an hour out of Las Vegas while Montana got the details on the casino job. Pahrump was famous for dust, a winery, and independent folks—folks who didn't ask too many questions, questions that didn't always get straight answers anyway from those who came over the mountains to play. Bowling, golf, and slot machines weren't the only diversions Pahrump had to offer. That flat congregation of souls included some of the best legal whores in Nevada. Located just outside of Las Vegas's Clark County, where prostitution was illegal, Pahrump, unhampered by convention, continued its plodding course toward the twentieth century in proud defiance, its single traffic light winking at the pompous pretensions of less pragmatic places.

"Remember the time we did that sicko?"

Arthur smiled. He remembered. Montana had taken the contract from two vice cops working North Vegas. Six years ago. "Can't forget that one."

Montana laughed and slapped the steering wheel. "Christ, that was a beaut, wasn't it?"

"It was that." A local mortician with a nasty habit of papering his apartment with photographs of deceased residents in various positions of naked, if nonobjecting, sexual display had presented a problem for the local police. They couldn't figure out how to handle the situation without causing a lot of agony for the citizens whose relatives had been compromised. The mortician had begun to sell his artwork. Busting him legally would probably have put the whole business in the press. Sex trials had a way of doing that. One of the victims had been the mother of one of the cops.

"Sometimes I got to wonder about you, Wolfer."

"You thought it was pretty effective."

"Effective." Montana laughed again. "Not so pretty."

Arthur got into the mortician's office. The fellow used a thirty-five-millimeter camera that Arthur found on top of a stack of particularly detailed photos. While the deviate was drooling at the dancers in a topless strip bar, Arthur had popped a healthy C-4 charge into the camera body under the film and wired the detonator to the shutter release. He was pleased to discover, when he located the camera, that it was a range-finder type and not a single-lens reflex. He was able to load the full charge, not halve it to clear the mirror. All they found of the bastard's head were seven teeth and one ear. The cops destroyed the photos.

They rode through the bright light of the Mojave noon, taking in the strange, lunarlike scenery, their friendship a reserved, uncomplicated thing. They shared many traits. Both were deliberate, self-disciplined. Both were patient by nature—patience being the mark of an efficient sniper crew. Both were, above all else, unemotional. If there was, in fact, any real difference between the two, other than Arthur's slightly bigger build, it was that Arthur had the edge when it came to self-control. Montana was cool; but Arthur was beyond that.

"Four hundred twenty yards."

"Not bad. Four hundred thirty." Montana stuffed the scorecard back in his pocket.

Arthur addressed the golf ball, waggled the driver a few times in the dry air, then hit a low draw down the fairway. The ball hit the cement-hard ground and took a long bounce into the rough. He shook his head and made a practice swing. He bent down and retrieved the stub of his broken tee. "Another hook."

Montana followed with a shot that soared high to the right, piercing the clear sky in a banana-shaped arc. It landed far from the fairway and rolled under a scrub pine. "One tree on the whole layout, and I'm under it. Shit."

They walked off the tee together pulling their golf carts.

"Good thing Charlie can't see us now," muttered Montana. "He'd get a charge out of this."

After a few strides they parted company and angled away in pursuit of the errant tee shots. Fifteen minutes and several shots later they met at the green.

"Like the way you played that tree," Arthur said without looking at his partner.

Montana yanked his putter out of his bag and headed for his golf ball, which lay on the back fringe of the burned-out green. "Sue me. I'm not going to bust my nuts trying to knock one through that scrawny green bitch. I paid to have a good time. Stupid fucking game anyway."

Montana knocked his first putt ten feet past the hole. Then he hit the next ten feet past the cup coming back. He rimmed the hole on his third attempt and the ball spun five feet away to the left. He glared at the ball.

"Mind if I putt one?"

"Hold your ass." Montana punched his ball at the hole. It smacked into the back lip of the cup, popped two feet straight up into the air, then fell down into the hole. And bounced out. Three inches away. He picked the ball up.

"Putt it." Arthur grinned.

"Fuck you."

"How far?" Montana held his palm over the card.

"Five hundred and forty yards."

"I say five hundred sixty." He removed his hand and looked at the yardage. "Five hundred fifty-five. You lose."

"You looked at the marker."

"Bullshit." Montana teed up his ball.

"Last hole. Par four. Double or nothing."

Arthur studied the distance. "Three thirty."

"It's three twenty-five." Montana looked. "Shit."

"Well?"

"Three thirty. Lucky guess, butthead."

"That's twenty bucks, loser." Arthur reached out with his club and knocked Montana's ball off the tee. It rolled under a bench off to the right.

"Stupid fucking game." Montana ripped up the scorecard and threw the pieces over his shoulder.

They sat together at the clubhouse bar. Four beer bottles. Two empty, two working.

"We ought to be able to play this game, Wolfer."

"Tough game."

"We can put a .308 up a rat's ass at five hundred meters. I don't get it."

"Tough game."

"Numb-nuts game. Waste of time."

They watched TV from the twin beds in their room at the Saddle West Hotel in the center of Pahrump. Shoes off. Shirts off.

"We got too much sun." Montana inverted his beer bottle and shook it above his head. A few remaining drops sprinkled out onto his face. "I told you we should buy hats. But we don't need hats, says you. Just because you got a tan sailing around after those beach-bozos, you think we can't get sunburned. Nice call."

"Sunshine is good for you. It gives you vitamins."

"Good for me? I suppose fucking cancer's good for me, too."

"You can't get cancer. You're too ugly."

"Two days from now I'll be shedding skin like a snake. Face like a piecrust. I'll probably get leprosy."

They watched a news story on the latest casino robbery.

"It's three days until you have to meet the contact in Vegas," Arthur pointed out. "So, do we play tomorrow?"

"Nine o'clock, Wolfer. I hear the other course has sand traps."

■ ■ ■

During the next two days they managed to lose twenty-two golf balls between them.

Montana sagged onto the stool next to Arthur. The horseshoe-shaped bar, its dark surface inlaid with Pahrump's coldest video poker machines, was sparsely populated by semiconscious drinkers. The after-midnight crowd was quiet, eyes glazed, most of them lost in various stages of introspection or simply numb with gambler's fatigue. The early morning hours rolled over the beaten players and their soft problems. A few slot machines clanked, and country music jangled out of unseen overhead speakers through air comfortably ripe with the stale aroma of cigarette butts and fried food. Liquor bottles lined the shelf behind the bar and gleamed in the flickering light of neon beer signs.

Arthur sat beside a lanky, leather-skinned man who looked to be in his mid-seventies. The man had a wiry, hard frame wrung out by the ravages of alcohol, manual labor, and desert sun; eyes alive and intense above a white-stubble beard; long, muscular arms ending in callused, strong, vein-piped hands; quick, alert movements of head and shoulders more suited to a boxing ring; and, like Arthur and Montana, was out of place in the bar's desultory group of early morning drinkers.

"You should have come with me, Wolfer." Montana grinned and lit a cigarette. He waved at the bartender for service. "I think I'm in love." He stuffed the cigarette pack and lighter back into his shirt pocket. "Who's your friend?"

"Just barstool buddies . . . Montana, meet Frank."

The man stubbed out his smoke in a wet, full ashtray, reached past Arthur, and grasped Montana's hand. "Pleasure." Eyes sharp and knowing. "Been whoring?" Firm handshake terminated.

Montana bent his head and peered around Arthur to look at Frank. Montana waited for some opinionated remark.

Frank lifted his drink and drained it. He placed the empty glass on the bar, then jerked his head at the barkeep who was there for the order. "Same, Harry. I'll get these."

The barman dealt three new napkins onto the wet wood.

"Beer," from Montana.

"Draft?"

"Sounds good."

"You? Same as before?"

Arthur nodded.

The bartender moved away.

"The Castle?" from Frank, not looking at Montana. "Ask for Emily next time." A matter-of-fact tone. "She'll break your back. She used to be a diver. High board. Olympics."

Montana blew a smoke ring toward the ceiling. "Two of 'em. Salt and pepper, they call it . . . and my back's broken already."

"That'd be Fran and Coot. You get your hook into Emily, sonny. Write it down." Frank fired his swizzle stick at the bartender's back by snapping it out of a pinched hold between thumb and forefinger. The missile ricocheted off the target's neck and bounced into the row of bottles above the cash register. The barkeep turned around and gave Frank a dead look. Frank stared back and slowly raised a middle finger at the man. No expression from either one. The man turned and finished building the drinks.

"Yeah. You got a real pair, those two." Frank flicked a fingertip through a pool of water on the bar. Droplets of liquid sprayed through the air. "Integration in action. Best damn double-pump in the valley."

Frank turned his head and looked across the casino floor at a short man in western dress about to leave through a side door by the cashier's cage. "Hey, Martin!" in a loud voice. "You still sucking cocks?" The man glanced over his shoulder in the direction of the bar, then continued out the door without reacting to the question—the type of question apparently expected from Frank despite its vigorous premise. Frank was no stranger to the regulars of the place, and no one looked up except a middle-aged male tourist who stopped pulling on a quarter slot handle behind the twenty-one pit. The slot player's face showed alarm, anxiety, violence anticipated. Startled by the remark.

Frank, no smile, no explanation, pushed a ten-dollar bill toward the bartender who delivered the new round of drinks.

Montana laughed, too tired to keep the straight face that Frank's words needed for best effect.

The three men, mostly Frank, made small talk for the next twenty minutes while they drank. He rambled on, never asking what Arthur and Montana were doing in Pahrump, not asking where they were from, what they were about. He talked about his thirty-five-year job with the Atomic Energy Commission, how he'd been a civilian test engineer who had worked at the Nevada test site at Yucca Flat until his retirement eight years ago. Arthur registered the fact that Frank must have been someone with a lot more on the ball than his present appearance and behavior indicated. People didn't hang around a federal job that long unless they had something special to offer . . . not in the mandatory retirement atmosphere that culled all but the indispensable.

"Got me a turquoise mine up near Tonopah. Best stone in the world. Know what? I ship most of it to Russia. Yeah. Russia. They work it up, polish it, sell it back here in the States. Makes it special. Coming from Russia."

Without pausing, Frank abruptly turned the monologue in a different direction. No transition. "People in Nevada, up in the state capitol, Carson . . . " He finished his drink. " . . . them jerks make all sorts of noise about the feds dumping on Nevada, putting all that hot waste under the mountain, burying that radioactive shit here. They bust their ass trying to get it shipped somewhere else. Know what?"

Arthur answered the question with a question. "That stuff could be valuable someday?"

Frank barreled on, not acknowledging Arthur's comment, not about to surrender the looming revelation. "I'll tell you what, boys. That stuff is going to be valuable someday. Too much energy there to ignore. We'll figure out how to use it. Write that down. Pretty soon, too. It's better than gold. Write that down."

The hour slipped away. Montana couldn't stay with it. He began to nod off, excused himself, and went up to the room. The Vegas trip was tomorrow. Except for an obese couple sitting on the other side of the horseshoe bar taking turns sticking tongues in each other's ears, Arthur and Frank were the only ones still buying.

"They told me I'd be dead by now."

"How's that?" Arthur turned to look at Frank.

"Too much time on the sand. Too much gamma."

Arthur went back to stirring his drink.

"Shows what them MIT boys know." Frank found a place in the ashtray for one more butt. "Showers. Lots of showers. Vitamins. Antioxidants. Vitamin A. Vitamin E. Exercise. Plenty of exercise. A man can feel death coming into hisself."

A minute passed. Arthur realized Frank was looking at him.

"What do you think about death, Arthur?"

The man called him Arthur. The tone was different. The dust was blowing away from Frank. The question was too sudden.

"My death?"

"Any death. Death in general."

Arthur pushed his empty glass toward the bartender, who slouched against the cash register reading a newspaper. The man didn't see the move, kept on reading, and Arthur didn't try to get his attention.

"And don't tell me you don't think about it. Everyone thinks about it."

Arthur paused for a long moment. Then, "I don't give it much thought. Not anymore."

"When did you stop?"

"A long time ago."

"Think you're immortal?"

"No," Arthur said, laughing. Then he denied the negative. "No. That's not right. I read somewhere that all these atoms ... " he spread his hands on the bar and looked at them "... these atoms were there when the Big Bang happened. That means my parts were there at the beginning and they'll be here after I'm gone. I don't know about souls. Souls I leave to priests. But the pieces will always be around. That I do know. Maybe pieces make a soul. I haven't found any facts about souls." He looked at Frank and smiled. "That makes me immortal, far as I can tell."

"The thought give you peace?"

"All the peace I need."

Frank directed his attention to the barman. "Hey, jerkoff. You still working? Do we have to pour our own?"

The man put down his paper and began to put together another round.

Frank smiled at Arthur. "If you think like that, you don't much need to care what happens to folks."

"I care." Arthur pushed money forward for the drinks.

Frank waited until the drinks were delivered and the barkeep went back to his paper. "I killed a man once. He was fucking my wife." Frank was serious and snapped a toothpick in half.

"Killing's a hard word," said Arthur.

"For some. Comes a few times in life a man gets the green light. Don't happen often. Comes a time, though. The state thought so, too."

"What state?"

"Texas."

"Texas is a lot like Nevada," Arthur said, sipping his drink.

"It used to be," Frank replied and lifted his glass.

Arthur caught Frank's stare. "Killing's just tinkering with time, Frank."

❚ ❚ ❚

Montana sat back on the dark green leather couch. He slowly leafed through the dossier pages and paused to study the full-front and side-view color pictures of Michael Patrick Henry. The man appeared normal, pleasant, somewhat intellectual in wire-rimmed glasses and short beard. Medium height, more slender than stout, pleasant facial features, but with a hint of arrogance, maybe boldness, in the sharp lines of his hazel eyes. His light hair was cut short, close, and trimmed neatly across the neck and sides. Angular shoulders beneath a square jaw crowned a confident athletic slouch that carried the strong hint of lean muscle under his loose-fitting sport shirt. Montana looked at the data below the pictures. Thirty-two years of age. Single, but with a five-year-old daughter who lived with him in a single-family house in an upscale community ten miles northwest of Las Vegas. Though unmarried, the man shared his home with a steady companion, a woman about his age, also divorced and with a three-year-old son.

The remaining pages of the profile sheet contained a detailed listing of the man's habits and known physical characteristics, including a description of his ability with firearms. A right-handed, right-eyed shooter. A USMC tattoo on his upper left arm. Some background was there on his history in the military. The man had trained as a recon Marine, short tour, did peacetime service from 1981 to 1984. An honorable discharge. No bad paper. No brushes with the law.

"Mr. Henry is a bad person." The words, matter-of-fact and cold, pierced the cloud of cigar smoke rising from the jowls of Anthony Sgro, security chief of the Crystal Casino. Sgro was the contact man for the contract on Henry. A snow of cigar ash dusted the expensive gray suit that draped a short, bulbous body behind the oversized oak desk. "He's a genuine asshole. A major meth lab supplier in San Bernardino County up until three years ago. Likely he's killed a few hundred kids with that poison trade of his. And the bastard walked. No record. No time. He walked." Anthony Sgro put a pudgy finger into his nose and pumped at some unseen accretion. "Now the prick is playing with us. He's smart. Uses his scum-money to cut us up. He's on to something. More than lucky." Sgro's finger drew back from its excursion, moved to some unfortunate surface on the edge of the desk. "No justice in this world if a man can walk after something like that."

Montana looked at the pictures again. If what Sgro said was true, it was equally true that Michael Henry didn't use what he sold. That face and body seemed hard as steel, the closer Montana looked.

"Where'd this come from?" He drew attention to the dossier by raising it slightly.

"Two years ago. Credit ID file. Before we knew the bastard was
going to make a living screwing us." The fat man rose in his seat as
he farted. "Do it on all our big gunners. Always get paper on the
heavy hitters. Routine."

"Who's in on this?"

"Two other casinos besides us. But I'm the only one who knows
you and your man. Just me and the chief at the Forum. No one else.
And don't let it concern you boys. We know our nuts are in the sling
on this one just the same as yours. You go down, we go down."

"When do we take him out?"

"Before the college season gets rolling big. Forty days, most.
We'll eat his shit till then. Have to. We know you boys need time to
make it right. We don't want no fuckups." At the sibilant "ups"
another shower of ash rained down. Sgro wiped the front of his suit
and smeared the residue in a gray streak.

"We get half up front." Montana watched the fat man. Looked
for a reaction.

"No problem."

"Cash."

"Cash we got."

❙ ❙ ❙

"How come you don't whore with your buddy?" Frank, bourbon in
hand, leaned his chair back against the wall of the darkened lounge.
As he did so, his knee hit the small round table and nearly upset
Arthur's gin and tonic. Arthur caught the tipping glass with a cat-
quick grab.

"He likes to hunt inside the fence. That's not my style."

"Not your style. A shot of leg's a shot of leg, my opinion."

"Different strokes."

"Snooty son of a bitch. Whores too easy for you?" Frank balled
up a wet cocktail napkin and threw it on the floor. "Pussy's a lot
more dependable on the pro circuit. And a lot less complicated."

"No challenge."

"Getting screwed ain't no challenge nowadays, sonny boy. You
can write that down. More beaver running loose these times than

when the Pilgrims hit the fucking rock." Frank tried to balance his drink on the palm of his hand. "Challenge? Only challenge is to keep 'em off your back. More bowlegged broads out there than at the ladies' rodeo final, you ask me. Christ."

"You're reading the wrong newspapers. Seeing too many movies."

"Wrong newspapers? Tell you what. You put a bug in every hotel room in Vegas, it'd sound like a pogo stick race in a swamp. Wrong newspapers. Where you been?"

Arthur saw Montana enter the lounge section, saw him squint into the dim, smoky air as he looked for them. Arthur waved. Montana headed their way.

"You got it right about Emily, old man." Montana shook his head as he sat down. A meaty odor of industrial-strength sex settled over the table. "All my time poking around overseas, I never did the basket. Not till tonight. What a lively lady!"

"See? What'd I say? Bet you didn't have to tell her you'd marry her, either," with a triumphant, raised eyebrow look at Arthur.

"Marry her?"

"Your buddy and me's discussing the merits of professionals as opposed to amateurs, is all." Frank brought the front legs of his chair back down. "She spin for you?"

"Like I got it caught in a blender."

Frank nodded sagely. "Takes a set of muscles, that does. Up and down, too."

"Up and down."

Arthur laughed. "It couldn't have been too far up and down."

"Go screw yourself." Montana waved at the cocktail girl.

"Yeah, boys." Frank looked serious. "Quite a sight seeing that thing pushing through the net, ain't it. I sure don't reckon I got the strength to work that rope . . . hefting myself up and down on a pulley . . . going around like that all a-hanging from a ceiling hook. Maybe for a couple of seconds, is all. Don't reckon I could do that. No way. No sir."

Arthur stared at Frank, a thoughtful expression on his face. "That'd be a real ugly thing to have to see, Frank. You in the basket." Arthur liked Frank. He saw war in those eyes. And pain.

"You son of a bitch. You know what I mean."

"Ugly . . . real ugly."

Frank affected a conspiratorial look. "What's the difference between a blonde and a bowling ball, boys?"

They waited.

"You can only get three fingers in a bowling ball." Frank raised a fist in the air . . . the punctuation mark common to all his sex jokes.

Montana looked at Arthur. The challenge was to keep a straight face.

"What do you call a blonde with a runny nose?" Frank was off again. They knew he wouldn't stop until he'd offered up at least a dozen zingers. They waited.

Frank looked at them both, knowing there would be no response. He let a few calculated seconds slip by. "Give up? . . . Full!"

Up went the fist.

The waitress had come over from the bar to take Montana's order. She was blonde. She stood there with her cocktail tray pushed into the curve of her hip, her free hand tapping the eraser end of her pencil impatiently on the cork surface of the tray.

"No offense, Gaileen," from Frank. He chuckled at his last recitation.

Arthur knew Frank had waited until the girl was within hearing range. Gaileen gazed at Frank with glassy-eyed indifference.

"Know any jokes, Gaileen?" Frank reached out and down and grabbed the waitress by the bare knee. The girl didn't flinch.

"I'm looking at one." She stared placidly at him.

"She can't get a man," Frank said with a concerned expression, and he nodded in Gaileen's direction while looking at Arthur and Montana.

"What'll you have?" Gaileen to Montana.

"Bring me a pitcher, please."

"Please. A new word. That's nice. Very nice. And sitting with Frank, too. A pitcher it is." She looked down at Frank's hand, still on her knee below the short skirt, then looked up into his face. She smiled sweetly. "And you, Frank?"

"The usual. And another one for the cowboy." He pointed to Arthur.

"Okey-dokey. One pitcher and another gin drink for the two gentlemen, and one more bourbon for the goat-faced baboon-butt on my left." She put on a stage grin and directed it sweetly at Frank.

"She wants me." Frank removed his hand.

"I'd rather do it with a pig."

"Won't happen, Gaileen. Some things even a pig won't do."

"Will that be piss with your bourbon, Frank?"

"I'm offended."

"That's not possible."

"In that case, piss will be fine, my dear."

"Piss it is." Gaileen walked away.

Frank watched her as she went to the bar. "We've been friends too long. A Philadelphia girl. Main Line." He looked at Arthur. "One of your 'outside the fence' types, no doubt."

Ten minutes later Montana and Frank sat alone. Arthur had gone to the men's room.

"You boys be leaving soon?"

"Tomorrow."

"Coming back?"

"Maybe."

"Hope so. Good to see new faces." Frank picked a piece of ice out of his drink and popped it into his mouth. "It ain't none of my business, but if you two need somewhere to stay after you done your business, you can stay at my trailer."

Montana didn't look up. Aware now. Careful. "Nothing wrong with this place," Montana said. "Good room. Nice bar. Making new friends every night." He waited.

"Trailer's out of the way. It's real private. Up in the north valley. You're welcome to use it. I told your buddy that, too."

"Thanks, Frank."

"My number's in the book. Elder. Frank Elder."

At three in the morning, Montana woke up. Tired as he was, the moan, low and drawn out, painfully constricted, penetrated his deep sleep. He didn't turn on the nightstand light between the two beds; the white window drapes, though drawn, allowed the passage of a soft orange glow, enough to illuminate the interior of the room. A metallic hum emanated from the room's window-mounted air conditioning unit and quavered in eerie resonance with the haunting, building groan coming from Arthur. Montana, instantly awake, sat on the edge of his own bed and watched Arthur twist in the pale light. The sound was brutish, inhuman ... something between a bleat and a howl. Montana shivered.

And he waited. He had seen it before, Arthur like this. Many times. A thing always unexpected and random, not connected to stress or liquor or to any sorrow in the waking world that Montana could determine. The ghostly intonation built. And still Montana waited, waited to see if the sound would go away. Sometimes, in times before, it would stop, fall back, diminish on its own. But on those nights when it didn't go away, when the unearthly discord built toward a scream, then Montana would hold Arthur, hold him tightly in his arms until his friend came awake. And the holding was a dangerous thing. It had to be done with strength and resolve because when Arthur came back from that place the first moments were violent and powerful.

On this night the howl died.

And Montana lay back down. And fell asleep again. The cool air of the room quickly dried the sweat on his brow.

9

The Writer

I need a favor, Melody." The shift boss with the steel-gray eyes affected a solicitous smile.

Here it comes, she thought. She clenched her teeth . . . she hadn't had to bunch up those jaw muscles in weeks. Melody waited for the proposition.

"The Sports Book needs a fill-in writer. I owe Bill a favor. You're a fast study, kid. You won't have any problem picking it up. No problem at all. What do you say?"

Melody didn't say anything. She was relieved not to have to tell him to blow off the expected request for sex. But she didn't want to be taken off the tables. She was confident dealing twenty-one, had just begun to get comfortable with the cards, with her co-workers.

"You still deal," he said. "Take your pick of shifts. You can still deal as much as you want. But give the Book three days. Friday through Sunday. Ten to six. That's all."

"Any tokes over there? I don't know anything about writing."

"If you take a turn on the cashier cage, you'll get tokes. Keep what you get. I'll tell Bill to let you rotate."

Melody pulled at her black bow tie. She wondered what would happen if she refused. Nothing good, she figured.

"How about it, Melody?" The sleek smile was still pasted there. Menacing. A shark smile. "This gives you good experience. It never hurts to branch out. The more training you get now, the more options you got later."

"When do I start?" No sense waffling over the inevitable.

"Atta girl. Go see Bill after your shift. I'll tell him you're coming." His smile expanded by three atoms of cheek on one side. A tic? Or was he happy? "I really appreciate it, kid."

The Sports Book manager was a thin, nervous-looking man. He appeared ten years older than Melody knew he was. His eyes flicked constantly up at the towering game board as he talked to her. He seemed to have a fearful regard for the ever-changing numbers that twinkled and rolled every few minutes behind the rows of weekend matchups of college and pro teams . . . as though his future depended on tracking the numbers' every nuance, every sparkle. Which it did. Melody hadn't seen such tension, such ill-concealed fear, on anyone so high up in the casino hierarchy. It made her uneasy. Mistakes in the Sports Book apparently could be big mistakes. The man wore a red bow tie that bobbled every time he swallowed . . . and he swallowed frequently.

"You're Melody." A statement, not a question . . . words spoken to fix Melody in his mind. "Sandy gets off in five minutes. She'll tell you what to do. Ever write before? No." Another statement that was supposed to be a question. Talking to this man was like being invisible. She didn't bother to suppress a glance down at her shirt bib, at her hands, which she spread, palms up, in front of her, as if checking to see whether she was really standing there. "I want to go over what she tells you later. That's my office." No gesture indicating where the office was. No nod. "Have her bring you in when she's through with you." His red bow tie bobbled in response to another gulp. His nervous eyes zeroed in on the numbers again.

"Is that Sandy over there?" Melody inclined her head at the only female behind the counter.

The man's eyes suddenly bulged. He took a step backward as if he had received a sharp blow to the face. He winced. He turned abruptly and scurried off toward a Teletype machine that had begun to chatter importantly on a cluttered desk in the corner.

Melody heard him mutter something about the Green Bay Packers as he rushed through the swinging wooden gate at the far end of the counter.

She wondered what she was getting into, wondered why her life couldn't stay simple for more than a few weeks at a time.

She liked it. She was amazed at the amount of cash moving over the steel-topped ticket machines. Most of the bets were small ones, ten or twenty dollars in crumpled bills placed by guys in T-shirts or by tourists uncomfortable and trying to bet for the first time while wives or "weekend wives" stood off to one side with confused, sometimes bored looks in the unfamiliar venue. But as game time neared, the heavy hitters moved up with their chewed pencils and clipboards and black, belt-carried portable phones; some dressed to kill in expensive suits; some not so well decked out, but with bets of a size that required her to turn and loudly request approval from the manager, who would rush over behind his bobbing bow tie for hurried appraisal.

"Five dimes on San Francisco."

"Three nickels on Minnesota."

"Two dimes on Atlanta."

A "dime," one thousand dollars; a "nickel," five hundred.

"Six dollars on the Cowboys." Six hundred dollars.

Melody got a kick out of the betting shorthand that always made the big money amounts sound small, insider shorthand that made a bet sound like it was no big deal. Sandy told Melody that the terms came from the phone bettors, the out-of-state call-forward traffic that ran to millions of dollars every season, wagers that were placed over telephones in an aura of paranoia because one never knew when the feds were listening in on the illegal out-of-state phone wagering . . . a bettor's lingo . . . transactions spiced with conspiracy . . . a taste of history . . . a remnant from simpler days when the country was young and betting parlors sprouted in back rooms.

The Sports Book was fun: careful work but carried on in a more relaxed atmosphere than at the tables; not as structured; not so many suspicious eyes; not so many goofball players who couldn't add up to twenty-one in less than sixty seconds, even when sober. More and more, Melody looked forward to the weekend work behind the ticket-spitting machines. The tokes weren't all that good. Not yet, anyway. But she had heard of the big few ... a fistful of bucks shoved over the counter by a cigar-chomping megatipper aware of the need to keep Lady Luck on his side, or by the T-shirted parlay winner, half-full of beer, expanding with largesse in the glow of a sudden, macho-building, garbage-in-gold-out victory.

She kept working part-time at the blackjack tables. She was nursing a respectable savings account, building it slowly. The dealing tokes helped a lot. She enjoyed the common persecution of the table dealer community, the friendship, the inside jokes, the story swapping, the "Us against the world" attitude.

"Five on Seattle minus five and a half." The bettor placed a neat pile of fifty hundred-dollar bills on the counter. Then he laid five more bills crosswise on top of the stack for the ten percent house vig. Five thousand five hundred dollars.

Melody looked up. Customer clean-cut, young, mid-thirties, lean, a tattoo high on the left bicep half-covered by a pressed sport shirt. U.S. Marine Corps anchor and globe.

She turned and looked for the red bow tie. He was standing by the Teletype machine pulling on the paper feeding from the rollers, trying to tug the latest line change out of the thing, trying to speed up the arrival of the most recent information.

"Five dimes on Seattle." She had to say it louder. Bow Tie was peering anxiously into the maw of the printer in an attempt to read the numbers before they exited the output rack. "Five dimes on Seattle!" she called once more.

Bow Tie's head snapped up like some hen suddenly aware of the flashing shadow of a chicken hawk. He hurried over, Adam's apple pumping, ticker tape abandoned, money pulling rank on numbers. His eyes tinged with anxiety, pupils wide.

Bow Tie looked at the money, looked up at the board, looked at the customer, looked back at the board. Once more at the customer. Looked through Melody. Again back at the board. Swallowed.

"Take it." Then he shouted in the direction of an open door that led to an office on the left side of the counter. Beyond the door, an assistant manager hunched over a desk under a wash of harsh fluorescent light. "Seattle to six!" The assistant manager looked up. Bow Tie shouted again, "Seattle goes to six!"

She counted the cash twice, then glanced up at the customer. He was doodling numbers on the edge of a pink parlay card with a short yellow pencil.

He was handsome. Composed. Showed none of the nervousness that the one-time-fling bettors displayed when they put everything they had on the "get-even" bet, a desperate stab at paying back company money or, perhaps, the kid's savings account. He seemed distracted from the business at hand, treating the bet as someone else might treat the purchase of a newspaper. Melody looked down at the tote machine and felt the betting slip with her fingers as it fed out of the slot. She tore the slip away from the cutter, separated the casino receipt from the customer's copy, and looked up into a pair of diamond-sharp hazel eyes that looked straight into hers. Not at the betting slip, not at the pink parlay card, not at the high rows of numbers—one of which went from five and a half to six as they stood there staring. The crystal eyes held her own. Her breathing grabbed. Stopped. She froze. His hand reached out and took the slip from her still fingers. The hazel eyes never left her face, never looked at the slip to check the printed numbers against the board in the manner of all players, big or small.

She was suddenly aware of what she was wearing. Was the shirt neat? The bow tie straight? Was her hair all right? Eyebrows? Lips?

Her nostrils flared as she tried to inhale him. The only part of her that moved.

He said, "Thank you."

She said, "You're welcome."

He waited, betting receipt in hand, silent, unmindful of the three impatient bettors in line behind him. He simply looked into her eyes and she looked back.

He smiled, then turned and walked away.

10

Karla

He walked toward the cashier's window.

Melody watched him come.

"Hello again. Looks like you brought me luck." He placed the winning ticket in front of Melody. He smiled at her.

Melody took the ticket, attempted to appear calm. She had tried to temper her memory of their first meeting, blunt the emotion, deaden the image and the feeling. She knew as well as any how dreams, especially romantic dreams, could self-polish and expand in the absence of daylight and good judgment. She was familiar with disappointment, had experienced the bitter revelation of reality not living up to expectation, of hope gutting itself on truth. She had been there before. She would not be fooled this time.

"I need a count. Cage count." She said the words loudly, her head turned toward the adjacent line of bet writers. The girl Sandy left her position and came over to the cage. Together they carefully counted, then recounted the money. The bettor had won five thousand dollars. Added to the amount he had invested when he placed the bet, the stack of crisp bills totaled ten thousand five hundred dollars.

Melody bounced the pile of new federal notes on the marble pay surface, tapped one side of the stack, then the other. She neatly straightened the edges of green paper. Riffed them. Then she put the pack down on the counter and pushed the money across to the customer.

"Nice win," she said. She looked at him.

"Just lucky. Thanks." He peeled three one-hundred-dollar bills off the stack, put them on his side of the marble surface, and pushed them in her direction.

"Have to keep the gods on my side," he said.

Melody reached out and touched the money. Her biggest toke ever. She didn't say a word. She picked up, then folded the three bills and put them in her shirt pocket. She stood there and looked at him.

"Well, guess I'll be going." He seemed confused because she hadn't said anything.

She still didn't say anything.

"So long." He hesitated, then turned and walked off past the waitress station that separated the Race Book from the Sports Book.

Once he looked back at her.

Melody stood there for a full two minutes staring out at the busy islands of slot machines in the center of the casino . . . not seeing them. Sandy went back to the writer's counter. No one else waited in line at Melody's cage to cash tickets.

She touched the folded bills through the material of her yellow blouse. They made a starchy, crinkling sound.

I I I

"How 'bout it? Can I stay with you for a week?" Karla's phone-voice betrayed her excitement. "Only till I get my own place." She was trying to sound nonchalant. Trying to sound as if Las Vegas was just one more bin of creeps waiting to do her in.

Karla continued before Melody could answer. "Pop's got me a day job slopping pizzas and subs off the Strip. Good pay. Probably a Mafia parlor."

"Promise not to smoke in my place?" Melody waited. Also excited.

"No."

"Okay." She laughed. "When do you get here?"

"I'm on the pay phone downstairs. I'll be up in thirty seconds. Be decent."

Ten days later, Karla was camped in a two-bedroom apartment one block from Melody. They shopped together. Hauled furniture in Melody's van. They scrubbed an oven and a refrigerator and a dishwasher . . . those appliances supposedly cleaned before she moved in, but cleaned to a male standard. One dead spider lay curled in a ball of belly and folded legs at the bottom of the dishwasher; two quite active pieces of fur-covered swiss cheese lurked beneath a paper towel and reproduced in the quiet, fetid air of a cracked vegetable bin in the refrigerator; a thin char of black, bubbled lava coated three of the four range-top burners, a mystery substance more mysterious because they also found it in the oven and in the overhead range vent.

"The guy must have burned virgins in here," Karla said, peering into the oven chamber on that first day.

"He probably just spilled something." Melody looked in over Karla's shoulder.

"Spilled something? Christ! This whole thing must have been on fire. A serial killer. I rented a serial killer's place. Nice."

Melody had begun to pop a few of the black carbon blisters on the range top with her fingernail. "Maybe you should have stayed at my apartment for a few more weeks. I think you could have found a better place."

So they scrubbed. Chipped. Scraped. Talked.

And laughed.

I I I

Melody's legs hurt. She was losing her endurance. Alternating with the stints in the Sports Book, where she was able to sit down for the entire shift, the constant standing while dealing twenty-one was starting to tell on her. She began to develop a habit of perching on one leg like a stork, then switching to the other leg for relief. She felt silly doing it. She was dimly aware that her subconscious mind was probably trying to tell her something . . . *go full-time to the Book.* But the blackjack table tokes were steady and predictable, and she was proud of the speed she had acquired with the cards and checks . . . not silver-dollar tokens now, but red and green five- and twenty-five-dollar checks. Five-dollar minimum bet table. Big stuff. She also enjoyed the interplay with the gamblers, even though it went against her grain not to chat with them beyond a few perfunctory phrases. The casino was strict about that.

He detoured around a small group of conventioneers who were watching one of their own playing at her table. He sat down at the open position to her right.

"Hello." And there was that soft smile.

"Hi." Both feet back on the floor. Alert. Pores opening. Heart shifting gears.

He played steadily. Intelligently. All the right hits. Not counting or, if he was, not pushing the bets.

She was seized by a sudden, dangerous urge to "tell" . . . to wiggle a finger when she had a hole ace, to cough, sniff, scratch her nose. *My God, where did that come from?*

Ten minutes later, the deck went cold. Two players, one the conventioneer, left the table. His crowd trailed after him.

Snotty comments from the fat lush on first base.

The cards stayed cold.

Only her Sports Book person pleasant, relaxed, steady.

Fat Lush lit a cigarette. Blew smoke at her.

She dealt the house three snappers in a row. Ace-king each time. Fat Lush beaten with an eighteen, then two twenty-counts. He cursed and left the table in a huff. Only one player, a one-legged Chinese lady, remained at the table with Sports Book.

Five hands later, she put China back on her crutch.

Only him and her now.

Three more hands.

"When do you finish your shift?"

"Forty-five minutes."

"Can I buy you a drink?"

"Not here."

"Where?"

"Across the street. Lounge. By the showroom."

Heartbeat. Bang, bang, bang.

"I'm Mike." He stood as she approached the small table in the low light. He pulled out her chair. He moved it smoothly under her as she sat down. On stage, a trio played a silk-soft jazz number.

"I'm Melody."

"What can I get you?"

Anything. "Bourbon and ginger."

"Bourbon and ginger it is."

For the first ten minutes they listened to the music, sipped cocktails, talked of the city, the smog, the casino construction boom, touched the small conversational bases that strangers touch in first moments. Talked to the air.

Then they began to talk to each other.

"You were in the service?" She pointed at the tattoo.

"Oh, that?" He laughed easily. "One night in San Diego . . . on a bet . . . and a little too much rum. No dashing dramatics, I'm afraid. No Hong Kong alley with spies and mysterious women." And he smiled again. "Just a weekend pass and not a lot of sense."

She watched his hands as he spoke. Strong hands. Clean. No ring. No watch. She looked at a small corral of veins that formed a "W" at the base of the knuckles of his middle and ring fingers on the back of his left hand. He moved his thumb tip slowly back and forth on the black surface of the table.

"How do you survive in this town without knowing the time?"

He rolled his wrist at her question as though he were wearing a watch and was going to read the time from it. He looked at the place where a watch would be. Then he looked at her eyes. Another super smile. "It's true, isn't it?" he said. "None of these places have a clock. Didn't believe it until I saw it for myself."

"Keeps the players from seeing how late it is. That's what they say."

"I've heard that."

"I suppose it makes sense." She took another sip of her drink. "Do you play twenty-one most of the time?"

"Never."

Melody looked down. She smiled.

"I bet sports," he said, "mostly football . . . only football."

"With no watch? Seems the customers are always checking their watches. Trying to get the bet down before kickoff."

"Think about it."

She thought. Five seconds. Ten seconds. Suddenly she tapped

her forehead twice and snapped her fingers. "That's right! The Race Book. Right next to us." She shook her head. "I never realized it. I've looked at those clocks a hundred times."

"Right."

"There's a whole line of them there."

"A clock for every track. Post times are important. I guess sometimes money counts more than psychology." Suddenly he raised his right arm high in the smoky air and snapped his fingers. A strong, rapid, aggressive action. A loud, sharp noise. No waiting for the cocktail girl to chance a glance their way. No hesitating half-wave. No trying to catch her eye. The abrupt crack of his fingersnap startled Melody, who was gently balancing reality, who was watching small things, who was spinning delicate "what-ifs" in her subconscious. The sharp noise made fear flicker in her stomach, and the sensation lingered for more seconds than she thought it should have.

She didn't say anything until the girl brought the order. In the odd silence that claimed that interval, almost three minutes, her partner took out his wallet, removed a hundred-dollar bill, and placed it under a corner of the empty ashtray. Then he studied a paper feathered into the folds of the clear plastic card holder in the center of his wallet. Somehow, she was alone.

The drinks came to the table.

Without looking up, Mike reached over and put one finger on the edge of the bill, snaked it from beneath the ashtray, and pushed it toward the waitress. "Take those drinks out of this."

"Yes, sir." The girl took the bill and headed back to the bar.

"What are you reading?" Melody spoke the words in a tone of voice that carried just a hint of irritation, and the sound of her question, the way it came out, surprised her.

He looked up. No apology for the distraction. "Checking this week's games. It's a short season. I'm glad it isn't longer. I'd probably be a confirmed addict if they played all year 'round." He glanced once more at the paper, then folded the wallet and put it back into his shirt pocket. He buttoned the pocket.

"Do you ever bet on the games?" he asked. She shook her head.

"Lucky you." He laughed. "It's fun, though . . . if you do your homework."

His attention shifted to the trio of musicians on a one-step riser at the center of the room, and he listened for a few seconds to the opening phrases of the song they started to play. The new number, a slow version of a forties torch favorite, caused a few heads to turn in response to the different sound.

A couple in their sixties got up from a table, walked to the parquet dance floor, and began to dance under the blue lights.

They watched the couple move to the music. The pair turned and swayed together with smooth, almost hypnotic ease. A testament to time, perhaps to love.

"May I dance with you?" His eyes on her again. A smile with teeth. An outstretched hand.

He led her through the maze of dark tables to the dance floor. He turned to face her, looked into her eyes for a few seconds.

He took her in his arms.

Her first three steps made her wonder if she was wearing snowshoes. Then awkwardness disappeared, and she drifted into the sensuous envelope of his easy grace. The music became part of the air she breathed, and she felt the hard structure of his shoulder beneath the thin fabric of his shirt. She became very aware of the pressure and position of her fingertips on that shoulder, and she moved them slightly on the angle of him as if her fingers were touching some magic, first-time thing.

They didn't speak.

After a delicate, floating minute his arm moved on her waist and drew her closer. She felt hips touch, thighs brush, his cheek graze, then press against her ear . . . and stay there. Their bodies seemed wrapped in gossamer. They moved together on the soft wings of the music. Silk on rock.

She breathed him in. Warm leather. Lime whispers. Clean fabric smell. October leaves.

The song fell away and the trio shifted pace, began another refrain, one faster, more alive in tempo, a doubled beat.

But he only cut the tempo in half, smoothly, no hesitation, and they continued moving in the same gentle way they started.

She allowed her eyes to close. She gave herself to the music, gave herself to him and to the measured agitation of what they did.

They danced a sweet mile in the blue light and never said a word.

When the trio stopped playing and went on break, Melody and Mike walked back to the table. A pile of bills, change brought by the waitress while they danced, lay between two half-full glasses.

Melody said, "Thank you. That was nice." Her heart said *Oh my.* Her brain said *Watch out* . . . but not much else.

"Do you like to dance?"

"Yes." She swallowed and dug her fingers into her thigh.

"You're a good partner. You make me look good." He ignored the money and sipped his drink.

"Nothing to it."

For some reason she didn't understand, she chose not to tell Karla about Mike. Not for two days, anyway.

"When did all this happen?"

"Tuesday. After work." Melody poured the contents of a can of mandarin oranges into a plastic Tupperware container and pressed the top closed. She set the empty can on the counter and looked out the window.

Karla stood by the open refrigerator door with a carrot stick in her hand. She stopped chewing. "Tuesday?"

"Yes."

Karla waited. Then she began to chew again. "No big deal, I suppose?"

"Maybe."

Another pause. Intuition in high gear. "Did he try to get in your pants?"

"No, he didn't try to get in my pants." Exasperated tolerance.

"Probably queer."

"I don't think so." She turned on the tap and rinsed the can.

"Are you going to see him again?"

"Next Tuesday." She finished cleaning the empty tin can and dropped it into the wastebasket.

"That doesn't go there."

"Oh, you're right." Melody fished the can out of the trash and put it into the recycling pail with the other empty cans.

"What's he do?"

"Do?"

"Yeah. Do. Like for work."

"I don't know."

"She doesn't know."

"It didn't come up."

"What didn't come up?"

"Karla!"

"Okay, okay." She tried to slam the refrigerator door shut, but it only bounced on the trapped cushion of air inside. The air whooshed out past the rubber door gasket. The door swung open again. Karla kicked the thing shut.

"Don't kick the door. It's the only new thing you own."

Karla pulled a chair out from the round kitchen table, spun it around, and sat on it reversed, the chairback between her legs, her elbows on the top of the seatback, skirt almost to her hips.

"Screw the door. What's he like? Another Craig?"

"Not quite."

"He better not be." She started to drum the fingers of her right hand on the top edge of the chair.

"He's got nice teeth."

"So's Dracula."

"He's a good dancer."

"That's nice. Does he come with a tin cup?"

Finally angry. "Why are you being such a little brat?"

Karla pointed a finger at Melody and sighted along it like it was a gun. "Don't call me little."

"He's a very nice man. He bets sports."

"Oh, my. He bets sports! How mysterious! He bets sports! I'll bet he's got a dick, too. Show me any guy in this damn town that *doesn't* bet sports. He bets sports."

"Tell me why you're being like this." But she knew.

Karla looked mean. "Tuesday."

"What about Tuesday?"

"I'd tell you if I met a guy Tuesday. I'd tell you Tuesday! On Tuesday. Not a week later."

"It's not a week later."

"Same thing."

"It is not the same thing."

"Yes, it is." A long pause. "Same thing."

Melody looked at her. "Don't sit like that."

"Like what?"

"Like that. Go put on some pants. Act like a lady."

Karla looked down at her lap. She got up and turned the chair around. "I'll sit any way I want. It's my house." But she smoothed her skirt over her thighs.

Melody failed to hold back a laugh.

Karla put on a soft face. "Do you really like him?"

"Yes."

"Okay."

11

The Hook

Montana waited for an oncoming truck to pass, then turned left across the highway onto a small feeder road. Another fifty feet and a right turn put them into a gravel parking lot in front of a small saloon that sat half-hidden by dust-covered trees. The roadhouse, a one-story wooden building hovering somewhere between quaint and seedy, boasted four cars in its sunlit parking area, all the vehicles nosed up like horses to the hitching rail that fronted the wide-planked front steps of the place. Above the dark, recessed entrance was a flat pinewood sign that tilted down and proclaimed to a generally disinterested world that this was the Mountain Springs Saloon.

The car crunched to a halt on the small stones. Yellow clouds of dust caught up to, swirled around, and investigated the shiny surfaces of the new arrival. As though finally satisfied with the dimensions of the visitor, the dust disappeared back into the gray rock. A black and white dog pressed its nose into a chicken-wire fence that defined an enclosure abutting the left side of the small tavern. The animal set its front feet apart, then barked loudly as Montana and Arthur stepped out.

"Fucking dog must be great for business." Montana closed the car door and stretched. The dog abruptly stopped making noise and trotted off toward the bar's side door. Duty done. Handout a possibility.

Arthur looked up at the snowcapped peak of Mount Potosi and slowly turned completely around. "If I ever decide to move out this way, this will be the spot." The air was crisp. A smell of pine sap and burning wood drifted in the bright sunlight.

They went up steps that squeaked, pushed past a beat-up door that was more concept than function, and sat down at one of the five tables. The place was dark and cool. Rough wood planks and brown overhead beams defined the interior. The wall behind the bar was crowded with signs and placards that displayed pithy slogans, gentle insults of rude humor, half-truths circumscribed. On the wall above an old jukebox were two eight-by-ten pictures of the tavern buried in snowdrifts from some past storm.

Four old men sat at one end of the bar and chatted in low tones with a stubby leather-skinned man who wore a stained apron. After an appropriate interval to underscore the casual mood of life at the side of a Nevada mountain road, the barman came over to the table with a frayed towel and wiped ashes and dust and water marks away.

"What's your pleasure, gents?"

"Bloody Mary," from Montana.

"Sounds good to me. Make it two." Arthur put a twenty on the table.

"Two red fuzzy ones . . . on the way." The man balled up the worn towel in a pudgy paw and went to make the drinks.

"You got a place for us?" Arthur pushed back his chair and crossed one leg over the other.

"Two rooms. A mile apart. Both with kitchens. I paid for six weeks in advance. Lots of football bettors in town this time of year. They come to Vegas to hang with the action and camp out till the money's gone."

The drinks arrived.

"What does our guy have working?"

Montana downed half his drink in a single swallow. "I think he's a middler."

"That's where someone bets both teams in a single game, right? With a different point spread on each bet?"

"Right. Our boy tries to get it both ways. Say he gets an early bet on Frisco at minus six and gets a late bet on the Giants at plus eight. If Frisco wins the game by seven points, he wins both bets. Figure it out. And seven is an easy number to hit. Even if the number doesn't fall, the worst he can do is lose one bet."

"How can he tell which way the line's going to move?"

"If I knew that, I wouldn't be sitting here watching you sip that Bloody Mary like some fairy-fart bluehair."

"Does he live alone?"

"No."

Arthur took another taste of his Bloody Mary, then shoved it across to Montana.

"One thing, Wolfer. We don't want to get made by the eye."

"The eye?"

"The eye in the sky, the videotape cameras in the ceiling. They're all over the place. Little black dome things. To nail scammers. No sense us being seen together. They save those tapes. It could be trouble."

"Is this guy Mike Henry bad news?"

"He used to be a pusher. He got his stake selling meth to schoolkids on the coast. He's a prime-cut scumball."

"Is he a shooter?"

"He's an ex-grunt, according to the buyer. I'll know more after I watch him."

"Watch him good."

❚ ❚ ❚

"Ouch!"

"They're hot. Be careful."

Melody shook her hand in the air, then stuck her fingertips into her glass of ice water. Four people at the next table turned to look. She hurt too much to be embarrassed.

"I'm sorry." Mike looked serious even though a half-smile played at the corners of his mouth. "When this place serves a bucket of clams, it serves them hot."

Melody rolled her eyes up and looked at the ceiling. She wiggled her fingers in her glass of ice water. "That's what I get for eating in buffets all my life. I'm not used to hot food."

They sat at a table in the Seafood Grotto in the Frontier. The pristine table settings and the sound of rushing water coming from the stone waterfalls in the dining room lent an air of elegance to the room, and Melody's "ouch" exclamation turned a few heads.

"Keep them in the water," and he put his hand gently onto hers to prevent her from removing her fingers from the salving liquid. "Ice is the best thing. It keeps the capillaries from breaking."

The pain began to die away.

"I'm a klutz."

"You're not a klutz." He lifted her hand and looked at her fingertips. And kissed them. He smiled. "I can't take you anywhere." Then he kissed them again, one by one. The hurt disappeared. It was replaced by a warm feeling that started in her stomach, then migrated downward as she watched his lips touch her.

Despite herself, she thought of Craig, of how he would have handled it. Probably would have laughed in her face and gone right on eating . . . then discussed the possibility of a lawsuit.

The people at the next table nodded and smiled and went back to eating pink crab legs.

He ordered wine and then dinner. While they waited, they shared a piece of sourdough bread after he buttered it and offered the first bite to her. They took turns at the single piece of bread.

The rest of the meal went better than the appetizer. He talked to her, not at her. And he listened to what she said. Listened to her adventures, her doubts, her muted but determined resolve to make a go of things in the casino venue. Her voice had carried a bit of challenge, a bristling note of strident wariness when she tried to justify the new attempt at independence.

And the bottle of wine lost its contents in silent increments.

Over pale sorbet, she learned he'd taken a room in the Atrium Tower suites above the palm-guarded swimming pool beyond the windows.

"Do you live here?"

He laughed. "No. I just like to try out different hotels. I hope to find my lucky room." A quick look of concern on his face. A look that said he might have said something that could be taken the wrong way. "What I mean is, I'm superstitious . . . if I do well betting the games this weekend, I'll come back here next time." Now that smile again. "All gamblers are hopelessly superstitious. I'm no different."

You're different, she said to herself. A last chunk of sorbet managed to evade her pursuing spoon tip at the bottom of the silver dish. "I've never been in one of those new rooms." Bold. "I hear they're really nice." Wine easy and daring in her veins. She grinned at him. Her tummy full and warm.

"They're real nice."

She stood by the big window that overlooked the pool. From the high tower, twenty-three stories above the blue-green water, she watched the Las Vegas Strip twinkle and bustle noiselessly as it ate dreams. A fat moon lazed in the blue-black sky above Frenchman Mountain to the east. Landing lights on airplanes floated over black mountains and drifted at McCarran Airport to the south.

She felt his heat as he came up to stand behind her, heard the soft rustle of his clothing as it came to press against hers. She could smell the clean smell of him.

"Would you care for brandy?" His arms encircled her waist. "I have some in the reefer."

"I thought brandy tasted better at room temperature." She rested her head back on his chest.

"I like it cold." Arms tight now. "I'm not that classy."

She felt the length of his erection press into the cleft of her backside. "You feel pretty classy to me," and firmly pushed her hips rearward and centered him.

He kissed the back of her neck. Lights twinkled. Traffic inched. Planes drifted. Dark mountains slept.

She felt his hand move in the tight space between them, heard his belt come undone with a leathery whisper. Then she felt a long ridge of pressure hot through her dress, felt it lengthen until it reached to the small of her back.

She reached down on either side, grasped a handful of skirt, slowly lifted the fabric, slid it up over her legs until it was bunched at her waist. The breath-thin silk of her panties seemed to dissolve against the thing pressing at her.

"I think I'll pass on the brandy."

"Maybe later?" he said, almost inside her ear.

"Maybe." Her hands didn't belong to her. They floated away from her arms and found her hips. Someone's thumbs, her thumbs, hooked into the top elastic of her panties, pushed them down. His arch of flesh cooked her curves, poled against her burning skin, reached from the hot place between her buttocks up to and under the edge of her blouse.

If there was a place where all the good feelings of wine spirits blossomed before the ache of excess took over, she was at that place.

She reached behind and encircled his sex, her hand not able to make the circumference.

Eyes cast down more in hunger than in innocence, she turned around. Her pupils widened in the dim light, light dim but not too dim. "I should go to the ladies room . . . shouldn't I?"

"No."

He gently unwrapped her fingers from him and he undressed her in a way that made her realize she had never known what undressing could be. She felt her own heat weave its way up over her bare flesh when he was finished with her clothing.

She watched him undress. He watched her watching him.

They stood naked under the moon. By the window. Soft above the sparkling lights beyond the glass.

He entered her there where they stood. Lifted her up with hard hands, then lowered her slowly onto him. She moved her legs apart as he began to fill her. She felt, because of his size, what should have been pain, but the filling was a thing undefined by pain.

Half-full with him, she raised her legs and wrapped them both around his waist. She dug clawed fingers into his shoulder curves and felt him swell still more inside her at the gouging ferocity of her nails' press.

She locked her legs and lifted partway up to wet the tight girth. Twice more. Slowly. Lubricated the brawny lust that fed into her. Then farther down. Then down all the way. Down until her insides moved, and male and female curves locked together.

The things of the room pulsed in dizzy spins.

Eyes shut. Her expression drugged. Her inside muscles feeding. The warm air around them heavy and weightless in the same moment, its currents filled with the salty scent of sex. Wet rawhide. Power. Desire.

Her nerves began to harden. A sudden tension straightened her fingers. Her hands broke from his shoulders. He cradled her weight in his strong arms as she bent back.

It rushed at her. A genetic snarl. Erotic was a new word. And then it was upon her ... took her mind ... took her soul ... took away everything except the violent, raging desire to have.

▮ ▮ ▮

Arthur Arthur pushed back the white drapes and stuck a finger into a gap in the Venetian blind level with his eyes. He moved his finger down, and the thin metal of three slats buckled in sequence with curt, tinny clicks. He looked out through the opening onto a world dark and wet with early autumn rain. From the second-story window of his room he could see the reflected marquee lights of an aged hotel across the street shimmer on the black surface of water along the far curb. It was midnight. Few cars moved. From those that did pass by, the hiss of tire treads on the wet macadam barely penetrated the streaked glass of his window. One couple, man and woman, then three solitary pedestrians, one of those with a folded newspaper held above his head as a shield against the drizzle, moved quickly along the sidewalk, heading toward the Strip two blocks away.

After a few minutes of watching bands of mist dance gracefully on invisible gusts of night wind, he turned away from the window and stood in the darkened room. He was naked. He was alone. Montana had dropped him off that afternoon and would begin to case the mark in the next few days. They would remain apart until Montana got what they needed.

He walked across the room and sat down on the edge of the bed. In the dim light penetrating through the heavy drapes, he stared at nothing in particular, waited for his pupils to dilate and build images of chair, nightstand, dresser. Unlike most, he did not find disconcerting the thought of spending the coming days in his room ... alone ... without his partner ... unable to taste the easy delights of the neon monsters, those voracious casinos that built a soft electric fire beneath the desert sky. He had learned to wait, to hunker down and let time move past him, to ignore that empty space he could not fill with people.

After a long interval in which he listened to the muted sound of a television set in the room below his, listened to a door slam, listened to the frame of the two-story building creak at a sudden nudge of outside wind, he switched on the bedside light and reached for the black nylon carrying case that contained Montana's "Yugo," the AK-47 spotter rifle. He unzipped and positioned the open case on his lap and stared at the weapon. Its metal bulk felt more than cold, sucked heat from his hands where he touched it. Finally he lay back on the bed, feet still touching the floor, and rested the nine-pound Mitchell semiautomatic on his forehead, balanced it at its midpoint so that it seesawed slowly and pressed onto his skin above his eyes. The axis of the rifle and that of his body formed a cross, a shape made of steel and human form. The nylon case tilted, slid off his thighs, and fell to the floor. He closed his eyes. He drew comfort from the weight of the weapon on him, from the smell of gun oil and teak loose in the air, from the icy pressure that pushed away the small headache that had begun to nibble at him an hour ago. He wondered how many other shooters in how many places used cold killing-iron like aspirin as he did in that moment. More than a few . . . a unique approximation, a pragmatic bond peculiar to those familiar with the mystique of man and weapon.

Ten minutes passed. He sat up and recased the rifle. He filled in a crossword puzzle and drank one can of beer. He showered. He shaved. He went to his overnight bag and removed a sound-activated tape player and plugged its adapter into a wall socket next to the nightstand. He turned on the player's standby switch, positioned the thing on the edge of the table near his head. Any sound in the room would cause the device to play a prerecorded sequence. He spoke a few words aloud. Words not important for their meaning but for their sound. The red light on top of the small machine blinked on in response to the agitation of voice noise, and Arthur heard the tape start to move. After a few seconds the moving tape stopped. But not before the tape player emitted three sharp cracking sounds . . . the noise of twigs being snapped . . . a sound that would bring Arthur instantly awake. And stop the dreams and the howling noise they brought.

I I I

Montana pulled into the parking lot of a pizza restaurant that sat behind a tall sign painted with a stylized rendering of the Leaning

Tower of Pisa. He stopped the car and put a sheaf of handwritten notes resting next to him on the front seat into the glove compartment and locked it.

The place was dark. A humid, dough-smelling aroma met him as he entered through the heavy front door. Highbacked wooden seats paired with brown tables lined the walls, and the center floor of the eatery was sectioned by a series of long slab tables with low benches on each side. All the tables showed the standard napkin holder, salt and pepper shakers, and matching glass cylindrical containers of grated cheese and red pepper flakes. A dozen teenage boys occupied two of the center tables and talked in loud voices distinct and raucous over the noise coming from beeping video game machines and a blaring jukebox that stood along the wall opposite the order counter.

Montana studied the menus that lay pressed flat beneath a scratched length of plexiglass next to the cash register. A short, compact, well-built woman in her mid-thirties stood beside the register. She was trying to make sense of a jumble of scribblings on a takeout order slip. She shook her head with undisguised annoyance as she attempted to decipher what the lanky, acne-pocked boy talking on one of two order phones had handed her as Montana came through the front door. Her black curls bobbled at the edges of a paper chef's hat when she abruptly turned in the direction of the boy on the phone. The tall white hat began to topple off her head, and she crammed it back into place with her free hand, an act of salvation that turned the thing into something resembling a smashed pie plate.

"Hey, Gumball!"

Gumball kept talking on the phone.

"Stupid! Yeah, you!"

The fellow looked over at her, the phone still in his ear. He looked frightened.

She waved the slip in the air. "English, Dartface! Try it in English! I don't read Chinese!" She stamped her foot, and crumpled up the order. "Where'd you learn to write? On a roller coaster?"

She wheeled around to face Montana. "What the hell do you want?"

Montana just looked at her.

She grimaced at him. Put on a dinky, false smile and adjusted what was left of her hat. Tried to smooth out the rumpled order slip on the edge of the counter. "Sorry, Clyde. Didn't mean to shout. Gumball there isn't the sharpest tool in the shed." She tossed her head over her shoulder in Gumball's direction. The boy stood transfixed. Small squalking noises came from the phone and carried over the noise of the restaurant to the counter.

"What can I get you?"

"What's good?"

"The place across the street."

He looked down at the menu again. "How about one of those garlic things . . . medium one. They any good?"

"They're wonderful. Great if you like garbage. Try the Hawaiian Delight. Give your stomach half a chance."

"What's on it?"

"Ham, pepperoni, canned pineapple. Ten bucks."

"Okay. I'll have one of those."

"You going to eat in this pigsty or take out?"

"For here."

"Anything to drink?"

"Serve beer?"

"Beer's flat."

"Flat?"

"Flat as snakeshit. Gumball's twin sister left the friggin' tap cracked last night."

"Ice tea?"

"Ice tea's okay. You want the salad bar? Buck ninety-five extra."

"No salad bar."

"Good choice."

She punched some keys on the register and handed him part of the slip that cranked out. "Number thirty-two. What's your name?" She waited with her pencil poised over her half of the receipt.

"Smith."

"Pick something else. I got a Smith waiting."

"Vader. Darth Vader."

She looked up. Then wrote the word "Vader" on the receipt. She shook her head. "Clowns. I get clowns."

Montana folded his part of the slip and put it in his wallet and put a twenty-dollar bill on the counter.

She made change.

He took the change. She wiped her hands on her apron. "Should be about fifteen minutes, give or take a half-hour . . . that's if this hole don't get shut down by the Health Department first."

She got him his glass of ice tea and shoved a straw at him after biting off the top inch of wrapper with her teeth. She spit the wrapper top into the air.

He smiled at her. "You got my name, what's yours?"

She regarded him seriously for a few seconds. "Karla."

"Thanks, Karla."

"Go sit down."

"Yes, ma'am."

"Watch your butt." She nodded at the table of noisy teenagers. "These hormone bags leave sauce all over the seats."

Fourteen minutes later, Karla brought the pizza to Montana's booth. She also filled his ice tea glass from a plastic pitcher she carried.

"Here you go, Vader. This is about as far as we deliver."

"Thank you."

"Don't let it go to your head."

She stood there looking at him for a few seconds, then set the pitcher of tea on the table and sat down on the seat facing him. She took a cigarette from the pack in her uniform pocket and lit up. "Time for my break. Smoke bother you?"

"No. Not if you give me one. Left mine in the car."

She gave him a cigarette and a light.

"Who's watching the counter?"

"The sun'll come up tomorrow." She reached over and picked a chunk of pineapple off the top of his pizza, popped it into her mouth, leaned against the seatback, and blew smoke up in the air by sticking out her lower lip. "What's your game?"

"Game? You mean do I gamble?" He looked at her with a deadpan, uncommitted expression. But inside he smiled. "I don't gamble."

"You eat *here*, you gamble."

"I'm in town on business. I sell outboard motors."

"Outboard motors?"

"Right." He let the smile come out.

She stole another piece of pineapple. "Okay, so it's none of my business."

"Well, I'm not here to gamble, anyway." He puffed at his cigarette. "Didn't mean to be a wiseass. Sorry about that. Thanks for bringing my pizza over."

"No big."

"Here. Have some." He pushed the hot tin plate toward her.

"Think I'm crazy? Most of that stuff's been walked on." She lifted another piece of pineapple. "Except for this. This just came out of the can." She popped the piece into her mouth.

She ate almost all his pineapple chunks as they sat there for twenty minutes talking about nothing in particular.

"Well, Vader. Better get myself back to work. Gumball's likely up to his dripping zits in alligators. Nice talking to you. Thanks for the junk food." She looked at him, a direct gaze, open, a hint of expectancy.

"You married?" from him.

"You sell outboards?" from her.

Montana opened the car door and stood there in the Pisa Pizza parking lot for a minute to let the heat escape. Then he got in, closed the door, started the engine, and let the air conditioner work on the interior. He removed the sheaf of papers he had locked in the glove compartment and thumbed through them. He removed two pages of notes. They were handwritten observations penned by one of the casino's PIs. The mark, Michael Patrick Henry, had been tailed for a week by the PI to build a habit profile. On two of those days the mark seemed to be following someone, but the PI hadn't been able to figure out who it was . . . he had his hands full keeping Henry under surveillance without blowing his cover.

Montana took a pencil from the center console and scratched out the Pisa Pizza name. *Nothing here,* he thought. *If the mark stopped at the Pisa Pizza, it had nothing to do with the betting. No "big money boys" in that joint, they'd stand out like Gumball's zits.* He thought for a moment more about Las Vegas, about how so many people tailed other people around the city . . . an invisible parade . . . all the way from the owners and politicians at the top down through the cops to the small-time pickoff artist following a jackpot winner out to the parking lot—or out to some dark, lonely desert road leading home.

Montana put the collection of papers back in the glove box. Then he took out his wallet, and on the back of the pizza receipt he penciled in "Karla" and the phone number of the place. He drew a star by her name and drew a circle around the star.

He smiled and shook his head as he looked at her name. Then he drove off.

▮ ▮ ▮

Montana pulled off his backpack and set it on the ground. He cleared a spot in the sharp shale talus with his boot and sat down with his shoulders resting against a large boulder. The hot slab of rock faced east, to the sun, and the heat pressing into the skin of his back through his shirt was uncomfortably warm. He leaned forward and took a pair of binoculars from the backpack. He raised the glasses to his eyes, then settled back gingerly against the rock. Tolerable this time.

From his perch low on the foothills of Mount Charleston he could see the mark's back yard. He fiddled with the adjusting knob on the binoculars.

Two hours later, baking in bright sun, sweating despite the dry air of the high desert, Montana verified that he had a problem . . . a thing that had bothered him when he first read the profile of Michael Patrick Henry in the buyer's office on the first day. A thing he hadn't told Arthur.

The mark had a daughter.

He watched the two playing kickball in the postage-stamp confines behind the house below.

The dollars were big. Their biggest contract yet. The money he and Arthur would get from the hit could set them up for the next five years.

And the mark had a kid. A goddamn kid.

Montana felt sick.

He watched the yard for twenty minutes. Henry's head turned toward the house. He said something to the little girl and went inside, reappearing a few moments later with a portable phone held to his ear. The mark crouched down and wedged the receiver between head and shoulder as he tied his daughter's shoe. The little girl lay back on green grass and pointed at a single white cloud.

Montana put down the binoculars and reached for his knapsack. In seconds, he had set a Bearcat portable scanner on the rock next to him, screwed its chrome antenna into place. He punched up the search mode bracketing the forty-six megahertz band and pushed the red search button. Green digits flickered, then froze on a wandering conversation between two women. He pushed again. Teenagers. Whiny. Giggly. Pushed again. Green numbers flickered, then stopped and twinkled 46.610 on the panel face. And he heard the mark talk.

12

Poor Choice

Arthur stepped out of the convenience store and turned left into a dark alley that paralleled the Strip and led to his room in the converted motel. He tucked a brown paper bag containing chips and a bottle of bourbon into the crook of his arm. 2:00 A.M. Windy. Crisp air. No people or cars moved in the narrow lane between windowless building walls. He pulled his jacket zipper up as far as it would go.

He stepped around a puddle left by the previous night's rain. On the surface of the dirty water a soggy, six-page pulp handout advertising female "escorts" floated in slow, desultory circles. The torn, wet pages shivered, then accelerated and moved fitfully across the tiny lake, pushed along by a chill kiss of night wind spinning through the alley. On saturated pages, telephone numbers in bold black print framed pictures of women, some legs spread wide, a rack of plump breasts bulging, two rumps high and curving, a pair of eyes promising . . . more truly, pleading.

A rat scurried.

Arthur passed a dark recess in a wall to his right and caught a brief impression of something moving quickly at him through the shadow.

Then the night air whistled as a dark force tore through it with vicious speed. His world exploded.

He went down.

His package hit the pale cement at the edge of the alley road and he could hear, as though from a great distance, the crack of the bourbon bottle inside the bag. His senses reeled and spun in ugly confusion. Bursts of red light flared through his brain. His sense of sound faded, then went quickly mute. He was down on his hands and knees in gray silence, silent. No breath came.

He felt himself kicked. He rolled and knew he was on his side. His right ear was warm and wet. He couldn't see.

A brutal impact rocked the back of his head a second time.

He sensed them, aware of two persons standing near. Kicking at him. He tumbled toward unconsciousness. The red light coming at his brain turned into blue fog.

The blue went to darkness.

He was looking up from the depth of some brutal place, looking up at a dim light far away, pinioned in a cold pit of hope-killing verticals.

He felt hands rip into his jacket front, then into the back pocket of his pants where his wallet was, and he felt the wallet pulled out.

He sensed alien movements swirling about him and he dropped deeper into the sucking helplessness.

"Got it, man. Got his stuff."

"Give it here. Lemme see."

"Pull his shoes. Fucking money there. Might be motherfucking money there. Get his shoes."

He was tugged at, shoved.

Arthur began to struggle for the light. He felt the first tongues of rage flicker in his gut, the first heat of vengeance. He sucked chunks of night air, and that air fed the thing that fed him. He concentrated on the yellow glow that spilled over the high edge of the pit.

A weight pressed onto his chest, the knee of one of them. They wrenched off one of his shoes.

The thing inside him expanded like an unwrapping steel spring.

On the dry, gritty pavement his right arm stretched out, his fingers walked desperate inches, scratched hard asphalt, found then hooked around the neck of the broken whiskey bottle.

A mean face turned, looked down. Eyes wide and white nesting black pupils.

Arthur drove the savage edges of the broken bottle into the space between the eyes. He pulled the bottle back. The eyes floated in a sea of hamburger. Mean angles of brown glass stuck out like amber slabs of slate pinned into a mountain landslide, like brittle fragments of pack ice thrust above a frozen sea, like plates of pain if pain had shape. Arthur drove the weapon hard into the man's side, felt it pop in steps through shirt and skin and muscle and into some soft place. He twisted the bottle clockwise as far as his wrist allowed, then counterclockwise, hard, deep, always deeper, pushing deeper. The weight toppled away to his right and squirmed on the roadtop.

Arthur raised up on his elbows, rolled left, and stood. The other one sat hypnotized, its backside glued to earth by the sight of the thing that writhed six feet away holding a screeching face. Sat and stared as though starched. Sat in a tetany of disbelief. Stunned. Iced. Paralyzed.

Arthur strangled the sitting one as it sat there, strangled it with a single hand: fingers curled under flesh anterior to the side muscles of the neck; the jugulars and windpipe trapped; spindly hoops of trachea crimped in the "V" between thumb and palm.

A light above a door came on. The sudden glare startled him. He picked up his wallet. He hurried away from the light.

He put ice in a towel and held it against the back of his head where the scalp was mashed. Then he stood in the shower, ran cold water, and cleaned away the grit. He rubbed stinging soap into the red lacerations. Rinsed with more cold water.

He stepped from the shower and without drying himself moved into position before the bathroom mirror and approximated the torn halves of his split ear. As he stood there squeezing the two parts of ear together, pressing hard to gel the tear, he saw a stranger in the glass. He looked into the eyes of the other, the one whose ear was split like his.

In that sharp moment anger swelled in his sore body, a sudden, fleeting surge of rage that melted slowly away to sadness. He willed the physical pain away. But he could not numb the pain that draped a foul realization on his soul of how he was changing. In times past, he would have rolled away from the blow that put him down on the alley road. He would have reacted, perhaps parried the attack completely. He would have taken them apart in those first violent microseconds like he was dining on lobster, dissecting each hard angle, every vulnerability, every static defense.

Mingled with the sound of the water still running from the shower spigot behind the plastic curtain . . . he thought he heard someone or something laugh. The walls were thin. Not that thin.

❘ ❘ ❘

"What the hell happened to you?"

At Montana's question, Arthur touched the scabbed surface on the back of his head, then fingered the black line bisecting the stiff flesh of his healing ear. An awkward, fleeting, but sharp guilt tinkered with his brain. What he had done in the alley wasn't the kind of thing that should have happened to someone trying to keep a low profile. He guessed that the police wouldn't spend much time looking for the public benefactor who'd taken out the muggers, wouldn't expend much energy or resources attempting to discover who was doing their work for them. But he knew he'd overreacted. Let his rage control him. It was the kind of thing that could make trouble. He didn't like the feeling of having made a rookie mistake any more than he liked having to make up some half-assed story to feed Montana.

"I slipped in the damn shower. Almost drowned myself." Arthur grinned, a weak smile. Sheepish . . . not at the proffered excuse, but at the new and unfamiliar discomfort of lying to someone he couldn't afford to lie to. Didn't want to lie to. He changed the subject. "What about our man?"

Montana didn't pursue the matter of the ear. He walked over to the window and peered out at the street, keeping his back to Arthur. "He's got a place on the northwest side of town. Backs on the slope of the mountain. It's in one of those stucco farms where the old farts hit golf balls and keep the cops chasing shadows all night."

"Anyone with him?"

"Just some girlfriend. She's got a kid. Guy's probably using her for a steady sleeve . . . and to keep the local fuddy-duddies off his ass." Montana kept looking out the window.

"Think he's working alone?" Guilt gone. Montana wasn't going to push the bathtub business.

"Haven't found anyone."

Arthur sat on the edge of the bed. He began to stuff dirty clothes into a mesh laundry bag. Busywork. Casual. "Got his phones?"

Montana turned away from the window and sat down on a wooden chair by a round table. "I left the scanner set up in the rocks back of his house. On standby on his frequency. Nicads and a VOX. Clear as a bell." He put his feet on the table. "He talks, we listen. I check the tape each forty-eight hours. Under the moon."

"Think he's got a hardwire phone, too?"

"Likely. He's got to have more brains than that. Wouldn't do much sensitive business on the portable, my guess. Not this one."

"Does he stay in town all the time? Does he do any traveling?"

"He goes north maybe every third day toward Reno. Early in the morning. By himself. He's gone about five hours. It wouldn't surprise me if he's greasing his lizard at one of them whorehouses over the county line. I haven't tailed him all the way, not yet. The road's too empty. He'd make me in a New York second."

"Does he go alone?"

"Alone."

Arthur twisted the top of the laundry bag closed. "I'll be back in a minute. I have to throw these things in the wash." He slid coins off the table by the bed. "Got any quarters?"

Montana found three in his pants pocket. He handed them to Arthur.

"Thanks."

Montana looked at him. "Don't fall down."

I I I

"Hey, Vader. Back for more?"

"Garbage hot?"

"Hot? What's 'hot'? You'll be lucky if the cheese melts."

"Where is everyone?"

"Word spreads fast. Customers are dying off like flies."

"Do you still steal the customers' pineapple?"

"It's on the house. Go sit down."

I I I

"A deal you can't refuse." Montana slapped Arthur on the shoulder.

"A double date? You want me to watch?"

"It will get you out of this hole for a few hours."

"A double date?"

"Just a movie and a few drinks. Maybe a show. You don't have to marry the bitch."

"Whose big idea is this?"

"It's my idea. Keep you from playing with yourself."

"No thanks."

"Look. This girl's a kick in the ass. She's got a friend. I figure we can both use a night out. Just like the old days. You'll go batshit staying here all the fucking time."

"Where'd you meet her?"

"In a pizza joint. She's funny as a sack of wet cats. She has a great ass, too. Know what they call a great ass in this town? The 'don't side' . . . like on the dice tables."

"That's real interesting."

Arthur looked at Montana and shook his head. Montana wore an expression of youthful expectation—a teenager's great idea. This teenager was fifty-six years old. Arthur tried not to smile. "I suppose you've seen her friend. Dogmeat, right? Do we have to swing by the pound to pick them up? Who buys the leash?"

"Do me a favor . . . look, I don't want to scare this one. She's different. You come along. We take her friend. That way, I won't fuck things up like usual."

"See that phone book? Ever look at the yellow pages in this town? You want a night out, all you need to do is use the phone. 'E' as in Entertainment. They deliver."

"This ain't like that."

The look on Montana's face wouldn't cave in.

"Okay. Once. Then you're on your own," said Arthur.

"All right! I owe you one."

"You owe me more than one."

"So I owe you two."

I I I

"No, Karla!"

"A favor."

"Favor?!?"

"Yeah."

"A favor? I'm seeing someone!" Melody stamped her foot.

"Let's not throw a wedgie, Mel."

"You just can't go around fixing me up with every pizza geek in town. No! I won't do it."

"Have I ever asked you to do this?"

"Yes! Of course you have."

"Maybe once or twice."

"Once or twice? What about that bunch of Navy SEALS in San Diego? You consider that once?"

"That was like a USO thing."

"USO!?! That was a grope! A grope!"

"So we went swimming."

"We went swimming in San Diego Bay! In the middle of the night! To get away from those oversexed maniacs! Swimming? Swimming you say!?!"

"They had some great buns."

"Great buns? How the heck would I know? I was swimming for my life."

"You shouldn't run. It makes them think you're afraid."

"That's what they tell you about animals, Karla . . . animals. You aren't supposed to run away from *animals!*"

"Yeah."

"And that gardener . . . that guy living in the bushes. What about that one!?! He didn't even have his green card. He had fertilizer in his shoes, Karla. He really had fertilizer in his shoes!"

"That was sort of a cross-culture thing. I didn't know you were prejudiced."

"Oh my God! I am *not* prejudiced! You could have at least let me ride in the front of the truck!"

"There wasn't room for the four of us. You didn't want him to ride back there alone, did you? He was *your* date."

"I can't believe you did that. Do you know what it's like riding in the back of a junk pickup truck? All those lights shining in your face!?!"

"I've ridden in the back of a pickup truck. Don't make a big deal of it."

"When you were *ten*, Karla, when you were *ten!*" Melody smacked her hand down on the tile top of the counter. "No! Go tell your hot little friend I'm busy . . . I'm out of town . . . I've got AIDS."

"Will you just listen for a minute?"

"And that clown . . . that mimic, or whatever you call him . . . the dumb freak making all those stupid hand things. He never said a word all night. I thought that stuff was for the sidewalk!"

"He was nice."

"Nice!?! How the heck would I know? He even ordered off the menu that way. Nice!?! Three *hours* of that, Karla . . . three terrible hours!"

"He thought it was cute, I guess. Like, it's what he does. He thought we'd get a kick out of it. You didn't have to give him the finger."

"Yes, I did, Karla. Yes, I *did!*"

"I thought you were above that."

"It cost me twenty dollars to get home! Twenty dollars for the cab. Twenty dollars was a lot of money."

A long pause. Melody went to the sink and filled a glass with water and drank it. She calmed a bit. "I'm sorry. I'm seeing someone. That's all there is to it."

"The sports guy?"

"Yes."

"Mel, this is special to me." Eyes on Melody. Hands clasped in front of her skirt. Arms straight. Cinderella leaning against the refrigerator. Soft voice. "My guy wants his friend to come along. Just this once. Says his buddy's been working too hard. He could use a night off . . . needs a night off. No funny stuff. Just dinner and a movie. Nothing else. I swear. My lug is trying real hard to act like a gentleman. It means a lot to him . . . being a gentleman and his friend 'n all . . . and my lug means a lot to me."

No reply from Melody. She refilled the water glass. Drank one swallow. Set it down in the sink.

"I know it sounds stupid," said Karla, "but I like this guy." Medium pause. "Can you help me, Mel? This once?"

13

Double Date

"Karla, this is Arthur. Wolfer, meet Karla."

"Hi. What is it? Arthur or Wolfer?"

"Arthur."

"Come on in, guys. Hey Mel! They're here."

"Nice to meet you, Karla."

"Sure. Have a seat on her new sofa. I'm not allowed to sit on it. Mel's doing her face. How about a drink? Beer? Soda? Booze?"

"Beer'd go good," from Montana. Happy smile at Karla. He looked at Arthur. "What'd I tell you?"

Arthur smiled. He nodded. "Nothing for me, thanks."

"One beer, one nothing. Coming up."

Montana sat on the sofa. Arthur went to the window and looked out at the street.

"Where are we going, Karla? What's on?"

"I thought we'd go over to the Rio. Hit the steak house. Then we walk over to the Gold Coast. They got a movie theater there. Got a dance hall, too. Bowling upstairs . . . if you want to get beat. Me and Mel can take you two . . . easy. You dance, Arthur?"

"Not very well."

"He can dance, Karla. Ol' Wolfer can do anything."

Karla poured half a can of beer into a pilsner glass. She brought it over to Montana from the kitchenette that opened onto the small living room. She carried the half-empty can.

"What's this?"

"That's a glass, Vader."

Montana looked at Arthur. "Ever drink beer out of a glass?" He held the glass up.

Arthur didn't reply.

Karla sat next to Montana. She took a drink from the can. "I hope you guys don't mind the tourist bit. If you'd rather go somewhere else, it's all right with us. There's other places. I know a nice Mexican joint out on Tropicana."

Montana shook his head. "We ain't been anywhere. You decide, Karla."

Arthur looked at Montana. A flat look. He went over and sat down in the easy chair. The possibility of being caught on casino videotape bothered him.

Montana read Arthur's mind. "It sounds great to me. I guess one night away from the Strip won't hurt."

Arthur didn't say anything.

"So, you guys are both in the outboard motor racket?" Karla raised her eyebrows and looked over the top of her beer can at Arthur as she took another drink. Arthur looked puzzled.

"Me and Wolfer . . . we're the best in the business." Then a quick change of subject. "Karla runs a pizza joint."

"Been in Vegas long, Karla?" Arthur tried to seem interested.

"Just a few months. Long enough to learn this place doesn't have a corner on the pizza market. I try to keep your friend here safe from ptomaine, but he keeps coming back for more."

Melody came into the room. She wore a black sheath dress and a single strand of pearls. She worked at hooking a pearl earring to her left ear as she entered. "Hi."

Arthur stood up. Montana remained seated, but his eyes ran a quick appraisal of Melody; his expression, initially hopeful, evolved into one of relief, then of smug confidence.

"Hello." Arthur extended his hand.

Melody took his hand, a gentle shake, a quick release. The earring fell off her ear and bounced on the rug.

"Darn." She bent and picked it up.

Awkward silence deadened the room as the three watched Melody refasten the thing.

"Melody works in the casino," said Karla. "She deals blackjack. She sells sports tickets, too. We know each other from San Diego."

Melody smiled, a distracted, noncommittal effort. "I'm sorry I'm late."

"I think we have the best-looking dates in Vegas," from Montana through a broad grin.

Arthur remained standing. Melody looked around the room, not sure where she should sit, if she should sit. The sofa and the single chair were the only places. Arthur stepped away from the easy chair.

"No, no. You sit there." Melody went over and perched on the arm of the sofa next to Karla.

Arthur sat back down. Silence. He rested his left elbow on the small round table next to his chair. A self-conscious move. He shifted his weight on the soft chair cushion. Next to the elbow, beneath a Tiffany lamp, a small Hummel figurine looked out from under a ceramic umbrella.

Karla slapped Montana on the knee. "Vader here, yeah, he's into pizzas. He refuses to die. Keeps me in pineapple chunks."

"She steals pineapple off my pizza." A dumb smile.

Arthur looked at Montana, then at Karla . . . on his face, a polite, expectant expression. Arthur waited for an explanation, a continuation, a reason for the comment.

More silence.

Melody shifted her position on the sofa arm. She looked at her watch.

Karla cocked her head and peered at Arthur. "What happened to your ear?"

Arthur involuntarily touched the scar with his right hand.

Montana laughed. "He got belted with a bottle in a whorehouse." Montana laughed again. The only one laughing. The others stared. The remark landed in the room like a dead cat.

"I hit my head in the shower. I fell down."

Melody gazed at Arthur, then glanced down at Karla. Eyes back on Arthur. Amazement growing.

"Get any stitches?" from Karla. Trampling on the remnants of Montana's remark.

"No." Arthur looked at Melody. She looked back. He noticed furrows of concern above her eyes, undisguised wrinkles of wonder on her forehead. She blinked, a not quite veiled look of alarm.

"Wolfer falls down a lot." Montana's weak effort at damage control.

Melody's frown deepened.

"Like they say," from Karla, "gravity sucks." And she tried to swallow that remark. She scrambled into retreat, conversational engines in full reverse. "What do you say, Mel? Let's get some food in these guys."

Melody nodded and turned to Karla. "What do you suppose they eat?"

Montana drained his glass. "Show the way." He stood up.

Arthur moved to rise. As he did so, he leaned slightly on the surface of the small table, and the table tilted forward. Half out of his chair, he watched the figurine slide into space. With his left hand he grabbed the lamp to keep it from toppling, and he stuck out his free hand to catch the falling cherub. He clipped the pastel ceramic with a glancing, upward blow, and the thing somersaulted in a flat arc across the room toward the sofa. The lampshade rattled. The spinning figurine bounced once on the rug, then popped high into the air and came down on a bare wood section of floor between living room and kitchen. It shattered into pieces.

The lampshade stopped clanking. The fragments stopped sliding. Nobody said anything.

Montana looked blankly at the pieces spread on the floor. Karla was startled, speechless.

Arthur, holding the lamp, looked perplexed and embarrassed.

Melody wore a blank expression. She looked over at Arthur, then back at the jagged sections of her murdered Hummel. Slowly, at one corner of her mouth, a faint smile rose.

Karla reached out and took Montana's empty glass. She looked at him, then at Arthur. "Maybe you guys would rather go down to Circus Circus."

*   *   *

"I thought we were going to stay clear of the casinos." Arthur looked around the restaurant room of the Rio steak house. He and Montana sat across from one another over empty plates and half-full water glasses. A dark bottle of red wine, two-thirds down, guarded the table center.

Melody and Karla had gone to the powder room.

"No problem here. It's the places over on the Strip could give us trouble. The joints on this side are more local trade. Loose. It's the other side of the freeway we worry about. No one going to match us up in here."

"This is a big casino."

"Classy, ain't it? How about those cocktail waitresses? Ever see outfits like that? Talk about flossing ass cheeks. Man, when I die, I'm coming back as one of those outfits. Makes you order drinks just for the view."

"What happened to your dream of coming back as a bicycle seat?"

"I changed my mind." Montana smiled and patted his stomach. "How about it? Sorry you came? Ever had a better piece of steak?" He didn't wait for an answer. "I think I'll stay right here and get myself a belly and hang it up. I've been in worse towns."

"You like her, don't you?"

"Karla? She's okay." He shrugged his shoulders.

"Jumped her yet?"

Montana looked up. "None of your fucking business. There's more to some girls than that." Offended. A hostile edge to his reply.

"My, my."

"That's not all there is, you know."

"Since when?"

"Since I say so."

"My, my."

"Your ass, Wolfer."

"You're too old. You have twenty years on her."

No reply.

"One more time . . . have you jumped her yet?"

"FUCK, NO! I AIN'T JUMPED HER." Faces at other tables turned to look.

Arthur smiled.

Montana picked up the wine bottle and drank from it. He lit a cigarette and eased back in his chair. "How about yours? Not bad."

"She's okay. She doesn't say much. A little squirrelly."

"Maybe because you tried to wreck her fucking house."

"What do you think, Mel?"

"About what?" Melody leaned over the row of sinks and tried to adjust her earring in the mirror.

"About *what?* . . . about *him!*"

"He's strange."

"Strange? Not that one, for Christ's sake . . . *my guy.*"

Melody looked at Karla's face looking at her in the mirror. "Your guy? Oh. I guess he's all right. Yes. He's all right."

"They're hardass. Both of them. Got secrets, don't they? Not your everyday truckers."

"This town's full of surprises."

"Surprises? You should know surprises, Mel."

"Probably a couple of serial killers."

"He makes me itch."

"Itch?"

"Yeah. Itch."

"Get a tube of Mycelex."

"Bitch."

Melody laughed. "Okay. He's a nice guy. Good luck."

"So, what'll it be, gang?" Karla rubbed her hands together.

They stood on the curb between the Rio and the Gold Coast. The black surface of the six-lane road separating the two casinos sucked in all the light that fell on it, reflected nothing, an invisible barrier, an abyss that stretched south to north and presented the peculiar illusion of something deep, a bottomless void that created uncertainty in those stepping onto its hard back. The Rio's red, blue, and white neon on one side, the massive bright white bulk of the Gold Coast on the other caused the pupils of pedestrians about to forge that gulf to constrict, to lose the reality of the macadam highway.

They waited for a single automobile to pass, then stepped out onto the dark road, Karla in the lead.

"You got your choice. You guys can get your butts whipped in the bowling alley, we can see a movie, or shoot some quarters in the slots. Got a dance hall here, too. Fifties stuff. Got some old guys who play pretty good Dixieland in one of the lounges. Nice place to toss down a few toddies." Karla led her small band of explorers past the two-story parking garage and toward the yellow lights framing the entrance to the casino.

"They got a bowling alley? In the casino?" Montana took Karla's hand. Tried to make the touching nonchalant, natural.

"The Gold Coast is big on local trade. Has to be. Being away from the Strip. Gets the natives away from the TV sets. That's how joints on this side of the freeway operate."

Melody and Arthur walked side by side, followed Montana and Karla past the valet area and into the lobby. No hand-holding for them. They trailed along like reluctant siblings behind overly enthusiastic parents.

The four of them snaked through the crowd of glassy-eyed, informally dressed casino patrons waiting, on the right, for a spot at the nickel video poker machines, on the left, for sugared confections at the ice cream parlor. A sticky, heavy smell of lactose and dairy concoctions permeated the air, overpowered the cigarette smoke, and mixed with the piercing beeps of the video machines.

Single file, Karla on point and Arthur bringing up the rear, like some probing combat patrol penetrating an odd, bright jungle, they wound through the crowd, then stopped to watch the Dixieland band tooting and thumping out a brass-heavy New Orleans jazz number in a dark lounge. The band ambled easily through the familiar riffs and ponderous slides of a melancholy dirge of love betrayed.

"Not bad, are they?"

"Good stuff," from Montana retaking Karla's hand.

They traversed the main casino floor. "Let's check out the bowling alley."

The four of them rode the escalator to the second level. Montana and Arthur commented on the size of the bowling complex. They sat next to one another on an elevated row of seats facing the alleys, Karla next to Montana, Melody between him and Arthur. Black balls thundered, pins clacked and spun, and people shouted and groaned as black spheres ran true or missed.

Montana left them and returned with four beers. They drank and made rude comments on bulging stomachs and errant shots.

"Look at that one!" Karla pointed to a sweaty corpulence in lavender pants, a pig-faced athlete of indifferent gender, female in fact, who tried to launch uncooperative orbs at waiting white pins. The pins, a distant phalanx on her alley, stood unmolested, an army of disciplined targets seemingly possessed of some supernaturally repellant antimagnetism that diverted anything she threw at them into hungry gutters leading to gray oblivion on either flank.

"I wouldn't go out in public looking like that." Karla shook her head.

Montana laughed. "You won't ever look like that."

"Check this one out," said Karla. She tugged Montana's hand in the direction of a threesome, an older red-haired man about fifty-five, a woman, probably his wife, and a younger man of thirty years who could have been the couple's son. The red-haired man seemed to be having trouble deciding which fingers to put into the holes of his bowling ball. He stood for a long interval after reaching a decision on what digit belonged where and stared with menace at the distant pins. Then he started forward, mystically appearing to move both feet ahead at the same time, defying all laws of physics and human locomotion. Short, choppy, confused shuffling steps. Balance precarious. Ball swinging rearward herky-jerky, like some helium-filled balloon.

"Aaak!" yelled Karla.

The man stumbled forward in the throes of a wild, disjointed, ten-step delivery, and the black ball arched high above the alley, a gravitational outlaw cutting through virgin bowling territory, a place unfamiliar, unintended, a place new and exciting. Bowlers up and down the row of launch sites froze in wonder as the renegade ebony moon began its descent. A third of the way down the alley the thing hit the planks with a murderous crash and bounced twice. A collective wince overtook all the watching faces. The ball skidded down the varnished boards. The red-haired man was down on both knees, one hand in the righthand gutter, eyes staring, hope alive above gritting teeth. The ball wavered left, then responded to the friction of the wood beneath it and began to roll. It bore down on the confident platoon of white soldiers. The ball barreled into the headpin, smacked into its scarred white chest, and put all the leader's comrades into shabby disarray. A strike.

"Jesus Joe Christ!" Karla was on her feet. She clapped her hands. "Great shot! Great goddamn shot!" above the din. She hit Montana on the shoulder. Gold liquid jumped out of the opening in the top of Montana's can of beer. "See that one, Vader!"

Montana grinned.

Melody looked at Karla, then right and left at the people looking in their direction. Embarrassment colored her face.

Arthur looked at Melody.

"Karla, sit down," from Melody. "Be quiet."

Karla crouched, still standing, both hands flat on the long rail in front of her. She bobbed up and down, then raised a thumbs-up salute to the red-haired man, now back on his feet and dusting off his hands. The man returned her thumbs-up and smiled broadly in her direction as he returned to his seat.

Karla whooped. "Atta go, Red!"

"For goodness sakes, sit down," said Melody.

Montana laughed . . . and Arthur smiled as he looked at Melody.

They finished another round of beer and went downstairs. Karla was full of bubbles, joking and alive.

"Follow me," she said and led them past clanking dollar slot machines into a wide dark ballroom where people danced to slow music.

They found an open table and ordered cocktails from a tall brown-haired girl. Karla held Montana's hand, then took him to the dance floor beneath a big, revolving chandelier that sparkled facets of white glare into quiet corners. Small panes of reflected light danced across their shoulders and across the shoulders and faces of older couples moving together on the shiny floor. The light splinters didn't dance on Karla's face or on Montana's. They were too close for light to get through.

"Boy, that looks serious," Melody said without looking at Arthur.

Arthur smiled. "Your friend enjoys herself."

"She's a kick." Melody sipped bourbon and ginger ale through a blue straw.

"Thanks for putting up with us," said Arthur.

"No problem." A pause. "What do you do? Why are you in town?"

"Just looking around."

"Been here before?"

"Here? You mean in this place?"

"No. Las Vegas."

"Oh. I've been here. A few times."

Melody looked at him. Then back at the dancers.

He shifted in his chair.

They watched Karla and Montana far across the floor.

"Is it good pay? Dealing blackjack?"

"It's okay."

"Hard to learn?"

"No."

A long pause. The band shifted into another set after a small interval while sheets of music were turned. The dancers began to move again. Same slow tempo. Same soft sound.

Melody looked up and smiled at him. "You really fall down in the shower?"

He laughed. A quiet laugh. Eyes down. "No."

"Get in a fight?"

"Yes." He drank some gin and tonic from his glass. He twisted at the cocktail straw. Fingers steady. He reached across the small table and took the straw from Montana's drink, began to make that a part of his work. "Guy jumped me in an alley."

"Tough town."

"Not if you stay out of alleys."

She watched a giraffe take shape.

"Did you lose a lot of money?"

"No. Not much."

"This town has more security than any place I've ever been. Town cops. State cops. Every casino has its own police force. Bet there's more cops here than anywhere."

"Guess you're right."

He looked at the dancers again.

She looked down at the tiny stick figure he held in his hand. She reached out to take the thing with her fingers. To look at it. A friendly, innocent gesture. In the low light he didn't see her hand moving. Her fingers brushed against his, and his hand jerked away. A quick, instinctive recoil at her touch as though an electric shock had jolted him. She was frightened by the sudden move.

He looked at her. "I'm sorry. I didn't mean to make you jump."

Her heart beat a fluttering tattoo. She was speechless.

He didn't know what to say.

He extended his hand and held out the straw figure.

She just looked at it.

"Here." He moved it a few inches more.

She slowly reached and took it from him.

She turned it around and studied it, then put it down on the table. A tiny leg straightened slowly and it fell over.

No one had ever done that to her . . . jerked away at her touch like that.

Small fragments of thought flickered. *Was she repulsive to . . . was he so turned off . . . was he afraid of . . . was . . .*

Wonder. Self-doubt.

In the turning silence between them, they both looked at the dancers dancing.

"I . . . "

"Don't . . . "

Both speaking in a single moment.

He laughed softly. An uncomfortable, lost laugh.

"Don't mind me," he said. "I . . . " and didn't finish the words.

She picked up the fallen giraffe and bent the leg a few times and made the thing stand on the table.

"There," she said.

The tall brown-haired girl came and asked if the table would like another round of drinks. Arthur said, "Yes." Montana and Karla nodded. But Karla and Montana were not talking as much as before. They sat closer, Montana having moved his chair into her sector of table, a move accomplished by subtle adjustments and repositionings under the smokescreen of dim light, conversational distractions, and turned heads.

After a fifteen-minute break filled with elevator music, the renicotined musicians filtered back to the cardboard parapets on the bandstand. A few honks from the brass, some drum taps, the sax burbled twice. Arthur looked around the room. Faces, pale disks like sunflowers turned toward the light coming from the stage, waited for the real music to begin again. Expectant faces. Older faces. Floating, detached but energetic faces creased by yesterday things, creases regal in the shadows and the smoke.

The honking stopped. The tapping stopped. The burbling sax was still. A hush.

The trumpet man, the leader, silver horn to his lips, bobbed head and horn four times, and in a soft explosion the sound came back to peel away the years. It unfolded from some magic place, spread its wings, and swept into the room.

Around dark tables, couples raised up like cobras summoned by the snaker's flute, swaying, already part of the rhythm, glazed by the moment and moving toward the sound.

Montana and Karla were gone from the table at the first notes. No words. Out to dance. Gone so quickly that a paper napkin fluttered off the table in their wake.

Arthur sat.

Melody sat.

The cocktail waitress came back to the table with the drinks. She picked up four empty glasses and reached for the giraffe.

"Leave that," said Melody.

The waitress nodded. Went away.

"That band is good." Not looking at Arthur.

"I'm not much of a dancer," he said, half-smiled, and shook his head.

"I'll teach you."

"I need teaching. We seem to take turns being embarrassed tonight, don't we?"

They latched onto each other like awkward eight-year-olds at a Sunday school tea dance chaperoned by the bishop himself. Arms straight. Eyes on feet. Bodies too far apart. And still he managed to crunch down on her foot with his first step.

"Jesus."

Melody laughed. "Relax."

She began to glide backward on the music. But he did the same and they popped apart. They stood there like two hitching posts, redundant verticals, straight and static in a place where everyone else moved. She put her hand to her mouth and tried to pinch away a laugh.

He looked down at his feet as though they were not his. Then he looked up at her and shrugged.

Melody had no idea what it was she saw flicker in his eyes in that moment. It was not helplessness. It was not humor. It was not rage. It was all three. Then he smiled and the thing was gone.

"Come here," she said.

He moved forward.

She put her arms on his shoulders and meshed her fingers together behind his neck. "Put your arms around my waist."

He did as he was told.

"Now. Feel the music. Don't take any steps. I don't have many toes left. Just stand here."

She began to sway, her shoulders gently turning to the beat. She made his body move with hers.

After a few moments, after they were together with the rhythm, she took a small step backward. He followed. Then she stepped forward, her body firm against his, forcing him to mirror her motion.

Then a drifting turn. And back. A composure-saving two-step. He learned quickly in the press of her. They moved smoothly with the rest.

After two minutes his body took over, and she gently followed his lead; now it was the pressure of his arms, his legs that decided where they would go, what turn would happen next. And they didn't think any more about where feet should be.

She felt hard muscle. His moves, awkward and childlike at first, now melted into easy motion. It was as though she had begun the dance with an ungainly young colt, but now she held something graceful, powerful in her arms. The image of a panther against black jungle shadows came into her mind. Against her will, with unexpected surprise, the image in her brain turned and looked at her with yellow eyes.

She shuddered.

She felt fear. Fear.

She almost stopped dancing. It hit her with the sharpness of a slap. She made herself not look at his face. She didn't want to see his eyes. She moved her head to the side of him that showed no ripped, healing ear. She had to breathe and when she breathed she could smell nothing of him . . . no cologne, no aftershave. No male sweat odor, no deodorant. No breath mint, no mouth smell. Only a hint of alcohol from the drinks.

Somehow, revealed by some instinct breaking through into her conscious mind . . . despite all the jokes and Karla's silliness, the small talk, the botched dance steps . . . she knew she held in her arms a thing that hunted.

And she knew it was alone.

And the next day she attributed the whole strange evening to red wine and beer and bourbon through a straw.

And went back to work.

14

Problems

Admit it, Mel. You had a good time. The guys were fun. I know when I had a good time. Dancing. I haven't danced with a guy who wasn't trying to cop a feel since I been out here. Come to think of it, I haven't danced with anyone since I been out here. It's sort of nice not getting a knee in the crotch every other step."

"Don't tell me I had a good time."

"Go to hell. You haven't laughed like that in a month. Who are you trying to kid? It's me . . . Karla . . . remember?"

They sat at the kitchen table in Melody's apartment. Melody watched Karla concentrate on cementing sharp fragments of broken Hummel together with Super Glue.

Melody stared and frowned. "You're going to bite your tongue off."

Karla positioned two pieces of ceramic umbrella, pieces almost touching but not quite touching, a scant, shaky millimeter apart above the tabletop six inches in front of her face . . . getting ready for the irrevocable commitment. Her tongue stuck into the angle at the right corner of her mouth and was trapped there between bared teeth as she worked. Melody saw the pink tongue-tip blanch as the two broken pieces moved closer, the intensity level high and rising. Finally, the immutable, pecking closure.

"Beautiful!" Tongue disappeared. Back where it belonged. Broad smile. Karla held the glued section up to the light, then thrust it in Melody's face. "Try to find the crack. Try to. Try to!"

Melody studied the repair.

Karla pushed it closer to Melody's nose.

Melody's eyes began to cross. "Okay. Okay. It's great. It's wonderful." Sarcastic.

Sarcasm unnoticed.

Karla snatched her restoration away and began to search for another piece.

"Don't you think there's something funny about that Arthur guy?"

Karla poked a finger through a dump of broken ceramic. "Funny? His ear was funny."

"Not that. Funny. Like weird funny."

"Everybody's weird. Except me. *You're* weird." She picked up a fragment, studied it.

"What do you think they do?"

"Mine does pizza."

"I think they're creepy."

"They're not creepy."

"Mine was creepy."

"You attract creeps, Mel."

"They didn't try to hit on us."

"So?"

"Why not?"

Karla suspended her search and looked at Melody. "They're decent guys, that's why." She shook her head. Tolerant. "Jesus, Mel, there's some out there who don't just dive headfirst into the clover patch first thing. Not many. These are good guys. Don't be so antsy. Give it a rest."

Melody regarded Karla for a few moments. "Would you? If he asked?"

Karla resumed her search. "Not on the dance floor."

Melody got up and put some pretzels in a wooden bowl. She came back and set them on the table next to Karla. "What do you talk to him about?"

"Vader?" Karla looked up, sat back in her chair, and picked a pretzel out of the bowl. She smiled. "You."

"Me?"

"Sure. Like I bet you and Arthur talked about me and Vader. Right?"

"We talked about you two. A little bit. At first."

"Happens on a double date. That's why people go out like that . . . in pairs . . . at least to start with. They get to talk about the other couple. It breaks the ice when you're sitting there with your thumb up your nose not knowing what to say. It gives you something to talk about."

"What did your Vader say about Arthur?"

"Well . . . said he's a great guy . . . as usual. Known him for a long time. Since in Vietnam. Talks like Arthur's some sort of eighth wonder. Something about being a great shot. Rifles. Bullets. Stuff like that. Arthur doesn't go out much . . . with gals . . . sort of shy. Lonely. Probably a bunch of bullshit. Probably trying to get me to get you to feel sorry for him, get you to give Arthur a roll in the sack." Karla smiled. She raised a cautionary forefinger in the air. "Kidding, just kidding . . . that's how they are, though. Guys. Even the good ones. Crotch warfare. They can't help it."

"I still don't know what they do."

"Guys who do something worthwhile, they don't tell you . . . not unless you ask 'em point-blank. Only the bullshit artists do that. Try to impress you. Snow your butt. You've seen enough of that with old Craig, or have you forgotten already?"

Melody didn't reply.

"So, tell me . . . not a bad night, was it?"

"It was okay."

"Want to do it again? Thursday?"

Melody whipped her head up and glared at Karla. "Absolutely not! I'm seeing someone Thursday. I told you. Just that one time only. Once. Go get someone else. Take them out yourself. You can handle two guys. You can probably handle twenty guys!"

Karla. Stoic. Nodding. "Oh, that's nice."

Head down. "Sorry."

Karla sat. Silent.

"Darn it all, Karla!"

No response.

"I don't need complications. Don't make me so angry."

No response.

"Look. Your guy is nice. Arthur's nice. You're nice. I'm nice. But I got this guy. I love him!" Melody halted, startled by her own words.

Karla stared in wonder, her eyebrows arched slightly.

Melody, softer tone, less volume. "I love him."

Karla watching.

"Well, I do."

Karla no reply.

"DARN IT ALL, KARLA, I DO!"

Karla resumed her search for another Hummel fragment.

"So leave me the heck alone!"

"Jesus, you're moody today." Still searching.

▮ ▮ ▮

Early morning. 7:00 A.M. Weekday.

Arthur drove northeast out of the city on Interstate 15. He relaxed in the bright emptiness of the thinly traveled highway, in the rush of motion, in the elevating feel of escape that came from getting away from his small room.

And he relaxed in the knowledge that this was Nevada, a state where the highway patrol thought there was something wrong if you *didn't* carry a weapon in your car. Not like California, where a single live cartridge rolling around in your glove compartment could get you popped . . . sent back to prison . . . "doing bullets," as the local recidivists termed it.

He thought about the past week.

Buried in that cheap apartment . . . alone . . . enduring an isolation he usually handled with professional, almost gloomy pride.

But this time it was different.

For some reason he was out of sync with the old routine. He had grown restless. Small things rasped at him. A dripping faucet. TV sound in the walls. Dogs barking. Dust floating in a sunbeam. The dust pieces in the air made him hold his breath . . . it bothered him that he had no choice but to inhale. Even the steady business of caring for the weapons—the AK-47 and the specially tuned Remington 700, the long-distance killer—became an exercise in irritation. Once, while he ran patches from chamber to muzzle, he got careless and pulled one back through the barrel, distracted, not thinking. On the day before that, he dropped the bolt of the 700, managed to catch it before it hit the floor. Then he listened to himself swear aloud at the bore-brush when he noticed the front bristle tips were worn and crimped. No backup brush.

Solvent, lubricant, oil.

Sleep, television, bourbon.

Over and over.

Dogs, dust, drips.

At night, a few times, he thought about the girl he'd danced with. The one called Melody. He didn't think deeply about her. Just looked at her in his mind. He turned her around, watched her laugh, remembered her eyes, tried to feel again the pressure of her arms on his shoulders as they moved to the music.

There had been women.

Some paid for.

Some used, by him, usually for a reason. He saw them as strong but strangely capable of sudden weakness. He wondered why they put up with the things of their lives. He wondered why they talked so much of change and hope, yet seemed afraid to trade security for dreams. They were like small, delicate animals . . . not painted in his mind as something inferior . . . not put down . . . only different and hard to understand.

Women were not a tangible part of his past. Or his present.

A rabbit flashed across the highway. He jerked the steering wheel, punched the brakes, and missed it by ten feet. The electric chemical loose in his blood made his fingers tremble. He felt a tiny bolt of panic. The feeling stayed with him. The sensation was like the one he experienced after drinking too much coffee. Five minutes later the feeling was gone. But it had lingered too long, bothered him in its persistence.

Twenty miles out of Las Vegas he turned north onto Route 93. A line of blue mountains marched northward on his left horizon. He drove with more care.

One hour later he left the highway and drove west on a dirt road, the sun at his back. The corrugated surface of the desert trail pounded at the car's tires with tooth-rattling hostility. He sped up, then slowed, then increased his speed again as he tried to find the optimal combination of shock absorber, rubber, and velocity to smooth his passage over the uniform rows of two-inch, wind-built sand drifts.

The road angled up as he entered the rocky foothills of the Pahranagat Range. Then, on a rising mountain flank, trees began to grow. Green became a color.

After forty minutes more, he found what he was looking for.

A broad valley. No sign of human enterprise.

Grass. Snow higher up. Yellow desert below to the east. A place between places.

He stopped the car. He sat in a chilly, clear silence, a velvet soft void brushed only by the sound of wind exploring branches and rock angles.

He got out of the car, opened the back door, and took the weapon cases and twenty-power spotting scope from the rear seat.

He walked away from the car and crouched beside a wind-scoured boulder. He set the weapons down, still cased.

Crystal air bathed the great empty space below. He studied the distant terrain, tried to estimate the range of objects across the void. He made calculations of scale ... desert landscape ... difficult to measure. The clear air made all things appear close, magnified. No cars, no telephone poles, no buildings to check the eye's assumptions. Only amorphous shapes of rill and rock. He looked back at the sandy expanse of desert he'd crossed minutes before and saw the glassy shimmer of a wavering mirage as the sun began to warm the surface. There were tricks to shooting here. Try to get above the target, shoot down into the radiating distortion, make the mirage effect more shallow by shooting high to low ... if there was a choice. Shoot early, at dawn's light, before the heat began to work the air ... if there was a choice. Look for sand drags that, like miniature snow-drifts, showed the prevailing wind direction over the surface. Remember that wind followed valleys, traced the long axes of depressions near the ground. And remember that the unreal clarity of dry space worked both ways, worked for the target as well as for the hunter. Look for a way out in case the hunt turned and stalker became prey. Determine cover, escape routes, new positions . . . if there was a choice.

He opened the AK-47 case and removed a black range finder. He estimated distances, then checked his estimations against reality.

Short.

All short.

He put the information in his brain.

Prone position. Spotting scope on its stubby tripod.

He began to shoot.

First with the spotter rifle. One shot only. One per target. Ignore the dangerous confidence induced by the seductive presence of the AK's thirty-round magazine. Treat the first shot like it was the only shot. No room for error. No second chances.

Dark rock slabs spit dust in the distance. Sound cracked around the valley.

Back to the spotting scope. Impact point white on black rock. Corrections clicked in. Numbers written down. Move. Shoot. Write.

He put away the AK and uncased the Remington. He uncapped the 10X M3A Leupold scope and chambered a round. He adjusted the sling and wrapped his left arm into the leather. His cheek welded to the stock. Almost right. He adjusted the butt pad. Cheek weld right.

Feel the trigger. Concentrate. Take out the slack. Fingertip on metal, two-thirds down the trigger; not touching any other thing; no other contact. Align the reticle. Shift the body to meet the sight line. Two deep breaths. Exhale. Stop. Steady.

Sear resisting.

Fingertip smoothly back.

Crack! Recoil.

Follow-through. Hold the concentration.

Again. New target.

Fresh loads. Match grade.

Seven hundred meters away, black rock cracked white. Thirty thousand years of waiting, waiting for this violence.

Twelve inches off. Then ten. Eight. Six inches.

Enough. No more shooting. Fifteen rounds. No more.

I I I

"Hold it steady, Vader. I got this crummy ladder at a swap meet. I don't want to fall and bust my ass."

Karla hooked stainless-steel hangers into the row of plastic loops on the traverse rod above the window. Montana steadied the rickety five-step ladder with both hands. She stood on the fourth step, legs between his arms, the back of her knees level with his eyes. She raised one foot to the top step. Her short yellow skirt slid up the back of her legs. Black lace panties.

She finished attaching all the fasteners on the left side of the gold and white drapery.

"Okay. Let's move it over." She stepped down onto the floor. She leaned back against him, her head tilted up, surveyed her work. He kept his hands on the ladder sides. He could smell the clean smell of her hair inches from his face as she stood in front of him between his arms.

She ducked under his right arm and stepped back three paces into the center of the room. One more look at the drapes. "Be right back. Move it down to the other end." She turned and walked off into the back bedroom. He moved the ladder to the right side of the window. Waited.

She returned a minute later ... after he heard her rustling around in the other room ... after he listened to a drawer open, then slam shut. She ducked under his arm and climbed up the ladder again. She stopped on the fourth step, then raised one foot and placed it on the top step like before. Legs slightly apart.

No black panties.

She began to insert more silver hooks into the row of plastic attachments.

He leaned forward and slowly pressed his lips against the back of her bare thigh. She turned and looked down. A playful smile. "What do you think you're doing?"

He kissed her there again.

The first time was fast, violent, hard, straight, and silent. Comforter and top sheets lay in a pile on the rug beside the bed. Hungry eyes locked on other hungry eyes. Staring. Small rims of tears. The crash of hearts. Passion-reddened skin. Teeth hitting teeth. Muscles straining against muscles. Hip bones sparring. Sweet angles. Delicious hurts. Her heels hard into his back, then away, legs close to cramp-ing. Quick gasps of air . . . not a breathing thing . . . a pleasure thing. Arms tight around shoulders, holding, crushing, pulling.

Fingernails raking pink lines.

The second time with kisses. Slow, full minutes. Minutes laced with half-sentences. Love sounds.

Gentle words painted the soft, spinning space between them.

"Love." "You." "Me." "More."

These words floated in air filled with clean-sheet smell and promises. White linen friction-burned his knees and her backside. They didn't notice.

"You sweet bastard." Her eyes full of tears.

"Karla."

I I I

Anthony Sgro fired up another cigar. Montana sat and looked across the desk at the security chief of the Crystal Casino and decided that the slob must have put on another two pounds of chin fat since their meeting twelve days ago. Sgro took time to assure himself that the obscene vegetable torpedo protruding between his purple lips was properly ignited.

"So you think it's a problem. A big problem?" Sgro blew a rolling gray bolus of smoke across the desktop.

"Straight up? Yes. It could be a big problem." Montana looked into the smoke cloud. Tried to find the eyes.

"How big?"

"Another fifty thousand big."

"For you, right?"

"That's right. I'm going to have to take the thing all the way through the setup. To keep him from finding out about the kid."

"Who's your fucking friend? Robin Hood?"

"Robin Hood it is."

"What if your man finds out about the fifty?"

"If he finds out about the fifty and the kid, it's over. He goes east, I go west. No more team."

"Couple of heroes."

"That's right." Montana thought for a moment. "That's right, partner. A couple of heroes. That's why the fifty just went to eighty."

"You think we're made of money?"

Montana looked slowly around the room. He looked back at the fat man sitting behind the desk, smiled, and didn't reply.

Sgro nodded, eyes hard above a suddenly deep-red glow of cigar end. "All right. But that's it."

Montana waited.

Sgro blew a boil of smoke.

"Now."

The fat man shook his head, stared at Montana, then opened a drawer in the desk and removed a block of bills. He counted, eyes never off Montana, snapped a rubber band around the extracted amount, and tossed the stack of hundreds on the desk.

"Thanks." Montana reached out and took the bundle. He put the four-inch-thick wad into his jacket pocket without counting it.

"We can buy a hit for a fucking lot less than that."

Montana rose from his chair. "Not on someone like this, you can't. You need this done right. He gives you the slip, you'll lose the handle on him. He'll get someone else to buy in."

The cigar end glowed red. Bright red.

Sgro pushed back in his big chair. He hooked the cigar out of his mouth with thumb and forefinger. "Is that all? Sure you don't want a house whore? A free room?"

"I have a room. Thanks anyway."

15

Favors

Melody knocked on the door of his suite in the Towers. He was there to open it before she knocked a second time.

Mike held the heavy white door wide, one hand still working to straighten the knot of his necktie. He smiled. "I thought you wanted to meet down . . . "

She stopped his words with her lips. She dropped her handbag to the rug and kicked the door closed behind her with the back of her foot. Her arms locked around him even before he could remove his hand from his tie, and his arm was pinned tight between their bodies. She kissed him hot and long. Kissed him with a blind, unchecked, neck-wracking fury. Kissed him so hard that the tissue of her upper lip split on the curve of his canine tooth and began to bleed. The salt taste of her blood flared on their tongues. She twisted her head on the pivot their lips made, twisted left, then back to the right, left again . . . she tried to core his lower face like it was an apple, right again, left . . . she ground his mouth flesh with her own, moved one hand up to the back of his head and pressed his face hard against hers. Her tongue forced its way past his teeth and arched over the surface of his tongue, moved from side to side in strong sweeps, drove deep into the warm depth of him, then deeper still. Her hungry passion forced them one step farther into the room, bodies welded together, the sheer material of her red dress crushed out of reality in the nonexistent space between them. She felt the muscle of his tongue respond, come alive, rise up and push against hers, and she let him force his way into her mouth, plowing her hot tongue backward with his.

As she took his tongue into her mouth, she felt a sweet, wrenching release of surrender infuse the entire length of her body. Her knees buckled. She felt moisture well inside the warm depth of her hips. She sealed her lips around the circumference of his tongue, suckled hard, pulled him in as fiercely as she could, tried to turn herself inside out with raw excess.

She wrapped one leg, then the other, behind his legs. His knees, their one support, flexed slowly. His strength lowered them gently to the thick carpet. They knelt, holding tightly, submerged in the dazzling hunger of that endless, furious kiss.

He reached behind her thighs. He lifted her slightly with his hands, made her legs extend straight on either side of him. Still they kissed. Her dress slipped up toward her hips, rode across smooth skin. He leaned forward, lowered her backside onto the plush rug. He put his fingers on her shoulders and pushed gently. She lay back on the rug. He brought her legs together, and she raised her hips to let his gentle hands take her panties away.

He spread her legs again. She watched him stand up. Watched him remove his shoes and all his clothes. Saw the curved length of his sex come free, watched it sway erect in front of his flat stomach as the last garment was thrown aside. He knelt again. His eyes explored her. She watched him look at her there. She bent her knees, parted her legs more to let him see every swelling curve of her. Open. Wanting. Deliciously lost for him. Swept by a consuming wish to share all she was and all that she could be.

He leaned forward, lowered himself to her . . . his lips a fiery fraction above the apex of her sex . . . a slow, hypnotic closing of impatient space . . . and he kissed her tenderly. A soft, pinpoint, slow-motion, breathless, feather-light touching . . . an electric blaze of lip to flesh. Her spine arched. Her head went back. Her eyes fluttered shut. Her neck muscles contracted and cut sharp patterns beneath red, tight skin. Time reeled, became a blur of shattered seconds.

Then a rage of white sensation. She let the slipping reins of last restraint fall free . . . and shuddered to a sparkling place.

Two hours passed.

Two hours near the door.

Things were knocked off tables. A chair was pushed three feet. A curtain was pulled and torn. Ice cubes melted in a plastic cup, and that cup then tipped over. Papers and a yellow pencil, once safe on a coffee table, were on the floor.

Then, worn and sweetly injured, like stragglers from some obscure, steamy battlefield, they limped side by side into the other room and slept on soft white sheets.

They woke. They showered together . . . then filled the tub and tried to scrub each other with a white washcloth.

But nipples turned to hard erasers.

Things swelled.

Lips found lips and feasted, and they made love once more, she astride his lap and facing him, he buried deep inside. Arms sore from hugging, hugged again. And water splashed on the floor. She turned around, her wet, shiny back to him, skin slippery, suds sliding down pale curves. She moved back on hands and knees, legs outside his legs, then reached between her thighs and centered him in the folds of her sex, pushed herself onto the heat of him, moved slowly down, then up, then down again, her fingers tight around the hard shaft that surged above the water . . . making him see the filling of her . . . making him see the lusty raid of flesh on flesh . . . making him see the glistening evidence of her passion . . . and making him see every-thing that had been private, guarded, hidden, hers.

She felt him grow longer, thicker. She felt his lean muscles trem-ble and shake beneath her.

Water rippled and shivered.

She lifted off him and moved the top of his rigid hardness to the opening in her bottom. She released him and reached out to the spigot of the liquid lotion dispenser fastened to blue tile above the water mixer. She pushed the silver plunger with the heel of her hand, filled her palm with cool cream, reached back. His hand touched hers, she tipped her palm.

She placed both hands on the enamel beneath the water, braced on all fours.

She felt one of his hands press down on her lower back. A lean finger on his other hand moved at and then inside her.

He massaged her slowly, stretched her, made her ready.

Then she felt the push of his erection between her buttocks. She tried to make herself relax, but she wanted him so much, lusted for him so much.

Her head hung down.

Bodies trembled.

Long delicious minutes mated. She grew dizzy, faint. Inside muscles began to accept the slow violation.

Then both his hands hooked around her waist, forced her back and down. His power began to slide into her, guiding fingers not needed now.

Down.

Her backside hard against his hips.

Impaled.

She touched herself. Unable to stop. Stoked the growing heat. And went to a place she'd never been before.

❚ ❚ ❚

"The salsa's hot," he said, looking over the top of his menu at her.

"*You're* hot," Melody said, smiling. She dug a tortilla chip deeply into the red mix, scooped too much salsa from the black wooden bowl between the full wineglasses.

She bit the chip in half.

Her eyes began to water.

"Told you."

She drank cold water.

He lowered the menu all the way. "I can hardly move my legs."

"I'll move them for you," and she reached beneath the white tablecloth and jabbed a fingertip into his knee, then grabbed a handful of his inner thigh.

He laughed, jumped, but didn't pull away. His laughter

stopped. Expression turning serious. He stared into her eyes. "I love you, Melody."

Salsa tears no more. Shiny, cheek-riding, love tears instead.

They'd slept for three more hours after the bath. Slept deeply on warm sheets, no dreams, not restless, sometimes with arms around, and sometimes with legs hooked together. Never awake, but always reaching out for the other. Touching somehow. As though their limbs weren't through with loving.

He'd awakened first, had dressed before he kissed her from her slumber, had dressed so he could run for the door should she awake naked, smiling. He was starving.

He studied the menu again. "I could eat a horse."

Melody made a soft whinnying sound, then two small snorts. She pawed her foot on top of his foot beneath the table.

The Mexican waiter came and took the order.

First a sixteen-ounce margarita, two straws.

Eyes locked. Cheeks hollow, sucking. Fingertips holding straws and icy drink flowing up. The other tables and diners and all the soft sounds around them dissolved away and they were alone in a private place.

Then the food was brought to them.

They ate.

Imperial lovers.

Served by captured Nubians. On silk and silver. Nightingale tongues and yellow wine. Icy goblets. The zinc smell of evening Nile waters mingled with a dry, sweet scent of desert air. As she watched him eat and smile and talk and drink, Melody felt the wild heat start to build again and was almost afraid. She had never known such passion, had never given herself so completely and with such unreasonable surrender. She checked the impulse to apologize, to say something even remotely defensive about what they had done, about what she had let him, *made him*, do to her. She checked the impulse to couch rapture in the excelsior of humor. She knew that she was in a place where lovers go when lovers fly . . . a place that lovers can't describe, won't describe, because words don't work, lose meaning, become useless, obtrusive, muted things . . . where questions don't need answers, don't even need the asking . . . where one body speaks to another body in some strange, clear hypersensory way . . . pressures, a nudge, the turn of a limb. A place where revelation unfolds like the morning glory and, like that mysterious flower, strangles all other nearby things.

They ate slowly . . . spending the night like gold.

Melody knew she had to say something soon or she'd go across the table.

"Do you make money betting?" Her words, frail and studied, as though from someone else.

"You want to talk about sports?" He smiled.

"We better talk about something." She closed her eyes and took a deep breath.

He watched her. He laughed softly. "I know what you mean."

Mike reached over and lifted, sipped from her wineglass, put it back down on the table. "I work hard at it. It's what I do. It's not a hobby for me." He was serious.

Melody looked at him. After a few silent moments, "I was born on a Wednesday . . . but not last Wednesday. You beat the numbers? Pardon me?" She surprised herself at the thinly veiled skepticism in her words. Challenging words. Doubting words. An instinctive relapse into the we-versus-them mind-set common to dealers . . . a distrust out of place in the magic night. "Gamblers lose. Always." She heard her own words and wondered who was speaking.

"I don't gamble," he said.

"You don't gamble." Not a question.

"That's right."

"How do you do it?"

"I middle."

"You don't bet often, then."

"Often enough."

"You have to know which way the line's going to move."

He smiled and speared a piece of green pepper, ate it, and lowered his fork.

She was curious now. "Middles don't happen every week. Not in this town."

"Yes they do."

She tried to think. The margarita and the wine wouldn't let the numbers come.

Mike continued. "Maybe not so much in the pros. In the college games. The people who make the numbers have a harder time with the colleges. I can usually find a hole there. But sometimes in the pros, too. Last week I had a pro middle. The Saints. They opened at two and closed at five. Remember?"

She thought. He was right. She remembered the scared look on the Book manager's face when a load of cash came in on the Saints thirty minutes before the game started. The red bow tie had bobbed out of control. The Book took the number across three and then even farther in a panic . . . a desperate attempt to balance the bets so the casino wouldn't get caught heavy on one side. "You're right. It did close across the three."

"It usually happens late. That's why most players aren't aware of it. They don't know where the number stops. They've already bet and are somewhere eating dinner." He smiled. "You sure you want to talk shop?"

She ignored the question. "You still have to know."

He pinned another pepper on his fork.

She watched him eat the pepper. He chewed and swallowed and smiled at her. "Well?" she asked.

"Well what?"

"How do you know?"

"Secret."

She pushed her lower lip out.

"Do you really want to know?"

She didn't say anything.

"It's not illegal, what I do. I don't do anything illegal."

Silence.

He smiled again. "I'm not trying to tease you."

"Tell me."

He looked around the room, then looked out of the corners of his eyes and squinted comically. "You'll turn me in."

"Will not."

"Will." He smiled. "Runners."

"The layoff guys?"

"Yup." Abrupt. Smug. Like a little boy with a secret.

"Tell or I'll beat you up," she ordered.

"I'll call the cops. They'll put you in jail. Lesbians will eat you."

"Tell."

"I know a few runners. Don't know them personally. Just know who they are. I watch them. They bet for themselves before they lay off the big money from the East Coast books. They know where the money's going to push the number, which direction. They take a free ride. Dangerous game . . . for them. Not for me. The bunch they are laying off for would dump them if they knew what was going on. So the runners don't grab too much . . . not enough to move the number early. They middle, I middle. I watch them."

She nodded and sipped tequila through a straw.

"I miss a lot, though," he said. "I can't just hang on their shoulders all the time. They'd get wise to me. They're pretty tense players. It'd be nice if I could read lips or something."

"Is that why you were in the Book when you bet at my window? That first time?"

He didn't hesitate. "Yes."

"Who was he? Did he bet at my window?"

"No. The one to your right. A few seconds before I got down."

"Why our book? We don't have the high limit the big-time books have."

"Your number held. At least until I got down. Then I ran the Strip. It's easy once you know where the runner's going to dump the bucks. These guys are pretty consistent."

"You try to get down just anywhere?"

"No. Some books don't panic. They hold the line. There's a few. Like Little Caesar's. And Dufty and Gregorka at the Sands. Gutsy. They hang tough, don't panic. They make their own number and stick with it. We can't press them."

"We?"

"Some friends help me out." He laughed. "I can't be everywhere at once. But I do the work. It's small-time, but it's a living. And it's exciting. Nothing beats watching a game where you have both sides . . . except maybe taking a bath with a certain beauty."

Melody didn't pick up on the remark. "I bet the real big casino books hold the line."

"You'd be surprised. Real surprised. Like maybe your three biggest? Two of them run like rabbits."

"And that's where you nail the other side?"

"Right."

She frowned. "It sounds fishy."

"It isn't. Not fishy at all. Where's it fishy?"

"Sneaky, then."

"Isn't sneaky, either. The books figure the number. We just chase it. Economics 101. Supply and demand."

She giggled. The wine? The hour? The delicious fatigue? He was surprised by her reaction. "What's so funny?" he asked.

"All you guys sneaking around." She emptied her wineglass. Set it down and giggled again. The room moved. Everything was hitting at once. "It seems funny." She grinned. "Like a little war. So you make ten, fifteen thousand . . . split it with your friends . . . so what's the big deal? You guys only make money when the number falls. And I know the number doesn't land inside the spread all the time. The season only lasts five months. If you're smart enough to figure that stuff out, you and your friends could all be dentists or something."

"It's more fun this way."

They left the restaurant and walked through casinos. They laughed, played quarter slots together, and held hands. They didn't talk of important things. They only moved through the night and later loved again.

11:00 A.M. Breakfast in bed. Limbs as sore as pleasure can make limbs sore. She'd jumped when the room service boy knocked. Mike went to the door. Her world was strangely brittle, delicate, fragile. She was suddenly close to tears. And she didn't know why. At first. And then she knew. Could she ever go back there? Back into last night's passion? Could any human soul go there more than once? That question was the morning's gift of melancholy.

"You don't want your orange juice?" he asked.

"You can have it." She sat with him at a small round table near the large window in the bedroom of the suite. She was naked under the fluffy white comforter from the king-size bed. Her arms, buried in the cotton material, clutched the big quilt about her body so only her head stuck out. She trembled. She looked as though she were freezing. She stared out the window. Eyes vacant.

"I know what you're thinking," he said softly. "I feel it, too."

"Oh, Mike." She began to cry with no sound. Tears ran down her cheeks. "I don't want to . . . I don't want to go out that door."

"I know." He looked at her. Saw the big tears. He got up from his chair and went to stand behind her. He knelt, naked and concerned. He put his arms around her and slowly rocked her from side to side. Tears sparkled off her cheeks and disappeared into the quilt. The white comforter drew up the falling drops and no mark was left where they had been. It was as though the tears never were.

Past the high window, a black bird flew.

"I'm supposed to go to work in three hours."

"Call in sick." He spoke the words close behind her ear, his chin gently on her shoulder.

"I can't. Three dealers are out already. I can't do that. It wouldn't be fair."

He said nothing.

"I hurt inside," she said.

"Hurt?"

"Not that way. I hurt because I don't want to go away. I can't leave you. I can't leave this room. It makes me hurt all over."

"I know."

"Has anyone else ever felt like this?"

"Some. Not many. Not like this. Some."

"Oh, Mike." More tears.

And then he did the sweetest thing she would remember from their time together. He lifted her up, carried her to the bed, and laid her down. He peeled away the comforter and walked to the thermostat on the wall and turned it up. Warm air moved from the heating grilles and rolled across her cool flesh. He went into the bath and came back with a small bottle of skin cream. As she lay there looking up at him, he rubbed cool white oil on her breasts, her neck, her tummy, her legs. He poured more in his palm and with a touch like silk he bathed the soreness between her legs. Not pushing, not even caressing, just moving with a grace so delicate that she felt her heart leap at the tenderness. His touch, too feathery to be called touching, put all the hurt away. And she didn't have any idea why the hurt dissolved.

He put her back together. Put her back together with his kindness.

Once, when she smiled through new, different tears and reached for him, he stopped her hand firmly in its travel, and lovingly pressed her arm back onto the sheet.

"Not now," he said.

He kissed her forehead.

He watched her dress and watched her do things to her hair, her lips, her eyes.

And when she was ready, when she could breathe again, when she could smile at him in the mirror, he took her to the door.

She turned and they kissed softly. A childlike kiss. A kiss that floated bare fractions above tinder-dry, explosive passion.

"Go to work," he said.

She smiled and stepped back and folded her arms across her chest so they would not reach for him. "Thank you." Looking at him. "I love you."

"And I love you," he said.

She turned away, then stopped. "Maybe I can help you see which way those guys bet . . . "

"What guys?"

"You know . . . the ones you watch . . . the runners. No one better than me to see how they bet."

"Oh, those guys. Yeah. That would be a help." He smiled. "Go to work, girl. I love you."

"Bye." A small wave. She turned and headed for the elevator.

16

Lessons

Arthur waited in line with his basket of groceries. He stood behind an old man and watched the grizzled senior count pennies. Knobby fingers, nails broken with age, hands shaking with the steady oscillation of ninety years took dirty copper coins from a frayed black purse and placed them one by one on the worn gray checkout surface next to the cash register. Each coin was put down with a tiny "click" next to three well-traveled one-dollar bills. Slowly, steadily, with proper precision, the sum built. At last, ransom sufficient, another fifth of apple wine was liberated from sterile rows of glass-bellied soldiers silent on dusty shelves behind the Iranian clerk.

Purse snapped shut. Carefully put back into coat pocket.

The expectant, time-trampled face looked up at the smooth skin and small eyes of the middle-aged clerk. *Is the money enough? Can anything go wrong?* The drinking so close. Veteran saliva glands began to sweat inside antiquated cheeks.

Bottle of mystery wine assigned to brown paper bag. Bag handed over to trembling hands.

"Thank you."

"Thank you, sir." Small, perfunctory smile from the clerk.

Arthur began to unload his shopping basket onto the counter. One by one, the clerk raked the items across the bar-code reading device.

"He's a steady customer," with a nod after the old man. Pause. "Did you hear about the killings?"

Arthur looked up from his migrating collection of goods. The clerk, eyes down, continued moving articles over the square glass window set into the counter. The device read fat and thin lines, added numbers, computed cost.

"Killings?"

"In the alley. North about two blocks. A few days ago."

"I hadn't heard."

"Probably a drug deal, robbery . . . something like that."

Arthur alert. Face calm. "Cops?"

"They were in here this morning. Fishing. Asking questions. I don't know what this town's coming to."

"The streets are full of animals."

"It's bad for business."

"I guess it would be."

Total complete. "Looks like $28.74. Do you want a separate bag for the bread?"

"No."

"I heard they were two tourists. One was some senator's kid."

"Everybody moonlights."

"The cops are going house to house. Big deal. Too many rooms around here for that. Don't think it could be anyone local."

A gaunt teenage boy sporting long dirty hair and a fresh crop of yellow-green pimples brushed against Arthur's elbow, shoved a pulp magazine toward the clerk. A fearsome picture of a red-eyed werewolf snarled without sound from the cover of the comiclike publication.

The clerk shifted his gaze to the boy. "Be with you in a minute, sir."

Eyes back on Arthur, then a nod at the picture on the magazine cover. "You don't have to look far to see where folks get their crazy ideas."

"Not far." Arthur shook his head and smiled. He put two twenties on the counter and the clerk made change.

Arthur walked past two police cars parked in front of an apartment building halfway between the store and his room. The cars were empty. He knew why they were there. The clerk was right. One of the muggers had a name, a big name. The cops were going full bore after the alley killer. It was time to find another place. Fast.

I I I

"How about I make a picnic lunch? I make a mean chicken salad sandwich." Melody twisted the fingers of her free hand in the coils of the telephone cord.

"Picnic?"

"It'd be fun."

"Around here?"

"Sure. We could go out to Red Rock Canyon. Some place like that."

"They probably have laws about making out in a state park."

"Laws are made to be broken." Pause. "I love you, Mike."

No reply.

"You need to get out of that room before we break all the furniture. You have to do something besides bet on sports and make love to helpless girls."

His soft laugh made heat build in the skin of her face. Her hand dropped from the phone cord to the seam of her black dealer slacks, and her fingers pressed into the hot curve between her legs. *God. This is crazy.*

"Helpless?" More soft laughter from him. Then a change of tone. "A picnic might be fun. We could drive north up 95. There's lots of open space up there."

"We could fly a kite."

She heard the sound of his breathing. She moved her hand against dark cotton. She pushed the receiver hard against her ear. She sat down on the edge of the bed.

"Do you ever shoot?" he asked.

"Shoot?" Deep breaths.

"Rifles."

"Rifles? Guns? Like bang-bang?" Hand halted.

"Like bang-bang."

"Sure." A lie. Instantly regretted. Anything to please him.

"It's fun, trust me."

"No, no, it sounds great."

"It's a hobby. It relaxes me. You'll like it."

"I like you."

"When do you want to do it?"

"I want to do it now." Hand moving again.

"Not that." More laughter.

"Next week? Wednesday? I'm off Wednesday," she said.

"Okay. Wednesday's good for me. I'll pick you up at eight in the a.m." A pause. "Will I see you this weekend? In the Book?"

"I deal tomorrow and Thursday. I'll be working the Book on the weekend. Friday through Sunday."

"I'll drop by then . . . Saturday morning. I want to get down on a couple of games."

"I can't wait that long."

"You have to."

"Can't." She lay back on the bed. Her hand moved inside the waistband of slacks and panties.

"I'll be out of town until Friday late," he said.

"Seeing somebody else?"

"Sure. Right. Three or four. Look, Mel . . . you got me so beat up I can hardly walk. You think I have anything left for somebody else?"

"I'm going to keep it that way. You'll never walk straight again."

"That a threat?"

"It sure is."

"I love you," he whispered.

"I want you," her voice changing, husky . . . her hips moving.

"Nope."

"Mike?"

"Nope. I can't swing it today."

"I'll swing it for you."

"I'm standing here hard already. I could get you for sexual abuse."

"I can't wait a whole week."

"I love you."

"Mike?"

"I think I better hang up."

"Twenty minutes? Only twenty minutes?"

"I can't, Mel."

"Twenty dollars for twenty minutes? I'll pay you."

"Go get in the shower."

"Mike?"

"*Cold* shower. Oops! . . . 'shower' is the wrong word, isn't it?"

"It sure is." She inhaled sharply, held her breath.

"I'll see you Saturday in the Book . . . Mel? . . . you there? . . . you all right?"

▌ ▌ ▌

"Hello."

"Arthur? Hi." Surprised. Very surprised. "What's with all the stuff? You leaving town?" Melody stood by the door. She looked at him, looked at the single brown suitcase by his feet and at the two large bundles partly covered by the topcoat he carried. She fingered the top button on her yellow blouse closed.

"Come in. I just got off work." She stepped aside. She was barefoot.

With his free hand, he pushed the suitcase inside the door. He followed it in. She closed the door.

"I would have called. I didn't know your number," he said.

"No problem." Unsure. "How's your friend, Montana?"

"Fine." Awkward silence.

"What can I . . . "

"I wonder if . . . "

Two sentences, one space.

He waited.

"What's up?" she asked.

He looked around the living room, then looked back at her. "I know this sounds nuts, but I lost my apartment. I wondered if I could leave this stuff here for a few days. Until I get another place."

She looked at the nylon cases. "Sure. Can't you leave them with Montana?" She felt embarrassed at the way the words sounded.

"No." No explanation. He couldn't think up a good reason for her.

She bent and picked up the brown suitcase. "We can put your stuff in my bedroom." The thing was heavy. The weight made her grimace. "You got gold bricks in this?" She started across the small living room. He followed. He didn't answer that question, either, and in the bedroom he placed the gun cases on the floor beside his suitcase after she had positioned it next to her dresser. She shoved things around, rearranged the three parcels. "There." She straightened up. "No one will bother them. Leave them as long as you like." She gently touched one of the gun-carrys with her foot. "What are these?" She wiggled her toes against the black nylon.

He waited for a few moments. "Rifles."

"Rifles?"

"Yes."

"Guns?"

"Rifles."

She looked at him, eyebrows raised. She looked back at the suddenly ominous luggage. He was in her apartment. His guns were in her apartment. She was alone.

He stared at his shoetops. Scratched his forehead. "Samples. I sell them." Cheeks warm in the fabrication. He was surprised by the fact that he didn't feel comfortable lying to her.

She gazed at the black nylon that felt slippery beneath her bare toes. "Rifles." Not a question. She pursed her lips.

He detected a subtle nod of her head.

"Nothing dangerous. I mean, they're not going to blow up. They aren't hot . . . stolen, I mean." He smiled.

"No, no. That's all right. No problem."

She took him by the elbow and guided him toward the bedroom door. Once she looked back over her shoulder, looked back at the nylon cases on the floor.

As they entered the living room she realized she was pushing him by the elbow and quickly let go of his arm. "Oh, my. I'm sorry. Thought I was teaching you how to dance again. Like the other night. Didn't mean to push you around."

"Don't mind."

"Would you like a beer? A soda?"

"Thanks. A diet soda if you got it."

She motioned toward the couch. "Sit down," and she went into the kitchen.

He looked across the room at the lamp table next to the single chair. "I see you got a new thing. That statue thing."

From the kitchen, "Oh, that. Karla glued it back together. It's the same one."

"Oh. Good job. Sorry about knocking it on the floor."

Melody came back into the room. She'd poured the soda into two glasses with ice. She handed one of the glasses to him and sat down in the chair by the Hummel.

He sipped his soda. "This tastes good."

She nodded.

"How's Karla?" he asked.

"She's back in San Diego for three days. She went to pick up some of her stuff."

"Oh?"

"Yes."

Silence.

"Did you drive over?" she asked.

"I took a cab."

"Oh."

"Montana's got the car."

Pause. She took another sip of soda. "So, you sell guns? Karla thought you guys sold outboard motors."

He looked at his shoes.

She looked at the window, looked at the Hummel. Looked back at Arthur. "I never shot a gun. Do you shoot them? Those guns?"

"Yes."

"Can people shoot guns around here? Around Vegas, I mean?"

"You can shoot anywhere around here, except in the hotel lobbies."

More soda. An ice cube broke loose from those stuck in the bottom of her glass and bumped into her nose. She leaned forward quickly, but some soda splashed around the sides of the ice cube and dribbled onto her blouse. She coughed and cupped her hand under her chin.

"Darn!" The word came out muffled in the confusion of glass, ice, soda, lips, and hand.

He stood up. A concerned look on his face. "Can I get you a towel?"

She brushed at the brown drops of liquid on her shirt front. "No. This shirt's going in the wash anyway. No thanks."

He sat back down.

She finished rubbing the dark stain into the front of her yellow blouse. "I always do that. Stupid ice."

No reply from him.

She sat back in her chair. "Would you show me how it works?"

He looked at her, a confused expression on his face.

"The gun. How the gun works."

"You want to shoot? Sure. Happy to. If you like, we could go out and pop a few someday . . . rounds . . . pop a few rounds, I mean."

"Really?"

"Any time."

"Good!" She thought for a few seconds. Made a decision. "If you want, you can stay here on the couch . . . you know . . . till you get a place. It's not very comfortable, but I'm gone most of the time. It won't be any trouble." She put her soda glass on the table, put it on a coaster by the lamp next to the Hummel. "It shouldn't take you long to find another apartment." She smiled. A nice smile under one squinting eye. "You can really teach me to shoot one of those things? Is it hard?"

"Nothing to it."

"I'd like that."

"When?"

"Soon. Real soon."

"You name it."

"Do you have any of those bullet things?"

"Bullet things?"

"Bullet things. For the guns."

"I have plenty of bullet things."

▮ ▮ ▮

They sat cross-legged on the living room floor. The AK-47 lay field-stripped on an old bedsheet covering the section of rug between them. All the rifle's components were arranged in neat, parallel groups.

"My God! I don't see how it stays in one piece when the bullet blows off."

He looked up at her remark. She was staring at the sleek gray parts. She reached out and picked up one of the empty thirty-shot magazines. She shook it. Peered into the loading slot. Shook it again. Held it up to the light. Looked into the slot once more. "There's a spring in there."

She sat in robe and pajamas, white pajamas, white robe. He was in T-shirt and jeans. She, white slippers. He, green socks. On the floor by the couch, scattered in a large cardboard box, were the munched crust-bones of a deceased pizza.

He pointed at the AK parts and told her what they were called. Receiver, receiver cover, magazine, carrier, bolt, gas cylinder, action spring, rod, kit. He could see by her expression that she wasn't going to absorb much of what he said. He remembered seeing the same look on the faces of the young Marines in his R & R classes on sailing. A person needed to experience the totality before the specific, needed to feel the life and action of an object before the association of terms could have meaning, needed to feel the power, the essence, the function of the whole before the particulars made sense. He began to reassemble the weapon.

Melody watched, fascinated by the speed and precision with which the rifle went together in his sure, practiced hands. He didn't appear to think, his blue eyes more distracted than concentrating. Some parts joined as he looked at her, not at them. He spoke the names of the pieces as they snapped together, but his fingers seemed to work without waiting for him to tell them what to do, as though attention was unnecessary, even intrusive. She had the impression that were those hands severed from his body, they would be able to work just as quickly in doing what they did.

In seconds the AK was whole.

"Wow." She stared at the assembled weapon.

"Wow?"

"You've done that before."

"Got to know 'em if you're going to sell 'em."

"Do that again."

"Break it down? Sure."

The rifle dissolved to pieces and reappeared put back together in seconds. *And this was the guy who couldn't get around a dance floor without hurting people? Who couldn't sit in a chair without breaking something?* She stared at the weapon, then at him. "You could do that in the dark." A statement.

He smiled. "Yes."

She looked at him as though she were seeing him for the first time. He seemed shy in his manner, almost afraid, but there was a power in him, and she thought again of the night she first touched him in the dark as they sat at the small table in the casino, as they watched others dance under blue lights. She recalled her feeling of surprise, of hurt, of rejection, when he had pulled away from her, when he jumped at her touch like some beaten animal, when he was startled at the innocent contact in that moment.

She looked again at the eyes and tried once more to understand what she saw there. Sorrow? Loneliness? Fear?

Or was she painting something between lines that only existed in her mind?

"Is something wrong?" He looked concerned, puzzled.

She blinked twice, refocused, and snapped out of her trance. "I'm sorry. I was thinking of something at work."

"If you're tired . . . "

"No. No, I'm not tired." She smiled and looked back at the rifle. "How does it work? How do you shoot it?"

"Lie down. Stretch out on the rug."

She uncrossed her knees, put one hand on the floor, and lay down on her back, legs straight, together.

He stared.

"Like this?"

He didn't speak for a few seconds. Only looked at her. Then he laughed out loud. "No, not like that. On your stomach." He tried to swallow what was left of the laugh.

She felt the color heat her cheeks. "Darn." And she continued to lie there staring up at the ceiling.

"It's my fault. You haven't done this before." He chuckled.

She rolled over, facedown, pressed her nose into the pile of the rug. "That is embarrassing." She stared into fabric an inch in front of her eyes, her words muffled by the pressure of the nap against her lips. Then she started to laugh too.

As did he. Again.

She jiggled against the floor. She couldn't stop. Their laughter filled the room.

He tried to speak, but had difficulty. "That's how you shoot at birds. Let's start out with something simple."

Tears ran down the side of her nose and onto the rug. She propped herself on her elbows, her face red, her breathing compromised. The more she tried to stop, the more she realized she could not. She rolled onto her back and put her hands over her face and gave in to the absurdity.

It took long minutes.

He laughed with her, lost what was left of his reserve, and in the course of his outburst knew it had been a long time since he had broken up like that . . . a very long time.

"My God!" when she could form words again. "I must really be out of it." She uncovered her eyes and looked at him. His face was wet with tears, and he brushed at them with the back of one hand. "I need a drink," she managed.

Melody got up on her hands and knees, then got to her feet. She collected the two empty soda glasses and staggered out of the room.

"Rum and Coke? It's all I got," from the kitchen.

"Rum and Coke sounds good."

He heard ice cubes pop out of ice trays. Another burst of laughter came from the kitchen. A bottle cap clattered.

"My God," again, from the other room.

She came back with the drinks. She handed one to him and flopped onto the sofa. "I'm sorry." And her eyes squeezed shut, and she began to giggle.

"Don't be," he said. Now back under control. "People who haven't shot are the easiest ones to teach. They don't have any bad habits to unlearn." He wiped away tear tracks with the edge of his hand that held the drink.

"Right." She looked at him. Broad smile. "You can be honest."

"It's true."

"I think I know which end the bullet thing comes out. I think I know that."

"We better be sure."

And they both started up again.

He sat on the floor with his back against the front of the couch, sat beside her legs. She leaned forward and put her hand on his shoulder and watched him sketch lines on the back of the empty pizza box. Almost undetected, he jumped again at her touch. She felt his

shoulder muscles tighten, a shudder, uncontrolled and quickly passing, but she felt it.

He drew a picture of a rifle. Above the rifle he drew a straight
horizontal line. Then he drew a shallow curved line that started at
the muzzle of the weapon, rose above the horizontal line, and then
descended below it again at the far side of the box.

"You look through the sights. What you see is the target. The
straight line is what you sight along." He pointed at the straight line
with the eraser end of the pencil. A serious expression. "The bullet
thing . . . " He started to laugh.

"The bullet!" She pinched his shoulder hard.

"The bullet leaves the barrel heading up. Like this curve. That's
because the barrel points above the sighting line. It has to. If it didn't,
if the barrel and the sights were parallel, then gravity would pull the
bullet down before it got to the target and you'd miss low. See?"

"Yup."

"So there's only two spots where the bullet and the line of sight
intersect. One up close," he pointed at the crossing of lines in front of
the barrel, "and that one way out there where the target is. That one
is the one you need to figure out."

"So?"

"So that's why the sights are adjustable. Different distance, different settings."

"How do you know what's right, how to adjust them?"

"You experiment at measured distances till you get it right. On
the range. And you guess a little."

"No problem."

"Oh, there's problems . . . like wind . . . cross-wind."

"Wind can't blow bullets. They're too small. Go too fast."

"Wrong, white girl."

"How wrong, sahib?"

"At four hundred yards, a ten-mile-an-hour cross-wind can
push you more than a foot off-line. Just a ten-miler. And that's using
the best-grade ammunition. The good stuff."

No reply.

"That's why these sights don't just adjust up and down, they
adjust sideways, too."

"Sideways?"

"Here." He picked up the rifle and showed her the sight mechanism. "You turn these."

"Those doodads?"

He craned back his neck and looked at her. "Those doodads." He smiled, his shoulder against her knee. He set the weapon on the floor and picked up his glass and chewed up an ice cube. "Then you have to crank in the temperature, altitude, elevation, humidity, whether the target is moving, how fast it's moving, up angle, down angle . . . stuff like that. There's times the heat makes the air wiggle . . . like a mirage. Plus there's wind, the distance . . . like I said before."

"I'd just point it and pull the trigger."

"You could do that." He laughed. "That might work."

"How about that other gun? Same thing?"

"Same thing. Different settings, though. That's a long-range weapon. A thoroughbred. This pony's a little bit of everything."

"You need a better gun. One that doesn't take so much fiddling around." She pinched his ear and stood up. He didn't jerk away. "I need another drink," she said. "You too?"

"Me too."

She made the drinks. He showed her how to load the magazine, how to rock it into the receiver, how to chamber a round, how to remove the magazine and clear the chamber. She learned, timidly at first, as though the AK were some sort of bomb, but she learned.

And he watched her. Clinically. Objectively.

At first.

Then he found himself looking at her fingers, not at what her fingers did.

At her eyes, not at what those eyes studied.

At her hair when it tangled around the trigger guard and spilled over the stock as she raised the AK to aim.

At the skin below her cheekbone where the teak nestled against the side of her face each time she positioned, then repositioned, at his instruction.

At the way her legs stretched and moved inside the white material of the pajama bottoms . . . bathrobe abandoned in the name of efficiency . . . legs that stretched and moved each time she aligned herself with the weapon as she lay prone on the rug and he kneeled beside her.

At the way her breast filled the space beneath her arm, moved then stopped moving under the white fabric as she held her breath in the moment before she pulled the trigger back.

At the smooth curve of back and neck and arm.

How those curves seemed to flow and extend the graceful lines of the weapon.

How her lips parted and mated and moved so slightly at the corner of her mouth when she asked him things.

How the swiveled rifle sling wrapped like a strong dark snake around her forward arm, pressed into her flesh, then tightened as her muscles tightened against it.

How she smelled . . . a scent of woman soap that laced the air of the room and flirted with the aroma of the AK's oiled teak, with the metallic, smoky nitrate odor of cold steel.

All these things made him think of where he had been, of what he had done.

And he knew that the few inches separating him from her were really miles.

17

Secrets

No answer. Three calls. Arthur hung up the phone, fished his quarter out of the coin return slot, and left the phone booth. He had mixed feelings about telling Montana of his move to Melody's apartment. Montana would want to know the reason for the change. Arthur knew he could come up with some workable excuse—nosy neighbor, too much noise—but Montana would wonder. And the lie, the secret of the killings, would grow.

The decision was a nondecision. Montana needed to know where his partner could be reached. To wait the few extra days until another apartment was found was to take too big a chance. There was an understanding ... surprises, the unexpected, confusion ... the automatic "mission abort" signs. And this job was too lucrative to jettison. Montana had to know. Even though there was plenty of time, he had to know where Arthur was.

"Hi." Yellow blouse unbuttoning. Purse flipped onto the couch next to him.

"Hi yourself. How was work?" Arthur folded back the second page of the classified section of the newspaper and put a pencil mark by an apartment listing.

"Turkey Central. You don't want to know."

"Turkey?"

"Goofball players. Finger counters. Slow and stupid. Give me the twenty-five-dollar tables any day." Shoes kicked off.

"Any good tippers?"

"Tippers? What's a tipper? More tips dealing a cemetery."

Melody continued into the kitchen. He heard the pop-fizz of a soda can opening.

"There's a fifty on the stove. My rent for three days."

"Don't be silly. I'd pay that for the gun lessons."

"I'll hide it in the phone book."

"Then I'll kick you out. No money!"

She came back into the room and sat down in the easy chair across from him. She rested a bare foot on a knee and massaged her toes. The top three buttons of her blouse undone. Her nametag off. Shirttails out. "Any luck with the house-hunting?"

"Got two to look at tomorrow."

"No hurry. I want to be like Annie Oakley by next week. You can't go anywhere till I say so."

"Why the crash course?"

She looked at her toes. "Just something I always wanted to learn. Won't get another chance like this."

They ate meatball sandwiches for dinner. Melody showered and put on a blue tracksuit and a pair of worn-out running shoes. Arthur wore a sport shirt and black slacks. She'd agreed to let him order the sandwiches from the deli on the corner, her one concession to his insistence that he pay his way. He studied the ad section in the news-paper as they ate.

She got him to put the newspaper down by insulting his table manners. So they talked about her job. They talked about shooting. Then the phone rang.

She got up from the table and went over to a telephone that sat on top of a small toaster oven on the kitchen counter.

Arthur had nagged her that morning before she went to work

about the wisdom of cooking telephone equipment. She said she'd move the phone off the toaster oven as soon as she could find a place that sold extension cords. She promised.

Melody picked up the phone.

"Karla! How's it going? . . . Rain? It never rains in San Diego." She rolled her eyes at Arthur. One finger tapped on the black phone next to her ear.

"Oh, no! Darn! Is it ruined? . . . An extra couple of days? Sure, I'll bring in the paper. . . . No. No mail. . . . Did the car run okay for you guys? . . . Wonders never cease. . . . Secret? Of course I can keep a secret. . . . Karla! . . . Not in the desert!"

Melody looked at Arthur and shook her head.

"On the ground? In the sand? Are you nuts? You'll rub all the skin off your butt."

Melody laughed and put a hand over her mouth.

"It's never too late. Put some Bactine on it."

Another laugh.

"Okay. . . . Okay. . . . Right. . . . About the same. Lousy. . . . Nobody tokes. Must be the recession. . . . Okay. See you next week. Don't get any scorpion bites!"

She hung up the phone and came back to the table with a big smile on her face.

"Hey! Guess what!" she said.

Arthur put down the paper. One corner settled on the edge of his paper plate and began to turn red with meatball sauce. He lifted the paper and turned it over, wiped at the stain with a napkin. Then he looked at Melody.

"Guess who Karla's with?" A teasing little-girl smile played on her face.

"Who?"

"Guess."

No reply. A flat look. Curiosity quickly dissolving.

"Montana! Isn't that neat?"

"I want to see the other gun."

"Rifle."

"Rifle."

"No."

"Why not?"

"It's all wrapped up."

"Unwrap it."

"Maybe later."

"Grinch."

"This one's got everything you need to know."

"I'm going to take it apart." She set the AK-47 down on the bed-sheet on the floor. They sat cross-legged on either side of the sheet.

"You don't need to do that."

"Want to."

He exhaled in mild exasperation. Shook his head. "You need to know how to use it, not how to take it apart."

"Want to."

"Go ahead."

She broke a fingernail when she extracted the bolt.

He smiled.

She didn't complain about the broken nail and kept on working. It took her twenty minutes to take it down and ten minutes to put it back together. Smug look. Then twelve minutes to do it again. Start to finish. More smug.

"Piece of cake." She grinned.

No comment.

"I'm ready to kick butt."

He had to smile at that one. "Not yet."

"What else?"

"Stoppage. If it jams, you have to know how to clear it. If you can't do that, you're dead."

"Clear it?"

"That's important. That's the most important thing."

"Show me."

He showed her. It took six tries before she learned to strike the charging handle at the correct angle so it functioned as a forward assist. The palm of her hand was red. Another fingernail broke. Again, no complaints.

"Not bad." He nodded his head, eyes on the rifle.

She settled her rear end back on her heels, the weapon across her thighs above her knees, which pressed onto the edge of the sheet on the rug. She looked at the abused flesh of her right hand, then at him, and she smiled.

"Now I can kill gooks."

He looked at her. Looked into her eyes with a hard look that surprised her.

"Don't say that."

"Say what?" her smile gone, chased by the steel stare.

"Gooks."

No reply.

"They're people . . . just like you . . . and me. Not gooks."

She waited. He waited. He felt confused. She didn't deserve his anger.

Finally, he shrugged. "Sorry. You did good." Weak smile. "Rum and Coke?"

She put the AK down on the sheet. "Okay." And she got up from the floor and went into the kitchen and made drinks.

They sat side by side on the sofa. She talked about small things, about how she had learned to deal twenty-one, about how nervous the manager of the Sports Book was when big money came in, about how the pit boss scared her, about Karla. Once, when she looked over at him, she thought she saw tears, but she wasn't sure . . . a glitter on his lower eyelash . . . she wasn't sure.

He followed along behind her words and didn't say much. He was polite, but lost.

Suddenly, from no place she knew, she felt a desperate, aching urge to take him in her arms. The idea pinned her heart to a stop.

It was not a sexual thing. Not man and woman. It was a human thing. She was struck by the brutal realization that the person next to her was alone, horribly, dangerously alone.

She looked down at her lap, at the drink in her hand. "I didn't mean to say gooks."

He didn't look at her, but his hand moved across the cushions and took hers.

"Oh, my," she said. "I'm sorry."

In the night, she came to look at him as he slept on the sofa. Wind chafed against the outside of the building. Light from a passing car moved across the white ceiling. A cat screeched, and the lid of a trash can rattled. The ceiling went red in the glow of a traffic light down the block.

Her heart hurt.

Her vision adjusted to the low light, and she saw that he slept with an earplug in one ear, and the wire from it trailed down to a small black portable on the cushion. She moved across the rug and knelt down beside the couch. She studied his face as he lay there. She wanted to touch his face. She didn't.

She bent and looked closely at the portable, found the switch, reached out, and clicked it off. Gently she lifted the wire, and the earplug slipped away from his ear. She smiled and coiled the wire and placed it next to his arm.

She stood with her arms folded across her chest and looked down at him. She thought of the music that put him to sleep and wondered what he listened to.

The room seemed cold. She shivered. A gust of wind rocked the building. She thought to move his blanket higher so it covered more of his chest, his arms, but she didn't want to chance waking him. She would let him rest, would let him find a refuge from the memories that made him weep at words. Safe. Protected by the night.

And finally she went back to her bed and lay in the dark and then fell asleep.

She began to dream of gun parts. Of the glitter of tears.

"Vader?"

"Ummm?"

"You awake?"

"No."

Karla grabbed a fistful of Montana's chest hair. She twisted.

"Ow! Goddamn it, Karla!"

"There. Bet you're awake now."

She put her arms around him and pulled him close, snuggled her nose into his neck, wrapped her naked legs around his.

The muffled roar of a tractor-trailer rig on the freeway in front of the motel built to a throaty pitch, then faded as the truck powered north through the fog toward Los Angeles. The room was dark and cool. The aromas of cigarette smoke, sweat, and sex worked in concert to override the lingering tang of room disinfectant and air freshener put there by an overworked maid with too many rooms to clean. Despite the hour, an endless ribbon of Latin music pulsed wistfully along the outside corridors of the place, wormed under doors, filtered past window frames—guitar and trumpet-rich phrases of love and loss spun above the muted rustle of a maraca. The sound drifted like wind, now soft, now softer, changing direction . . . perhaps coming from another room, a car, maybe from some nearby bush camp where migrant field hands took small pleasures from wine, sound, and memory while sore muscles ached under brown skin.

She pulled his body against hers as powerfully as she could. She felt hard sinew tighten, felt his arms press back, felt the skin of his neck move as he smiled in the darkness.

"Love you, Vader."

He replied with more pressure, his arms forcing her breath out.

"You and me?"

"Me and you, Karla. I never had nothing like you to love."

"Can we make it?"

"We can make it, honey. We sure can."

"Crazy, isn't it?"

"Good crazy."

"What'll you do? What about Arthur?"

"I need to stop sometime, need something different. When I finish this job, the one we're doing now in Vegas, then I'll have enough to get us set up. This is the big one. Big bucks. I've got some saved . . . we'll have enough . . . me and you."

"Have you told him? Told Arthur?"

"It has to happen sometime. I think we're both sort of burned out, me and him. I know I am. We do too much moving around. I think he knows it. It's time to settle somewhere." He hugged her. "I don't want nothing 'cept to love you."

She moved against him and didn't reply, only smiled and sighed and kept her eyes closed.

"When you talked to Melody tonight? . . . She say it's all right? Your taking an extra couple of days?"

"Uh-huh." Another squeeze. "Said she'd get the mail 'n all. No biggie."

"She's a nice gal. Sort of stuffy. But okay. Nice."

"Ummmm. I love her. Lotta laughs. I told her we did it in the desert." She giggled. "I told her you made my butt raw." She pinched his arm and snuggled closer.

Montana smiled in the dark. "She's pretty . . . sort of."

Another pinch. Harder this time.

"Ow! Not as pretty as you."

Karla let go of the pinched skin.

Arthur began to dream.

It started not with images. Nor with sound.

It started with a smothering pressure. No air to breathe. No way to move. His body unable to turn. Paralyzed by the force of his own will. Blood screeching silently at lungs for something, anything to use, even the water that covered his mouth. Even to inhale that foul liquid that stank mere fractions beneath the openings of his nose. Even that.

A rage to breathe. A ragged, urgent rage almost stronger than the urge to live.

Trapped by the mud and the sun.

Muscles aching, muscles licked by flickering tongues of bright shiny pain . . . muscles in a fiery vise of limitless agony not from exertion but from being made motionless.

Motionless.

Twenty-eight hours.

Only the rhythmic push of arteries, the barely discernible swell of veins under mud-caked skin and cloth. The metered, locked expansion of his chest under the water of the rice paddy . . . a mad exercise full of resolution and desperate purpose. Breathe. Enough to live and no more. Enough to live yet keep the water still as glass.

Waiting for the nudge of a bayonet. Of a rifle muzzle. Of a boot tip.

His own weapon pressed along his body . . . pinned between the mud bottom of the paddy and his chest . . . each angle and projection of the rifle magnified and harsh and stabbing like stiletto steel where it touched him . . . the fingers of his right hand frozen into claw shapes, all the feeling gone, the cramping total.

Voices.

Singsong phrases. Charlie words. Laughter.

The sound of boots bending reeds. Four times the sound of piss gurgling and boring into the water only inches away. So close he smelled the ammonia and tasted the bitter flavor through his sealed lips. So close he heard the rustle of cloth as a penis was put back behind black fabric.

And once the whine of an animal, a dog. A goddamn dog. No!

Sniffing. A tail hitting brittle stalks of grass. No!

Things of the mud moved into his sleeves and burrowed past his pulled-out pants cuff. They crawled behind his knee and up to his groin. Things that scratched and fed. Things that ate his blood, things that marveled at the warm, pliant feast they'd discovered in the midst of their sordid universe . . . things that stayed and moved and bit and didn't go away and seemed to get bigger as he tracked their progress over his flesh.

The snake. It slithered from the pale grass in front of his face. He heard the reptile coming before he saw it. Then it was there, black in the water. Its flat head stretched five inches above the surface of the dank pond as it glided through brown fluid. Neck glistening, swaying from side to side. It forged a silent passage, trailed a V of wake, small lines of wave that looked to him like surf . . . ripples that could key his death if they were seen and not understood. The viper bumped his forehead, then wrapped behind his neck and coiled onto his left shoulder, the one that stuck above the water. Weight pressing down. Heavy snake.

The thing sunned.

Once, late on that first afternoon, Arthur felt the maddening tickle of the serpent's wire-thin tongue flick about his ear. Felt the dry body push against and roll the beaded chain of his dogtags behind his neck . . . chain and tags painted black . . . pulled tight and taped for silence. The snake touched its feathery tongue to his ear just before it unwrapped itself and disappeared into the water somewhere beyond his feet. Arthur felt the heft of the dry coils leave his back and he was sad when the thing slithered off because now it was just him and the predatory pain again.

"Hey, Vader?"

"What?"

"When you guys went in the war . . . you and Arthur . . . they make you be a sniper? . . . You ask for it?"

"What do you want to talk about that for?"

"I love you. I want to know."

"Everyone shoots. They can see. You go to school. Most of it's learning how to sneak around, much as shooting. The docs have a go at you ... the head docs ... you know ... see if you got the patience."

"Shrinks?"

"Yes."

"To see if you're crazy?"

"To see how much you can take, endurance stuff. To see if you got the patience and can make yourself be a bush. Most of the time we don't go out to shoot at all, more to scout a target before the air comes in. To see what happens when it goes down, intel junk. So the brass and the wing know what they hit."

"Are you good at it?"

"I'm good at it."

"What about Arthur? Is he any good?"

"He's good. Maybe too good."

"Can't be too good."

"He got himself fingered once or twice. Special trips."

"How's that?"

"Special is all."

Arthur lay on the couch in Melody's apartment, his white face pressed hard against the cushions, muscles rigid, skin like stone sheet, eyes crushed shut, lips welded in a hard line, his breathing not a visible thing, his fingers starched hooks.

Awkward shadows chased across the ceiling as cars went by. The weak light sifted through the air, light preempted in its silent travel over room-shapes by a thing more silent than itself.

He cracked his lips to make an entry for the rancid water. He didn't suck, but only made an opening in his face and let the vile stuff flow into his mouth. Sound-free. Wave-free. He took in bits of floating grit and stalk and a small spider that walked like a spindly Jesus on the surface and came too close.

He wondered as he lay in his mud-hell how long they'd taken to kill Jankowitz. His spotter.

The image of his partner snapped like a frame of sepia-colored movie film into his brain. Jankowitz, palm turned in, four fingers straight and pointing up, arm pumping up and down for Arthur to see. Punji sticks. Jank turning, making sure his partner saw.

Then the slip.

Jank went onto the sticks with a low moan. No scream. No curse.

Three penetrations. Through and through. The smell of shit on the green wood. Jank's and Charlie's.

"Vader?"

"Ummmm?"

"I need some more of that stuff on my rump. It hurts. The feeling's coming back."

"I know I got all the sand scrubbed out."

"Sure felt like you did. It hurts anyway. Be a buddy."

"Where's the cream?"

"By the sink."

"Okay. Stay on your tummy . . . " He left the bed and crossed the room in the dark. From the bathroom, "You just want to be on top all the time."

"Be nice, lover. It stings."

"I told you we should have been careful."

Arthur had his arms under Jankowitz and was working him off the sticks when the first shot exploded the earth at the rim of the pit. Dirt peppered his face.

"Go, Arthur, go!"

"There's only one of them, Jank. Only one!"

"The rest are coming. Go!"

Arthur talked and tried to lift again, but his eyes were in the trees. "I've got to get you off."

Jank yelled in pain. Adrenaline diluting. Arthur stopped trying to lift. In the same second another round splattered dirt in Arthur's face, but he saw leaves jump.

He grabbed his spotter's rifle and fired a burst into the delicate, hanging mist that bathed the still-shivering leaves one hundred meters to the west. A clatter of metal and the crack of branches crossed the space. Charlie was hit. Or his weapon was hit. No time. No time to be sure. Back to Jankowitz, but Jankowitz had the .45 to his chin.

"I'll blow my fucking head off if you don't get the fuck out of here!" A froth of expanding blood bubbles rolled from the corner of his mouth . . . graceful, slow-moving pink bubbles. Jank's skin was white under the bush grease. "Go! Go now!"

"Jank . . . "

Safety off. Hammer back. "For Christ's sake. Let me get at least one more of them. You got to give me that, you useless son of a bitch!"

The shrill sound of a ball whistle cut the air. Voices.

"You stand there and make me waste myself? You lousy bastard! You know what they got. It's the bunch we been chopping." Jank's eyelids fluttered. "Please, Arthur, please go." A soft voice.

Arthur watched the trigger finger blanch as it tightened. He scrambled out of the pit and ran. No choice. Ran until he found his hellhole of mud.

Karla fell asleep after Montana smoothed the ointment onto the turns of her behind. The cool analgesic took the sting away. She dreamed of sitting beside him as they crossed the desert, dreamed of touching him, dreamed of the heat and the taste of him in her mouth as they drove, and heard again the sound of wind moving past the windows of the car. In her shallow slumber she heard the fall of footsteps on the walkway of the motel as someone passed by the door of their room, muffled voices, a soft laugh, female, a door closing farther down. Tourists? Lovers? The warmth of the man next to her bathed her in a peaceful, liquid calm.

In the night, the water sucked his heat away. The hot sun gone, a numbing cold took him in cruel arms. The foul water was still warm, but it was colder than the inside of his body . . . cold enough to shift the balance . . . cold enough to start him shivering.

He fought the cold. Battled against the jerking contractions. Faces drifted at his mind. Faces twisted in pain. Faces that looked flat and wavered in the glass of his sniper scope.

His brain tried to escape the faces. It traded the images of those he targeted for faces from long ago . . . faces twisted, black and frozen by the flames of the circus fire. Faces caked with carbon and flecks of straw. The smell of death.

Image rejected. New image. A professional face. A satisfied look of discovery on that face ... on the face of the Navy shrink who asked questions and wrote things on a yellow pad of paper.

Then that vision dissolved. Arthur's mind spun, hunted across a dark place, searched for reasons. Gray shadows. Hard-packed earth passing close beneath his eyes. Something in his jaws. Salt taste. Fur. Broken bones. Flesh still warm. A sliver of cold moon high to the left. Shapes of rock and mesquite branch on either side. The depth and reach of time strong on his senses.

A twig snapped.

The images jerked away, deserted his mind in a swift speck of dispatch.

Instantly alert.

The falsetto of Charlie.

So close.

Almost on top of him.

One eye unsealed and peeled open. Just above the water ... water that surely roared with the turbulence of his shivering limbs.

He waited, suspended in a stark, furious silence.

Another twig broke, a brittle cracking retort, a spear of sound that would stay in him all his days ... driven deep by dark import. The second most vivid sensation of his life.

Second only to the faces in the scope.

The faces of the children.

Arthur sat on a wooden bench outside the Regimental shack. The arguing voices barged through the plywood walls.

"I don't care what the fuck you think, Commander. We take them out."

"You got your head in your ass, Colonel."

"Watch it, Commander."

"You're dead wrong on this one. Eight of them, Colonel. Eight kids hanging from trees. In plain view. You want to make that village hate Charlie, that's the way to do it. Their kids! Their own fucking kids! We couldn't ask for a better piece of luck."

"They'll fold, Commander. That village will fold. They can't stomach any more. If they fold, we lose the whole sector. They're caught in the middle ... Charlie at night, us during the day."

"Hate works! The NVA fucked the dog on this one ... trying to scare those people back to their side full-time . . . fucked the dog! The people in that hamlet won't forget what's happening on the mountain. Never! Not seeing their own kids skinned alive a piece at a time. Not hearing those screams every night."

"Wrong."

"Not fucking wrong!"

"Pacification, Navy. Do you know what that means? It doesn't mean this! Not this shit! We put those children down, put them out of their goddamn misery. You take that beautiful, cold-blooded animal you got outside and get it done . . . do it right and those people won't even know who did it."

"Bullshit!"

"No more, Commander. Make it happen! End of discussion! Get him! Get the shooter!"

Water cold as ice. His soul abrading. Waiting for the touch that meant death. Maybe not a touch. Maybe a bullet, close range, turning his chest inside out. His body a ruptured mushroom of muscle and bone, a red blossom of confusion, and the water flowing in. Cold winning. Bugs winning.

The snap of another twig next to his ear, the scepter sound of death. Quick death . . . if he was lucky.

In his frozen world he cradled each new millisecond.

The night dragged through that coldest hour, the one before dawn. His mind drew in upon itself, found refuge in some protected grotto deep within the coiled chemistry of genetic memory. His body accepted its icy metamorphosis and became part of the muddy world of the rice paddy . . . at one with the earth . . . no more pain.

Arthur closed his eye. A small insect wiggled, trapped inside his eyelid. Arthur contracted the muscles of the eyelid. Relaxed and squeezed once more. The bug stopped moving . . . only a rough bump that floated beneath his skin.

18

Night Lights

Melody thought it was the wind.

A low moan. From no direction. Faint. Haunting.

She raised her head from the pillow.

In the living room, nothing moved. The street outside was empty. The night wind had dropped away to a fitful breeze. On the end table, beneath the turned-off light, the ceramic boy smiled out from under his pastel green umbrella. The top of the umbrella took on a deeper shade of green as the traffic light at the corner changed to that color.

On the couch, Arthur. Beside the bunched muscle of his forearm lay the coiled wire of the small, sound-activated tape player. The earplug rested on the edge of the cushion where Melody had placed it when she took it from his ear. On the coffee table fronting the couch, the nylon gun case with the AK-47 zipped inside sat with its black surface eating up what was left of light. The ink-dark hue of the case rendered it invisible to human eye were there a human eye to look.

*   *   *

She heard it again.

A cat? A dog? The wind hitting a corner of the building or moving across a drainpipe end?

A strangled, wavering sound. Not human.

She got out of her bed and went to the bedroom window and pulled aside the curtain. Looked out. The sound gone. She was standing there when the noise made her turn around. It was behind her.

Coming from the hallway.

She shivered at the twisting resonance. She clasped her arms across her chest and pulled her hands up into the cuffs of her white pajama top as if she were standing in a winter landscape before a chill north wind.

The crawling, muted howling stopped.

She waited.

Silence.

She went to the bedroom doorway. Stopped to listen. Nothing. A step at a time, curious, somewhat afraid, she started down the hall.

She turned the corner slowly. One step. Waited. She looked at the living room window. Perhaps the shadow of a cat would be there. At times the cat love-noises sounded like cries from some other world.

No cat shadow.

And then it came at her.

More snarl than howl. A tight sound. Compressed. Boiling up through the black air . . . lifting from the couch.

The strangled intonation froze her limbs and made her lungs stop.

The realization that the source of the demonic wail was next to her, so close, frightened her. Then she relaxed.

Thank God, Melody thought. *It's only Arthur.*

She took two steps toward him and stopped with the coffee table between him and her. She looked down.

He was quiet now, a dark form not moving.

Arthur waited. Asleep and not asleep. He waited for the touch of the bayonet tip, the rifle muzzle, the boot. Waited. The hands. Cramped hands. That was the problem. *Would they work? Would they respond to orders from the brain? Would they be able to strike and kill when the world exploded?*

A howl rolled up from some low place. Eerie. A pain-laced lamentation built deep in the soul of some black horror.

The earplug mute, lifeless. A disconnected alarm. A saving thing unsaving now.

She couldn't allow the pain to continue.

She bent from the waist and leaned toward him, leaned to touch his arm, leaned to wake him from the nightmare that hurt him so.

Her arm reached out.

Her finger straightened.

And softly in that dark room the tip of her finger closed the last, outrageous inch between them.

She touched him.

He was ready.

In those next savage moments his world altered the character of time, his seconds became minutes. The professional.

Her world exploded into blunt, numbing disarray. Her seconds didn't exist at all. They were compressed out of existence. She was put behind time, trailed reality. Helpless. The amateur.

His hands, claws now, shot out and buried talons in the coarse fabric of the enemy's shirt front. As his fingers filled with cloth, his arm muscles began to contract . . . to jerk the opponent toward him. He bulled up to head-butt the face pulled down by his hands.

Something was wrong! The shirt front tore away. Not stiff burlap, not harsh canvas. Something else. His lunge thwarted.

The hands had come at her so fast. Her white cotton top had been stripped away from her body. Only the weight of her torso, off balance though she was, was enough to start the ripping, was enough to keep teeth in sockets, to keep blood inside constricting veins, to keep brain in skull.

White breasts rippled, liberated in the instant, naked in the cold air, but cold had no meaning.

Head-butt aborted, hands full of stripped cotton, he jackknifed his body in a vicious horizontal sweep. His slashing legs would seek and shatter knee . . . destroy ligament . . . crack bone . . . turn pink cartilage into disheveled mush.

His legs crashed against the nylon gun case instead of flesh. The gun-carry lurched across the tabletop, absorbed most of the brutal, maiming force. The object was between his legs and hers.

The heavy nylon sheath slammed against the side of her right knee, but anatomy held together in the face of mayhem.

She was spun completely around and then some. She buckled to the floor and came to rest with the back of her shoulders against the outside edge of the coffee table. Her legs twisted under her body. Half-sitting. Stunned. Facing away from him.

There was nothing in her mind. Nothing at all. Only the shredding image of her hand moving toward him in the hanging half-second before her world had turned to chaos.

Time moved a tiny segment more, moved one small click forward, and in the next insane moment a steel forearm crushed against her throat . . . locked into the crook of his other arm . . . the hand of that other arm cupping the back of her head . . . and pushing . . . more than pushing. Bending her neck forward. Blocking her breathing. Making her cervical vertebrae splay apart like a deck of fanned playing cards.

She was locked in a vise, and the vise was closing.

Breathing was not an option, protest not a choice, defense nothing but a sad joke . . . death a monstrous, probable alternative to tomorrow.

For those who know the pristine intensity of the secret war, the war that puts warriors alone behind enemy lines, that allows not even one mistake, that teaches by simple attrition that every human sense—sight, hearing, touch, taste, smell—is critical—for them, the sense of smell is no small item, not a thing played down. Especially when other senses go mute in night and noise. The smell of Charlie's breath laced with nuoc mam, the rotting fish sauce odor that carries far and puts sentry dogs on go; the deadly giveaway of cigarette smoke; of aftershave; of soap—all can be front-row tickets to oblivion. When real killers kill, the senses work to keep feeding facts, to keep faithful watch as fury swirls.

It came to him.

The smell of her hair.

The delicate aroma of her clean hair.

That small thing.

It saved her life.

The vise stopped its murderous travel.

His mind leaped forward and came up hard against the wall of real time, present time, the now. Awake. Aware. He saw the shadows of the room and knew.

He released his stranglehold. He moved beside her.

He took her in his arms.

She pulled air, held the sides of her throat with both hands, and tried to restart her brain.

They sat on the floor in the dark living room. He rocked her gently. They did not cry. There was nothing left to cry with. No intellectual energy strong enough to waste on words. No emotion strong enough to overwhelm the import of what had happened.

They were two people impaled on the sword of something they didn't understand.

Her shoulders and her bare breasts were pale in dim light. A nakedness not thought about. Not in that silent room where a distant traffic light brushed green and red and yellow color across the ceiling in gentle repetition.

He lifted her to her feet, then picked her up and carried her to the back room, carried her to the bed and gently eased her down onto the edge of it. She sat there. Small, silent, head down. He moved a blanket and covered her legs.

He stood before her, his hand holding hers.

He stepped back to leave.

But she held on and did not let him go.

She looked up and saw sorrow glitter in his eyes, on his face.

She pulled him back.

Slowly she began to undress him. When he was naked, she took off her own torn clothing. And made him lie with her.

Beneath warm covers, she put her arms around him and held him. Bodies pressed together. Her head on his chest.

Not a word was said.

Not a single word.

They did not make love.

They just held on.

And waited for the day.

Waited for the sun to dissolve that fearsome night away.

▌ ▌ ▌

"They said I have no heart."

She sipped coffee from a blue cup. She looked at him as he sat across from her.

He didn't turn away, but looked back at her with no shame, no excuse building in his expression, no defensive challenge in the tone of his words, and simply said, "I think they're wrong."

"They *are* wrong."

But he said nothing in reply.

"How long has it been like this?"

"The nights? I don't remember. The war, I guess. That's why they made me leave. I couldn't sleep. Couldn't keep quiet. They couldn't use me anymore. But there was always something. Always something there. Even before the war. I just don't know."

"That thing, that radio thing. That's what you use when the dreams come . . . to wake you up. Am I right?"

"Yes. I should have told you."

"You just did."

She buttered toast pieces and put grape jam on top. She pushed the plate across the table to him.

"I'm not out of it. I mean, I know what's going on. When I left the service, they made a real effort to get me straight."

He ate one piece of toast.

"The tape player was their idea. They said I should use it until the nights got better, but the nights didn't get better."

"I guess not." And she smiled a soft smile and touched her throat.

"They gave me a pretty good going-over. Sometimes I dream things I've never seen. Like I'm some kind of animal."

For the first time he looked embarrassed.

"I think we're all animals once in a while." She thought of her and Mike twisting together, making love, burning hot hours, and she was taken by the realization that she hadn't thought about Mike since yesterday. She felt a mild despair come into her. She shook it off.

"It's so real. The guy who worked with me, Captain Harrigan, he said we have genetic memory . . . something about evolution, stuff like that. Said it's like birds—you know, how they know how to fly? Sheer instinct. He told me there's something in everyone, something that remembers. Nothing magic about it . . . not anything weird. Real. It's just stronger in some people."

"Could be."

He began to swirl the last of his coffee in his cup, held the cup in his hand and made circular motions in the air. Now his eyes stayed away from hers. "He said another thing, too. He said some people just get wired wrong. Some are crosswired from the start, are born that way; he said I'm not one of those. Others get burned out by life, can't handle things that happen. To keep from checking out, they make a break with reality."

She saw color rise in the skin of his face.

"Like psychos do," he said and set his cup on the table.

"You mean schizophrenics."

"Yes."

"I read something in a magazine about it once, but I don't know much about it."

He looked up, and her smile left her face when she saw his expression.

"Do you think that could be it? I'm one of them?"

"You're asking the wrong person."

Silence. Awkward silence.

"The captain said he thought it was more the genetic thing . . . the memory thing we have."

"We? What's this 'we' stuff?" She smiled and poured coffee into her cup so it was full. Her remark made him smile, too. She stirred her coffee. "I guess we all have things we're afraid of," she said, "things that make us weak, things that make us weird."

He was silent for a moment, then softly spoke. "I'm not afraid of being weak. It's more the other way around."

She laughed, and the sound of her laughter sparkled in the small kitchen. Unexpected laughter. Disarming. She picked up the spoon she stirred her coffee with, and she reached across the table and whacked him on the back of his hand. Hard. "You ain't so tough. I could take you, soon as you learn to fight fair. I could kick your butt." She squinted across the table and pointed her spoon at him. "You don't scare me, you big goof."

He stared. Then he rested his chin in his hand and began to chuckle. He felt the muscles in his back go slack and felt the skin of his face soften as a quick, delicious feeling of physical release washed over and through him. His mind relaxed, then untwisted in a way he couldn't understand as it escaped from somewhere to somewhere else.

Her bold look dissolved into a grin. They just looked at each other for a moment.

"Do you remember anything bad?" she asked. "Anything that happened to you? . . . Way back? . . . When you were a kid?" But her words were easy, light, warm. Gently curious.

"Nothing happened. Just the usual stuff." His voice sounded different to him.

"Did the shrinks give you pills? You know, pills?"

"Once." He smiled. "It didn't work. The pills just made me sleep all day."

"Did you have a bad time in the war? Vietnam?"

"Everyone had a bad time, most guys worse than me. But I don't march around looking for . . . whatever. I feel funny when I see that. Crying. Hugging. I try not to be hard-assed about it. Everybody's different. Guess it's good to cry, but I don't think it's good to cry too much . . . you have to hold something back, something to use, something to keep you pissed off. Men know that. It's our secret." He sipped coffee.

"That stuff was twenty-five years ago," he said. "That's a long time. Nam didn't bother me. I've still got all my pieces. Not like some." He took a bite out of the second piece of toast. "Some guys won't let it drop . . . but hell can do that to you."

"Does Montana know? About your trouble?"

"He knows."

"Were you two guys always together? Over there, I mean?"

"He was my third spotter."

"Who were the other two?"

"A guy called Fratello. And Jank."

"What happened to them?"

Pause. "They got out."

"Ever kill anybody? With your gun?"

"Yes."

"Bet you were a holy terror. Ever think about it?"

"No."

"Were you scared?"

"I guess."

"Those people had it rough, didn't they? The ones who lived there, I mean. The Vietnamese. Especially the kids."

Longer pause. "The kids."

"At least you tried to help. I guess you have to feel good about that . . . about trying to help them."

He drank more coffee and scratched behind his ear. He moved his chair and tapped on the tabletop with his spoon. "I tried to help."

"Did you ever think of staying in? If you could figure how to sleep?"

"Guys like me, we're only good for fighting. When the fighting's done, we just get in people's way. I guess we make guys who weren't there feel left out." He looked at his coffee cup. "They think *they're* left out? That's a laugh." He didn't laugh.

"Got a bunch of medals? Got a bunch, I'll bet."

"Got some."

"Hero. I never knew a hero."

He looked up. His expression was flat, without emotion. "Now you know a hero."

19

Practice

"That's a neat gun," said Melody.

Arthur looked at her. She tried too hard to look serious and gave away the fact that she was tweaking him by using the word "gun."

They stood next to her van in the middle of the Big Empty, a silent and barren stretch of desert one hour out of Las Vegas. The place was a glittering stillness, a reach of yellow, brown, and mint green beneath a steel-gray morning, the sky a pristine cymbal waiting to be struck. A red sun floated. A single gun-puff of white cloud drifted slowly east like a lone sheep grazing on unseen wisps of grain in a high blue pasture. A brown dust devil danced on distant sand, a twisting tentacle playing with dust and sticks and meandering to the whim of obscure circumstance.

She studied the compact black rifle as he removed it from its nylon case. He unwound its muslin wraps. It was not one of the two weapons he had left in her apartment. It was smaller than those. She wondered where it came from. She was taken by the look of the new weapon, excited. She wanted to reach out and touch it, but she waited to see if her "gun" word would get his goat. He didn't take the bait.

"Oh, I forgot . . . rifle." Her fingers over her mouth. "This is my rifle, this is my gun. This is for shooting, this is for fun." She pointed a finger, first at the rifle, then at her hips and over again, as she minced the lines of the boot camp chant he had taught her before he realized she was playing games with him. Her eyes sparkled in the crystal air.

A false look of concern clouded her face. "What do they do now that there's women in the military? What do the ladies sing if they get mixed up? . . . Gun instead of rifle? Girls can't march around holding onto their . . . their . . . you know. What do they do, Arthur? Huh? What do they do?"

He looked at her with a calm expression.

"Huh, Arthur? Huh?"

"Are you through?" he asked.

"Tell me, Arthur. Tell me."

Instead, he held out the rifle to her. She reached for it and gently took it from him with both hands. The weapon absorbed her full attention.

"It's a Ruger Mini-14. It's yours."

"Mine?" She looked up.

"Since you're going to learn to use it right, you might as well own one. I got it for you yesterday. It's new."

"You didn't have to do that."

"I know. I'm sure I'll regret it. You'll probably shoot me."

"It's expensive."

"No, it isn't. I mean it's expensive, but I didn't have to pay for it. It's a sample. I get them wholesale." A minor fabrication, but a comfortable lie. "Credit it toward my rent."

They lay side by side on the hardpan desert. Prone. Propped on elbows.

"That's right. That's how to wrap the sling." He reached over and tested the tension in the web strap. "Remember to hold it snug against your shoulder so the recoil won't bother you. If you hold it loose, it's going to kick you silly, and you'll start flinching when you pull the trigger."

She seated the rifle butt firmly into her right shoulder.

"Nope. Try this." He reached over and pulled the barrel so it pointed up and away from the line of fire. The move rolled Melody up slightly onto her left side. "This opens the pocket. The pocket is the place on your shoulder where the butt rests. If you do it this way it makes the pocket easier to find." He moved the barrel back to the line of fire and pushed the rifle rearward against her shoulder as she settled in. "See how it fits? Always roll it down like that when you start. You find the right spot every time."

She moved the rifle forward away from her shoulder and repeated the sequence without his help.

"Like this?"

"Like that."

She squinted along the sight line. "Do I keep both eyes open?"

"That's up to you. Whatever feels natural. Some of the pros say you should keep 'em both open so the pupils dilate the same. I don't think it's all that important."

"Do you keep both eyes open?"

"Yes."

"Me too."

He smiled.

He reached over and cupped his fingers against her face and wiggled them into the junction where her cheek pressed onto the stock. "This is what's called your weld point. You have to make the spotweld the same each time. Remember how it feels on your skin. You want your muscles to remember where they touch the stock so your eye is always the same distance from the rear sight."

He took his hand away. "We can put some cuts in the stock if you want . . . something to help you feel the right spot."

"You're not going to cut on my gun . . . rifle."

"Your trigger finger. Don't wrap it like that. Do it like I showed you . . . just the tip."

She moved her finger.

"Something else." He reached out and pressed on the little finger of her trigger hand. "Keep pressure on that finger. Use it to hold the rifle back against your shoulder to keep the tension off your trigger finger. And don't jerk the trigger when you fire. Just pull back nice and smooth. Straight back. Don't move the rifle. Straight back."

"I want to shoot a bullet."

He rolled on his side and studied her from head to toe.

"Give me a bullet. I'm ready."

He reached down to her right knee and put his hand there. He grabbed a handful of blue jeans and tugged gently. She didn't jump at his touch, let him bend her right leg forward.

"Put your leg there. Keep it bent. That takes the pressure off your upper body. Feel the difference?"

"Okay. Great. Give me a bullet."

"Stand up."

She turned her head and looked at him. "Stand up?"

"Yes. I want to see you get into position by yourself."

She got to her feet. As she did so, the barrel of the rifle swung around and pointed at him.

"Watch it!" He reached out and smacked the business end of the weapon to one side. She jumped at the sudden move, startled by the quickness of the impact of his hand on the barrel.

He grinned at her. "That's so you remember. If you point that thing at me, I'm not going to give you a bullet."

"Sorry." She looked embarrassed.

"Look, lady. You're a piece of cake. Like I said before, nobody I'd rather teach than a beginner. No bad habits. You're doing great. Just don't kill me, okay?"

She nodded. Then she kneeled down, went prone, and got into position.

"Good. Fingertip."

Her finger moved.

"Lower down. About two-thirds down." He positioned her finger on the trigger. "Great. You're doing great."

"Bullet. Need a bullet."

He ignored her request. "When you shoot, breathe normal. Then take a few deep breaths just before you squeeze off."

"Squeeze off?" She kept sighting down the barrel.

He looked at her.

"Never been 'squeezed off' before." A straight face.

He shook his head. "Before you pull the trigger."

"I like 'squeezed off' better."

"Then breathe in about halfway and hold it while you fire."

He watched her practice the breathing cycle a few times.

"My bullet. I want my bullet."

"Give it here." He reached over and took the rifle from her.

She lay on the sand and watched as he loaded the twenty-shot magazine with fifteen rounds. He snapped the magazine into the lower receiver. It seated with a sharp, metallic click. He handed the weapon back to her. "There you go, tiger."

She held the rifle, a new look of respect and anticipation in her eyes as she regarded the curved magazine protruding from the belly of the Ruger.

"What do I shoot at?"

"See that piece of sandstone? Shoot that."

"That's not so far away. I want to shoot something far away."

"No, you don't."

"Yes, I do. How about that bird?" She sighted along the rifle at a hawk dipping and holding in the air three hundred yards to the east as it searched for ground squirrels in the sage.

Arthur followed her line of sight, saw the hawk, then looked back at Melody.

"Okay? That bird?"

"No."

"Yes."

"The sandstone."

"No. The bird."

"If you miss . . . and you're going to miss . . . we won't know why you missed, which side, high or low."

She kept tracking the bird. "I can get him."

"Okay, shoot him." He waited. "Not the killer type, are you?"

She lowered the rifle and looked at him. "Well, I don't want to shoot dirt. I want to shoot something far away."

He stared at her.

She pursed her lips, then aimed at the lump of sandstone.

He rolled into position beside her.

She exaggerated the breathing cycle.

"Not so deep. You'll get dizzy."

She slowed her breathing.

She shot quickly. The crack of the rifle ripped the air, and the sand in front of the rock splashed up as the round hit low.

Two echoes, then a third, ricocheted through the crisp air.

"I killed it! I killed the mother!"

He turned his head. "You were low. You closed your eyes, didn't you?"

"I did not. I nailed that darn rock."

"This time keep your eyes open and don't jerk the trigger. You pulled the barrel down."

She lined up. Then she stopped and looked at him. "That was neat. It was a pretty loud bullet, though. It made me jump."

No reply.

"I saw a picture in that gun book you got me. Shouldn't I get some earmuffs like the guy in the book?"

"No."

"Why not?"

"Because they screw up your spotweld . . . get between you and the butt stock. If you're going to be a hotshot killer, you won't always have earmuffs in your purse. That's for competition when you shoot all day."

"I'm going to shoot all day."

"No, you're not."

"Can't stop me . . . I got my own gun . . . rifle."

"I've got the bullets."

"I'll rob them off you. You don't have a gun."

"Shoot."

She fired again. Then three more times. The last shot tunneled through the middle of the soft stone target.

"Not bad. You're still jerking."

"Am not!"

He rolled on his side and fished around in his pocket. He pulled out a quarter. He took the weapon from her, removed the magazine, and cleared the chambered round. He gave her back the Ruger. "Aim."

She aimed at the sandstone. He reached out and balanced the quarter on the forward top end of the slotted barrel guard.

"Now do your thing. Breathe and pull the trigger."

She lowered the rifle and the quarter fell off. She looked at him. "I don't have any bullets."

He looked at the quarter lying on the sand. Then at her. "I know you don't have any bullets."

"Oh."

She aimed again. "Long as you know."

He retrieved the coin and placed it back on the barrel top.

She started the breathing cycle. She began to giggle. The quarter fell off again. "This is stupid."

He folded his arms and rested his forehead on them, closed his eyes as he lay there facedown, not moving.

"Okay, okay." Giggles gone . . . but not far.

He reset the quarter.

Four times she went through the firing routine and four times the quarter fell off the rifle before the trigger released. He showed her how to cock the charging handle between each cycle. On the fifth attempt, the coin stayed put until the trigger clicked.

"I've got it!" she said.

"Not yet. I want that thing to stay there even after you're finished."

"After?"

"After. It's called follow-through. You might as well learn about it now, despite the fact you're so great." He looked at her and smiled.

"Follow-through? Teach me."

"Remember. Even after the trigger is pulled and the sear releases, it takes time for the firing pin to move forward and detonate the round. Then it takes more time for the bullet to get down the barrel. Not a whole lot of time, but some . . . enough to screw things up if you jerk out of the sequence. Just think of the whole thing in slow motion, and don't relax after the trigger lets go. Concentrate. Keep steady. Ignore the shot. Refocus. Look at the target. Freeze. Imagine that the weapon never fired. That makes the difference between good and great. You can do it."

"Get real."

"Do it." He reset the quarter as she aimed again.

It took ten tries. Finally the coin stayed in place.

"Not bad. Not bad at all." He put his hand on her head and pushed it into the ground.

She spit sand. Her face split in a broad grin. "More bullets."

He refilled the magazine and gave it to her. She snapped it into the receiver. Tapped it hard with the palm of her hand as she had seen him do.

She put five consecutive rounds into the middle of the target. The soft rock split apart in the violence of the last impact.

"I broke it."

"Stay here. Don't kill me." He got up and went to the van. He rummaged around in the glove compartment and found a worn-out road map. "Okay if we shoot this?"

She nodded.

He walked out behind the sandstone target and stuck the map onto the branches of a mesquite bush. He smoothed out the folds so the target presented a broad face toward Melody. He came back and crouched next to her. "Shoot."

She looked at the target. "That's pretty far off."

"You'll hit it. Shoot."

As Melody sighted at the road map, she hesitated. "This is all different. What do I look at? If I look at the map, I can't see the sights. If I look at the sights the map gets all blurry."

"Look at the target, then focus on the sights, the forward sight. That's the last thing you see. The forward sight. Keep steady. Don't sweat it. Just get lined up like before."

She aimed. He reset her left elbow more firmly in the sand.

She fired. He looked at the target through the small set of binoculars he had brought back from the van.

"Look." He lifted the strap from his neck and gave her the field glasses.

She set the rifle down on the ground and peered at the road map. "I don't see anything."

"Just above that red section. North Vegas."

"That little hole?" Excited. "That's it? I hit it first shot?"

"You hit it."

"Gee whiz. I hit it!" She kept looking through the binoculars.

"And you screwed up. Big time."

She turned and looked at him. "Screwed up?" Bewildered.

"The rifle."

She looked down at the rifle.

"You put it in the sand."

"Oh."

"That's not good."

"Oh."

"Look." He turned the Ruger over. Small sparkling grains stuck to the lightly oiled metal surface of the weapon. A twig of sage angled out of the recess behind the bolt.

She began to pick at the debris.

"Twenty laps."

She peered at him. A guilty look, a cookie-jar thief look.

"Yep. Twenty laps around the grinder. Full pack." But he was smiling.

"Now, rookie, you're going to learn how to clean a rifle."

"Now?"

"Now."

She brushed at the sandy grit. "There."

"No. Not 'there.'"

"More bullets!"

"No. No more bullets. First things first."

"It's my gun. Gimme bullets. I'm hot. Got to kill."

He picked up the rifle and headed for the van.

She stood up. "Hey! Where you going? Come back here."

Without turning he waved for her to follow. "Break time."

Melody trailed after him. Once she stopped and looked back at the target with the binoculars, a big smile under the eyepieces. They set up two folding chairs next to the open side door of the vehicle, and Melody spread a white towel on the floor inside the sliding door. From a styrofoam cooler she unloaded her supply of chicken salad sandwiches, chips, pickles, and pretzels. She took a bottle of white wine from a brown paper bag and unscrewed the foil top. She put two plastic cups on the towel, put ice in the cups, and then produced a delicate long-necked crystal vase into which she placed a single rose she took from a narrow box hidden beneath the driver's seat. She looked at Arthur.

"Guns or roses?" she asked.

Arthur had watched the picnic materialize, a smile on his face, not saying anything. Now he laughed. "Nice . . . the gun can wait."

"The *gun?*"

"The gun."

He set the rifle on the floor of the van next to the white towel. "We can't let that ice melt. Let's eat, rookie."

She poured wine for him. Cut his sandwich in half and put it on a paper plate. She gave him chips and pickles and pretzels.

And they ate in the shade of the van.

The dry, clean air carried aromas of sage and mesquite to them. They watched the red hawk hunt and soar. Melody kicked off her shoes and dug her toes in the warm sand. She nibbled pretzels and refilled his wine cup when his cup was half-full. She gave him a paper napkin when a piece of chicken salad fell from a corner of his sandwich and took the napkin from him when he finished corraling the wayward dollop. She emptied her cup of wine, and when she was finished leaned back in her folding chair and made the aluminum joints of the thing squeak as she held her empty cup high above her face and tried to catch the last few drops as they sparkled down toward her lips. Then she set the cup down and stretched like she would stretch if she had just awakened from a delicious sleep, her toes and feet pointing down, her arms rigid behind her head and in line with the rest of her, her fingers balled in little fists, and her head back. The folding chair squeaked again. She purred. He heard her purr. Her feline stretch collapsed in segments and she went limp. She stared at the horizon and said without looking at him, "God, it's beautiful out here."

He didn't reply at first. He had watched her turn into a cat and back into a woman again. Then he said something that wasn't true. "I knew a girl like you once."

She smiled and looked at him. "Like me?"

"Yes."

"How so?"

"She was pretty. Beautiful. She could make a chicken sandwich. We used to go on picnics and drink wine."

He was dismayed by the stark invention of his words. He had known no such person. Never. Why had he said that thing?

"She used to stretch like you just did."

More words free and false. His skin felt numb on his face. But he smiled at her with that same skin and she smiled back. His mind stepped away and watched. Took no part in what he said.

"She couldn't shoot, though." His eyes finally going to the tops of his shoes, eyes no longer willing to play the strange game.

She looked at him for a long, quiet moment.

He could not remember the last time he had blushed. His skin grew hot. Squeaks wailed from the metal rivets of his chair as his feet pushed the sand.

"You make a good friend, Arthur. She was lucky. I'm lucky, too."

She looked at him a few seconds more, then bent forward in her chair and picked up a dry branch of piñon pine. She asked him what it was and he told her about it, using lots of words—true words about how this type of piñon had solitary needles instead of clusters or pairs like other pines and how the thin-shelled seeds fell to the ground where they would die in the hot sun if it weren't for the squirrels and jays that gathered them up and hid them in cool places and how the Indians ate the big seeds for food and how these "pine nuts" were important things and how the piñon cones were egg-shaped.

All true words.

"How'd you learn all that?" Her eyes properly wide.

"Bush school."

"Bush school?"

"In the service. I used to read books, too . . . when I was a kid. About trees, animals, things like that."

She laughed. "You were a kid? You must have been at the head of the class if you knew all that stuff."

He looked at her. No reply. He felt foolish and wondered why.

After they finished eating, Arthur showed her how to strip and clean the Mini-14. Then Melody shot some more. She did as he said, learned quickly, showed a steady hand, and he was pleased to see her adapt to the shock of the recoil without flinching. "That's a rare thing in a beginner," he told her. "You're good, real good."

"Look," and he took the weapon from her. He used the tip of a live round to deliberately click the drift and range dials off center. She watched as he inserted the nose of the bullet three times into square notches on the rim of the small black dials. Then he gave her the rifle while he walked out on the desert and moved the target map to another bush 150 yards away. He walked back, and she handed him the weapon.

"There's two important things I want you to remember. That's why I'm showing you now . . . at the end . . . so you won't forget." He carefully aimed at the target. "I taped over the holes in the target with white tape. Look at the map."

She looked through the binoculars. "Okay. No holes."

"First thing, this is how you zero a rifle in the field. When you don't have time to get fancy."

"Zero?"

"That means adjusting the sights for the conditions. Wind. Distance. Stuff like that. Zero."

He braced the weapon by setting three chunks of rock beneath and along the barrel. Then he aligned the rifle. The Ruger seemed to melt into position against his cheek.

"I'm aiming dead on . . . at the center . . . right where those two creases meet."

She found the intersection in the map as she looked through the field glasses. "Gotcha, cowboy."

"Cowboy." He snorted, then went ice-steady and fired.

He carefully released the weapon so that it stayed in its braced position. "The sights are still on that center crease. Where's the hit?"

She set her elbows into the sand and refocused the glasses. "You just shot Nellis Air Force Base. They're not going to like that."

"Top right?"

"Yes."

With the tip of a round, he gently nudged the wind and range dials into new positions. He sighted the target again and took great care to keep the rifle in position on the bracing rocks as he did so. He made another adjustment and sighted again. "Give me the glasses." He examined the map, then made one last click on the top dial. "Now get over here and look at the target. Don't move the rifle. Don't move it at all. Leave the strap alone. Just look."

She moved into position. She touched the weapon only enough to keep it from tipping when her cheek brushed against the stock. "It looks like it's not aiming in the middle anymore. It's aiming at Nellis, isn't it? It's aiming at the hole your bullet made."

"Right."

She turned to him.

"Move over, rookie." He picked up the Ruger from the support rocks and wrapped into the sling. He didn't go prone, but sat cross-legged and aimed. "Guess where I'm aiming."

"At Nellis?"

"Think, rookie."

She thought, then snapped her fingers. "At the middle, at the crease. That's because you fixed it."

He aimed. "You got it." And he fired almost before the last word left his lips. He eased the rifle down. "Check it out, lady."

She raised the field glasses. "Yikes! Right on the button! Right in the middle!" She kept looking at the map. "Right on Casino Row. Cool!"

He walked out and taped over the two holes in the map and returned. "Now you do it."

She did. She ran through the procedure three times.

He stood up and smiled. "That's the sneaky way to zero a weapon . . . but it works in a pinch."

She put her nose against the breech. "I love the smell of this stuff." She closed her eyes and inhaled.

"That's enough for today, shooter. Help me pick up these empty casings." While they retrieved the brass he told her about the quirk in the Ruger's safety, the subject he saved for last so she wouldn't forget.

"I know about the safety. See?" She pulled back the thin blade mounted in the forward trigger guard.

"That Ruger is a nice piece of work, but I almost shot my foot off with one."

"You?" Her voice was all shades of disbelief.

"I was shooting tin cans. I'd knock them over, then set them up and knock them down again. I got sloppy. I walked out to reset the cans and thought I was pulling the safety back. My finger went into the trigger space when I thought I was out front on the safety. I pulled back and the round missed my foot by two inches. Close call. Stupid."

She looked at the trigger arrangement. Put her finger there.

"That's when accidents happen," he said. "When you don't expect it. Shoot enough and sooner or later you're going to screw up. It'll scare the hell out of you."

She examined the safety release. Snapped it back and forth a few times.

"Don't forget it, rookie. Always keep your brain in gear."

"I'd never do that . . . shoot my foot off."

He shook his head. "Hope not. Might ruin your dancing career."

❙ ❙ ❙

"My dad told me. It helped a bunch." Melody's words. Gentle words.

The lounge was dark, and two drinks sat between them on the

little table. Gooey elevator music oozed through the smoky air, but neither narcoleptic sound nor stale smoke could take the glow off that day of a single rose and wine and friendship.

"He was a neat guy. My dad. You're a neat guy, too."

Arthur traced lines in the moisture on the side of his glass.

Melody tapped a plastic straw on the tabletop.

"Did it really work?" he asked.

"It took awhile. About a month. Maybe more."

"What were you dreaming about?"

"Some green thing . . . a skeleton or something I saw in a comic book. I couldn't stop dreaming about it. It really scared me."

He kept making lines with his finger.

"I had to concentrate. Every night. Right up until I fell asleep. I kept telling myself I could do it . . . because my dad said I could." She reached out and poked the back of his hand with her straw, gently stuck him with the end of it as he drew patterns on the glass.

"Concentrate?"

"Not on something sweet or nice, not on flowers or a lake or anything like that . . . you concentrate on pulling the dream toward you, making it come, making yourself want it to come. You force your way into it, take over, break the rules, eat it up. My dad said dreams are like dogs, they chase you if you try to run away."

He was silent.

"Pretty soon I could make it stop. Then it got to be fun. I could do what I wanted in my dreams. I could make elephants dance. I made my chair fly all over the place. Everything." She laughed. "I did horny things, too." She laughed again.

Her revelation made him smile. "Horny things?" he asked.

"Yeah. Horny." She dropped her straw into his drink. Then she leaned forward, an expression of conspiracy on her face. She shifted her glance from side to side through half-closed eyes, her head not moving . . . a cartoon spy. "Really horny."

He looked at her for a moment. "You're a goofball."

"It's worth a try." She sat back and smiled at him. "I did it. You can. I bet you can . . . rookie."

20

Wondering

Melody left to deal the graveyard shift. The day of shooting and the time spent with Arthur had left her upbeat and full of energy. She'd only had time for a quick two-hour nap after they'd returned to her apartment from the lounge, but the nap had been enough to charge her up. She'd covered her boast to Mike, had learned enough to show him she could shoot. The lie was safely buried. Everything had worked out. She felt relieved, excited again. Her world made sense once more.

Her time with Arthur had been more than fun, more than just a con job to get him to teach her how to handle the rifle. She felt she'd given him something, had broken through the pain he lived with— the pain she didn't understand but knew consumed his hours. She'd read him like a book, read him as only a woman who cares reads a man who needs caring for. When he laughed with her, it was more than laughter. When he talked with her, it was more than talking. And when they were silent together, something moved in that silence. She knew it and he knew it. She could tell. In their short time together she'd discovered that being needed was a feeling too long out of her days. She'd been there for others before, others who cared for and needed her, but this was a need so stark and desperate that she could touch it, so sudden and vivid that it made her fearful in her heart. And somehow bold. Afraid and hoping.

As she dealt cards that night, as she smiled and made small talk with early-morning players, she wondered when he would go away. And he had to go away. There was no room for him and Mike. Not those two. She was not enough for that. A fleeting shadow shivered through her mind.

Suddenly she stopped dealing, and the players at her table looked up. Her eyes were cast down, seemed to be trained on the green felt with its red and yellow squares, but her eyes didn't look at squares and cards. Unseeing eyes. Her hands still. Her breathing not perceptible.

A man from Arizona looked to his right at a woman from New York, then back at Melody.

"Miss?" he said.

No reply.

"Miss?" again. "You in there?"

Melody blinked and looked at the man. Then at the card in her fingers. Looked back at him. She extended her arm as if to pass the card to him, to hand it to him. The card hung in the air, unclaimed, against the rules. The man looked at the card.

"That's her card," with a nod to the woman at his right. "Not mine."

"Oh. Oh! I'm sorry." Melody began to deal again.

❚ ❚ ❚

Arthur was out of the apartment when Melody came in. A note lay on the table in the kitchen.

House-hunting. Arthur. Get some sleep, goofball.

She showered. Walked naked into the bedroom. Got into bed.

Sleep wouldn't come.

She got up and went to the bedroom window, moved the drapes aside, and looked out at cars moving in bright sunlight and at people walking.

She went and knelt by the dresser and moved the larger gun

case from beneath the one that held the AK. She sat down on the rug and looked at the sleek nylon carry. She leaned forward and took the metal tabs in her fingers and spread her arms. The twin zippers sizzled in opposite directions around the periphery of the container and met on its back side. She lifted up the top. She unwrapped a gray cotton cloth from the rifle. The weapon lay dark against the black interior. On its top, a telescopic sight. She did not take up the long rifle, only peeled farther back the cloth that partially covered the scope. With one finger she engaged the lip of the rear cover cap and pried it up. Three-quarters of the way through its travel, the cap snapped away from her finger and clicked into position above the body of the optic tube. The glass surface of the ocular lens gleamed black in the uncleared scope, the forward cap still in place. The surface looked hard and shiny and clean. A filament of lint floated in the air in front of her face, and she reached out and caught the mote before it might settle on the glass. She looked again at the ocular. Black glass. Bottomless black glass.

She wondered what things his eye had seen there. She bent down to look into the lens. Deep in the glass, her own eye looked back.

I   I   I

"How long you need it?"

"Three weeks."

The one-eyed, stubble-bearded man looked at Arthur and pulled at a thick leather belt curled along its top edge by fat and time. The man wore a black eyepatch held in place by a thin round cord, also black, that cut into the skin of his forehead, the cord set deeply in a fold of red flesh that said the eye was lost a long time ago. "I let 'em go by the month. Like the sign says."

"What sign?"

"There." The man pointed at the door. Arthur turned and read a small cardboard placard on the wall next to the throw lock.

"Okay. A month. I'd like to see the room."

"Number twelve." A brass key with a brown tag wired to it slid across the top of the counter.

Arthur picked up the key. "Number twelve. Thanks." He turned for the door.

"One person?"

"Just me."

"Pets?"

"No pets."

"Good. No goddamn pets. Make a mess."

"That stove work?" Arthur back to the counter.

"Worked last week."

"How much?"

"Two hundred. One month."

"Much noise?"

"Friday, Saturday night a little. Payday. No kids, though." The man looked past Arthur. "Fucking cops."

Arthur followed the man's gaze and saw the rear end of a patrol car going down the street. "Cops?"

"In here this morning. Ever see one of them scanner things?"

"Scanner. Radio scanner?"

"Nope. One of them paper scanners. Looks like a vacuum cleaner end."

"No, I haven't seen one of those."

"Little ol' thing. Run it over my records. The sign-in book. Copies words."

"No kidding."

"Yeah. Copies 'em right up. That's our taxes, buddy. Fucker probably goes a thousand bucks. Bleed us dry. Lazy fuckers."

"What do they want your records for?"

"Who the hell knows? Make-work. Waste of fucking time."

Arthur looked at the man and waited.

"Said they's looking for someone might have checked out last week. Usual shit. If I knew, bet your ass I wouldn't tell 'em."

"Trouble here?"

"Here? Fuck no. Ain't had no trouble here. Couple hookers is all. Short-timers. Two hours, out the door. Wreck my good sheets. Charge the holes an extra fiver. You want number twelve?"

"Maybe. Got to see if I get something back on my other place."

One eye looking. Long pause. "Nice room. Quiet. Real private."

It was past three. Late afternoon. Arthur had been two hours sitting in a dark bar downing bourbon and ginger ale. Thinking. The bar was tucked into the corner of a cutesy Las Vegas shopping mall, and he'd been able to sit alone, an unobtrusive shape lost in a boredom of brown Naugahyde, mahogany tabletop, and sepia wallpaper. Dim light. Terra-cotta lamp base. Tan lampshade. Bronze trim. Russet cocktail napkin.

Another bourbon and ginger. Brought by the nut-brown Filipina waitress who sat at the end of the bar smoking a cigarillo while she read a Spanish novel with a copper-colored cover and never bothered him with small talk . . . not even when he clucked at her and she had to put down her book, get up, and make another drink for him.

The only other customers passing through that auburn oasis were women shoppers, mall warriors, always in pairs, packages and bags rustling, the smell of perfume, never more than one couple in the bar at any given time. Like the bar gave appointments. One pair of shoppers, max. Speed drinkers. Credit cards still warm. Two quick cigarettes. The second round. In-flight boozers refueling. Hit and run. Rustle, rustle, rustle.

Arthur enjoyed watching the aromatic parade from his cryptic brown fortress. Only twice in two hours had a shopper looked his way, then performed a double take as he was discovered. A furtive lump of man skulking in their clandestine reserve. A harsh look. A surprised look. A look that told Arthur the female pairs at the bar regarded the place as they would a ladies' restroom.

His first experience with a mall bar.

He was getting drunk.

And it felt good.

It had been some time since he'd gone bottle-killing. The unquestioned repetition; the endless supply; the loyalty of taste despite days of separation; the welcome feel of cold, heavy glass against thirsty skin; of muscle warming and nerves unwinding; a flower unfolding in the gut with gentle-slow explosions of genial pleasure; the rippling kiss of those first sips on lips tight with failure; the sweet release of having to focus only on the next drink and screw tomorrow.

Arthur mulled the wisdom of stoking his drinking habit. He knew he'd come close to alcoholism in the early days—days when he drank to get past that first hour of sleep when the dreams would come, but the booze would bring morning before morning was ready. A night got through. A victory. But a wearisome victory. An enervating triumph. A treadmill of exhaustion that a young body could handle for a while. Cells rebuilding in the alcohol-fed flame of cells dying.

But not now.

Not anymore.

Now days were lost getting back to normal. Dull hours stepped on dull hours as liver worked overtime, ever more slowly.

The ominous rasp of pain in throat, stomach, and bowel. Bitchy little storm flags flown by Mother Nature.

Elation and hope turned to depression and confusion.

But there were times when the soul needed a vacation and those were times when biology had to lump it.

This was one of those times.

Arthur tried to put things in order.

His mind. Still twisting in too many directions, somehow aware of more but understanding less.

The contract. Lucrative but disjointed. Lots of questions to be answered still. The mark unknown, a faint image dimly hovering.

His own skill. The one constant. Compromised a bit, but at least he knew where the compromises lay, and that was critical. More than enough ability for this.

Montana. Unpredictable. A new worry. Perhaps it was his own fault more than Montana's. Perhaps his moving in with Melody was the source of the mix-up. Perhaps they just missed connections. He pictured Montana trying to call to say he was going with Karla to San Diego . . . and Arthur not there . . . not there because he hadn't told Montana about killing the muggers, about having to run, about the heat coming down.

The buyer. Smart. Powerful. Rich. And odd. The casinos were run by corporations these days. Big, respectable corporations. With few exceptions, the mob was out. He knew from what he'd read and from Montana that the casino industry was the most regulated industry in the country behind the nuclear energy folks. Why this? This fifties-style hit? Out of place. These were necktie-and-briefcase days. Cement shoes and loose kneecaps were supposed to be movie stuff. Corruption was still the game, money and power still moved above the people, but this hit was out of place. Why?

And Melody. All of a sudden he had a goddamn den mother.

He gulped the last of his drink and clucked at the Filipina. She set down her copper-colored book. Went behind the bar.

Melody. He'd found a place away from women. A place where he could concentrate. What he thought was put away for good, was trying to come back. The confusion of caring. The hurt when it was gone. *Goddamn it all to hell.* He had no room for that. He needed to keep the isolation he had won. Not again. He couldn't protect him and her. Not at the same time. Not do that and live.

Melody had left a note on the lamp table. *Night shift. Only four hours. Lock up. Got the other key. Back at eleven. Eat!*

Arthur showered, took three aspirin, and ate an apple. He had not had time in the bar to sort out the immediate problem.

Where to stay?

The cops were taking this one seriously. Someone might have seen something. He remembered the light coming on in the doorway after he'd persuaded the second mugger to enter the food chain. All it took was one pair of eyes. What did they have? Description? Prints? A trace to the store that sold him the bottle of whiskey?

And he *had* moved. That might put them onto him. That's what they'd been looking for. But moving out had been the best of two lousy choices.

He couldn't stay here with Melody. Not much longer. Not for as long as the job was going to take. If he was made around her, she would be wrapped up in the thing. That wouldn't be fair. She didn't need him screwing up her life.

No car. That didn't help.

Damn Montana!

He turned on the TV. He knew he'd have to stay where he was.

The bourbon wrestled with the aspirin.

At 10:00 P.M. he stripped down to undershirt and shorts, unfolded the blanket, and turned off the light.

He lay in the dark room. He put the earplug in his ear and stared at the ceiling. *Where to go next?* Sleep came. But before it came he tried to imagine the dreams. The mud. The snake. The punji sticks sprouting from Jank's chest and gut. And the faces. The faces of the children. But another dream came instead. A face. A man's face. Yellow shadows from a fire. Shapes of mesquite bush. A moon shining. Fragments of words . . . "None of my business . . . if you need a place to stay . . . welcome to use it if you need to . . . "

He remembered waking in the night. The electric jolt of the breaking stick sound. Eyes open. Melody going through the room. On tiptoes. Like a kid at Christmas. Yellow blouse. Sleep came back.

Sunshine. Morning. Friday morning. He sat up on the edge of the couch. He stretched his arms above his head. He walked down the hall to the bathroom and carefully closed the door behind him. He urinated on the slope of the bowl so as not to wake her with his noise. He washed his face and brushed his teeth. When he came out into the hall again, he stepped to the door of her bedroom. He looked in and saw her there. She was sleeping. On her side. She was naked and he saw one bare breast. He saw her arm and the soft hair that fell to her shoulder and framed her sleeping face. The fingers of one hand were curled around one of the magazines from the Mini-14 he had given her. The curved metal container rested close to her face, under her nose.

Arthur smiled.

And then went into the kitchen and put coffee on. He cut two oranges in sections and popped out the seeds with the point of a paring knife. He made toast. Buttered it. Found a jar of apple jelly and put that on the toast. He put all the things he'd made on a wooden tray and put cream in the coffee when it was ready and emptied one envelope of sweetener in and stirred it with a spoon. He took the tray into her bedroom.

He sat down on the edge of her bed, the tray balanced on his knees. He did not look at her but looked at the window.

"Hey." Softly.

No move from Melody.

"Hey, goofball." Louder.

"Hmmmm?" She moved. Sheets whispered.

"Melody. Wake up."

"Hmmmmmmmm?"

"You'll be late."

Silence. Then, "Arthur?"

"Breakfast, goofball. You have to be in the Book in one hour."

A hand touched the back of his neck.

"Got you some chow." He lifted the tray and held it out from his side so she could see. He kept his back to her.

"Oh, no." Soft protest. "What time is it?"

"Eight-thirty."

Her voice fuzzy, "Sleep. I want to sleep." Fingers moving on the back of his neck. "Got to sleep."

"You're the one who wants to work two jobs. Wake up."

He could feel the covers stir as she moved. Then two arms went around his waist. Her cheek on his shoulder. Eyes peeping over. "For me? That's for me?"

"I can't let you get fired. Take it." He raised the tray two inches.

A piece of toast was lifted up. The brown slice with its cargo of butter and apple jelly disappeared behind him.

He felt her cheek muscles move against his back. Full breasts pressed gently.

"It's good toast. Still hot." Sleepy words.

He leaned to one side and set the tray on the nightstand, one of her arms still around his waist. He sat straight again.

"You always sleep with live ammunition?"

"It smells good. I like the smell." More munching.

He eased her arm away and stood up . . . still not looking, but wanting to look.

"Thanks, cowboy."

He walked toward the door. "Turn to, goofball! Go make money."

He heard the coffee cup click against the saucer as he went out into the hallway. Then her words, "Not bad coffee. Not bad at all . . . for a rookie."

21

Good Friday

Hey, Diane, it's for you. It's Suzy. She wants to know when you're taking the kids to the park."

"I'll get it out here, Mike." Diane finished popping a green dome of gelatin from the last of a dozen aluminum molds lined up on the counter next to the sink. The tentative finger of a five-year-old reached over the edge of the counter and poked at one of the mounds of green. A defenseless bulge of emerald quivered, its crenulated surface gently wounded and showing a small dent. "Don't do that, Sarah! That's for dessert!"

The foraging digit retreated.

Diane crossed to the portable phone on the other side of the kitchen. She wiped her hands on a dish towel, then draped the towel over her shoulder and picked up the phone.

The disobedient finger appeared above the counter edge again. Another puncture victim wiggled. Two casualties. The finger drifted left and aimed at the next target.

"Suzy? . . . we'll be by in ten minutes. Nick's going to go potty first." She lowered the phone. "Sarah, get Nick to the potty. And stop poking those desserts!" The small finger hesitated, the missile abort request under consideration. Diane, back to Suzy, "Kids! I don't see how you handle four of them."

Diane leaned back against the cabinet door. She stood on one leg, her other leg bent at the knee and pressing a worn running shoe sole against the front of a cabinet door. She was a dark-eyed woman whose classic beauty was somehow made greater by her usual "let's-grease-the-car" wardrobe. She showed long legs and shapely arms, delicate fingers and short black hair, alabaster skin and the same sharply defined lashes as those of her brother. Though two years younger than Mike's thirty-two, she had the same straight-ahead look as he. The sleeves of her oversized sweatshirt were bunched high on her forearms. Her right arm was folded across her flat stomach and rested beneath her full breasts, and the palm of that hand cupped the elbow of her other arm, which held the phone receiver, held it close to but not touching her ear, another trait shared with Mike.

"Mike . . . please get Nick on the pot."

"He's your kid," from the other room.

"Mike! . . . Sorry, Suzy. He's worse than they are."

Mike's voice resounded with more volume, but was laced with open disinterest. "Sarah, do Daddy a favor and help Nick." A half-hearted male concession to current share-the-load theory.

"I can be there in ten minutes, Suzy. . . . Yeah, that should hold the little fiends. . . . Paper cups? I have some. . . . I'm on my way."

Twenty minutes later they were gone, the potty evolution aborted by a more dignified need to murder bugs and throw rocks.

Mike and Diane, brother and sister. Their divorces of two years ago, only days apart back then, had resulted in the present loose-knit commune that provided uncomplicated freedom for both, an amalgamation of circumstance surprising in its comfortable assumptions, the habits of a lifetime understood and tolerated; small irritations made smaller by the recollection of frayed marriages gone threadbare.

Money now a game where it was war before.

Sensitivity a cause for compliment, not suspicion.

Insensitivity chalked up to a bad day, not to a bad love.

Pretension unneeded.

Jealousy the stuff of soap operas.

Michael Patrick Henry sat on the living room sofa. He finished wiping down the flanks of the H&K PSG-1 sniper rifle with a soft cloth to remove all but a thin film of protective gun oil from its metal exterior. Satisfied with his work, he carefully recased the expensive semiautomatic weapon . . . the finest piece for its purpose that money could buy . . . the crème de la crème . . . 1/2 MOA, minute of angle, able to shoot one-half-inch groups at one hundred yards . . . the boss.

He carried the weapon in its leather case to his bedroom, which was located toward the back of the house. In the bedroom he opened the door to a large walk-in closet that contained a five-foot-high gun safe bolted to an interior support wall. He dialed in the lock combination and pulled the door open. He placed the PSG-1 on its rack next to five other cased rifles beneath four handguns that hung in precise, stepped array on felt-covered holding pegs. The floor of the safe was occupied by numerous boxes of ammunition labeled with easy-to-read numbers put there by him with a black indelible marker pen, and the boxes were separated, one caliber from the other, by thin metal dividers. A Marine Corps ceremonial sword sheathed in its metal-tipped scabbard centered a field of smaller blades . . . lethal, sharp blades, some curved, some straight, some serrated, some smooth and clean and as definite as hate.

Michael Patrick Henry closed the safe. Friday. Telephone day.

▌ ▌ ▌

Arthur left the apartment. He wanted to walk. He headed west in the direction of the Strip, no destination in mind, only a desire to move and breathe the late September air. That air was colder than he'd guessed, and he stepped into a shop that sold jackets and athletic gear. He selected a hooded sweatshirt with the UNLV logo on the back and tried it on. Tried another. He paid for the sweatshirt and wore it out of the store. Once on the sidewalk, he pulled the hood over his head and tied the drawstring tight beneath his chin. The heavy material felt snug and warm, and he wondered if he was going soft in his old age. But the sting of the cold morning was still in the flesh of his ears, and he welcomed the building heat inside the hood. He shoved his hands into the front pouch of the shirt and continued toward the west, the morning sun warm on his back.

After walking two miles, he had decided three things.

He would call Frank Elder in Pahrump and take him up on the offer to use the trailer as a place to stay. Next week.

He would tell Montana about the muggers.

He would get away from Melody because she was too much in his mind. He would put a stop to that.

He removed his hands from the fleecy pouch. He rolled up his sleeves. He untied the drawstring knot and pushed the hood off his head. Thoughts clear. Ears warm. Problems put to rest.

But still he walked toward the Strip, toward Melody.

I I I

Melody watched a young couple point at the red letters and yellow numbers on the electronic odds board high on the wall behind her. The two held hands and talked and looked confused as the numbers occasionally changed to reflect the shifting opinions of bettors and the Book manager's attempt to keep the action in balance. The couple's perplexed expressions betrayed the fact they weren't familiar with betting the games, and Melody waited for the questions she knew would come. Still holding hands, the pair approached the counter, the man tentative but leading the woman, who lagged behind and looked up at the big board.

"Miss?"

Melody smiled at them.

"Could you tell us how this works? How to bet?"

"First time?" An unnecessary question.

"Yes. We haven't bet football before. Just slots."

"Staying at the hotel?"

Hesitation. The man looked at the woman, then back at Melody. He appeared uncomfortable. "No, we're not. Do we have to be staying here to bet?"

Melody looked at him. Mike's eyes. Arthur's chin.

"Oh, no. We let anyone bet. Always happy to have new players." She looked over her shoulder at the board. "It's pretty confusing, isn't it?" Soft smile.

"Sure is." He shook his head.

"The teams that are playing each other this weekend are in red. The team on the bottom is the home team. Like up there, the Cowboys are at the Eagles . . . the Philadelphia Eagles. That number in back of the Cowboys? . . . the one that says minus six? . . . that means the Cowboys are favored by six points. The minus means you have to subtract six points from the final score to see if you win. If the Cowboys win the game by seven points or more, you win the bet." Melody looked at the man's fingers; they were long like Mike's fingers.

"What if the Cowboys win by four points?"

"Then you bet on the wrong team." She looked at the woman. Her fingers were laced in his. A round bruise showed on the side of her neck. A pretty fair hickey. Lovers.

"So if we like the Eagles, we can bet on them and we get to add six points? For our bet?"

"That's right."

"What if the Cowboys win sixteen to ten?"

"Then it's a tie, a push. You get your money back."

"All of it?"

"All of it."

"How do you guys make any money?" A gentle suspicion that he was missing something.

"You have to bet eleven dollars to win ten. Or a hundred and ten to win a hundred. Or eleven hundred to win a thousand."

"A thousand dollars?" from the woman. Eyes wide.

"The house makes ten percent on the losing bets. That's what pays for the lights."

"Can we bet twenty dollars?"

"Bet twenty-two to win twenty. Give me twenty-two and if your team wins, you bring your ticket back to the cashier over there after the game and you get forty-two dollars back. You win twenty and get your bet back." Mike had nicer ears.

The man looked at the woman. "Want to do one?"

"You pick it. You watch football."

"We can watch the game on TV, go back and get in bed and watch the game. We can gamble lying down."

A red glow built with pastel softness on the woman's cheeks. It deepened as Melody watched, a delightful rush of embarrassment around a childlike smile. "Bryan!"

Bryan beamed. Then color started in his cheeks, but his blush was no match for his companion's.

Melody smiled. She winked a mischievous wink. "That's the way I'd do it, if I were you."

Red cheeks got redder.

I I I

"Looks like the Bears game to me. It's hanging right at two and a half. Not much action." Mike cradled the phone between his ear and his shoulder and tapped code letters into the computer keyboard with his right hand.

"The weather's lousy, and it's going to get worse. Chicago's a mudhole. They'll push it big, sure as hell." He leaned back in his chair and watched an image take shape. "The total's thirty-two."

Isobars flowed onto the screen. The projected weather pattern flickered and changed and migrated across the glass as the two-day forecast unfolded. He picked up a pencil and scribbled numbers on a pad. "Right. Me too. That's got to be one of them . . . he'll be there, trust me. They hit last week and have lots of green to play with." He tapped the eraser end of the pencil on the desktop. "Chicago's going to be the game . . . a real gold mine."

Arthur turned right onto the road behind the casino. The day had warmed up considerably, but he pulled the hood of his new sweat-shirt forward onto his head anyway. He looked at the looming walls of the hotel. The dull hum of heavy heat exchangers on the adjoining casino rooftop drummed powerfully in the morning air. He shifted his gaze to the employee parking lot as he walked along a chain-link fence. He spotted the silver top of Melody's van next to a light pole. He smiled and continued through the casino grounds and exited the property on the north boundary. He stopped and looked back at the casino for some reason he didn't or couldn't acknowledge, then headed back east toward the apartment.

Bits of paper fluttered on white cement, and the gray-green tops of trees swayed in a wind that had begun to move east as the big desert heated under brilliant sun.

"So you like the Steelers?" Melody looked up at the board.

The young couple had returned to her counter. She had watched them share a large white concoction at the long bar located at the back of the Sports Book . . . a creamy, foamy drink put together in an oversized, long-stemmed margarita glass . . . the shadow of cinnamon, brown on top of the foam, dark spice barely visible across the distance . . . a pair of straws . . . them laughing . . . a quick kiss, then another kiss . . . her head bending once and touching his shoulder. Melody's heart had flown and hurt in the same moment as she watched them.

"We like the Steelers." His arm around the woman's waist. She smiling. Shy. Pretty. Young.

"Nope," from Melody.

"Nope?" Confusion back on his face.

"Bet something else."

Lover's eyes looked into lover's eyes, then back at Melody.

"The Steelers aren't on TV." Melody's eyes sparkled above a gentle smile.

"What difference does . . . ? Oh." Then he laughed. "I see."

The woman looked at them both. "What . . . ?" And the red began to build again.

"Then who's on TV?" His eyes moved back to the board.

"It's up there . . . See? . . . Right behind the teams . . . See?" Melody pointed.

"I see." His hands on her shoulders, his strong hands turning his lover back toward the bar. "Another conference!"

Melody laughed. "Take your time. It's two days before the game kicks off."

Friday wasn't going to be such a bad day after all. She didn't feel tired anymore.

And tomorrow she would see Mike. He said he would be at the Book to make some bets. She wondered how it would feel to simply stand there and sell him a ticket while she thought about his arms around her, about his strength inside her, about his naked heat warming her skin as they snuggled in the afterglow of their sweet passion. Images danced, faded, danced again, and dissolved.

She wondered what she and Arthur would have for dinner.

"Okay. We're going to bet on the Seahawks. They're on TV on Sunday night, right?"

Melody looked at the board. "Right. Sunday night. The late game." She turned back to them. "How much?"

"Can we bet eleven dollars? Eleven to win ten?" A ten-dollar bill and four quarters on the counter.

Melody took the money and tapped up the bet. The tote machine hummed and offered up a ticket from a dark slot. "Seattle it is. Eleven bucks."

"Think we'll win?" He took the ticket and studied it.

Melody looked from him to her and back to him. "You've already won."

"Charlie? It's Mike. Can your man handle twenty dimes? Right. Chicago. . . . Twenty thousand. . . . How about your small shops?" He wrote numbers on a pad. "Five dimes? . . . Good. Later." He pushed the disconnect and dialed again.

"Hey, Brooklyn, how's the beans? . . . Sleep alone, tell her it's for her own good." He laughed. "Okay, Tony, looks like we'll be loading Chicago. . . . Sure they'll take it. . . . The Giants are top-heavy, they're on a roll. . . . You and me both, pal. Tell your store we'll be there with the limit, let him load the locals, we'll bail him out when it goes to four. The limit. . . . If he wants to, sure. Another twenty's fine. Work it. I'll call with the go late tomorrow. Same time. Won't go inside that last hour, though. Nothing after twelve noon. . . . Right. . . . I like it, too. . . . Same to you, buddy. *Ciao.*"

He hung up the phone. His hands went back to the keyboard. His fingers moved. Numbers ticked onto the blue screen.

Friday. Money Friday. Good Friday.

Arthur began to jog. He trotted at a steady pace and jogged in place on the sidewalk when stoplights made him wait. He'd stay with Melody until Montana got back after the weekend, then he'd have Montana drive him over the hill to Pahrump. Montana could keep the car. It wasn't necessary to rent one for himself. Too much visibility. Keep it simple.

Montana would set it up right like always.

Stay low.

Get some sleep.

Maybe buy some groceries for Melody. Surprise her.

22

Sweet Dreams

"Shrimp? I love shrimp!" Melody stared at the kitchen table.

"Damn! I was hoping you wouldn't. Then I could eat it all myself. Lousy guess." Arthur tried to look disappointed.

She took his hand and kissed him on the cheek. He rubbed at the spot. "Don't mess with the cook, lady. You get what's on your plate and no more. Go change your clothes so we can eat. You smell like cigarettes."

"You'll just have to lump it. Not with that wine sitting there. And those candles. This goes down right now."

"Change."

A pout. One shrimp stolen from its bed of ice. Dipped in hot red sauce. "Okay. I love it when you're like this! Brute." Shrimp bitten in half. "Ummm." More sauce. Shrimp gone. She hurried down the hall. He heard her open and slam a dresser drawer in the back room, heard her scamper into the bathroom, heard water run and heard her singing softly.

She ate like a bandit, devoured her shrimp like she was on the run. He refilled her plate from a large square glass container in the refrigerator.

"Arthur . . . that's my candy dish."

"So?"

"So . . . more shrimp."

"I found it in the living room. Don't give me a hard time."

"Men!"

He watched her dig into the second helping. "You'll get sick. Slow down."

"Won't."

"Don't they feed you?"

"Not like this. Not big juicers like this."

"Big juicers? Nice."

"They only feed us the little ones. Bait."

Melody finished the bottle of wine. He cleared the dishes and began to rinse them off under the tap. She didn't offer to help, only sat and watched him and let him treat her, start to finish; it was his show.

"That wine was good, Arthur. You just buy *one?*"

He turned from the sink and casually dried his hands with a towel that showed the figure of a big yellow duck leading three little ducks. "Don't push it. Yes, I just bought one. I didn't know you were a frigging wino."

She got up from the table and went to the refrigerator. She retrieved a brown paper bag from the vegetable bin. She removed a bottle of wine from the bag. "I was saving this for a special occasion. This is a special occasion." She handed the bottle to him. "Open it. I'm going to sit on the couch in the other room and put my feet up. Don't make me wait."

He stood there holding the wine bottle. He looked at her. "Do you need anything else? Maybe I could play the violin for you?"

"Maybe you could. It wouldn't surprise me." She turned and went out of the kitchen.

He opened the silverware drawer and rummaged around until he found what he was looking for. A corkscrew. This one had a cork.

"Have a good day?" He leaned back on the sofa. Two pair of bare feet on the coffee table.

"It got a lot better since I walked in here."

He didn't reply.

"So what did you do with yourself while I was working for a living? Sell any guns?" She licked the rim of her wineglass. Pink tongue tip framed by white teeth.

"I goofed off. Went for a walk. Bought a sweatshirt."

"And got me shrimp."

"And got you shrimp."

She bent forward and refilled her glass. "More?" The bottle tipped in his direction.

"Still got some."

She leaned back and settled next to him, pushed into the warm cushions of the couch. Their shoulders touched.

The room was almost dark, lit only by the light coming from the kitchen and the single candle he'd placed beside the bottle.

"This is nice." She wriggled her toes.

"Have you talked with Karla in the last few days?"

"Nope. They should be back Monday. Unless they ran off to Mexico."

He was silent.

"Think they're going to do it?" she asked.

He turned his head. One eyebrow up. "*Going* to do it?"

Melody laughed. "Not that. Get serious, Arthur. I mean, maybe go for it, get . . . you know . . . married."

It was his turn to laugh. "Not him. Not Montana."

Melody put a fingertip to her tongue, wet it, then began to slide her finger around the rim of the wineglass.

Arthur watched her. "You need expensive glass to do that."

She wet her finger again. Back to the rim.

"K Mart?" he queried.

"K Mart's got some pretty good stuff." Defensive, her finger moving.

"Good car parts."

"You think you're so hot." Concentrating.

He watched.

The glass began to sing.

Later, after Melody had gone to her room and as he lay on the couch, he tried hard to make the dreams come. She'd asked him once, earlier in the evening, if he'd been trying to do it, if he'd taken her seriously when she told him how her dad had helped her beat the thing with the green face that scared her when she was a child. Arthur had smiled noncommittally, made some small comment. He hadn't told her how hard he was working at doing what she said, how intently he pulled at the memories in the hour before he fell away to sleep.

Finally he drifted off, the earplug of the small tape player in his ear. For the past two nights the dreams had not come. It was as though his spirit were cautiously trying to fathom what was happening, to evaluate the new energy, to interpret the change.

She'd told him it would take months. But he was desperately more motivated than she'd been. He wasn't fighting something from a comic book.

And that night he drifted into the dream ... drifted into the dream aware that he was dreaming. He moved toward the images. First they, then he, then they again dominated unsteady sequences. A rush of fear, then a backing off; a sense that he was watching from another level; a feeling of relief; a subtle, sweet defense that let him be an observer and not merely a terrorized part. He couldn't overpower the dream, but he was not helpless in its dark weave. Excitement took him as he hung in that shifting twilight. Conscious of his unconsciousness. Distanced. Asleep yet somehow not asleep. Perdition taking one step backward. He acknowledged the first tentative feelings of discovery. He moved farther away and higher up, drew off from the images that seemed disorganized and jumbled. They would swell and cover him, try to eat him alive as they always did, but he would break free, flicker up to that God-sent aerie and look down on the horror from a high place. His mind ricocheted and spun in the fiber of the struggle. The faces would take him, then he would escape. The astounding alternation pulsed and wobbled like a frantic optical illusion that reversed reality in blinks of time.

But a real fragment of control glimmered.

Elation spilled across the banks of frightful precedent.

And then he became aware of something else.

Something else.

Something that hung almost beyond his perception.

Something depraved and dark.

Not something else. Someone else.

Someone else was there.

Someone who knew his soul as completely as did he.

Melody showered and dressed.

Noises emanated from the kitchen as she made her breakfast.

"You're sleeping late. Did the wine get to you?"

No reply came from Arthur. He lay on his back on the couch with his eyes open and looking up.

"Sleep it off, cowboy. See you later."

She put two of her fingers to her lips and transferred the kiss to him. She touched his forehead. "Be good," she said.

His skin was cold.

▮ ▮ ▮

"Hi." His voice.

Melody stopped counting the money in her cash drawer. "Mike!" Her heart bounded. "When did you come in? I didn't see you."

"I've been watching you from back of the bar. You're beautiful when you count money. I could watch you all day."

Melody stuffed the bills back into the cash till. "Can I help you?" from her. Ridiculous words. Words as good as any other words when words didn't matter. She felt dumb but didn't care because she knew he didn't care.

"Matter of fact, you can." He stepped closer and rested his elbows on the counter, his face so near, yet light-years of propriety distant. "In about thirty minutes a ratty-looking guy with a clipboard is going to get down on some games. He's short. About five foot three. Thick glasses. White guy. No hair on top. Potbelly. Hearing aid. Short right leg. Limps." Mike smiled. "You could spot this guy in a coal mine. Find out who he's playing." He paused. "God, you're beautiful, Mel. Is it against the rules to kiss the employees?" Eyes staring into hers.

She stared back. "Jump over this counter and we'll find out if it's against the rules."

"Easy, Mel." He glanced over his shoulder. "Look. Give me a ticket. Twenty-two straight." He took out his wallet and put some bills on the counter.

"What team, Mister?"

"Any damn team. Someone's going to see us. I'm supposed to be a player."

"They've already seen us. And you're a great player."

He looked past her at the odds board. She studied the muscles of his throat. He looked back at her. "Okay. Make it five-five-seven. Twenty-two bucks. Straight."

"I'll make it straight."

"Five-fifty-seven. Give me the Chargers. I'll be back in one hour. Tell me how he bets."

"Who?"

"Mel! The rat. Tell me how the rat bets."

"I go on break in forty-five minutes. Meet me by the dealers' lounge past the showroom. Be there and I'll tell you what he bet."

"The dealers' lounge," he repeated.

"And I just might pull you in there and make you do me . . . so the other girls can see what they're missing."

"You're crazy."

"That's right. I'm crazy." She took his money, punched up the ticket, and pushed it across to him. "Now get the heck out of here before I fall down."

She was chatting with two twenty-one dealers as she came down the hall. Mike leaned against the wall in a narrow space between a pay phone and a cigarette machine and nonchalantly scanned the sports section of the morning paper. She didn't even look at him, ignored him completely, and went into the lounge with her two friends.

Five seconds later, before the door had completely closed on its hydraulic arm, it was pushed open again. Melody's smile popped around the corner. "Chicago. The rat bet Chicago." A thumbs-up sign.

And she was gone.

I I I

"Hey, Mister."

A boy, about ten years of age, offered up his hand-carried box of trinkets for Arthur to examine. Saturday's bright sunlight caused rings and bracelets to sparkle gold and silver on a black felt lining. The four o'clock sidewalk crowd was sparse as workers and tourists alike prepared for evening diversions.

The boy worked a corner far from the Strip, far away from the gamblers who wandered between the massive casinos seeking fortune, not souvenirs. To them, a few dollars, even a cup of quarters, were sacred tokens, things not to be wasted on goods. Those coins, perhaps all that remained of an optimism-ravaged stake, were the keys to salvation, the tiny catalysts, the magic disks that might yet defeat the imposing, indifferent numbers that stood between elation and despondency.

Brown eyes set in brown skin. Hopeful eyes. Optimistic face. A brave smile. A soul still believing that honest effort deserved one last chance before the lure of illicit enterprise made its damning pitch, before the temptation of easy, though immoral, gain should spread its lustful legs. He lived where drugs were sold, where money was passed through rolled-down car windows, where mothers railed against ungodly opportunity, then wept beside small caskets in some green place between stone markers where words were too late.

Arthur always looked first at the eyes.

"Good rings, mister."

Arthur reached out and steadied the box, tipped it forward.

"Good buys. Maybe something for a lady?" A white-toothed smile.

Arthur picked up a gold ring with a green stone. He turned it in the light, a zircon emerald with two small glass diamonds on either flank. "Are these real stones?"

"They're good stones . . . not real, though." Eyes blinking.

"Not real? They look real to me."

"The gold's real . . . real enough." An excuse made before the young salesman realized an excuse wasn't necessary. The guy had said the stones looked real. That was a good sign.

"How much?"

"That one?" appraising Arthur's selection. "That one's twelve dollars."

"Twelve dollars?"

"It's on special today. Ten dollars today."

"Hummm. Do you have one with a ruby?"

"Right here, sir." Thin fingers darted into the top corner of the box. "Here's your ruby." A stone was shined on a shirtfront, then held at an angle so the sun could make the sale.

Arthur slipped the emerald ring onto his ring finger. It wouldn't fit. He slipped it onto his little finger.

"This feels pretty good. Is that red one the same size?"

"It sure is. The same size. You want the red one instead?"

Arthur took the ring with the red stone and held it beside the green one on his finger. "Which one looks best?"

The boy took Arthur's hand, tilted it slightly, and studied both rings with a serious expression. "I think the green one goes good with your hair. Orange and green, you know?"

"I'll take them both."

"Sir?"

"I'll take them both."

"Yes, sir! . . . Both! Good idea. Both."

"How much?"

"For two." Not a question. "For two is twenty dollars. No, sir, two is eighteen dollars." He looked at Arthur with a hopeful expression and waited for the sale, now so possible, to conclude.

"Here's twenty. We'll call it even." Arthur took a twenty-dollar bill from his wallet and handed it over.

"Eighteen out of twenty . . . for two rings. Two bucks change." A corner of the black felt was lifted up, and two one-dollar bills appeared after the twenty went under the material. A brown hand extended across the case. "Two dollars change."

"Keep it."

"No. Eighteen is the price. Fair and square."

Arthur took the money. The red stone ring was handed over, and he put it in his pocket. "Thanks."

"A box . . . a box for the ring . . . that'd be two dollars." An empty ring case was produced from a shirt pocket. "If the red one's for a friend, a gift . . . better you should have a box. Two dollars. Last one. Ain't got me but one."

The two dollars passed the ring box in the air. Arthur fished the red ring out of his pocket and placed it in the slot in the middle of the tiny case. He held it at arm's length and tilted it so the sun got at it. "Good! It looks good." He nodded and walked off across the intersection as the traffic light changed.

"Thanks, mister."

Arthur waved without looking back.

*   *   *

As was his habit in the days before a contract hit, Arthur liked to relax, to walk, to wander and explore. It was his way: It allowed him to focus, to cultivate the intensity needed to perform. The buying of the rings had provided such a distraction. It had interrupted the sense of unrest he was feeling and had been feeling all through the morning, an uneasiness that was unfamiliar to him because it was really fear. Arthur had some trouble recognizing fear. Fear was something he only experienced in the dreams . . . until now. Now he was awake.

Last night that fear had been partly controlled by his concentrating. It was the first time he had ever been aware, ever been an observer, ever been free to pull back, to separate himself from the dreamscape. The first time. And then, only for brief moments. But in those moments, wandering through the ego-purged world of the subconscious, in fact, he brought his ego.

In that macabre realm of disjointed image and partial memory, of tumbling anxieties and veiled recall, of things horrible and things erotic . . . he'd discovered something more frightening than all the dreams . . . had discovered something that caused fear to spill into his waking hours.

Someone else was there.

One who shared that hideous desert below the intellect.

He had found the other one.

Arthur walked into a bar. He sat in a booth near the back of the place. Images of a Saturday football game flickered on a black-and-white TV above the bar. Six men sat there and smoked and talked and watched the play. Cigarettes. Shot glasses. Hard swearwords. When no one came to the table to take his order, Arthur got up and went to the bar and purchased a bottle of beer. He returned to the table. At the bar some pushing and shoving started between two customers. Unfriendly, drunken shoving. The dispute dissolved in a flood of excited words from the TV as a long pass play went for a touchdown.

His bottle of beer half gone, its gold label partly peeled away by his idle fingers, Arthur got up and went to the men's room. As he stood relieving himself, someone came in and walked behind him.

The person went into the commode because there was only the one urinal in the rest room. The rickety door to the john slammed shut. A drunken curse came from the stall, then the sound of a zipper going down.

The heavy sound of urine drilling into water emanated from the commode. The strong smell of ammonia fouled the air. The room was hot. Very hot. Arthur focused his eyes on the wall a foot in front of his face. Numbers, telephone numbers. Profane scribbles chipped in paint and written in pencil. Two pictures of female genitals. A penis and testicles drawn next to one. A girl's name on the side of the penis. His gaze shifted left as he surveyed the graffiti. A picture was there, a realistic picture of a coiled snake drawn with a felt-tip pen. The snake's eyes looked at him.

The world compressed around Arthur. Sound and smell and light changed. And he changed.

Arthur came out of the men's room. He sat down and finished tearing the gold label from the beer bottle. He balled up the paper scraps and drank more beer. He drank again, and as he held the bottle to his mouth he noticed a green stone ring on the little finger of the hand that held the bottle. He set the bottle down, pulled off the ring, and looked at it with eyes that did not seem to comprehend, eyes that were not the eyes in that skull ten minutes earlier. He turned the ring over in the palm of his hand. He finished the beer with a final gulp, then squeezed the ring flat and dropped it into the empty beer bottle. He looked around the room.

From the bar, a roar went up. All eyes there were on the TV. Somebody had fumbled. The other team recovered. Important stuff.

Arthur got up from the booth and walked to the bar. "Beer," he said. The bartender did not hear or pretended not to hear, his attention on the game. Arthur spoke again. "Another beer."

This time the beer was brought. Arthur returned to the booth.

He sat down and drank slowly in the dim light and looked at nothing in particular.

The uproar at the bar died down. One of those watching the football game got up and stumbled toward the rest room. As the man came near the booth he lost his balance and lurched against the table. The half-full bottle of beer on the table tipped sideways at the impact, and Arthur reached out with his left hand and grabbed the bottle around its middle before it fell. His right hand shot up and took hold of the drunk's upper arm in a grip of iron that prevented the unsteady one from falling into the booth.

"Leggo o' me, scumbag!" from the drunk.

Arthur looked up.

The drunk righted himself. "You fucking asshole! What the fuck do you . . . "

Then the eyes of the drunk looked into the eyes of the sitting one, and the drunk man seemed to freeze. "Oh . . . sorry . . . sorry about that," he said, "my fault, buddy . . . I didn't mean . . . " and he took two backward steps. The boozer hurried toward the back of the place with a gait more steady than before.

Arthur walked along the sidewalk. He felt tired for some reason, and the harsh sunlight hurt his eyes after the dark atmosphere of the bar. He rubbed at his forehead with the back of his left hand and noticed something. He looked at his hand.

He stopped walking.

The green stone ring was gone.

He tried to remember. *Where was it?* But his mind couldn't reconstruct the event, couldn't recall the moments of the last half-hour. A hole had been punched in his reality, and he couldn't fill that hole with memory. He realized he was afraid . . . of what or why, he didn't know. He knew that something must have happened to the green stone ring back in the bar.

But he didn't go back to look for it.

23

Weekend

Arthur didn't return to the apartment after the loss of the green stone ring. Instead, he continued west, and when he came to the Strip he turned south and headed toward the newly constructed megacasinos that bracketed the intersection of Tropicana and Las Vegas Boulevard. He'd prowled the area on one of his earlier explorations, and what he wanted now was to submerge himself in the homogenized chaos. Flagrant architectural exaggeration began to bully the horizon as he passed by the old Aladdin in the late afternoon. Up ahead, the twin Trop towers guarded by two massive and sleepily tolerant Tiki heads ... then Excalibur's gaudy battlements, her spiked parapets stoically waiting for that first, off-line skydiver ... then the concrete and steroid bulk of the hybrid Grand with its green-eyed cat eating two-legged mice and their corn-fed offspring at a disappointing rate. Big casinos. Casinos that showed there really was such a thing as "too big." And all this "too big" surrounded by vehicles idling bumper to bumper in eye-watering witness to the limp foresight of traffic engineers.

He moved at an easy pace, not business-fast, not loser-slow, and kept his head down. He avoided stepping on sidewalk cracks except when to do so would have caused him to stutter-step like some nomadic spastic . . . *step on a crack, break your mother's back*; tried to keep his memories from swarming like blackbirds trapped in an old barn after a gust of wind had blown shut the door . . . *four and twenty blackbirds baked in a pie*; tried not to panic. Instead, he tried to re-create the instant of discovery made in the dream, to let intuition rather than logic feed understanding.

He didn't believe in ghosts, couldn't allow a desire for easy answers to create mystique. That was for people who possessed the luxury of small stakes. He wouldn't yield to that. He dealt in consequence. There was enough mystery in the real world without the distraction of building weak-walled castles in the air. This was survival.

He pictured the face of the Navy shrink and reran the words. The two probables. Genetic memory. And the other.

He stopped and looked up at the garish casinos.

People elbowed past him.

Cars crawled in serpentine lines.

High banks of flickering neon gained rowdy definition in the dying day.

Twilight.

On the corner of the castles.

He put quarters into a video poker machine, sat inside the bright casino called Satyr, sat between a man in a wheelchair and a Chinese woman. Arthur ran his two rolls of coin up to a cardboard bucket full, then steadily lost it all and bought another roll. He filled in a straight flush and won two hundred and fifty coins. More than he'd started with. In quick succession he hit four tens, a full house, and then four aces. The four aces was a bonus hand and credited him with four hundred coins. A yellow light on top of the machine began to blink.

The man sitting beside him leaned over. "Nice to see somebody win." He was well-dressed, neat, sixty. Arthur could see no obvious disability despite the wheelchair. The man edged closer.

"Even I have to win once in a while," Arthur replied.

The man stopped playing his own machine. "Our first time here for the wife and me. We shouldn't have come."

Arthur looked at him.

"It took two hours to check in. Two hours." The man lit a cigarette. "There was no way to get me to my damn room. The bastards rolled me a mile, took me down to the basement on a service lift, wheeled me through all that junk. Water. Dirt. Then they load me on a supply elevator and take me all the way up on that. They roll me another damn mile to my room." He inhaled deeply and blew gray smoke at the video screens. "This place ain't ready. It ain't ready."

"Where's your wife? Did she have to go down there with you?"

"Her? Hell, no. She's off playing twenty-one. Ain't seen her since the check-in desk." A fierce rush of smoke this time. "I'll be lucky if I see her in the room. Lucky? Did I say 'lucky'?" A crafty smile. "Hell, I won't see her till it's time to head for the airport . . . unless she runs out of money. Then I'll see her. Bet your ass I'll see her then. She'll find me if she runs low." The man shook his head and played a hand on his machine; he lost. "Bitch."

Drawn to the blinking light, a tall girl of metallic beauty put her hand on Arthur's shoulder. She was costumed as Cleopatra. She was accompanied by a stumpy official in a black suit.

"O great Caesar," she intoned, "you've won the gods to your cause. Four aces! The keys to the kingdom are yours. Satyr has a gift for you."

The stump suit scribbled words on a pad, then ripped off the chit and handed it to Arthur with a grand sweep of a Rolexed wrist. "Compliments of the Satyr, sir," he said. "Dinner for two in the Pharaoh's Buffet. Have a royal day." Arthur took the slip.

"I could use one of those," from the man with the wheelchair. "I've been playing for two hours." A beaten, hangdog look.

The black suit frowned. He looked at the man, looked at the wheelchair, looked over his shoulder at Cleopatra, who rolled her eyes, then back at the petitioner again. A serious expression; a pause pregnant with corporate condescension. More scribbling. The slip of paper was handed over. "Compliments." A face of stone.

"Oh, thank you." Eyes soft with gratitude. Chit clasped to chest. "You're very kind."

"No problem." Cutting words. The official pair turned as one and headed off.

The wheelchair man smiled, turned to Arthur, and nodded in the direction of the departing pair. "Pig fuckers." Arthur watched as the man took a collection of similar chits from his shirt pocket and folded the new paper in with the others. "You'd think I was asking to screw his daughter."

They played the machines for another forty minutes before the man ran out of quarters. "Let me play some of those," and he nodded toward Arthur's supply of coins. "They might bring me some luck. Lucky quarters. You mind? If I win I'll split it with you."

Arthur glanced over at the man. The same look was there that was used on the black suit. Arthur took a handful of coins from one of his cups and deposited the money in the empty tray of the other machine.

The man began to play. Four twos. A flush. Another flush. A straight. Then four twos again. The man's tray was half-full.

Arthur's machine had gone cold.

"Honey bag?" Sugary words from behind them. A willowy female of thirty years and platinum-blonde hair. Breasts at war with an outgunned silk blouse. Peach-colored lipstick over full soft flesh. Big dark lashes. Wasp waist. Long fingers dressed with gold. Legs that went all the way up to a rump that could sharpen knives. Expensive scent. "Honey bag?"

"What the fuck do you want? Go away. I'm winning."

"Silly honey bag!" White arms encircled the man's wrinkled throat, his ears beyond viewing . . . submerged beneath hills of buoyant mammary gland. A kiss on top of his head. Peach lips pressing. White teeth nibbling. "I won a bunch!"

"Go away."

"At the craps table. A nice man showed me how to play. He gave me chips to play with."

"Chips?"

"These!" Long fingers uncurled. Eight black chips rested in one hot palm. Black chips. Hundred-dollar chips.

Head pressed back into breast tissue. Eyes squinting down at the black chips held under his nose. Trying to focus. "Hey. That's pretty good. Any more?"

"More in my pocket." Inane snicker.

"How many more?"

"Bunches! He won bunches, too. A sweetie pie!"

The man leaned forward and punched the cashout button on his machine. Quarters clinked down and added to the pile in his tray. "Let's go eat, kid. I got freebies for the buffet." He disengaged his neck from the long smooth arms and stood up.

Stood up.

Arthur's eyebrows raised.

The man scooped quarters into cups. Three cups. He studied his take. He looked at the wheelchair. He turned to his lady. "You ride, sweetie . . . I'll push. Carry these on your lap. Where's the goddamn cage?"

The hardbody backside settled into the wheelchair. A giggle. Long legs longer. Nipples threatening design limits. Long hair pushed back. Eyelid-glitter sparkling. Money cups on her lap.

"It's over there, hon." Graceful finger, red nail. "Past the bar."

The man positioned himself behind her. He made a move to push off. He hesitated and looked back, an expression of friendly forbearance on his face. "So?"

"So what?" replied Arthur.

The man tilted his head in the direction of the wheelchair. A smile. "So, it works. No waiting in lines. Good parking spaces. People like to help the handicapped. Makes 'em feel good."

No reply.

"Besides."

"Besides what?"

"I'm an asshole."

Arthur nodded slightly. "Okay. You're an asshole."

"Right. But it ain't my fault. There's too much bullshit in life, too many rules. Let the guy in the chair deal with it. He gets things done." A wink. "The world don't fuck with cripples." The man turned and started to push the wheelchair.

"Hey, partner," from Arthur.

The man looked back.

"Forget something?"

A perplexed look. Then a smile. "Oh, yeah." He reached over a creamy-princess shoulder and rummaged in one of the cups. He grabbed some coins and handed them to Arthur. "Thanks for the stake."

Arthur looked at the coins. Not as many as he had loaned out. The man paused as if to say something else. His hand started for the pocket containing the free meal chits, then stopped. "I'd give you one of these," fingers patting his shirt front, "but you got one already."

And off they went.

Arthur played the machines all night long. He ate a chicken salad sandwich, then walked across the street to another casino and drank bourbon and listened to a girl sing soft songs in a lounge. He walked back to the Satyr and won more quarters. In the early morning hours he bought a Sunday newspaper and started on the big crossword puzzle, but he couldn't finish the thing. He wandered into the Sports Book and watched a replay of one of yesterday's college football games.

But mostly he thought about the man's words. *Let the guy in the chair deal with it. He gets things done.*

Arthur began to understand.

I I I

Sunday.

Mike and Diane sat side by side at the big desk in the den. Each worked the keyboards of two separate computers.

Mike transferred figures to a yellow legal pad. He punched up another display, studied it for several seconds, then reached for one of three phones and lifted the receiver. He keyed two digits into the memory dial.

"Charlie? How's things in Bridgeport? . . . What the hell do you expect? It's winter. Hey, you see what I'm seeing? . . . Yeah, the Bears-Giants game is really opening up."

He crossed out numbers on the yellow pad.

"The Bears are getting five points in New York and Jersey, too. Pretty damn nice. Give it twenty more minutes, then let 'er rip. We'll get that extra half-point, bet you a bottle of Chivas. Take another hundred dimes if they'll sell the six . . . I'm looking at their action right now. It's just like looking over their shoulder. Tocci dropped in a new horizontal sync restorer last Tuesday. No more drift . . . you got that right, pal. I think I'll get one of those personalized license plates next year. Van Eck. A real computer thief. Ain't science grand?"

Mike laughed. He pushed back in his chair and winked at Diane who had looked up at the remark about the license plate. She smiled at her brother, then returned to her computer screen. She quickly scribbled something on a slip of paper and handed it across to Mike. He read the numbers.

"Charlie! Listen up, hotshot. From Evanston. The Bears are pick-'em all over Illinois. We've got DiNatale's numbers on the screen now. He can't turn off the action. It looks like a college homecoming game. That poor son of a bitch is really hurting! Go to work, baby. *Ciao!*"

He hung up the phone. "This game is going to fall, little sister, I know it is. Five, five and a half points to work with . . . it's a lock! It looks like a million-dollar play. Maybe more." He winked at her. "And we have five points to work with, at least. If the Giants win by one, win by five, or anywhere in between . . . we hit both sides. What do you think?"

"I think you might be right. Look at this weather." She nodded at her video display.

∎ ∎ ∎

"It wasn't his fault."

"Ma'am, I don't care whose fault it was. He was driving all over the road."

Montana sat with his head pushed back against the driver's headrest and studied the patterns of small holes in the fabric liner inside the car roof.

Karla leaned farther over between his chest and the steering wheel so she could better see the young Highway Patrol officer. "I don't see why he should get a ticket. Give me the ticket."

"You weren't driving. He was."

Karla batted her eyes. "But, Officer," and Karla put on an innocent, embarrassed look, "I was just paying off a bet on the football game. He won. I picked the Bears, but the Giants won by three points. It was just a silly bet." She pouted. "Weren't you ever in love, Officer?"

No reply. Only an uncomfortable glance to either side.

"A guy with your looks . . . that bod . . . I can tell . . . you sure been in love."

Pen tip to tongue tip. Carbon paper folded under. "Just doing my job, ma'am. Maybe next time you should bet for money."

"I'll never do it again. Never. I'll ride in the back seat if you want. Promise."

Pen tip to tongue tip again.

"I'll ride in the trunk."

A hint of smile under the sunglasses.

"We're going to Las Vegas. His mother had a stroke."

Waiting.

"His dad's in a home. Wets himself. Nine hundred dollars a month."

Waiting.

"Cat got run over last week."

Waiting.

"Two kids. Sweet kids. Both simple. One's an imbecile. Needs special treatment, nurses."

Waiting.

"One leg. Kid needs crutches."

Pen tip retracted into pen barrel.

"Can't afford real crutches. Uses a stick."

Pen into pocket.

"Stick from a tree out back of the trailer."

Ticket book closed.

"Tree's sick. Caterpillars."

Sunglasses off. "Go."

"Green caterpillars."

"Go away."

Montana started the engine.

24

Homecoming

Arthur returned to Melody's apartment late Sunday afternoon. She would finish her Sports Book shift at six, and he took comfort in having the apartment to himself. He wanted to sort out his thoughts and get ready for the night. Despite not sleeping for a day and a half, he wasn't tired. An energy fed into him, an overt sense of anticipation almost approaching excitement. It was as though he were about to embark on a recon mission into new, dangerous, and therefore fascinating territory. The passion to know, to confront the dream, was as strong in him as was the avenging passion he directed at society's monsters. But beyond those twin passions lurked the ominous possibility that evil was not, after all, the real enemy; that the true horror might be a universe that was indifferent. If such were the answer, then pain, love, and justice didn't matter; it was all a waste of time.

Once, only once, Arthur had come up against written philosophy—that was when he'd let himself be signed up for a Navy literature course. The training, aboard a transport ship as it crossed the

Pacific, was part of a program aimed at giving the troops a chance at college credits. It was a way to make the transition back to the real world easier, to burn time and learn of things gentle after twelve months of cutting throats. The civilian instructor, one of two the Navy paid to ride the ship home, seemed lost, afraid, out of place in that cynical community. And when he and Arthur talked one night as they leaned on the mess deck rail watching black water rush along the hull, Arthur felt sorry for the man. No one wanted what the teacher had to offer. Too few had signed up for his course. No one wanted to read the classics and fend off images of blasted limbs, avulsed chests, and enterprising maggot squirms at the same time. Not then. Maybe never again.

Three students.

The four of them met at night in an empty room that doubled as ship's chapel. The compartment was small, but still too big to make the cause seem anything but lost. Arthur sat two chairs apart from a Filipino deuce who sat two chairs apart from a black lance corporal named Peter Biggs.

"Good evening, gentlemen. My name is Matthew Crenshaw. Please call me Matt."

Blank looks.

"This is your class. If you want to ask something, speak up. We're here to exchange ideas." Crenshaw displayed a hopeful smile.

"The wise teacher is he who learns from his students." A wink. Forced. A thumbs-up sign. One of the boys. Three months ago Biggs had bitten off a VC thumb about that size in a pitch-dark laterite tunnel under Cu Chi. He still carried the dried part in his shirt pocket. Tunnel rats had a thing for souvenirs.

"How many of you gentlemen have taken college-level courses?"

The ship rolled gently to starboard.

"Well . . . I thought we'd work on this first." He held up a blue book with the title *Principles of Philosophy* lettered in gold across the front. "Who knows the author?" The ship rolled gently back to port.

"I'll give you a hint." Another wink. Expression alive with conspiratorial revelation. "*Cogito, ergo sum.*"

Starboard.

"I think; therefore I exist."

Port.

"No takers?" Silence. There were no takers.

In short order Descartes was shelved in favor of Sir Walter Scott, who in turn quickly gave way to Melville because Biggs asked why they couldn't study an American writer. Why did they have to talk about foreigners?

Melville fit.

Moby Dick. The ship. Their ship.

The ocean. This ocean.

The evil whale. They knew evil.

Then, later, a gift for Mr. Crenshaw. The teacher, in fact, learning from the students: not the *evil* whale, the *indifferent* whale . . . not an *evil* universe, an *indifferent* universe.

That conclusion haunted Arthur through all the years.

"Where were you last night? I was worried." Melody, housekey in hand, stood there with one yellow shirttail out.

"I got the bug, the gambling bug. Video poker. I couldn't sleep." He smiled. "I guess they're right about the casinos putting something in the air. I never got tired."

"There's something in the air, all right. Greed. I wish you'd left me a note." And she did a thing neither of them expected. She went to him and hugged him. He put an awkward arm around her.

"I won about two hundred dollars."

She made scrambled eggs and she cooked sausages. She heated two slices of ham and some home-fried potatoes. "The Gambler's Special," she said.

In the early evening they sat in the living room and drank red wine.

"It helped. What you said about the dreams." He looked not at her but at his empty glass.

"Dreams? Oh. You mean about trying to stop the dreams?"

"Yes."

"It couldn't happen so fast. It takes more time. It took me a few months."

"Maybe I just hit it right."

They didn't speak for long moments.

"What do you dream about?" And she didn't look at him.

Instantly, Arthur was aware of everything in the room: the way the light fell; the way outside sounds came in from the street; the texture of the rug; the design on the cushions of the couch; his skin; the feel of the empty glass in his hand; the warmth of her body next to him as her soft heat radiated across the space between them. He could smell the linger of wine and the fry-smell of the skillet half-submerged in soapy water in the kitchen. He registered her perfume, the aroma of female powder, the faint tobacco scent, and the musk of distant sage.

He was quickly alert, tense, sharply aware of her words, and now of the way she breathed after the words. His senses reeled, and he felt dangerously off-guard despite the sharp focus of his world; her question, natural and innocent to her, had turned his composure to thin glass. Everything seemed to be happening too fast, her words expected, but brutally sudden. He wavered on the edge of a deep precipice more startled by the threat of falling than by the consequence of falling, more startled by the question than by the consequence of revelation. Once again in this strange week, he was afraid. In his soul, something scurried. He could feel the harsh alarm, and he drew out of his body and watched from a distance, his brain like hot cotton, numb like a face hit by a basketball. In those unnatural instants he wavered in a vortex of frightful indecision. *Tell her!*

Images unspooled. A young face blown silently away . . . a patch of flesh with hair hooked by a branch and hanging for a slippery moment before falling out of the scope picture. The scope drifting left. The next face—that of a six-year-old. A girl, her eyes wide and looking right. Her bruised arms pulling and tight with terror. His own arms hideously steady. Her head snapping back in a splash of red. *Tell her!*

More images. A boy. Eight. Olive skin. The olive skin suddenly peeled back in ragged flaps. White bone. Scope drifting left again. Five-year-old girl. Eyes squeezed shut, head jerking, her face a pale sheet of fear, trying to make the horror go away . . . in the lower edge of the sight picture a leather binding cinched deeply into the swollen skin of her young throat . . . and then the small skull motionless but intact as the chance tumble of the projectile entered on its long axis to kill cleanly. Blue hole in forehead. Drift left again. Past a wrist wired to a tree limb. But this time brown eyes that looked straight at him. Older eyes. Ten-year-old eyes that stared across the killing space and held his own. The involuntary hesitation of the shooter. A breath taken, deeply, slowly. Wait for breath to be over. Steady hands again. Squeeze. The shot low. Slightly left, Into the neck. *Oh, God, no!* The eyes still staring. A ravaged jugular emptying onto a brown, lean shoulder. Eyes fluttering, rolling up. Head pitching forward. A second shot into the field of black, shiny hair now fronting him. Unnecessary shot. *Tell her! Please tell her!*

The wineglass shattered in his hand. The faces flew away.

"Arthur!" Her sudden fingers cupped his bleeding flesh. "My God, Arthur!"

Melody on her feet, then straddling him as she bent to his cut hand. Her face white, her eyes wide. One knee on the couch to his left, her other leg angled and still on the floor to his right, the lower edge of her white robe in her hands and wrapping around his cut fingers, the robe pulling up in the center, the inside of her thighs and the dark junction where legs met exposed.

"Arthur. Oh, Arthur." His hand wrapped now and pinned between their chests as she kneeled astride his thighs and leaned hard against his chest as if the pressure of their bodies on the hand would stop the bleeding. His legs between her knees. Her tears. Her breathing uneven, confused. Her fear. She pressed his injured hand in the folds of her white robe. His own robe spread apart in the press of her position. Modesty unaware. Naked parts close.

"Sorry about the glass." His lips barely moved with the words. Their foreheads touched. Her eyes closed, but tears escaped the soft closing and moved down her cheeks.

"What happened?" A small voice. Her hands squeezed his cut hand with pathetic intensity. Her arms trembled. The white robe stained pink between their chests.

"I . . . " *Tell her.* "I don't know." His eyes also shut.

"My God, what have they done to you?" Foreheads pressing.

"I don't know."

And in that delicate, charged moment he felt a sweet shudder of emotion stir awake in his heart, felt himself start to swell and lengthen against the warm contours between her legs, felt desire build unbidden and uncontrolled, and he was made awkward by his erection and what was happening.

She did not move away.

"Let me fix your hand." But not taking her forehead from his. Not opening her eyes. Neither releasing her grip on his hand nor easing the press of her body on his.

"It's all right. It's stopped bleeding. It doesn't hurt." His breathing shallow. Desire running inches more. Confused. Wondering where embarrassment had gone when embarrassment should have been there.

And he knowing that she knew what was happening. And she not moving away.

Both rampantly aware.

His sex grew long against the naked curve between her legs, and that part of her pushed firmly back as she rode the topside of his filling flesh.

Reserve dissolved.

She moved gently there, and wetness came from her like honey. She rose slightly onto her knees and placed her cheek against his. She hooked his shoulder with her chin and pushed softly into the curve of his neck; then softness passed to urgency.

She freed one hand from the tight space between them, and that hand floated somewhere down. He waited.

They trembled.

That electric piece of time ended as her fingers found and guided him to that place, only guided him, didn't have to raise him because his flesh hunted her center with brute purpose. Her hand moved away from there and slipped behind his neck.

She lowered herself.

Hot, wet muscle ate his length.

The supple circlets of her inside swarmed his senses and held him tightly with contractions as involuntary as they were fierce. That hot surround released and contracted again when she lifted to wet the last length. Then she pushed all the way down.

They stopped breathing.

Hot rawhide laced his circumference. Sweet strength filled and anchored her. Pleasure lanced each flesh with graceless power.

"Don't move." Her voice ragged, deep, cracking. Her arms shaking, her chin still crushing into the rise of his shoulder. "Don't move," again. Fierce instruction.

His sex bulled into her.

Both her arms were around his neck, and her breath finally returned in jolting gasps hot on his cheek. Her hips a fiery vise.

He was lost. An avalanche of need raced through his tissues, unstoppable, unstopping.

"Move! Move now!" Guttural sounds in his ear. Her words half-words. Demanding words. Genderless sounds. Orders more animal than human.

Spots of light. His muscles bucked. Cuts reopened on his hands as they raged her backside. New scratches like fine spider webs welled red on the skin of his back from her nails . . . on his shoulder from her teeth. A wild convulsion twisted them together.

For one half-hour after, they stayed motionless. No words. He inside and still erect as though every sad stone in each sad wall placed during each lost year would be dismantled in those minutes.

She was aware of how he was. Hard into her body. Deep. She kept her arms around him and only twice did she move her hips to renew her wonder.

Tell her.

He didn't tell her.

She stirred. She lifted slightly, leaned and switched off the single lamp that was on the table next to the couch. His erect and full part only half left her body as she did that, and she settled back onto him in the darkness, buried his length and reclaimed the strong magic. Arms once more wrapped around. A soft cheek nestled softly on a lean shoulder. Eyes stayed closed. Their breathing stepped along in sweet rhythm. On him, an expression of complete acceptance, of compliant surrender; on her, a soft swallow of comfort beneath a sleepy smile.

More minutes passed. She nudged the side of his neck with her nose. "Hey, roomie," she whispered.

"Ummm?"

"Broken glass. Wine. Blood. Me. You. I'm going to have to buy another couch."

He felt the muscles of her face move in a smile against the lower line of his jaw. "Ummm," a deep, throaty, male rumble that made her chest vibrate against his skin.

"Sleep with me?" She nuzzled closer.

No reply.

"I won't pull any funny stuff."

"Let's sleep here." And his arms pressed hard around her and crushed down. His voice seemed different, harsh, changed.

She felt him expand inside her. She wriggled her hips in sultry trust, then gasped and trembled against his hard shoulder as she felt herself spread by his quick desire.

His arms were suddenly stronger, his hardness new and pushing deeper.

"Arthur?" A word alive with wonder and even fear at what was happening. "Oh, my God," as she absorbed a brutal thrust. Her mind shivered, hesitated for a lost, uncomprehending second, then gave way, and her body, more his than hers, pressed down to engulf the urgency of the man beneath and inside her. Her teeth bit into her lower lip. Lust flared, raged without love, and worked to strangle the male part.

His legs straightened, and a jolting tremor racked his body. She ground her sex against his and rode hard behind his ecstasy with her own . . . a communion quickly done, but done with an intensity that frightened love and buried reason.

She began to cry.

She cried with sad fury and could not stop. She hugged, then pushed herself away, then hugged again. She drew back and smashed a small fist against his chest. Hit him twice more, then collapsed against him in a shimmer of tears.

She struggled to her feet, her face wet and pale and twisted. A glass shard cut the bottom of one foot, but was not felt.

She drew her robe tightly around her nakedness and without a word left him, hurried to her room, and closed the door.

He slept.

In the early morning hours he awoke. He was deeply tired and knew sleep would come back quickly. He closed his eyes and fought his way into the dream.

The place was different. No green jungle. No dark sky. No fetid smell of vegetation. More a barren, open plain where large black boulders bulked on red sand beneath lurid, orange air. Three shacks, hootches of reed and stick, stood not on stilts but on the scarlet sand. A bed, a double bed, empty, out of place and neatly made up, inconsistent, far away. A flock of thirty birds, seagulls, bobbed yellow beaks into red sand and strutted. Some scattered trees were there, all brown and without leaves, but a thin stand, spread out, stunted and of no worth as cover. Deep silence over all.

He was aware of something or someone to his left and he turned that way. The presence rotated in the direction of his turning, and he couldn't come to it. He stopped his turn. Then quickly snapped around, and there beside a dark thrust of rock was a man. A filled-in silhouette, filled in with black, no details of face or form visible despite the bright orange air.

The other was still.

Did not appear afraid.

Seemed determined to stay.

Arthur knew the other was looking at him, though he could see no eyes in the depth of that featureless shadow. The crenulated surface of a knit watch cap defined the top of its head, and the slabbed shape of a three-quarter coat stood out against the backdrop of crimson sand.

Arthur took a forward, slightly sideways step, then two more. The thing shifted to front him and didn't move away. They faced each other on the silent landscape.

With no words Arthur tried to understand. Who? What?

A screech pierced the orange air, the screech of a hawk. The quick black shape moved above them. Arthur looked up and saw the predator flash through the flame-colored ether, a broken nestling in one talon, neck floppy, broken, dead. The dark bird with its lifeless cargo receded into the distance.

The silence settled in again.

Each regarded the other for long moments.

Then the shape moved one step away from the rock and extended its arm toward a dark place behind the boulder.

And waited.

A small hand reached out of the shadow, the hand of a child.

The hands touched. Locked. The child moved out to stand beside the other. A boy. A young boy. Six? Ten years of age? Arthur could not tell.

He strained to see who was there, squinted in an attempt to make out some detail, but could not. Arthur made no move, said nothing.

The two forms stood before him. Thirty feet away. Watching.

The small one shifted in the orange light, the bright orange light that lit nothing. And Arthur saw it was not one of those he had killed, knew it was not one of them.

The small one moved the arm that was away from the other, moved it from behind its back.

Arthur stared through bronze air that began to swirl with force, though the swirling could not be seen and the red sand was still.

He saw that the left hand of the boy held a cord.

The cord was a leash and on that leash a small black dog.

Arthur spoke to the shadow man. "Who are you? Why are you in this place? This is my place."

"We share this," said the shape. "We have to share this." The words didn't make a pleasant sound; they came into Arthur's mind with mean spirit, anger was there, hate was there. He didn't know what else to ask. He didn't understand.

The man spoke again. "We have nowhere else."

"I am afraid of you. Why am I afraid of you?" Arthur waited for an answer. A long moment unreeled in air that swirled and pushed and made him fight to keep his balance. The large form drew the hand of the boy closer. The building gale caused dark streaks to flare, and twisting black gaps opened in the orange air between him and them.

"*You're* afraid of *us*?" The voice seeped hate.

The dark shapes turned and drifted . . . did not walk . . . drifted quickly over the red-sand distance toward the sector where the hawk had gone. Then stopped.

The man looked back across that great separation.

Arthur heard the man's words as though they were spoken inches from his ear. Words sharp with hate, but urgent now. *"Tell her."*

When the first gray ray of morning came into the room, Arthur got up from the sofa. He walked to Melody's bedroom and knelt down by her bed. He looked into her face. "Melody?" Her red eyes opened. Crying eyes. "I want to tell you something, Melody."

She turned her back. "Go away. Don't come back, Arthur. I'm trying to be in love. Just let me be in love."

25

Monday, Monday

J ust one message, sir."

"One?" Montana leaned on the manager's desk, elbows between a wire rack of tourist pamphlets on one side, a small statue of the Virgin Mary on the other. Someone had stuck a cocktail garnish, a pink umbrella, into the praying hands of the Holy Mother. Propped against her ceramic robe were some black and white business cards promoting an outcall escort service. On each card, a contrasting logo in red . . . puckered lips simulating a lipstick imprint.

"Yep." Wet cigar stink. "You had some last week, but we chuck 'em after twenty-four hours. Can't let 'em build up. Only makes a fucking mess." The mauled cigar stub migrated in saliva-wrapping rotations to the opposite corner of the man's chancre-speckled lips. His large, wet frog-eyes glistened.

"Well?"

"Well, what?"

"Where's the message?"

"Wastebasket." The cigar stub pointed left and down.

"Why?"

"No need. Look behind you."

Montana turned.

Arthur.

"Have a nice trip, partner?" The look was cold.

Montana stared back. "Don't give me any shit, Wolfer. Where the fuck were *you?* I went to your place twice before we left."

The frog-eyes blinked with an audible wet, sucking smack.

They sat in Montana's room. The place smelled of cigarettes and something else.

"You brought her up here?" Arthur asked.

"Yes, I brought her up here. What's the fucking problem?"

"No problem. Nevada prisons aren't the worst in the world. Not if you like to dig trenches in hundred-degree heat and get your nuts kicked off at lockdown. Not bad at all."

Montana lit a cigarette.

Arthur walked to the window and looked out. "I moved out because I killed two guys."

Montana stared. Arthur turned from the window. "I got jumped in an alley."

No words from Montana.

"That's why I took off. I had to find another place. The cops were doing a door-to-door. I think someone might have seen it go down."

Montana took a deep drag on his cigarette and launched a cloud of smoke toward the ceiling. Still no words from him.

"I tried to get another place real quick. Wanted to get an address first. So I'd have something to give you. That's why I didn't get up with you right off. I guess that's when we missed each other. Part my fault."

"*Part* your fault?"

Arthur ignored the urge to come back at Montana. "One was a politician's kid. Both about thirty. Tourists."

Another cloud of smoke. Montana's eyebrows arched, his eyes wide in sarcastic mime. "You had to kill them, of course. You had no choice, right?"

Silence.

"Probably had a gun stuck in your mouth, right?"

Arthur leveled his eyes at Montana.

"Show me any two civilian motherfuckers who can take you out; show me three. *Had* to kill them? It's me, Wolfer. It's me you're talking to."

"It just happened."

"Just happened. Christ!" A pause. "Where're you staying?"

Arthur turned back to the window and parted the dirt-gray curtains. He spoke without looking at Montana. "I stayed with Melody for a few days. At her place. The cops are checking all the motels. She kicked my ass out this morning. I'm still looking."

"At Melody's place? You stay there and you get on *my* ass for bringing my girl up here for a thirty-minute rubdown?"

No reply.

"I can't fucking believe it. This town's got more eyes than a fucking field of fucking potatoes. And you spend your free time killing tourists for amusement. Biggest damn contract we ever had, and you're out collecting scalps. Christ on a stick!" Then a change of tone. "How'd you do it?" Curious.

"Hands. And a busted bottle."

Montana went into the bathroom and threw his cigarette into the commode. Arthur heard the sizzle of the butt when it hit the water and then the heavy sound of urine drilling into the bowl. Montana would be pissing on the butt, chasing it around inside the toilet with his urine stream. He always did that.

"Jesus," from the bathroom. "He kills tourists."

Then a chuckle.

They left the room and went to a small bar two doors down from Montana's place.

"So, you want to stay at my dump for a few days? We could hang a sign on the door. KILLERS FOR RENT. REFERENCES ON REQUEST."

Arthur didn't smile.

"Then we could invite the girls over. That way we all go into the bag together. A package deal. Makes it nice for the cops when they finally figure everything out. And they're going to figure it out easy, the way we're going."

"I want you to get me over to Pahrump. That guy Elder said he had a trailer. I have his number. You finish the setup, then I'll take off from there. That's my plan; get the hell out of here before something else happens."

Montana finished his beer and set the empty bottle on the tabletop. He thought for a moment. The idea was a good one . . . for more reasons than Arthur knew. He was to talk with the buyer late that afternoon to nail down the time frame. With Arthur gone, he could relax. Just as in the lobby when he went to pick up his messages, Arthur had an eerie habit of seeming to materialize out of thin air when he least expected it. "That sounds like an okay idea. Not bad. Where's the equipment?"

"At Melody's place. Under the couch. She doesn't know it's there. No one knows it's there. I stashed it before I took off. She was still in bed."

"Gee, Wolfer. That's great. Real nice. Melody's place."

"I've got a key. You or me can pick the gear up when she's at work."

"You've got a key. Why not just go to a fucking casino and check the stuff at the bell desk? Give everyone a chance at it?"

Arthur looked hard at Montana.

Montana saw a look he had seen before. He didn't push any further. He waved for another beer. "You fuck her?"

"Matter of fact, yes."

"Was she any good?"

"Yes. Very good." An honest answer. Very macho. No attempt at courtly discretion. No honorable gesture . . . even though the words made Arthur's chest ache . . . even though pain constricted his throat as he spoke . . .

. . . to talk that way of someone who meant so much.

It hurt. It physically hurt.

He was determined to put stones back onto a broken wall.

"You believe these numbers?"

Diane smiled and looked more closely at the sheet of paper Mike waved under her nose. She continued to wash the breakfast dishes.

"Look at this!" He pointed. "One point four mil. Can you goddamn believe it?"

"Don't get a big head."

"I can afford a big head. I can afford two heads."

"Tonight? Monday Nighter?" Diane lifted a wet plate out of the sink, held it to her apron front, and strummed at it like it was a guitar, "Are you ready . . . ?" in a raucous, singsong country music imitation.

"Sure. Why not? It's seven points. Right on the button. We got them on the run."

"Can you get together with the girl in the Sports Book? Can she spot the rat's play for you?"

He shrugged and folded the paper. "She's not working the Book tonight. She's dealing tables. Blackjack."

"They're going to be watching after the hit they took on that Chicago game. Do you think it's smart to push it like this?"

"Let 'em watch. They're probably still in shock. Who are they going to bitch to? If the Gaming Commission got wind of the fact that those two casinos are banking illegal books out of Nevada, they'd be fried. Big-time. Their golden goose gets its ass cooked."

Diane stopped washing dishes and placed her hands on the edge of the counter. She stared into the soapy water. Glassy bubbles popped. "How much is enough? When do we stop? We have the kids to think of. What if something happens?"

"Nothing's going to happen, Sis . . . except the kids will own their own damn casino someday."

Diane shook her head.

"And they can buy a retirement for their dotty old parents. Let them change our diapers for a change."

"I'll be glad when this stuff is over."

"So far, so good."

"So far." She picked up another dish. "What about the girl? What's her name?"

"Melody?"

"Yes. Melody. The casino watches the ticket writers. What if they get onto her?"

"What if they do?"

"She could get messed up. You don't want that. You like her. I can tell you like her."

Mike looked at her. "You're right. I like her."

*   *   *

Anthony Sgro tossed a second bundle of hundred-dollar bills through the cloud of blue smoke. The packet bounced off Montana's chest and landed in his lap on top of the first bundle. Montana stared at Sgro. The man defined ugly.

"That's another eighty grand. Will that get your ass moving?"

Montana picked up the two money packs and made them one. He looked at the money, then at Sgro, "Why the Christmas present?"

The fat man leaned forward and, with a vicious sweep of his pudgy, ring-studded fist, knocked the bronze Crystal Casino curio piece to one side. The heavy logo paperweight careened off the desk and clunked onto the rug, bounced twice, and separated from its oak base. Montana looked at the broken thing, Anthony Sgro did not.

"The rotten motherfucker is ripping our guts out. We want him done. Right fucking now! Like yesterday! No more time! We can't take another day like Sunday! You get that hotshot butt-buddy of yours and do it! JUST FUCKING DO IT!" The man's face bulged in red, quivering billows of tensed flesh. Distended veins cut hard lines at the start of his temples and along his fat throat. The purple cigar trembled and angled upward as the man's teeth crushed down on its wet end. Snakelike eyes narrowed to slits and black pupils shrunk to pinpoint pips beneath a moist accumulation of rage-driven tears. "JUST FUCKING DO IT!"

Montana wondered if he should call for help when Sgro dropped dead from the probable heart attack. He decided he would just leave with the money. Let the office staff handle it.

Sgro rubbed his face with the sleeve of his suit. Then slammed his fist onto the desk. "ANY FUCKING QUESTIONS?"

Montana leaned forward and snubbed his cigarette out in the massive glass ashtray. As he leaned back, Sgro's fist swept the desk again and the ashtray flew away in a shower of ash and gray dust. "No questions," was Montana's calm reply.

"WHEN?"

"I'll try to take him this weekend. Maybe Monday."

"NO FUCKING GOOD!"

"You want it done before the weekend?"

The man began to choke. The red face went to crimson. Sgro tried to form words but couldn't. A squawk came out.

"I guess that's a yes," from Montana, quietly.

A strange minute rolled by as he watched the security chief struggle for air. The face before him began to lose its florid hue and recover some of its usual hospice-yellow pallor. The face went past yellow to death-white, then back to yellow.

"Where is your friend?" A different voice, a small voice.

"He's staying with me tonight. Tomorrow I take him out of town to keep him out of trouble. He tends to drift."

"Drift?"

Montana nodded.

"He drifts," from Sgro. A beaten expression.

No reply.

"Please do your best."

The man must have almost died, thought Montana. He got up from his chair and left the office.

Sgro waited for a few seconds, then mopped cold sweat from his brow once more.

He leaned forward and pressed a button on the intercom box.

"Sir?"

"Tail him. Tail him everywhere."

"Going somewhere?" Montana looked over the top of Monday's local newspaper at Arthur, who stood by the door.

Arthur finished zipping up his jacket. "I think I'll take a walk. One last look at the lights. I probably won't be back here anytime soon. And there's not much for me to do over in Pahrump."

"You don't do much anyway."

Melody felt a wave of panic come. *No.*

The pair settled onto the two open chairs at her table. The methane smell. The chewed, grease-lined fingernails. The brown teeth.

And the other. The walking corpse. Half-asleep. Almost as repulsive in his own right. But not quite.

The fat one was the one she'd hit over the head with her cocktail tray many weeks ago ... the one who'd cost her her first job ... who'd jammed the lime slice in her crotch.

Would they recognize her?

"Hi, sweet tits."

Deal.

Keep dealing.

The game moved along without a hitch. The startled faces of the other players who'd turned at the "sweet tits" remark were calmed in short fashion by the stink-blob. "We're old friends," he said to all, with a knowing wink at Melody.

Deal.

The table smelled like the town dump.

Keep dealing.

Thirty minutes later, the corpse picked up his dealt hand and held the two cards a couple of inches in front of his face. His eyebrows showed above, his chin showed below the cards. Melody looked at him.

"Card, sir?"

No reply.

"Would you like a card?"

She saw the tip of his tongue appear beneath the lower edge of the cards. More of the tongue appeared. It hung like a thick slab of gray-green meat and kept extending downward. It lengthened past his chin and kept going. Now the exposed surface was populated by something that looked like tiny alfalfa sprouts, like the sprouts on the veggie salad bar, only black.

She felt her stomach flip.

The fat tick tried to suppress a giggle, but he couldn't keep it in. A filmy spray of saliva filled the air over the table. He giggled with glee as his companion's anatomical monstrosity kept rolling out toward the table surface like some slime-covered eel.

Six inches.

Everyone was hypnotized and stared. Everyone except the great, bulbous, methane tick who squeezed his eyes shut and continued to spray the air with spastic exhalations.

Seven inches.

The lady on third base screamed.

One more inch. A gel of mucous coated the newly exposed area.

The round one gained some breath and leaned at Melody. "How'd you like to saddle that ol' thing, sugar crotch?"

Third base screamed once more.

Melody's head spun. "Checks play!" she howled, the call for

help that would summon the boss when something needed attention; those words chased after the wail from the woman on her right.

The words weren't necessary. Before the echo of the scream from third base died, two security guards appeared behind the tongue-monster. Two strong hands, one on each shoulder, gripped the emaciated body.

Without warning, the fat slug turned and punched the nearest guard in the ribs.

Third base screamed again. Checks clattered. Cards flew. Drinks spilled. The brawl was on.

The wonder tongue followed its keeper backward onto the floor of the casino. Melody watched the glistening organ flop in a heavy, slobbering arc as it went up and over and disappeared below the table edge. Methane-man got in two more punches before he went down beneath a heap of black suit jackets. The mass of men rolled and thrashed on the carpet. Two players, a man and a woman, tipped backward off the player chairs into the writhing pile and merged with the mess of noise and curses.

After two wild minutes the clot of violence gained a multitude of legs, and all those legs marched off through the banks of excited onlookers toward the back of the casino.

Melody felt a gentle hand on her shoulder.

She looked around into Lou's kind face. Lou, her break-in friend and buffet buddy, his cherubic face wearing a calm but quizzical expression. His black bow tie, his nametag, his yellow dealer's shirt just right.

"Trouble, Mel?"

"TROUBLE? . . . TROUBLE? . . . ME?" Close to tears.

Lou gazed in the direction of the fading commotion.

"Gee, Mel. That guy had a big tongue, didn't he?"

She finished her shift.

"Why not?" she said to Lou. "What else can go wrong?"

She was beat. Exhausted. Monday night wasn't her favorite night anyway. Now this. The shift boss had oozed over to her table after the incident to calm everybody down. Everybody but her. He handed out passes to the country music show in the main room, saw to it that anyone who wanted to get a complimentary meal in the roach cafe got a chit, made sure that all the players had the desired drinks and warned the cocktail waitress that she'd better see to it that the table got special service. He assured all those present that the miscreants had been escorted out to the parking lot and sent on their way.

To Melody he said, "Keep better control of your table."

She ground her teeth together and felt a filling break. She tracked down the small chunk of silver and discreetly pushed the piece out of her mouth with her tongue. She picked the chip off the tip of her tongue with thumb and forefinger and flicked the fragment at the receding back of the shift boss. Then she turned back to the table and was embarrassed when she saw all the players looking at her.

Since the pit powers had expansively showered freebies on the players, they in turn assumed a subtle but definite air of wounded importance; the show of concern served to convince the customers they'd been wronged and were owed . . . certainly *they* didn't owe anybody . . . and Melody left the table without any tokes when her shift ended twenty minutes later.

A cold night. She still wasn't used to the radical temperature changes that came with the dry desert air and cloudless night skies. She promised herself she'd bring her lightweight coat next time she dealt night rotation.

It was a considerable hike to the employees' parking lot. *Of course . . . can't make the customers walk . . . friggin' casino piranhas might lose an extra two minutes of feeding time.* Melody recognized the unfamiliar bitterness in her thoughts. It had been a very confusing last few days. Confusing was too weak a word. *What the hell is going on?* One day nobody, next day too much. *Feast or famine,* she thought. She needing somebody, somebody else needing her. She was so mixed up. She wanted to scream. *No one would hear me anyway with all this friggin' wind and these friggin' trees blowing around.* She folded her arms over the purse she pressed against her chest and hurried through the whipping shadows of urban trees.

A squat bulk suddenly appeared out of black bushes to her left and blocked the pale ribbon of sidewalk twenty feet in front of her. She froze. Despite the wind, a rancid whiff of methane made it through the turbulence to her nose just as a pair of bony arms vised around her waist from behind. Something long and wet and grainy forced its way between the back of her shirt collar and the skin of her neck . . . something warm and slippery and quivering and muscular and alive . . . something about eight inches long . . . a tongue.

The skeletal arms pushed the wind out of her. The blob waddled toward her on the sidewalk, its thick arms bowed and stubby shapes against the glow of the parking lot lights far away, too far away. The vile abomination down the back of her collar slathered from side to side between her shoulder blades. Her stomach tied in knots and tried to empty.

One of the bone-hands moved quickly down the outside front of her black slacks and buried long fingers in her crotch. The thin fingers squeezed hard. The looming shape coming at her from the front blotted to nothing what little light there was. Six feet. Three feet away.

She kicked as hard as she could where testicles should be and that was where testicles were. Amazement rode through her terror for a brief moment. The pungent blob seemed to deflate in slow motion and assumed the character of an amorphous lump at her feet. The flubbering hiss of a great and lengthy flatulence rattled the air with industrial-strength force. A groan came up from the lump. Then wheezing words squeaked in the night air from below. "Kill the bitch, Basil! Rip her tits off!"

The slimy tongue jerked out of her collar.

"Timothy?" a halitosis-wreathed word close to her ear. The fingers came out from between her legs. "Timothy?" A confused word, an unsure word.

Melody freed her right arm, her left hand holding her purse, and drove her right elbow backward into what felt like a bag of chicken bones. The encircling arms let go. She jumped over the pile of stink and landed on the other side of him.

"Get her, Basil. Break her cunt!" from the sidewalk, more groans than words.

She began to run, to run toward the lights of the parking area.

At first she thought she was free. Then she heard the fearsome slap of leather soles on cement. The sound grew closer as she ran. She angled off the sidewalk and raced across the empty service road. She stumbled and almost fell as the camber of the dark asphalt surface forced a shortened stride, but she regained her balance and ran faster. The sound of steps was so much nearer. She could hear the whistling intake of breath. The image of a disembodied tongue strobed in her mind, a foul, thick malignance that licked her fear now as it had licked her neck before. Closer. She hurtled past the high gray bulk of a dumpster and veered onto the opposite sidewalk. She had the brief impression of someone standing there by a black tree in a dark shadow, but all shadows had monsters now and she kept running. Her lungs burned. She plunged toward the light.

No more following sounds.

Just her own sounds.

Don't slow down!

Run! Run! Run!

Don't stop running!

She got to her car and fumbled in her purse for her keys. She cast a quick look back into the darkness.

No one. No sound.

Terror still crowded her sensibilities.

Key into lock. Bile coming up. Door open. Into the car. Door locked.

She keyed the ignition in a nightmare of lost coordination and slow motion. The engine started. The transmission took the high idle shift with a smash, and the van sprayed a salvo of gravel into the grills and off the hoods of two cars whose owners would stamp and swear in the light of morning.

The light of morning.

Siegfried poked a cautious eye above the top edge of the dumpster. Her whiskers caught for a moment on the rough lip where the heavy steel top had gouged the metal. Then the whiskers popped free. The other eye came up to peer.

Look right. Look left. All clear.

The cat knew the big noise would come soon to take all the good stuff away. Time to move.

Siegfried was boss of the lot. She defended her territory against all comers, though it had cost an ear and two claws when that psycho-Angora tried to move in four months ago. She wound up gutting it with her hind claws, killed it.

Siegfried spotted a rubbery thing that was sandwiched between two soda cans. She locked it in her jaws, crouched, coiled, then leapt over the edge of the dumpster and crashed onto the top of a large cardboard box. She half-fell, half-slid the rest of the way to the ground. She looked around. An awkward jump. Quite uncatlike. But this thing was heavy, whatever it was.

Eight inches long.

Meaty.

Sort of wet . . . like a tongue.

And it didn't smell too good.

26

Tuesday

Montana stopped the Taurus in front of the Pahrump casino. Across the lot, a pair of ranchers got out of a rust-eaten pickup truck, hitched up their dusty jeans, spit as one into the gravel, and crossed in front of the Taurus. Valley boys. Straw cowboy hats. Working western boots. Flannel shirts. Rough hands. Rolled cigarettes hanging loosely and pointing down from sun-cracked lips. Classic beer guts, not soft but hard, blossoming imperiously over turquoise-studded silver belt buckles six inches wide and sparkling in the morning sun. Montana watched the beer guts enter the casino.

"You sure he'll be here?" he asked Arthur.

"I'm sure."

"We're early. How about I come in and we'll toss down a few cold ones? Hassle a cocktail waitress. Make her day."

"Guess again. From here on out, the less we're seen together, the better. Besides, you have a lot to do that needs doing quick."

"So, be an unreasonable, antisocial bastard. See if I give a rat's ass. Maybe I'll swing by The Castle on my way back to the big city. Give Emily one last chance to put my back right."

"Karla's not enough?"

"A little R & D, Wolfer. It never hurts to stay in school."

"Get your sorry ass back over the mountain. Get me what I have to have and get it straight . . . or you can do this one yourself."

"It's not my fault they want it done yesterday."

"I don't like plans that change this fast. It's not the way I work. It's not the way *we* work."

"They're paying, they got a right."

"When it's set, pick up the shoot gear from Melody's and get it out here. Brief me then. Call this number." He handed a slip of paper to Montana. "Elder gave it to me when I called this morning. It's the phone at the trailer." Arthur opened the car door and put one foot out. "I'll be there. All day, all night. Twenty-four hours. Call me as soon as it's ready."

Arthur entered the bar area of the casino. Frank was sitting slouched over a small round table talking to Gaileen, the blonde cocktail waitress. Other than two customers at the bar, the lounge was empty.

Gaileen looked up as Arthur approached the table. She winked at him over Frank's shoulder. "Hey, cowboy."

Arthur nodded.

"Your friend's back, Frank. He must be a psychiatrist."

Frank turned. Smiled. "Howdy, partner. Alone?"

"I'm alone." Arthur pulled up a chair and sat down.

"I'm trying to ease Gaileen's heart." Frank reached out and took one of Gaileen's hands and patted the back of it. "Her dog died. Ol' Hump. He was a real good dog. The best guard dog in the valley. That dog was the only critter, man or beast, could put up with Gaileen for more'n two weeks." Further hand patting.

"I'm sorry," from Arthur.

"Me, too." Gaileen's words were far from remorseful. She looked at Arthur and smiled. "Got his ass in front of a Corvette. No big. The monster ate like a horse. Dug up the yard. But he was a buddy. He kept me company. Hey, can I get you something?"

"No hard stuff," said Arthur. "Maybe some tomato juice."

"One tomato juice." Gaileen detached her hand from Frank's

and got up. Frank's hand immediately found Gaileen's bare knee as she stood there by the table. She only looked down, didn't pull away. "Frank, don't you think it's a bit early for that?" Then she looked at Arthur, a solemn, resigned expression on her face. "He's a knee freak." The words were clinical.

Frank frowned at Gaileen's knee. He addressed the kneecap in concerned tones. "What's a nice joint like you doing in a girl like this?"

Gaileen continued to look at Arthur. "That was a joke, see? To Frank, that was a joke."

Arthur nodded.

Frank cackled and released his grip. He slapped the table.

Gaileen tilted her head in Frank's direction. "He's harmless. They'll come for him soon. Every morning he takes his hormones out to play like this. Management says we have to humor him. If he starts to foam at the mouth, give me a wave . . . I'll bring his towel." She headed for the bar to fill the order.

Frank watched her go. "That dog? That ol' Hump?" He nudged Arthur with his elbow. "That dog didn't die . . . he committed suicide."

"Got no TV. Got a radio, though . . . on the counter, by the sink. You'll find a phone and two beds in back. The beds ain't made up. There's sheets in the dresser if you think you got to go first-class. Booze in the cupboard next to the reefer. You ought to be able to find everything else."

"Thanks, Frank. I appreciate it."

"Stay as long as you want. I got me another trailer over to town. My main trailer. I'll be keeping myself there for a few days. Got me a lady. Canada lady. Snowbird is what they's called. Come down this way every year. Bunch of 'em. To get away from that north winter."

Arthur grinned at Frank. "You're not robbing the cradle, are you?"

"Nope. Not that I couldn't handle it. Nope . . . fact is, she's near my age. Talks too goddamn much, but she's good to be with. She sort of got my heart, I guess you could say."

"Good for her."

"Anyone got *your* heart?" Frank didn't look directly at Arthur when he asked the question. The old man pulled back the curtains over the sink and brushed dust off the windowsill.

Arthur didn't answer.

"A woman don't always fit, do they? There's some folks can't afford gettin' soft. Woman makes a man soft. No doubt there. Nope. Some boys can't carry soft . . . not doin' what they do."

Arthur looked at Frank.

Frank stopped pushing dust and turned to meet Arthur's eyes. "Maybe we can just sit and talk some night. I'd like that. Got me a pit out back, a fire pit. Plenty of wood. Maybe we'll smoke a few and work down a bottle."

"Maybe."

"Your buddy got my other number? The number for the phone at the other trailer?"

"No."

"It's all right with me if you figure you should give him that one, too. No reason he should need it. Might be good he has it, though."

"I'll do that."

"Map's in front of the phone book. Not much of a phone book. Red circle marks this place. He needs to pick you up, you can use that map for directions, tell him how to get here."

Arthur nodded.

Frank grinned and winked. "That's so you two boys won't bother me case I get messin' in that snowbird's feathers. Figure I can sneak up on her if I can just get her talkin' fast enough. Woman goes into a trance she starts talkin'. Never seen nothin' like it."

"Good luck."

Frank went to the door. "Reckon I'll need it. Been tryin' to poke her since three winters now. I get two weeks' shot every year about this time. Ain't brought her down yet. Goddamn challenge, that one." He went out through the screen door with a wave.

Arthur watched him drive off. Frank sang aloud in the cab of his pickup truck. Arthur could hear the discordant notes of the man's tuneless effort waver with great energy above the sound of the old truck's engine as the vehicle bumped down the dirt road, lifting a powdery dust cloud that drifted across gray sage and made the sun a brown disk.

*   *   *

At first, Montana had no problem. The late morning traffic heading north from Vegas on 95 was heavy, and the cover was good. But as sprawling housing developments in the northwest sector claimed commuter after commuter, he became uncomfortably aware that only two other vehicles were between himself and the car driven by the mark, by Mr. Michael Patrick Henry.

Montana fell back another half-mile.

After dropping Arthur at the Pahrump casino in midmorning, he'd directed all his energy toward the hit. He went first to the scanner/VOX setup located in the hills above the mark's house and listened to the taped messages on the monitor that recorded the portable phone activity. Most of the tape talk was junk, except for a short segment where the woman, Diane, mentioned to one of her friends that Mike would be going north to shoot on Tuesday.

Only one road went north.

Montana had spotted Henry's car easily.

The mark drove fast. Seventy-five, then eighty as the desert highway traffic thinned to nothing.

Fifty minutes outside the Las Vegas limits, after winding out of a narrow pass, Montana almost lost him. A quick glance left and he saw the mark's car disappearing into the distance heading southwest on 160. Montana continued north until two southbound cars passed by, then turned and headed back toward the cutoff.

Henry's car was no longer visible against the purple bulk of the Amargosa Range. Gone. A sick, angry feeling came to Montana. The ribbon of highway undulated straight and far and was empty to the point where it merged with foothill shadows. He looked at the map on the seat next to him. The road led southwest, then south back toward Pahrump. His trip with Arthur and now the tail had formed almost a complete circle around Mount Charleston and the Spring Mountain Range.

He accelerated to eighty. The Taurus sped over the blacktop. Five quick miles ticked off the odometer. No car. No mark. The thin line of highway took shape in sections before him, but each new vista remained barren of the other vehicle.

Then off to his right he caught sight of a car top moving west, away from the main road. Sunlight flashed off the other's roof and barely pierced the thin scrub brush as Henry's car moved at a right angle to Route 160. Montana slowed. He came to the head of the cut-off, turned onto the secondary road, and stopped next to a modest wooden sign. He read the words, an advertisement for the Cherry Patch Ranch and Mabel's Whorehouse. The paved road led to the two brothels, names familiar to any Las Vegas tourist whose curiosity prompted a usually furtive reading of the spirited brochures available from sidewalk newsracks along The Strip and Glitter Gulch, newsracks that periodically and stoically endured the righteous assaults of visiting church conventioneers whose choice of Las Vegas as their convention destination seemed obtuse to some of the more secular in the general population. Twenty-one miles past the Clark County line, in geographic but certainly not sexual isolation, fantasy and reality did their level best to merge. Montana remembered reading in one of those pamphlets that the two establishments combined to entertain upwards of two hundred thousand men, and some women, annually; he remembered how he thought the word "upwards" funny when he read the phrase to Arthur. Nothing funny now. Henry's car had passed by the brothel lots and was proceeding onto the unpaved extension road leading into the desert, a road that generated telling clouds of billowing dust when any vehicle drove it at any speed. A problem. A real problem. He could find Henry. But Henry could find him.

Montana knew the mark shot every Tuesday and Friday. He'd picked up that much from his earlier stakeout and from the sketchy habit history given him by the buyer. But no one knew where. Not yet. This was the first time he or anyone else had run the tail this far.

He drove past the Short Branch Saloon and came to a spot where the paved road ended. He stopped the car. To the west, a hanging yellow cloud marked Henry's progress across a dry basin. Montana checked the road map resting on the seat beside him. It wasn't specific enough to delineate the patterns of the unimproved desert trails. He opened the glove compartment and took out an NOAA aeronautical chart for the Vegas sector. The detailed terrain and scale information showed that the dirt road Henry traveled cut through a National Wildlife Refuge called Ash Meadows. The trail led across the Nevada/California border and terminated twenty or thirty miles away at Death Valley Junction. Aside from a few small feeder trails, the road had no obvious outlet or switchback. It didn't seem likely to Montana that Henry would be shooting at a spot other than along that road. The time parameters wouldn't allow for it.

He decided to turn back to the saloon and have a cold one. Let the dust settle. Let Henry get set up. Let him relax. If he got to Henry too soon, he'd raise Henry's suspicions.

Michael Patrick Henry couldn't be far.

A brew wouldn't hurt.

The more he thought about it, the more the saloon visit seemed a good strategic move. It might provide a chance to learn some details about the refuge, about who or what might be out there. So far, this looked to him like made-to-order takeout country.

And he wasn't thinking about hamburgers to go.

I I I

"Damn, Mel! That's scary. Where in hell was casino security?" Karla blew cigarette smoke at Melody, but Melody didn't complain. She was relieved to have Karla back, to have someone to talk with. She wasn't going to quibble about cigarette smoke in her apartment after the roller-coaster ride she'd been on the last few days.

"Security? What security? The ones who weren't on break were probably out parading their hairy faces around the customers' lot. You think they give a darn about us? Fat chance. We only work there. They can always get dealers, we're a dime a dozen. So we get mugged and raped and killed . . . just don't bleed on the sidewalk."

"Why do you think you got away?"

Melody reached out and lifted Karla's cigarette and took a long drag on it. "Why? I don't know why. I hit him in the stomach with my elbow. Maybe he got a cramp."

"Right. You're a real threat."

Melody shuddered. "God, I'll never forget that creep. Never. I get sick thinking about it."

Karla pursed her lips, folded her arms, and looked at the ceiling. "Well . . . maybe with a bath, a haircut, a nice suit, some training . . . who knows?"

"Jeez, Karla."

They ate some donuts and drank coffee. Karla talked of her trip to San Diego with Montana. She told Melody about being stopped by the cop and why, and Melody got a detailed description of all the lovemaking, including the stop in the desert on the way over to San Diego. She showed Melody the scrape on her backside. The minutes grew into an hour, then a half-hour more. Karla did all the talking while Melody shined her dealer shoes, made a shopping list, and ironed clothes.

Finally, "Okay, Mel, what the hell gives? How come no wiseass remarks?" A tinge of irritation colored Karla's voice.

No reply from Melody.

"So where's the lecture? That thing last night with those two creeps ain't enough to shut you up like this. You're still in one piece. Cat got your tongue? You're not your usual Mary Poppins, wet-blanket, virgin-queen self. Don't you give a hot toot that I'm acting like an idiot over this guy? Getting sand up my butt on the damn side of the road? Sucking myself silly all the way from Riverside to Barstow like some teenage punk groupie?" She lit another cigarette and deliberately blew a cloud of smoke at Melody, who folded clothes on the ironing board. "I'd feel a hell of a lot better about me and him if you'd try to talk me out of it. You're usually dead wrong, you know. Are you trying to make me nervous?"

"I think it's nice . . . you and him." She stopped folding clothes and stood still, really looked at Karla for the first time since Karla had walked into the apartment. "I think it's nice. I think it could work out. I'm happy for you."

"Christ, the kiss of death."

"I mean it. He's nice. It's so . . . so . . . "

"So what?" and she saw tears build and sparkle in Melody's eyes. But the tears were in a tired face.

Melody looked at the floor. "So . . . simple," and teardrops fell onto the folded pile of cotton on the end of the ironing board.

Karla went quiet. She got up from the couch, put her beer can on the coffee table, and walked over to Melody. The ironing board was between them. She put a hand on each of Melody's shoulders and shook her gently. Karla scrunched her head down to one side so she could see Melody's face. "Hey, kiddo. What's going on?" Serious words, no challenge. "What happened?"

Melody startled them both with a wild sweep of her hand that propelled the freshly folded pile of clothing off the end of the board.

Karla didn't look at the clothes spread in disarray on the rug. She made no comment, only steered Melody past the end of the ironing board and over to the couch. They sat down together, and Karla put an arm around Melody's shoulder and held one of Melody's hands.

"Hey, Mel." Soft words.

Melody began to shake with sorrow and she wept and bent her head forward, and Karla saw all the silver tears fall.

I I I

Montana sat at the bar in the Short Branch Saloon. A middle-aged man at a table along the wall to his left played cards with a younger woman who wore jeans and a white blouse. The woman looked to be about thirty and had a hard but attractive face. Montana wondered if she was a pro and decided she was. The only other person in the place was a slim brunette who tended bar and had been kissing a short, rough-looking cowboy-type goodbye when Montana had come in from the parking lot.

"Take it easy, Sal." And the cowboy had patted her on the behind and gone out the door.

Montana asked the girl for a glass of draft beer.

She brought the drink and took his money. Montana looked at the change she put on the counter and he was surprised at the cost of the round. Cheap. For some reason he couldn't explain, he'd assumed it would be expensive.

"Miss?"

The girl looked up from the sink where she rinsed glasses. The sink was about fifteen feet down the bar, and after Montana spoke she kept working on the half-dozen tumblers until she was finished with them. Then she walked over to him as she dried her hands on a towel. The slow response was not remarkable, but the small delay made Montana feel as though the girl wanted to enjoy or keep private those few seconds of silence before she began again with whatever it was she was going to begin with. Another man.

"Yes?"

"What's out that road?" and he nodded in the direction Henry had driven.

"Out there?" She looked straight at him, eye-to-eye contact. The girl had a lean, angular frame; high cheekbones; shiny hair. She was a raw beauty up close, and, like the price of the beer, that fact surprised him too because he hadn't really looked at her when she brought the drink and then the change.

She waited, studied him for a few moments. Another peculiar delay. "Not much. The gravel road goes through Ash Meadows. The place isn't developed yet. When the state gets some money, it's going to be a national park. There's some mining out there, a few lakes. Some small springs. Bole Spring, Big Spring, Point of Rocks, School Spring. That's where the river comes up."

"River?"

Once again the disconcerting pause. "There's an underground river system that flows under the desert. We're right on top of it. The ground water is thousands of years old; it's called fossil water, and the channels run a hundred miles to the northeast."

Montana listened to her more, watched her talk. No dizzy affectations. A relaxed tone, but no smile. She was articulate and knew what she was talking about. She looked him square in the eye with those coal-black pupils and fed him facts with personable but clipped efficiency. And that weird hesitation. Here in the middle of nowhere, sitting on a barstool and trying to conduct his covert little fact-finding exercise, he realized he was being hypnotized, was witness to one of the most intriguing bits of web-spinning he'd ever encountered. The eyes, the tone, the timing, the stance, the knowledge; what he was feeling was a testament to what she was doing. In thirty seconds, she had roped him. He was suddenly aware that he was in the big leagues and was quietly stunned and full of admiration . . . and he wished to hell he didn't have to chase Henry.

"Anybody out there? Any houses?"

"There's the refuge manager. Sometimes a maintenance guy, too. They show up at the refuge office at Crystal Spring weekdays. Just a cabin." She leaned back against a low shelf that supported the cash register and looked at him, waited eight seconds, then talked again. "The Refuge manager, she lives over in Pahrump. Nobody's there weekends, especially this time of year . . . in the spring and summer, that's when a few tourists show up to look at the hole."

"Hole?"

"Devils Hole. They call it a National Monument, part of Death

Valley, but it's probably the scrawniest monument in the country. It's just a deep pit with some water at the bottom. No trees. No grass. Sand and grit. Hot as hell itself in summer. Colder than outside brass in winter. Most folks get torqued after driving all the way out here to see it."

"What makes a pit special?"

"Fish."

"Fish?"

"Desert pupfish. They have a long name . . . something *diabolis*. I can't remember exactly. The pool is fed by the underground river. They live in that. It's more puddle than pool."

"Fish in the middle of the desert?"

"That's what makes them special. It's the only place in the world where that fish lives; it's special because that pit is the most restrictive environment on earth . . . that's what the government sign out there says. I've been there."

"Devils Hole?"

"That's what it's called. Some names fit."

"Anybody else?"

"A few hunters. They shoot dove, quail, rabbits, that kind of thing. The season runs September to January."

"Hunters." Not a question.

"That's right. A few."

"I'd take the guy with the most money."

Melody sat with her head resting against the back of the sofa. Her eyes were closed, on her cheeks the dry tracks where tears had run. "Don't say that. Money isn't what it's about."

Karla put her feet up on the coffee table and folded her arms across her chest. She put her head back also. "If you can't make up your mind, go for the gold."

"Oh, shut up, Karla."

"Well, I'm not going to sit here and tell you he's too old. My guy is the same age as Arthur. I'm the same age as you. Nope. I won't tell you it's an age thing. But that Mike guy is tossing around the big bucks. Who knows what Arthur's got going for him? Big hat, big boots, no cattle . . . go for Mike."

"That's the stupidest thing I've ever heard."

"You just told me Mike is hot. He's about your age. You never knew sex could be like that, says you. He's nuts for you, says you. I say Arthur's just nuts."

"Do you know what you sound like? Listen to yourself."

"I'm listening. It's Mike."

No reply.

"So, who turns you on?"

"I can't even think when Mike and I make love. It's almost insane ... like feeling everything I ever dreamed I could feel, more than *anyone* could ever feel. I'm so alive it hurts. He takes all I give him and he gives it back to me with fire on it. I feel things I've never even read about. It's like I'm the only female that ever was."

"I rest my case."

Melody was silent. Then she reached over and took Karla's hand. "With Arthur, I'm ... special. I'm ... he needs ... I don't know."

Montana drove slowly. He kept the windows open even though the desert powder came in to coat the seats when the crossing breeze shifted and overtook him. The windows were rolled down so he might hear a telltale shot, an echo, might see the extra distance that the car's glass would obliterate. He drove slowly to keep the folding cloud of dust as low as possible. The big car was new and quiet and it moved west with only the sound of an occasional rock being shot sideways by the press of tire on roadbed.

Four miles. Five. The road curved up from the flat basin into the foothills, climbed over gentle rises of rock more red with iron oxide than white with the alkali of the lakebed below.

In a three-sided valley where wild mustard and sturdy creosote bush mixed with tufts of lean grass, Montana came upon the mark's car. The four-wheel-drive Bronco was parked between two rust-colored boulders near the road, each boulder larger by half than the car itself. He didn't see the Bronco until he was almost next to it.

Montana slowed. A rifle shot cracked in the northern apex of the triangular basin near a stand of broken rock. He kept the car moving and continued out of the basin on the road.

Montana decided to proceed into the refuge proper. The map showed that the wildlife refuge boundary was only one mile ahead.

The place called Devils Hole lay just inside the boundary line. Later, he'd return to the valley and follow Henry's tracks to the spot where the shooting was done. Montana was a tracker, a better tracker than Arthur . . . and Arthur was good. His thoughts went back to his early days, the days before the war, days spent following wolf spoor in the wilderness on his family's ranch. He touched the wolf ear on the cord at his neck. His father paid two dollars for each right ear. Two dollars.

The price of ears had gone up. Way up.

But he missed those days. The ranch boy had come to see things a boy wasn't meant to see, things no one was meant to see. Montana thought perhaps the two-dollar deal was the better deal after all. But going back was not an option.

He would know each step Henry took . . . if he always shot in the same spot . . . where he urinated in the rocks . . . where he sat down to rest . . . where he slept if he napped there . . . where he aimed . . . whether he took home his brass or buried it . . . and what weapon he fired even if the brass was taken home because Montana could understand how shell casings imprinted dirt as well as children understood how snow angels took shape on morning lawns after the first white night of winter.

He drove down a gentle incline and on the right side of the road he saw a brown wooden sign with block-carved letters painted yellow.

He stopped the car and read the sign.

DEVILS HOLE.

And under that a yellow arrow pointing.

Montana came to the place.

One hundred yards from the road sign, down a still more primitive road that led to a small parking area roughed out of dirt . . . he stopped the car. Before him stood a seven-foot-high chain-link fence topped by three strands of barbed wire. The sturdy fence enclosed a square of earth one hundred feet on each side. The fence abutted a rugged shale hill to the north. Inside the area was a sign of thick wood and professional preparation.

IN THE SMALL POOL AT THE BOTTOM OF
THE LIMESTONE CAVERN LIVES THE ENTIRE
POPULATION OF CYPRINODON DIABOLIS, ONE

TYPE OF DESERT PUPFISH—THIS IS THE
MOST RESTRICTIVE ENVIRONMENT OF ANY
ANIMAL ON EARTH.

Montana got out of his car and walked along one side of the fence where the earth was worn into a path. He followed the trail fifty feet and came to a narrow walkway that extended and ended over a steep gorge that angled beneath the walkway and was itself blocked by more steel fencing, making the pool inaccessible. The cut dropped sharply down to the bottom of the pit thirty feet below. Both catwalk and fence traversed the cut on pipe runs, as though the gorge had appeared after the fence was put up. The catwalk was lightly built, and Montana was surprised by its rickety construction, considering the government connection. The whole area seemed unreal, and he had the feeling, perhaps it was the light, that he was standing above a place beyond his time.

From the catwalk, he looked down at a narrow, six-by-forty-foot rectangular pool . . . black water . . . still water . . . water that carried a soft mantle of desert dust . . . water of concealed depth, but seemingly shallow. The east end terminated against a steep rock wall. The girl at the saloon had told him that beneath the east end of the pool was a dropoff leading to a series of underwater caves—caves more than seven hundred feet deep and filled with cold black water where men had drowned in powerful subterranean currents.

He saw no sign of life, no ripples. He knew the fish were tiny, minnow-sized—the girl had told him that—but nothing moved. He stood on the catwalk with his fingers meshed in the metal lattice of chain-link fence and stared. Silence, broken only by the whisper of soft wind on sharp rock, drew in around him. He shivered.

The walls of the hole were vertical rock and, except for the rift that angled sharply beneath the catwalk, seemed unscalable. He wondered how many animals had been lost in the pit. He thought that many must have drowned in that place because the water was there and the walls were steep. He tried to imagine what happened when something fell into that place. Did those unseen fish eat meat? Were they aware? Was there anything that passed for intelligence in that tiny community?

A wave of vertigo came over him; the dry air seemed suddenly thick, and he wondered if the beer he had drunk back at the saloon was bad. His fingers involuntarily tightened in the links. He had a fear of heights, a fear that made him ashamed, a fear he tried to hide from others. He pressed his face against the wire and steadied himself on the flimsy catwalk.

The dark water did not reflect the sky above nor the sides of the pit. Something in Montana's mind shifted, and he had the strange illusion that the black surface below was the eye of something alive. The illusion passed.

The beer, the damned beer.

Montana swore and went back to the car.

"A picnic?" Karla stopped filing her nails and looked over at Melody.

"Tomorrow. On my day off. We made the date last week. Mike said he'd take me shooting."

"Shooting? Shooting craps? Dice?"

"Rifles, shooting rifles. It's like, you know, his hobby."

"You get to watch him shoot? That sounds real romantic."

"I'm going to shoot, too."

"You? You can't even shoot spray paint out of a can."

"I have my own rifle."

"You have your own rifle . . . right. And I own a Sherman tank."

"It's in the bedroom closet."

"I keep my tank parked at the airport."

"I'm not kidding. I'll show it to you. Arthur gave it to me. Like a housegift for letting him stay here."

"Arthur gave it to you? Nice. Some guys give flowers, maybe a bottle of wine. Not Arthur. Arthur gives you a gun."

Melody looked at her. "Not a gun, Karla, a rifle."

Montana studied the imprints in the soil. Henry shot thirty-caliber stuff. There were no spent casings, but the shooting had been done on soft earth, a mix of dirt and sand that even without the full impression of the stepped-on shell told him what he needed to know. Other signs told him that Henry had fired there before, often; he knew it was Henry's spot because of the clues and because a pro needed to shoot with known range, measured distance. He looked at the bluffs. This was measured. This was it.

He sketched the terrain and indicated on the drawing where Henry fired and where that fire was directed. He fleshed in as many details as he thought necessary. He indicated sunline and ambient wind currents. He used binoculars, range finder, and topographical map to establish landmark distances. He looked critically at natural cover in the immediate area and extrapolated Henry's likely escape routes if escape became an option. He did all those things.

He prepared to leave, prepared to cross the basin and select the hide, the position Arthur would use to command an effective field of fire. Montana stooped low and lightly swept a mesquite branch across his own footprints as he backed out of the site.

It caught his eye.

He bent close to the imprint pressed into white sand at the base of a red rock . . . an imprint almost four inches in length from casing rim to lip edge. A fat furrow. He realized he was looking at the impression of a fifty-caliber shell casing. Probably match grade. A 750-grain load. Personnel-effective to fifteen hundred yards and probably a hell of a lot more than that. Some of the new stuff coming out of Phoenix was really pushing the envelope.

Montana stared at the imprint. He began to regard Henry in a new light.

Arthur would have to shoot closer in. A first-shot kill was more important now. With the fifty-caliber involved, the last thing Arthur could afford was a long-range war. Not only did the fifty shoot long, but even at one mile it hit with more power than a .44 Magnum fired three feet away.

A tipped fifty could shoot through trees. Not through the branches. Through the trunks.

27

Tuesday Night

Arthur closed the tattered book on gem-cutting he'd taken from Frank's desk. He put the old book down on the kitchen table, got up, and turned off the radio on the counter. The low rumble of an engine died away in the front yard outside the trailer. Arthur recognized the wheeze of Frank's pickup and went to the door.

Elder stumbled out of the night and brushed past Arthur. "Goddamn that woman to hell! All the way to hell!" He carried a half-empty bourbon bottle and proceeded to the kitchen, where he grabbed an empty tumbler from the cabinet.

Arthur watched him fill the glass.

"You need some bourbon, boy?" The bottle tilted toward him.

"Don't *need* it. I'd like some, though."

"Good." Frank pulled another tumbler from the shelf and poured whiskey. "Take anything with it?"

"Water."

"Get it yourself," and Frank set Arthur's glass next to the sink and sat down at the kitchen table.

Arthur added water to his drink and sat across from Frank.

"No feathers?" from Arthur through a smile.

"Christ! They say air pollution's a threat to the human race. Well, it ain't no threat to her . . . she don't stop talking long enough to take a goddamn breath."

Arthur laughed. "Maybe you've lost a step or two."

Frank glared at him, "Maybe so, young fella, but I had a few to lose." Then he smiled. "What the hell. I'll nail her yet. Stuff a damn sock in her mouth." He shook his head. "Never seen nothin' like it."

They worked on the bottle, three of Frank's drinks to two of Arthur's. Frank rumbled away about opportunities lost, not his but theirs, the women who somehow managed to avoid the wondrous range of his zoological experience. Arthur listened and drank and zinged him whenever Frank left an opening.

His mentor poured a fourth drink and stood up. "Let's go make a fire out back. I don't take to being cooped up like this."

"It's pretty cold out there."

"Drink it up while you got breath . . . ain't no whiskey after death. I say you can write that down, boy." Frank raised his glass in Arthur's face, pushed up from the table, and headed for the back door. "Man don't need but a shot glass full of hurt to put down cold. Write that down, too . . . 'less you don't need to."

The wind-whipped fire danced. A mesquite branch pinned beneath a pine log curled like a closing hand as it bent on itself in the heat. Arthur looked across a flare of orange flame at Frank's silhouette. On the side of the silver trailer, behind Frank, fire shadows danced in wild, silent skirts, and Arthur could not see the features of the man because the trailer bounced back more light than did human skin. In the black night and not so far away, a dog howled.

"You're a shooter," said Frank.

Arthur was still. Only flame and shadow moved.

"You wonder how I know?" Frank's words spread like hot acid through Arthur's mind. Things asleep came instantly alive.

Arthur looked down into the red coals. He drew the serape he had taken from the trailer more tightly around his shoulders. The two men sat cross-legged, one opposite the other, the fire an orange veil between them. "I think I already know," said Arthur. His eyes moved up, and in a gust of flame he saw the glint of firelight reflect from the pair of eyes looking back. "You're a shooter too, aren't you, Frank?"

The shape across from Arthur leaned forward and prodded hot coals with a stick, then moved a burned log to a new position. The face, closer now to the fire, almost one with the blaze, became visible and detailed and washed with orange light. "I shot with the Brits . . . in France, Germany . . . seems like yesterday."

Arthur watched the eyes. Frank stared into the flames.

"You never forget them, do you?"

"Forget who, Frank?"

Arthur saw Frank's nostrils flare and the head jerk back slightly, the exhalation of a derisive laugh aborted and stopped short of making facial muscles move.

Frank ignored the question that needed no answer. "No matter how much bullshit they feed you, no matter how much you get to hate the other guy, if you're close enough to kill, you get to see them in the glass . . . if they're close enough to see, they're close enough to remember." He didn't wait for Arthur to comment. "What we did still has a face, don't it, son? Not like the boys dropping bombs from a plane . . . them and us, we're both doing long-range killing . . . but for us, not long enough." Arthur said nothing and Frank stirred the coals once more. "What do you do with 'em, boy?"

No answer.

"There's some shooters it don't bother none. A few. Not many. Like as not they're dead by now, that type don't last 'cause that type don't quit. Can't stop. End up on the wrong end."

Arthur formed his words with care, "There's still some call for a shooter."

Frank looked up. From his pocket the old man withdrew a brown cigarette and stuck it into a tongue of fire. He withdrew the thing and examined the lit end. He took a deep drag and white smoke billowed out. "Still some call? . . . With the law, maybe. Or pulling a paycheck with some uniformed outfit, mercenary work." Another deep drag. A longer pause. "Not like you're doing."

Arthur made no reply.

"Don't get me wrong. I ain't making judgment. Ain't saying what you do is no good. Not my place." Frank leaned forward. "What I'm saying is, you ain't hard enough. Maybe you was, but you ain't now."

Anger boiled in Arthur, and he thought to leave before it came to no good end.

"I ask you again, boy . . . where do you put 'em? . . . What do you do with 'em? I've seen the look you get. Don't bullshit me."

Then Arthur said a thing that seemed unwilled and uncalled for. "I dream. What do you do?"

Frank smiled. "I get old." Another drag. "And I drink."

Tell him.

Frank nodded. "It gets scarred up. I give it a chance to die."

"It takes a long time, doesn't it?"

"It does that. Especially if you stay doin' it. I guess it makes a difference what you did."

Something seemed to crowd Arthur's mind, seemed to elbow and fight forward. Seemed to take the moment from him.

Tell him.

Frank spoke. "Yes . . . it makes a difference. There's things happen to some don't happen to others." A pocket of air in one of the logs exploded. Sparks flew through the air and bounced off the legs of the sitting men. Frank averted his eyes, looked at the fire. The question came gently.

"Arthur? What did you do?"

"I killed kids."

The words, so unexpected, raped the silent night. They came soft and controlled, but came from his throat with the rancid push of erupted vomitus. His nose stung; his tongue arched up as if to catch the escaped words and triggered the start of a gag reflex; saliva ran, and he felt it coat the inside of his mouth; his eyes burned as though lye soap and raw whiskey were there.

"Kids?" Now Frank looked at Arthur. "You killed kids?" A pause and then with force, "You bastard! . . . Kids?"

"They were dying, Frank! They were being skinned!"

"Kids! How in hell could you do that?"

"Jesus . . . " quick thin tears of rage, ". . . they were being gutted, tortured, cut to ribbons!"

"Not kids. Nothing makes that right."

"You're wrong! Fuck you, Frank, you're wrong!"

"Children."

"So fucking wrong . . . you're so fucking wrong!"

"Go burn in hell."

"Frank, listen to me! You don't know how it was! It had to be done!"

"Fuck you, shooter."

"No! I loved them! I loved them! One minute, one minute was all it took and I loved them!" The words began to live.

"Shooter," repulsing, distancing, degrading word.

"Fucking wrong," from Arthur.

Frank got to his feet, bourbon bottle in hand. Lit from below by flames, his face took on grotesque, fearsome shadows. "WRONG?"

And Arthur scrambled up. "WRONG!"

Frank leaned forward and glared at Arthur. The fire flared and framed his face. "OF *COURSE* I'M WRONG!"

The shouted words stopped Arthur's thought.

"LISTEN TO YOURSELF. OF COURSE I'M FUCKING WRONG!" He stepped around the fire pit and grabbed a handful of serape folds under Arthur's chin and yanked him forward. Nose to nose. Arthur smelled the fog of bourbon and a hint of snowbird perfume. Frank said his words like words were steel. "Just listen to yourself." The bottle lifted, tipped up, was drained inches in front of Arthur's face. Bottle down. "I wish to Almighty God I had a chance to do what you did! I wish I could have done something decent with my shooting!" Frank let go of the cloth, put that powerful arm around Arthur's neck and shoulder, hauled him close, and crushed him in a bear hug filled as much with rage as with compassion. The strength of the man almost raised Arthur from the ground.

Frank released his grip, took two steps backward, and threw the empty bottle high into the night. Far out in dry darkness it thudded onto the sandy earth and bounced and did not break.

Frank turned from the night and looked again at Arthur. "Go to bed, shooter! I'm off to get me some feathered pussy! No way I ain't!" A hint of smile softened the hard lines of his face. "You want bourbon, son, you're shit out of luck 'cause there ain't no more in there. Tough!"

And he stomped off.

28

Wednesday

Where are we going?" Melody asked. She turned and reached back through the opening between the front seats and tried to push down the top of the styrofoam cooler as the Bronco picked up speed and merged with the freeway traffic. She couldn't get the thing to close properly. She lifted off the passenger seat, turned, and knelt on the seat so she could use both hands. Her light print skirt rode up the back of her thighs as she bent to secure the cooler top on the seat behind Mike.

"That's one hell of a shooting outfit." He took his eyes off the road and glanced over at the smooth sweep of legs that rose to disappear beneath the hiked-up hem. The filmy material stretched in a tight line two inches below the curve of Melody's buttocks.

"It's my picnic outfit. You want me to look like a cowboy? I don't have any chaps. All my heavy leather's in the laundry."

"That's definitely not chaps."

The hem tightened more and rode higher. The beginning rise of a rear cheek showed. Bare skin.

"When a girl goes on a picnic, I think she should dress casual, be comfortable . . . don't you want me to be comfortable?"

"If you don't turn around and sit down, you're not going to be comfortable for long. You're going to cause a wreck."

"You don't like my clothes." Injured words.

"Get back here. I like your dress, I love your dress. Now sit down before we get a ticket."

"Okay, Grandma," and she turned around, sat down, and smoothed the print skirt material over her legs. She looked over at him. "What's that?"

"What's what?" his eyes back on the road.

"That bump. What's that bump?"

He looked at his lap. "That's your fault." Eyes front again.

"Oh my, what a nasty man." She leaned over and poked the bulge with a tentative finger. "You like picnics, don't you? I can tell."

Without looking, he reached down and pushed her finger away. "Don't fool with the driver."

"Who's fooling?" She said the words in a serious tone of voice. Then she laughed softly. "Where are you taking me?"

"There's a good spot to shoot about an hour up the road. It's where I usually go. No people."

"Hmmm. No people."

"Up past Mercury. Part of Death Valley."

"Death Valley? Gee, that sounds like a great place for a picnic."

"It *is* great . . . Do you know you don't have any pants on?"

"I don't? Darn! I forgot again! I'm always doing that. Do you want to go back?"

He smiled and shook his head. They drove onto the turn of the connecting ramp off Route 15 and headed northwest on 95.

"Is that your gun on the floor back there?"

"That's right."

"Do you have a big gun, mister?" Little-girl-sounding words.

"Big enough for you, kid." An evil laugh.

"Oh, aren't we special!"

The Bronco sped north through thinning traffic.

▌ ▌ ▌

Montana knocked on the door to be sure. There was no answer. He knew there'd be no answer. He'd called Melody's number three times from the pay phone across the street. He unlocked the door with the key Arthur had given him and stepped into the apartment. The rifle cases were under the couch, as he'd been told.

He retrieved the gun-carries and set them on the coffee table. He was about to leave, then stopped and looked around. The only sound came from the ticking of a wall clock in the kitchen. He felt thirsty, but knew better than to drink anything, even water, because he didn't want to leave any sign, however slight, of his having been there. He wanted to sit down and enjoy the silence and listen to the sound of the clock that reminded him of the clock his father kept in the den back when he was a boy, but that also would have been a mistake for the same reason ... a cushion shifted, a table moved, some small thing inadvertently pushed out of place that a woman, especially a woman, would notice ... all signs, maybe unimportant signs, but signs of trespass nevertheless. He stepped to the kitchen entry and paused to look down the hall toward the bedroom. The urge to look at her bedroom was there, but the shag hallway carpet had been vacuumed and he would have left imprints in the fabric. He stepped into the kitchen. He walked to the sink and looked out the window. He went to the front of the refrigerator and smiled at one of the magnetic message minders stuck on the front that showed an angel with a halo around its head and holding an axe in one hand, the words "I'M A HOLY TERROR" across the base. He saw a toaster with a telephone on it. Next to the toaster on the counter was a notepad. He walked over and looked at the pad. Scribbled on the top sheet were three stick figures, probably doodled there while she talked on the phone. One figure was female with curls drawn around its head. The female figure had the word "Melody" written beneath it. Under one of the other figures, the word "Arthur." Under the third, the word "Mike." Under "Mike" was written "Mike Henry" and under that, "Michael Patrick Henry." Three lines connected the figures and formed a triangle.

Michael Patrick Henry.

I I I

Mike pulled off the road and parked the Bronco between the two boulders. "Let's go, lady. I'll tote the food, you carry the rifle."

He locked the car. She held the black nylon gun case he'd given her, and he picked up the cooler by its folding aluminum handles.

"Follow me, Tonto," he said, and started off across the scrub plain. She fell in behind him.

They walked northeast over basin land that rose in a gentle curve as they proceeded toward an upthrust of rock three hundred yards from the road edge. The air was cool and dry, and the sun shone with bright winter light that warmed them as they walked.

Once, Melody stepped up close behind him and reached out and pinched his backside. "You got nice buns, white man."

"So do you, Tonto." He laughed and didn't turn around.

He unzipped the gun case and removed a muslin-wrapped bulk that was shorter by a third than the rifle Arthur had given her. They knelt facing each other in a spot between slab rocks of different sizes, none more than five feet high. She was barefoot, had removed her sandals and put them on the ground next to the styrofoam cooler. A carpet of thin, wiry grass covered the soft desert topsoil. Three hundred yards away and slightly below them to the southwest she could see the top of the Bronco. Directly west and four hundred yards away was another upthrust of similar rock with two small trees growing there. The two rock outcroppings, theirs and the one to the west, formed a triangle with the spot where the Bronco was parked.

"Is it legal to shoot here?" she asked.

"It's legal. Just about anywhere in Nevada is legal. Behind that other bunch of rocks is the boundary of a wildlife refuge." He nodded at the west outcrop. "I usually shoot here. We're outside the refuge. You can hunt over there . . . quail, snipe, rabbits . . . but you need a license. This is okay."

"Anybody else out here?"

"Not likely."

"Then who will save me if you decide to take advantage of a helpless, innocent girl?"

"No one will save you. I'll rape you and scalp you and take your money."

"The scalp part sounds scary."

"Do you have any money?" He smiled and placed a box of rounds on top of the gun case.

"You can have my money right now."

He began to unwrap the muslin. "What about the rape part?"

"Any time you're ready, mister. Just tell me what to do." She raised up on her knees and pulled up her skirt to a level above the middle of her thighs.

He laughed and finished unwrapping the weapon. She settled back down on her haunches, the back of her bare heels against her dress.

Her heart skipped a beat when she saw the rifle. It was exactly like the one in her apartment, the one Arthur had given her, except that the butt end of this one was folded forward along the body of the weapon. Everything else was the same as far as she could see. Even the safety release in the forward edge of the trigger guard was the same. A feeling of confidence, then anticipation, took her.

Mike held the rifle in one hand and with the other pushed down on a round black button at the rear top end. The stock swung back and snapped into position, making the rifle look like a rifle.

"This is a 5F Mini-14."

"A Ruger," she said, trying to sound nonchalant.

He looked up. "That's right. A Ruger." She tried to keep her eyes on the weapon, only glanced quickly up, then back down. The glance had revealed an expression of mild surprise on his face.

"Got to watch that safety," she said. "It's too close to the trigger housing." She nodded her head wisely, eyes on the rifle.

He turned the weapon so one side faced up and he regarded the safety design in silence. He didn't say anything. He looked up at her again.

"You shoot a lot?" she asked.

He waited a few moments before answering. "Not too much. I usually shoot an HK-91, sometimes a McMillan M-88, the fifty-caliber. Five-shot, fixed magazine." He kept looking at her.

Melody trapped one side of her lower lip between her upper and lower teeth and looked very thoughtful. She nodded a few more times and stroked her chin between thumb and forefinger. "Hmmm. McMillan. Yes. A McMillan. Very nice."

Again, he didn't reply.

"You buy it new?"

"Buy what new?"

"The McMillan." She'd already forgotten the numbers.

"Yes, I bought it new."

"Expensive." A reasonable guess.

"Yes. Expensive."

"What made you pick that one?" She didn't look him in the eye.

"What one?"

"The McMillan."

Another moment of silence. "It breaks down quick, which makes it easy to carry. It's reliable. It's lightweight, too."

"How much?"

"How much?"

"Yeah," she said. "How much does it weigh?"

"Less than twenty-five pounds."

"More like twenty."

"Twenty?"

"Twenty pounds." She felt safe with that. Twenty was less than twenty-five. She nodded again.

He tilted his head slightly and looked at the rifle in his hands. Then squinted at her. "Do you like to shoot reds or blues?"

Oops! What the hell does that mean? "Mostly reds."

"Reds . . . why?" It was his turn to nod his head.

"Oh, they're not so loud," with a flip of her hand.

"Not so loud?"

"Yeah."

"What kind of range do you get with reds?"

"Range? Range. Maybe three miles."

"Three miles? That's pretty good."

"That's with the wind." She scratched her ear.

"With the wind." A statement. He rested the rifle across his thighs. "I like the plaids."

"The plaids? Not me."

"Not you?"

"Couldn't get me to shoot plaids on a bet."

"Melody!" Exasperation in his voice.

"Mike?"

"Melody, there's no such damn thing as plaids."

"Hmmm."

"*Or* reds! *Or* blues!"

"Who says? Maybe you don't know everything."

"I know there's no such thing as reds and blues and plaids."

She reached out and picked up a loaded magazine. She gave him a challenging stare. "Bet I can shoot better than you."

"No such thing. No reds, no blues, no plaids. I made them up."

"What do we shoot at?"

For a moment he didn't seem to know what to say. He shook his head, then fastened the shooting sling into the hook rings of the Ruger. "Skins."

"Skins?"

"Rubbers. Condoms."

She looked at him.

"They make great targets . . . like balloons. We'll blow some up and I'll stick them on that bank out there."

"Sure. I bet I know how we're going to blow them up. That's my job, right? This is a trick. You have some sort of device to hold them, I suppose?"

He laughed. "*We'll* blow them up." He took a cellophane box from the gun case.

"You go first." His words carried a hint of smugness, but his eyes showed doubt as he handed the rifle to her. She had him off-balance.

She took the weapon and looked at him for a second. Then she stretched prone on the soft grass. One hundred yards away to the east, on a vertical bank, a population of inflated white condoms bobbed in the light breeze. Melody wrapped her left arm in the sling as Arthur had taught her. She rolled onto her left side and extended the Ruger upward and outward, then brought the butt end of the stock into her shooting shoulder. She settled into position and chambered a round. She aimed. "Is this piece of junk zeroed?"

The reply was delayed in coming. "Yes. It's zeroed for one hundred yards."

"Wind?"

"No drift."

"You sure?" Still sighting. "I don't want you making me look bad."

Melody slowly pulled her right leg forward. The move wasn't entirely meant to take the pressure off her shooting side. She felt the hem of her skirt ride high on the backs of her thighs.

Three shots. Three broken targets.

Mike said nothing.

She rolled left and unwrapped. With her eyes still on the target bank she extended the rifle to him. "Your turn." Her words dripped disinterest. "Watch your elevation. The zero is a bit high." She had no idea if it was high or not, but she couldn't resist saying the words.

▌ ▌ ▌

Montana tried to figure out the connection between the girls and Henry. It was a connection he'd written off to chance back when he'd checked out Henry's itinerary on Sgro's tracking report, the track that included the stop at the pizza parlor where Karla worked. Henry had gone there for a reason, not for a pizza. And Melody must have been that reason. She must have given Karla a ride to work that day.

It was starting to make sense. Henry was a sports bettor and was hurting the casinos big-time, real big-time. Somehow he was anticipating the line moves; it was the only way it could be done. Even the wiseguys couldn't do what he was doing. The oddsmakers made too good a line, especially in the pros where the teams were basically the same from year to year. Henry needed some sort of inside information. Melody worked in a sports book. Henry's name was in her apartment. That had to be it.

How did Karla fit in with the scam? Did she know? She didn't fit in, he decided. She just happened to be there. She and Melody had known each other for years. That part he knew for sure.

But there was a lot that wasn't sure. Melody seemed too damn straight from what he'd seen of her, too damned real. If she was part of the big-buck action, where in hell was the money? The lady worked her butt off, lived from paycheck to paycheck, drove a tin-can van, counted her change. It didn't figure.

Unless she was good, damn good.

Or didn't know.

Montana didn't like what he was feeling. He was cutting himself off from Arthur, not being up-front. The fact that Henry had a kid. The extra cash he'd weaseled out of Sgro for himself. Now the business about the fifty-caliber, which he'd already decided he was going to keep quiet about rather than take the chance Arthur might back off. This job meant too much. It was his ticket out, the stake he needed to give himself and Karla a real start. He knew Arthur could take Henry down, Arthur could take any son of a bitch down.

And something else ... he was certain the stuff about Henry being a meth pusher was bullshit ... he'd checked with his court connection in San Bernardino. Nothing. Even if there'd been a dismissal or a plea bargain or a nolo ... there would have been something. Nothing showed.

There were too many aborts. Given any of those facts, Arthur would pull out. Arthur had to have a reason to kill. It was how he was.

Too late now.

Just do it.

Get it over with.

"Bet I can get five in a row. One dollar."

"You're on." He watched as she bellied down on the sand and aimed. "Don't let the pressure get to you, hotshot," he said.

"Make it two dollars." She moved her right leg forward, and the hem of her skirt pressed tightly against the rise of her buttocks. She fired. A condom disappeared. She bent her shoot-side leg still more, and the pressure of the material suddenly eased as the lower edge of her dress rode completely up over her backside. The warm sun and cool air played over her naked skin. She fired again. A second target disappeared in a splash of copper-colored dirt. Then a third shot. A fourth. Hits. As she lined up for the fifth shot she felt him move on the sand between her legs, and almost in the same moment his hardness pressed at her sex. The front sight wavered, and she had to use all her concentration to put the peg back on line. She began to move her trigger finger back, but stopped and inhaled sharply as with one endless, sensuous thrust he completely ran the hot, waiting, wet depth of her.

She steadied the rifle once more. His strong hands were flat on the grass-covered sand on either side of her shoulders.

"Some guys will try anything to win a lousy two dollars," she said; soft words, but words half an octave higher and wavering.

The fifth round ripped the ground ten feet short of the bank.

"Keep shooting. Let's see how good you are when the pressure's really on." He started to move ... slow, long, deep strokes.

She lined up again and fired. Halfway to the target red rocks cracked and spun into the air. Her hips and the swelling curve between pushed against the earth.

"Nice shot." His words were harsh and strong. Male sounds.

She pressed the center of her body down, and the unyielding world beneath connected with her center. Sweet sensation rose in shivering waves.

Shot number seven plowed through shale ten feet in front of the rifle barrel and whined high into the air. She dropped the weapon on its side and spread her legs as far as she could and let the earth and him take her.

They lay together on their backs, naked and looking up at a powder-blue sky. He held her hand. "You owe me two bucks," he said. "You missed the fifth shot."

She squeezed his hand. "Double or nothing?"

He laughed and squeezed back.

Then she thought of Arthur. She wished he could have seen how she hit the targets. He would have been proud of her.

29

Wednesday Night

"C ongratulations." Arthur leaned forward onto his elbows. The kitchen table squeaked. "How'd you do it?"

Frank took a drag on a brown cigarette, then turned and spit a shred of tobacco onto the floor. "Earplugs."

"Earplugs?"

"I should have thought of it before. All that damn talking was breaking my concentration."

Arthur sipped bourbon. "Well, was it worth it?"

"You bet your ass. Tightest damn run I ever had. That thing hadn't been riled up in years, by the feel of it. I figure no one's been able to break the goddamn sound barrier till me."

"She ever quiet down?"

"Not for one second. Hummed along like a wet hornet." He spit another piece of tobacco. "Not till she went over the top. Just like a runaway diesel. I reckon she was pushing two hundred words a minute up to that point . . . 'course I couldn't hear too well."

Arthur smiled.

"She bit me." Frank turned his head to one side and showed his neck. "See it? That's a major league hickey, son, you can write that down. She put it on me right after. While she was talking, too." He turned back to Arthur. "I been showing it off over to the casino. Ain't answering no questions, though. I ain't the type to kiss and tell."

"You must have heated her up pretty good."

"Heated her up? You could have peeled paint with that thing. I can pick 'em, I can. Write that down."

"Are you going to keep after her?"

"You think I'm going to let that go? After all my work? Not after I got the secret! A man needs a good woman at my time of life." Frank fixed his eyes on Arthur. "Got you a woman, boy?"

Arthur nodded. "Maybe."

Frank picked up the bottle and filled both glasses. "You be damn careful, then."

"What's that mean?"

The old man sat back in his chair. He looked across the table for a long moment. "You want it straight?"

Arthur nodded.

"You ain't fit. It'd kill a *real* woman to try to bring you back from where you're at."

Arthur said nothing.

"I seen it. You ain't ready. More'n likely, you ain't noplace *close* to ready. Might never be." He crushed the brown cigarette into a clamshell ashtray. "A woman lives by soft things, little things. That's what makes 'em special. You got to be able to help 'em over spots that don't seem like nothing to you." He fired up another smoke. "You got no room for that. I seen it. You still got one foot in hell." He leaned forward. "She'd have to throw in with you or you'd have to throw in with her. That would be one long stretch, either way." He took a large swallow of bourbon. "If you tried to meet her halfway, you'd lose the edge. You can't afford to lose no more edge. Not yet." Frank drank again. "Ever see that car over to Whiskey Pete's, son? That Bonnie and Clyde car? All them bullet holes?"

"I haven't seen it."

"Go see it."

They sat on wooden steps and leaned against the trailer front. Two hours passed. The night wind was cold but came out of the north from the other side of the trailer, and the drink was enough to keep them warm.

"Some boys, they try to wait it out," said Frank. "If nature sees fit, she sort of dazes 'em . . . lets 'em be. Those boys don't ask questions, they just try to get along. Others? They keep looking back like they can change what happened. They're trying to move time around. That's a real hard thing to do, boy, move time around." Frank hiccuped. "The killing weren't their doing, anyhow, not really . . . wouldn't have done no killing if there weren't no war first." Another hiccup. "Rememberin's okay, but a day comes you got to get out of bed and start over." Frank drank again. A gust of wind howled around the end of the trailer and made small sticks move. "Sooner or later, a person has to look at things real hard and decide that fixin' tomorrows beats fixin' yesterdays."

The remark made Arthur turn. Frank was looking at him.

Frank laughed a small laugh and looked away. "Listen to me, boy. Hootin' like an ol' hoot owl. Good liquor, ain't it? What the hell was you askin'?"

"I didn't ask anything."

"Seems you was askin' me something." Frank hiccuped again. He was fading fast. One more hiccup, and then he emptied his glass with a mighty guzzle and slid off the step onto the ground. "Go get me a blanket, boy, I just run down."

30

Thursday

Montana crouched in the rocks overlooking Henry's tract home. He activated the tape monitor and began to play back the recordings. He was irritable and nervous. He cursed the fact that he didn't have access to the mark's hardwire phones . . . things would have been a good deal easier. As he listened to rambling gibberish about department store sales and kids' toys, he used a stick of sage to free up a crusted glob of white bird droppings on top of the scanner cover. In the center of the dung scab was a soft core of ooze. The vile yellow slime smeared across the black vinyl case. He swore.

" . . . and, can you believe it, I left all my coupons in the car . . . "

A six-inch banded gekko scurried from under the tape recorder and darted between Montana's legs. The sudden movement of the lizard made him jump, and he hurt his hand on a chunk of shale as he tried to maintain his balance.

" . . . She was a holy terror . . . I thought the dentist was going to have a canary! I don't see how they can work on kids, do you? . . . "

He crouched down again and saw that in jumping away from the lizard, he had kicked sand into the bird goo.

". . . Have you tried that brownie mix? . . . "

He looked for some leaves to wipe off the mess. No leaves.

". . . Why don't you bring them over here tomorrow? . . . Mike is going shooting again Friday; we'll have the place to ourselves, just us and the kids . . . Make it ten o'clock, he'll be gone by then . . . "

Montana nodded. *Friday. Tomorrow.* He turned off the switches on the recorder and the scanner. He packed the equipment into his knapsack. *Fuck the birdshit.*

He left the mountain.

"Take Friday off." The shift boss did something with his mouth that tried to be a smile. "You had a rough night Monday. I guess we owe you one." Pinstripes. Black tie. Dead eyes, each centered by a sliver of steel.

"I can work." Melody looked at Lou, then back to the suit.

Lou smiled and put a hand on her shoulder. "I'm taking your shift. Don't give me a hard time."

The shift boss nodded.

"It's better you take the day off," said Lou. "That fat guy? One of those two who gave you a hard time Monday? He's coming back tomorrow. He called the admin office and complained. Says he's going to sue the casino for tossing him out on his ass."

The steel eyes of the boss went to diamond, cold diamond. "The gentleman will be straightened out. Nothing to worry about. The cameras have it. He threw the first punch."

Lou shook Melody's shoulder gently. "No reason for you to be here." He smiled. "It might start a ruckus. Besides, the fat guy is huffing and puffing about Security doing something to his friend. He hasn't seen him since Monday night. Says it's the casino's fault."

"I'd rather work." Melody put her hand over Lou's. "Really, I would, I need the money."

The alloy eyes went to Lou, then back to Melody. "Miss, we don't want you here tomorrow. Read my lips. You have the day off." About-face; the suit walked away.

I I I

"This isn't exactly resort living, is it?" Montana surveyed the barren land surrounding Frank's trailer. He flipped his cigarette onto the ground and set the stock end of the gun cases on the toe of one boot.

Arthur looked where Montana was looking. "It grows on you."

"So does fungus. Where do you want these babies?"

"Bring them inside."

Arthur studied the map and the sketches. "When does he show?"

"He should be in the rocks sometime after eleven in the morning. That's if he doesn't stop at one of those Crystal City whorehouses for a hum job."

"What does he shoot?"

"NATO 7.62, standard, centerfire. Maybe a scoped HK-91."

"Five- or twenty-shot magazine?"

"Don't know. I think five but you better figure twenty. I didn't find a lot of brass sign ... I don't think he's a hoser, but figure twenty."

"Wind?"

"Not a factor. It's a shallow basin. Prevailing wind is out of the northwest, but it's blocked by that ridge."

"Sun?"

"It's his sun, but it won't be in play after eleven."

"He parks here?" Arthur touched a mark on the map next to the graded road.

"That's right. You'll see two boulders ten yards off the berm. He leaves his Bronco between them, more or less out of sight till you're right on top of it."

"Where's the nearest set of ears?"

"Eight miles east to the highway. Four miles northwest to the refuge cabin. The wildlife manager is a gal, Susan something, she lives in Pahrump ... she won't be there Friday. You got the place to yourself unless some tree-hugger gets loose. I don't think you'll be crowded. The place is dead till March."

"Air?"

"Not as dry as you'd think. Probably because of the reservoir and all the springs just over the ridge. Even though it looks like high desert where you'll be shooting, the place used to be a damn marsh. There's still a river under it."

"This stand of rock with the two trees. That's it? That's my hide?"

"It puts you four hundred yards west of him. You back out by going west over the ridge and down into the refuge. The border is about a mile in back of your position. Straight west. You can put the car somewhere in the refuge. There's plenty of cover there, lots of trees and washes. I marked a few spots . . . depends on how much hiking you want to do."

"Secondaries?"

Montana paused. "Not much to choose from unless you want to stay on the ridgetop and shoot seven hundred yards." He grinned. "Or get in his shoot site and wait for him to come to you. I don't know how accurate you'd be at six feet . . . probably miss the bastard."

"And leave a lot of footprints."

"Use the primary. It's you, Wolfer."

"So that's it." Arthur kept his eyes on the map.

"That's it."

Arthur looked up, looked into Montana's face. "No . . . that's *not* it."

Montana froze. He met Arthur's stare and did not blink, but his eyes were in retreat. *He knew! The fifty-caliber? The kid? The bogus history? The money?* He waited.

"This is the last one, isn't it? You're going to go with her."

Montana's mind went in two directions at once. Relief battled guilt. He looked away, looked at the map on the table. "You're nuts, pal. You been out here talking to bushes too long. How in hell do you come up with that bullshit?"

Arthur watched him.

"Yeah, I get along pretty good with her. Maybe I'll go after her someday." The defensive tone disappeared. "You'll be the first to know. Fuck you."

Arthur looked at him in silence, then nodded. "Where do I drop you off?"

"Give me a ride back to town. Pahrump. I got myself a room across from the casino. Room 134. Want to check my key, coach?" He fumbled in his pocket, pulled out a room key on a plastic disk, and dangled it in the air.

Arthur didn't look at the key. He looked at Montana.

*   *   *

Frank didn't come out to the trailer that night. Arthur used the twilight hour to go over the weapons. Then he sat at the table and studied Montana's sketches and committed the terrain map to memory. He folded the map so the area of the shoot faced out and placed it in the bigger gun case.

He ate an apple.

He went to bed.

It came toward him. Across the red sand. Arthur waited.

Six feet away it stopped. Light from the glowing ether made the face of the other take shape, and Arthur saw features that were like his own . . . only leaner, twisted, gaunt. The other was alone. Without being asked, the form made words that answered Arthur's question. "The boy will not be here."

It was not Arthur's place to speak, and he kept silent.

"I did that thing. I pulled out its tongue as you wanted. I cut it off with its own teeth. I put the body in the trash dumpster."

Arthur nodded slowly.

"But I will not do it again. I do not have to do it again."

Am I alone?

"Yes."

You know what I do tomorrow?

"Yes."

31

The Last Round

The timber wolf came in from the northeast. The hunting had been difficult, only a few rabbits and a lame bobcat in the last week. Water had been there in salty pools because the hard desert pan was holding the winter rain longer than usual. Although the drinking caused sharp, cramping pains to rack his gut, it had been enough to give him strength and keep him on the move.

In three weeks the wolf had covered better than 150 miles from the western edge of the Kaneb Plateau through the Virgin Mountains to the eastern boundary of the Ash Meadows Refuge. He traveled mostly during the nights, except for two days when hunger made him use the late morning hours to press on in search of meat. He hesitated a full day waiting to cross the hard ribbon of highway where lights moved through the night, had waited alert and puzzled and hungry until before dawn, when the desert road was silent.

He was the alpha male, the only survivor of his pack of seven. He had been unable to make the injured ones move after the noise from the sky had struck them down, after the men on horses had come to run the last two pups to earth. In the first days, fear and instinct drove him away from the place of the killing, drove him west because there was no option, but soon the need to find habitat that might sustain his need for food and water took charge of his direction. The land had been barren and cruel, and twice he stopped to dress with tongue and teeth sharp cuts in the pads of his forepaw.

The east boundary of Ash Meadows lay before him.

The wet smell of fresh water laced the air. He breathed the rich scent of prey. He heard the bird noises. The hard night was over, and though the need to feed was strong, the need to rest was stronger. Perhaps this would be his place.

He marked the shaded edges beneath a desert willow with urine, then curled up and slept.

In his fragmented dream the timber wolf heard once more the terrified yelps of his little ones as they died on the red sand far away.

▎ ▎ ▎

Arthur drove thirty feet down a curved spur off the graded road. He stopped the car in a stand of honey mesquite where it wouldn't be seen. He penciled a note on a piece of paper saying that he was taking photographs for a nature magazine and left the dated note pinched beneath a windshield wiper blade should someone chance upon the car. From the trunk he removed the M24 Remington sniper gear in its black carry. He put the camera and binocular straps over his head and adjusted them so they were comfortable around his neck. The gun case sling went onto his left shoulder, and he moved it to a position that allowed him to carry the case vertically and hidden by the long axis of his body. He walked out of the wash to the graded road and headed east toward the place where he'd shoot.

The sun was half-risen above the hill in front of him. It was a few minutes past seven. The site was two miles distant, one mile up a gentle grade to the sign with the yellow arrow pointing toward Devils Hole, then another mile to the valley beyond, the basin where Henry shot. The air was cool. The first rays of sun warmed his face.

As he walked, his mind was not idle but took in every detail of terrain and sky. He looked at the land and mentally recorded ground profile, potential cover, and backout routes. He stopped frequently and looked behind him to be sure he knew the land, since it would look different coming back. From the sky he gathered information for the shoot. The direction of cloud movement. The signs of wind currents in the way small birds flew, beating north, gliding south. And there was wind. Even in that usually calm hour after sunrise, there was wind.

When he came to the sign that read Devils Hole, he looked left at the fenced square by the cliff and halted. He put the dimensions of that place in his memory. He thought to walk the few hundred feet from the graded road to the pit, but decided against it and continued on.

At the crest of the final rise, Arthur stopped once more and removed the topographic map from the gun case. For the next five minutes he turned through 360 degrees, holding at each quarter-turn to match the land with the map. The east sector, the basin where the killing would be, took most of his attention.

He studied the near rock pile, the one he was to shoot from. The cover was good. The two trees growing there were of a type he did not know, but were squat and thick in their trunks. With the binoculars he examined the upthrust, then let the glasses travel to the place where Henry would be. All was as Montana had described it. A shallow basin sheltered by a high ridge to the north. Two rock towers, one on the east side of the basin and one on the west side, like a pair of granite forts, each twenty feet high and four hundred yards apart. He swung the glasses south and found the boulders where the Bronco would be parked. The killing-field triangle was populated by creosote bush and saltbush scrub. No other trees. Soil showed where wind had rubbed the land, and tufts of short, thin grass claimed most of the rest of the surface except where spills of flat red rock were scattered on the earth like oversized mah-jongg tiles.

Arthur spent twenty minutes studying the high ridge that formed the north boundary of the area. The ridge was irregular and mostly rock, and he could see how the wind had moved with great strength through that high place—a place where nothing grew. He looked at the clouds again and looked for birds flying through the air in the basin.

He saw no birds. The birds were gone.

He couldn't find the wind. Wind was critical. At four hundred yards, even a ten-mile-per-hour cross-wind would push his .308

round thirteen inches off-line. Through the binoculars he examined the area between the two rock towers. Two-thirds of the way along his projected line of fire, he saw it.

A drift of fine sand. The sand was rippled toward the ridge against the prevailing northwest wind above. A reverse wind pattern was not unusual below a ridge, but its presence made him uneasy, and the fact that he'd discovered it was not enough to dissolve the discomfort.

He lowered the binoculars and stood motionless, aware once again of the changes that came with age. Thirty years ago he would have simply cranked all the parts of the shooting parameters into a formula and gone about his business, confident, positive. Now he wondered. And no one was there to force the attitude of being sure; no young, awed trainee whose presence would make the older man young again in manner because old men don't let young men see doubt.

He moved down to his hide and melted into the rock.

And waited.

Melody had plenty of small stuff that needed doing . . . hang the new picture, take the blender to the fix-it shop, scrub the crud out of the refrigerator where the milk carton had leaked. The unexpected day off might be better used, but she wanted to get out of the apartment, get out and escape the memories there. The image of the fat slug and the thought of him bitching about her to the casino people made her uncomfortable, even afraid.

What to do?

She thought of the Ruger in the bedroom closet. What if that lumpy, evil man tried to find her? The idea seemed feasible; he'd ambushed her once, he might do it again. Could she shoot the creep if he tried to get her? Shoot him with the Ruger? She tried to reason the fear away . . . after all, the casino knew what he'd done . . . she'd told Security and the shift boss . . . the slug would be a fool to try anything. Still . . .

She wished she felt more confident with the weapon. Shooting with Arthur or with Mike was one thing . . . shooting by herself was something else.

She made her decision. She knew how to get to the place Mike had taken her. On her own she'd learn to handle the rifle better, maybe practice shooting at something up close, make believe it was the slug. Driving north to the refuge would kill two birds with one stone . . . she'd get out of the house and she'd get more familiar with the weapon.

"Why the heck not?" she asked the Hummel figurine.

The little fellow's smile beamed back from below the edge of his green umbrella.

Mike Henry slowed to make the turn that would take him past the low buildings that fronted silver trailers where working girls made ready to sleep alone after another night of enterprise and tolerance. He looked in the rearview mirror to assure himself the weapon carries didn't shift position as he applied the brakes. The barrel end of the PSG-1 case shifted slightly, then stopped moving as it came up against the bulk of the fifty-caliber M-88.

He turned onto the cutoff.

I I I

Beneath the desert willow the big wolf stirred. Four hours had passed in sleep. Hunger pinched his belly. He raised his nose and tested the air, smelled for water. That first. Then meat.

The cold water at the spring edge was sweet. The soapy taste of alkali and the harsh grit in the shallow desert pools he drank from during his long trek were absent. And there beside the water he trapped and ate a vole. He left nothing of it, then drank again.

Once more, he tested the air. Only the cold memory of horse scent came to him, horses once there but there no longer. No wild burro, either. Instinct told him that one or the other should have been in this place of water . . . but there was neither.

He turned and loped toward the dark lift of ridgeline to the southeast. His world was shades of gray. But nose and ear told him that this land beneath his silent paws was rich with fowl and rabbit, that ancient water waited in clean deep pools, and that the fearsome two-legged ones who killed without eating what they killed were not many. He smelled coyote and their leavings and their mating musk, and didn't smell the smell of his own kind . . . no female to take, no male to challenge . . . and if that beast knew loneliness he knew it then.

He began to climb the rising slope to the ridge crest. A gust of north wind pushed his fur forward in dark silken waves.

Michael Patrick Henry locked the Bronco and shouldered the weapon containers. The black carry that held the M-88 was stubby and unriflelike because that particular model was broken down into its portage mode. The Combo .50 was designed for Navy SEALS, who required a breakdown version to make transporting that lethal firepower more manageable. Henry walked away from the car and headed toward the rise of rock where he would shoot.

From his hide, Arthur watched the man cross the basin. He saw the shape of the .308 case on the man's shoulder and knew what it was. He was not able to decipher the other pack, but supposed it to be spotting gear and rounds, perhaps target material.

Arthur crouched behind a round boulder five feet wide, nested between the facing slabs of rock that formed the west tower. The wind-twisted pair of trees, the only two in the basin, were ten feet behind him. Henry moved across the land toward the east tower. Taking Henry out on the basin floor would have been easy, a prey without protection and targeted from above. But Arthur knew that couldn't be done. He'd have to go down into the valley and retrieve Henry's body, drag it to cover, and that would leave tracks an imbecile could follow. No option there. Take him in the shoot site. Take him as planned.

But Arthur didn't like the wind. It was gusting, and the air was very dry. He glanced at the ridge. Small things shifted and skittered . . . dead plant parts, twigs, grains of sand.

He snapped open the scope covers.

Mike set the shoot gear on the wiry grass. He looked east, away from Arthur's position. He looked at the sky, looked at a small bird that crossed the basin, looked at the way the tops of creosote bushes moved in the building breeze.

He uncased the PSG-1 with care and laid the rifle on top of its empty carry so it was protected from the sand. A gust of wind threw bits of leaf against his chest, and he covered the rifle with a sheet of plastic to shield it from the blowing debris. He stood and looked for a place to set up the fifty-caliber M-88, some spot where it would be sheltered by one of the jumbled rock slabs.

Arthur had watched Henry remove the PSG-1 from its container. Through the binoculars he could see it was not a weapon in the HK class, the butt blunt and in the shape of a square, the pistol grip exaggerated and flanged, the forward support-outline parallel, not tapered. But the sun, though not directly in his eyes, still blotted out fill-in detail. Arthur saw only the black profile.

Then Henry rose and carried the other bag into a break in one of the rock walls. Arthur couldn't see there. The upthrust was similar in formation to his own hide, with tall slabs facing and in the same plane as those he crouched between, but over there more broken blocks of stone littered Henry's site, and the amount of rock sticking above the earth was more.

When Henry came back out of the shadow, the bag he carried was empty and folded. Arthur could see that and wondered.

Melody held the steering wheel with both hands. Keeping the van on the freeway in the quartering north wind was proving to be a full-time job. Despite the difficulty she was having staying in her own traffic lane, she took one hand off the wheel and reached into the ashtray innards. She pushed in on the cigarette lighter. In the depth of a grocery bag on the seat beside her, from beneath three cans of diet soda and a bag of Poppa Bill's Potato Puffs, she located and extracted a pack of cigarettes. As she nibbled open the pack with her teeth, the lighter popped out. She pushed it back. It immediately popped out again. She finished opening the cigarettes, then tapped the batch of tightly packed smokes against the edge of the wheel. When no ends came forth she tapped harder, and five of them ejected from the pack, fell to the floor, and rolled around under the brake pedal.

She stared straight ahead.

By the time she reached the 160 cutoff that ran southwest from Route 95, she'd managed to get a cigarette going, but only after breaking its predecessor in half on the rim of the glowing lighter when a gust of wind pushed the van onto the road shoulder.

She slowed and turned onto the empty stretch of Route 160.

*   *   *

Mike Henry lined up on a talc stripe three hundred yards to the east. He centered the Hendsoldt cross-hair on the vertical white slash.

Arthur lined up on the back of Henry's head. The target was still. Arthur dropped the M3A's Duplex reticle a few millimeters to intersect the imaginary line between the earlobes that would center Henry's brainstem.

Henry fired. Arthur did not.

The wavering mirage lines shimmering off sand cooked by hot, dry air had reversed direction to the left in Arthur's scope as he started to squeeze down. As Henry shifted position for his second shot, Arthur concentrated on the mirage effect, tried to time the periods of reversal that revealed the shifting wind between the two rock stands. He ignored Henry as the man lined up and fired a second time into the talc. The wind pushed the lines up and past vertical, and they laid over to the right, laid flat, indicating a cross-wind of ten miles an hour or more.

In his prone position Arthur kept the reticle targeted over Henry's brainstem and waited to catch the dancing heat film at the moment of pure vertical, at the moment when the .308 projectile would fly true.

The moment came. The lines swung straight up, even hesitated in that position for delicate seconds. The sight picture was steady on the back of the target's skull as Henry went motionless over the PSG-1 in the act of readying his third shot. Arthur began to squeeze back on the trigger. His breathing halted in the middle of an inhalation. His weld was solid against the stock. The sling was tight and steady. The brace point on the rock was solid.

But he didn't fire.

He thought of Melody. Her face floated in his mind. The sharp realization of what he was doing and how it was a thing she could never understand stopped the trigger action in its travel. That thing he hoped would happen between him and her had no chance against what he was doing. No chance at all.

The heat waves tilted slowly left and laid down once more as Henry fired a third time. The detonation of his shot reverberated around the basin, and Arthur closed his eyes and rested his forehead on the stock. The trigger drifted forward as the finger pressure eased off.

In a darkness tinged red by sunlight that infused his closed eye-lids, Arthur, head down, willed Melody away and forced the mem-ory of Montana's words to come . . . how this animal he was sup-posed to kill killed others with his drug trade, killed young people who, intimidated or ignorant or both, had been started on that mean journey into hell. Then he thought of men he had hunted. Then he thought of the children in the wires.

"I wish to Almighty God I had a chance to do what you did!" Frank's words. "I wish I could have done something decent with my shooting!"

Arthur opened his eyes again. He made himself wait halfway to the objective lens, made himself wait until his pupils had time to fully constrict in the bright light, made himself wait past the point he felt he was ready until he was sure he was ready.

The big wolf had jumped, then crouched close to the red earth at the sound of Henry's first shot. But the terror, as sudden and intense as it was, had not been enough to make him run away. He knew that the sharp noise could mean food. The two-legged ones who made that painful sound often took only parts and left the rest to feed small things that crawled and buzzed.

His body trembled against the earth, but he held his ground and short moments later continued toward the ridge. He would see what lay in the next valley, would see what might be left to eat.

The next two shots froze him in his tracks, but he fought down his fear and moved forward.

He looked down upon them from the high north ridge. His prac-ticed eyes, honed to pick out the smallest of movements in his gray-black world, discovered them both. One he found instantly as its body shifted in the rock pile to the east. The other, in the west rocks, he was able to detect by the slow raising up of its head, a careful motion . . . the measured move of one who hunted.

The high sun warmed his fur, and the hair shafts separated in obedience to accommodative instinct. Dry wind swirling over the ridge pushed against him erratically, and he lay down on his chest beside a jagged rock.

The alpha wolf waited. And watched.

*   *   *

The scope intersect found the low middle of Henry's cranium once more as the man prepared to let go shot six. Arthur waited for the heat lines to start the climb from horizontal. He brought the trigger rearward and completed the motion smoothly as the waves approached vertical.

Mike Henry felt a tug on his right ear. That quick pull was followed instantly by the sharp crack of the rifle behind him as the sound chased the bullet east, and then by searing pain as ravaged sensory nerves recovered and did their thing, and then by the warm feel of blood cascading onto his neck and shoulder from mauled tissue. The lower half of his right ear was gone, and its minced remains oozed on tufts of wiry mint-yellow grass before his face. A red mist floated magically in the dry air, the atomized remnant of fluids traveling in the ear when it was struck. The highly vascular tissue still attached to the side of his skull poured blood, then checked its loss as shocked capillaries pinched shut, then poured again as the chemical of closure was abruptly lost in too much destruction.

While those capillaries exhausted their meager options, the red blood spouting from the ear stump painted picturesque arcs on the dry air as Henry rolled to the left with fierce urgency into the protective lee of a nearby boulder.

Arthur lost sight of the man before he could fire again. A sick feeling uncoiled in his gut. He slammed the bolt home and cursed. Intently he scanned the ground through the scope. No part of Henry showed. He waited. A miss. How much of a miss? He trained his eye on the broken silhouette of rock that was Henry's shelter and began to sweat.

A flicker of movement, an edge of boot. He fired quickly. The earth erupted there, and a dark chunk of something bounced crazily into the short grass. The distance was too great for the 10X scope to define what he had hit, and he was not about to go for the spotting scope and lose the visual field, not about to lose the chance to kill if that chance presented itself.

Henry ground his teeth together. The foot shot that had taken off the boot tip and two of his toes overrode the softer pain in the stump of his ear. Bone had been lost with the toes, and shattered bone had a pain all its own.

He heaved himself over a fallen slab of rock with an explosive burst of strength and rolled behind the main bulk of the north side of the upthrust. He edged right slowly and scanned the terrain to the west. Nothing moved on top of the western ridge, and he lowered his scope to study the nearer stand of rock. A splinter of light reflected from something close to the ground. The one who hunted him was there and was probably concentrating on the middle area between the slabs, concentrating on the area he had just vacated. If the shooter's sniper rig was standard, it was likely that its field of view was not wide enough to cover the spot he now occupied. He raised the PSG-1 and trained it on the place where he had seen the sun sparkle.

He saw a shadow move.

Henry opened up with his semiauto rifle and poured ten shots into the shadow as quickly as he could pull the trigger. The area centering the distant slabs disappeared in a cloud of hanging brown smoke. First to last, each shot rocketed into the crease with decimating precision.

The timber wolf shuddered at the ten-shot volley and hunkered as close to the earth as it could get. In the silence after the echoes died away its head came up again, and its predator's eyes moved to the dust cloud that was being sucked away by the dry wind above the west rock tower. Something alive squirmed and moved in the gray shadow. From his vantage point he could see it. He had seen things move like that before.

There would be food.

Melody had driven over the last rise and slowed as she descended into the basin on the graded road. She listened to music on her van's tape player and smoked a cigarette. The windows were rolled up to keep out dust. The music was full of life and loud, and she sang the words energetically and tapped her hand on the steering wheel.

She pulled into the area between the boulders and could only blink in astonishment when she saw the Bronco parked there. She had stopped beside the other car and turned off the tape player when, through the glass of the closed van, she heard the crack of a single shot, the shot that had taken off Mike's boot tip and toes. She waited for the road dust to settle and then rolled down her driver's-side window.

He was shooting up there in the rocks. Should she leave him alone? If he'd wanted her around, wouldn't he have asked her? Maybe he wanted time to himself. She could understand that. Then she jumped as the rapid-fire explosions of Mike's ten-shot volley tore the air. She picked up her binoculars and looked at the east tower. She saw nothing. *He must be on the far side of the slabs.* The burst of gunfire had unnerved her. The stark reality of weapons still made her fearful. She lowered the glasses. Should she walk up to the rocks? The idea of bullets whizzing around the basin made her pause. Then she had a cold thought. *What if he was up there with someone else? Maybe another lady?* Female thought. Lover's thought.

She remained sitting. She noticed a brown smear in the air over the west tower and knew Mike's bullets had impacted there.

Arthur hurt. He was flat on his back. The first round of the ten-shot volley fired by Henry had shattered the granite six inches in front of his support hand, and he had taken two fragments of rock in his face. One fragment penetrated his cheek, and he could feel the sharp point of it inside his mouth with his tongue. The other fragment laid open his forehead above the eyes on the midline. He twisted on the sand and pulled out the cheek fragment. Blood from the forehead wound ran in twin ribbons on either side of his head, filled and dripped from his ears. The pain was minimal. The surprise was not.

He realized the wounds were superficial, and that part did not bother him. What did bother him was the effect the forehead wound would have on his vision. He knew that as soon as he sat upright the blood would be in his eyes. And Henry might already be coming for him. He grasped a fistful of sandy grit and rubbed it into the opening on his forehead. He waited for a moment, then repeated the action. Still on his back, Arthur peeled off his shirt, then his undershirt. He wrapped the khaki-colored T-shirt around his head and knotted it tightly. He struggled back into his outer shirt and rolled onto his stomach. He checked the rifle. No visible damage.

He listened for any sound that might indicate Henry was closing on his position. Only wind whispered over silent rock. He didn't make an attempt to look for the other man. It was possible that by remaining still and out of view he could lure the opponent into the open. He lay quietly behind the boulder and wished it were closer to the forward end of the passageway formed by the standing slabs on either side of him. The rearward location of the boulder would seriously limit his peripheral field of vision should Henry try a flanking move.

After three silent minutes, Arthur edged forward and elevated his weapon with slow caution. He drifted the piece slowly right, then back to the left. A slight movement at the extreme north edge of the other upthrust caught his eye. Henry was there. Arthur settled into the sling with protracted deliberation. No sudden moves now. It was motion that drew the eye, not form.

Perhaps it was the sun, high but still in Henry's favor . . . or the residual effect of the forehead impact . . . or the wavering heat lines shimmering in the scope. As Arthur watched, Henry moved his head partly from behind the rock slab and worked on something with his hands. Arthur looked at Arthur. A young Arthur. The set of shoulder. The angle of jaw. The sandy tint of hair in the high red sun. Arthur stared, then tightly closed his eyes, opened them again. The illusion vanished. He saw Henry again.

The distant visage bobbed back behind the rock, then reappeared, a quarter of the face still looking down.

Arthur fired. Rechambered. Quickly fired again. The shape was gone. The double shots floated a bouquet of powdered rock where the face had been. No movement more than that. Arthur crouched low behind the boulder and waited for the swarm of semiautomatic rounds to come.

Nothing.

The double shots fired by Arthur made Melody cringe. She was standing by the front of her van and looking up at the other place, Mike's place, when the noise had erupted . . . sharp, unexpected, vicious retorts. Two shooters . . . one west . . . one east.

Fear. Fear swept through her, and her knees buckled and she slid to the ground in terror by the van's front left wheel. There was no second of hesitation; where confusion should have claimed a piece of time, horrible realization flashed. Only after she gained the ground did she wonder if there might be another explanation. But that wonder left quickly. Killing was in the air, and she inhaled that air. She was in the middle of a war.

Arthur inched upward and toward the boulder edge once more. Before his line of sight cleared the edge, the face of the north slab ten feet in front of him erupted in a flashing spray of rock, and in that stunning instant he felt his clip-belt tear away from his waist. The force of the hit began to turn his body, had only started to turn it, when the heavy sound of the round's firing got to his brain . . . more detonation than sound . . . more thunder than slap.

Guttural thunder.

Thudding.

Eviscerating.

Deep.

Arthur had been turned completely around. He sat with his back against the boulder, his rifle in the red dirt. In that position he watched as a second projectile exploded through the trunk of the tree nearest him, then through the tree behind that one. Once more the new thunder followed. The first tree shuddered and toppled forward with biblical majesty, a slow-motion testament to force, a blunt destruction full of revelation.

The branches whipped his feet as the tree hit the earth.

He knew. Then Arthur knew.

His clip-belt lay torn and ripped ten feet away. Crushed, dented, deformed shell casings lay like brass worms dead on the sand beneath the sun.

Thoughts flashed like spinning silver dollars on a marble floor.

A fifty-caliber weapon. He had walked into hell.

He had fired four shots at Henry. One round remained in the chamber of his five-shot Remington . . . all the others broken.

And most important, that first monster fifty-caliber shot had been no accident. Henry had deliberately used the slab face to turn the corner. It was a sniper's trick. It was the shot of a skilled distance man. The shot of a warrior.

Arthur's mind let go of those thoughts and focused on another thing. Pain. He looked down at his hip and saw the white curve of his iliac bone framed in angry flesh, an alabaster arch intact but denuded of cover, a thing his but foreign now in sunlight.

He reached out and picked up the rifle. On hands and knees he crawled out of that stone chamber, crawled past the fallen tree, crawled over the ruined shell casings . . . crawled west away from Henry.

Melody shook. She trained the trembling glasses on the west tower where the two heavy rounds had exploded rock and wood.

She saw a man crawling in the sun. She braced her right arm against the front bumper of the van. Her location at the apex of the shallow triangle put her closer to each tower than the rock towers were to each another. The binocular glass, its shaky motion dampened by the bulk of the van, steadied.

A woman who has truly loved a man knows how that man moves.

Her world was washed by a numbing narcotic of disbelief.

Reason stumbled. Explanation disintegrated. Supposition never took its first step. It was Arthur!

In desperation she swung the glasses east. She tried to hold her mind in place, tried to understand. She watched Mike walk through olive-green stems of creosote bush. He held a weapon. He moved toward Arthur.

With dreamlike motions, she opened the van's door and lifted out the Ruger.

His ears were up, his head off the ground, and he read the air with shallow breaths. The two-legged ones were deep in the hunting and wouldn't see him. The prevailing wind still pushed the fur on his back to the south, but coming up the slope, in the lee of the ridge crest, was the north-moving backwind. On that wind, the smell of blood. It bore the scent of freshly opened flesh, like red-rock iron, a tart smell he knew each time he opened the bodies of other living things. Both male humans were in the open now. Moving west. A new human was farther south of those. Female.

There would be meat.

Saliva ran inside ancient jaws.

*   *   *

Arthur fought the dizziness and kept crawling. He nursed his strength and prepared to scramble for the crest of the rise separating the basin from the refuge farther west. All his mental energy worked to keep himself in line with the abandoned rock tower, to keep it between himself and Henry, as cover, until he reached the point where the land elevated above the sight line and he would be seen.

He still dragged the Remington, and the Remington had one last round.

He glanced to his left and saw the place where Henry's car was parked. Two vehicles were there. A silver van. Her van? He stopped. He raised the rifle.

He saw her in the scope.

How? . . . Montana!

Montana was the only way she could have known!

But why, O God, why?

He didn't understand; and he didn't have time to understand.

She was drawing down on Henry. The man must be in the open.

Not this! Not her! Don't let her know this violence.

Even as she sighted into the delicate yellow flowers well in front of Mike—to scare, not to kill—she ran the options again in disjointed desperation. She could run at Mike or scream or drive the van up the rise. But she was terrified. Would she be shot? This was insane. Why was it happening? Horror swam in tight circles around her, its dorsal fin cutting the red earth.

Mike knew the man was hit. He'd seen dark shapes fly after the ricochet shot, had seen the twitching right leg. He had to end the thing, had to close it out. Get in tight and get in fast. If the sniper lived and escaped, he'd come again. All his concentration was directed at the rock ahead. The enemy fired a bolt-action weapon; the delay between shots told him that.

Henry carried the PSG, had left the M-88 in the outcrop. The semiautomatic power in his two hands was designed for close combat. The advantage was his, and he knew it.

She tried to hold the Ruger steady, but fear rattled the barrel on the top of the short, sloping hood of the van. She mustn't close her eyes.

And if he shot back at her? She buried the thought with a fervent act of will.

As she started to squeeze the trigger, the Ruger suddenly disintegrated in her hands in a vicious, shattering, bone-wracking explosion.

Arthur lowered his weapon. The shot had been downhill and with the wind. Three hundred yards. No variable except range. He'd fired at a point as far forward along the barrel support of her weapon as he could. If he had missed, he would also have missed her and blown apart the van's windshield. And that alone would have halted the thing.

He had stopped her. Stopped her from killing.

Now he had nothing left.

Only the threat of having something left.

He got to his feet and ran for the saving crest of the west ridge one hundred yards away.

32

Devils Hole

The sound of Arthur's shot at Melody startled Mike, and he dropped to the ground, tucked the PSG to his chest, and rolled several yards to his left. The violent motion prevented him from hearing either the impact of the .308 round against Melody's Ruger or the clatter of the weapon as it bounced down the hood of the van. He heard no whining passage of the round near him, saw no splash of earth in his vicinity, and he assumed the round had been fired at him and had missed badly. He still didn't know she was there, hadn't looked south at the place between the boulders where her partly hidden vehicle was parked next to his. As the echo died away, he raised his head above the tops of creosote bush and saw Arthur halfway up the slope beyond the west outcrop. The man ran low and fast, like something not human ... but like a human, purposefully zigging and zagging in erratic fashion and still carrying the rifle. Mike had to get above the brush to shoot, but as he moved to assume the shooter's kneeling position, the raw flesh of his foot wound stubbed hard on slate shards and dirt. Splintered bone raked small furrows in the earth. The pain buckled his frame. His rifle fell to the ground as he broke his fall with outstretched arms. When he picked up his weapon and looked again, the other man was at the crest. Mike saw the figure crouch and turn. To shield himself from the shot he knew would come, Mike was forced to drop and roll, to put the bulk of the west rock pile between himself and the shooter.

The shot didn't come.

Mike scrambled into the west tower that had been Arthur's position. He saw the blood, saw the torn clip-belt. He saw the scattered, deformed rounds and knew that even though the bounce shot had missed, it had caused useful damage. He began to wonder. How many rounds did the man have left? His adversary shot bolt-action, not a hose, and was a pro. A pro shooting singles wouldn't carry a lot of rounds. It was obvious the sniper was hit, but the man had managed to make it to the crest of the hill. Why hadn't his opponent shot when he turned and crouched on the hilltop? Was he out? A professional would have dropped and slapped one off. *He must be out of rounds.* Mike had underestimated how much his foot injury would slow him down in crossing the open space between the rock towers, an almost fatal error. And yet the sniper hadn't taken advantage of it.

Mike moved away from the cover of the west rocks and with a limping gait charged toward the spot on the crest where the man had disappeared. *Don't lose him! You've got the son of a bitch.*

Melody sat in a ball with her arms and hands wrapped hard over the top of her head, her knees up, her back pressed against the front tire, her eyes clamped shut, and her chin buried in her chest. Tears of confusion and panic still fell unchecked, and she shook as she tried to make herself as small as possible by pulling her head farther down and her knees farther up. The shock of the Ruger being shot out of her hands was not a thing that only frightened her, it was a thing that terrorized her, shattered her composure as it had shattered her rifle.

Her hands stung, her arms still ached from the impact, and the ringing in her ears seemed to grow, not lessen. But a desperate realization fought the panic. *Get up! . . . Move! . . . Stop them!*

The pain speared up Mike's leg above the shattered toes as he half ran, half limped to the top of the ridge. He dropped onto the ground and looked west at the broad valley before him.

Nothing moved.

Creosote bush, salt brush, sage, and rock.

Nothing moved.

Far away and below him the rich green colors of the refuge shimmered. The access road curved down from the ridge toward the lush meadows by the spring-fed lakes. But the one he hunted couldn't possibly have covered the distance to the saving, hiding greenery. It was too far away. There hadn't been time. *Where is he?* Near a jagged rise of sandstone Mike saw an enclosure defined by chain-link fence. He trained his scope there. High chain-link. Barbed-wire top. No sign of movement. There was no way an injured man could scale that barrier. No way. The man must be dug into the ground somewhere in front of him on the slope. He waited. He divided the land before him into sectors and carefully scanned each partition with his scope.

Nothing moved.

Melody got to her feet. Her legs were boneless stems. She leaned on the front of the van, her arms weak, her stomach heaving in painful, tight lurches, her eyes twin veils of fear and shock.

She saw Mike move the last few steps to the ridge top and go down onto the ground. He would kill Arthur. Arthur would kill him. She took three steps toward the ridge so far away and fell onto her hands and knees. Her stomach convulsed and tried to empty, but nothing came up except pain. Saliva strung from both corners of her mouth in the aftermath of the violent retching. She gasped for air. She got to her feet again and began to walk. Then to run. The unseen tops of desert brush spiked at her legs, and brittle slabs of slate snapped beneath her feet like plates of ice. Filaments of gunpowder smell drifted and stung her fear like soundless wasps. Tears still came and silently, but the dry air kissed them off her face as she ran toward Mike.

The big wolf rose and moved west along the high crest of the north rockline. Its eyes looked south and down at the moving shapes below, its nose worked the back wind and tested the moving air for blood smell, its ears pricked forward and tensed and made ready to lay flat should the painful, sharp sounds come up from the valley. Mixed with the lusty redolence of the blood was a familiar and terrible smell that had begun to recirculate soon after the shooting had started ... the hot, metallic smell that always came after the sharp noise. It rolled in acrid streaks on the wind currents, was trapped and recycled by the geometry of the land. The great wolf could smell the smell of all the shootings from the first shot to the last, sharp odors that mingled with the smell of sage, that almost smothered the sweet scent of the blood.

He moved steadily, kept pace with those below. He could see into both valleys from his high place. He watched them move, saw how the female ran from the east.

He tracked them with his sharp eyes and knew where each one was or had gone. He came to a spot above the area where the middle one lay motionless on the ridge top, searching. The wolf moved still farther west, then stopped and settled onto his strong chest again.

"Mike!"

The shout behind him, strangled and desperate and female. He rolled onto his right side and instantly centered her running silhouette without using the scope or sighting along the barrel. It would be a slap shot, a six-gun hip shot. Despite the position he was in, he knew where that round would hit with almost as much certainty as if he had used the scope. The trigger jerked halfway back and stopped. The sear quivered a fraction short of death.

"Melody?" He stared at her for only one second, then rolled onto his belly and focused again on the slope to the west as he'd been doing when she called his name. His mind churned with wonder, but his hand and eye and soul were steady on the valley where his would-be killer lay hidden.

Nothing moved.

The sound of her running steps came closer, and she crashed onto the earth beside him.

"My God, Mike, it's Arthur. Don't kill him!" The breathless words pushed and beat the air with frantic desperation, her words like dying wings. He kept his focus on the land below.

"Why are you here? Why are you here now?" he asked. Rough words; angry words; words tinged by fear and male impatience; words formed in that narrow instant before he realized what she'd said, what her words meant.

Melody raised her head and looked into the mangled remains of his ear. "God. Mike." And she gagged again.

"You know that son of a bitch out there?" his hard eyes never leaving the dry slope west and below.

Melody couldn't make words. Her world had shattered to pieces in the brutal minutes of the place. These men, the one she needed and the one who needed her, the men she could love, they were taking each other apart. She knew Arthur was hurt. She had seen him move like a speared animal. Now she saw the red-stained lower pants leg on Mike's left side. Unable to check the movement of her eyes, she looked down at macerated flesh bunched in purple folds around splinters of sand-covered white, all swollen and pinched by the ragged circumference of the exploded boot. As she watched the needles of fragmented bone, they moved and spread like the spines of a fan as Mike shifted position and his foot muscles tried to do things with toes that were no longer there.

The violence of the guns and this place and these men was spreading like a billowing, poisonous shroud across her soul. She felt a deep exhaustion, felt a great weariness take her, as though some horribly evil chemical had been injected into her veins. She was gored and made decerebrate by quick madness.

She stared at his torn foot. Her head began to bob up and down in slow rhythm. Up and down. Her eyes were suddenly dead and empty and did not seem to see. She was a nightmare child.

What he said next yanked her out of her trance.

"You! Did you set me up?" A growl of a question.

His words slapped her with more force than if he'd used the back of his hand. She stopped staring at his broken foot. She blinked and tried to understand what he'd said. She looked at him as he scanned the valley. She reached out to touch the drying trail of blood that crusted down his neck below his torn ear.

He smashed her hand away with a sudden backward thrust of his elbow. The angry impact turned her arm to rag, and it flopped back against her hip. But she didn't cry out and did not move or lower her gaze.

"Set you up?" Quiet words in the dry wind. She flexed her arm. Everything still worked, but the pain throbbed all the way up to her neck. Then her rage exploded. "YOU CRUMMY BASTARD! YOU CRUMMY, CRUMMY BASTARD!" She made a fist of her still-tingling fingers and pounded him once high on his back above his shoulder blades near the base of his neck. It was the only place she could attack. She pounded him with as much strength as she could. The single blow landed with all the force that terror and frustration and confusion could muster. That force was considerable.

His head snapped back, and a flash of yellow light sprayed through his brain. Her punch had the effect of a neck stinger. It had been delivered like a rabbit punch. His nose smashed into the top of the butt stock as his head rebounded to the front. He raised his head, shook it from side to side a few times, and looked at her. "I take it that's a no?" He smiled.

She looked back. A mute moment passed. Then a smile came to her face, but it had to come through many soundless tears.

He turned his eyes to the valley once again. "Who is he, Mel?"

She wiped her face with the back of her hand and looked where he looked. "He's a man I know. He has a lot of pain inside."

"He's got more than pain. He's a goddamn pro."

"You've hurt him."

"He's hurt me."

"I don't know why this is happening." She got to her feet before he knew what she was doing. He reached up and grabbed a handful of her jeans, but she stood firm and only covered his hand with hers.

"Arthur!" she shouted. The name echoed from the north ridge rocks.

"For God's sake, get down!"

She didn't move. "Arthur! It's me! Melody!"

Only the wind whispered softly in the sparse tops of brush.

Nothing moved.

"Arthur!"

"He'll take your head off, Mel!"

She dropped to her knees. "He can't hear me. He must be gone."

"He's not gone. He's here. There wasn't time for him to make the trees. He's here somewhere."

"He kept me from shooting at you. He knows I'm here."

"Shooting at me?"

"Arthur shot my rifle. I was trying to make you stop."

"You were going to shoot me? To stop me?"

"In front of you. To make you stop."

"He tried to kill me. Why would he stop you?"

"I don't know."

"Who is he, Mel? Level with me. Who the hell is he?"

She turned to look at him. "He's Arthur." She wiped her eyes again. "I don't know why all this is happening." She looked back at the valley. "Maybe we should go away. Get help. You're hurt."

"Can't do that. He wants me. It must be one of the books. Or the casino. If I don't stop this thing here, your buddy will try again. That's how these things work. I never thought they'd do it. This guy has to be stopped here."

"Then I'll stop it." She scrambled to her feet and headed down the hill. He watched her go. What she did happened so quickly that he couldn't stop her.

He got to his feet and followed. The pain in his shattered foot was fierce. The shock had worn off, and the pain was becoming pure. Though she only walked, he couldn't close the distance. He stayed low. He used the great pain to fire awareness. His every sense, honed in a furnace of agony, took on sharp brilliance.

She walked down the slope to its middle. She called Arthur's name many times. Finally she stopped near the edge of the gravel road that curved through the place and waited for Mike to catch up. Mike was limping badly.

"Could he have come this far?" she asked.

"No," he replied. "No farther than this. There wasn't time. We've walked over him. We've walked right over him." They began to trace a weaving grid pattern traversing the slope upward, back the way they had come. Mike stumbled and fell. The lacerated ear had reopened, and red blood ran down his neck to disappear under his collar. The entire side of his shirt was dark crimson.

She ran back to Mike. The sight of him made her wince and go pale. "Oh, God." She knelt in the sand beside him and looked at the destruction of head and foot.

"We have to stop," she said through tears. "I'll get my van."

"Not here. Don't leave me here. Not in the middle." His words were different. A small shank of fear was there. He'd lost a lot of blood. He was exhausted. And the eerie thought of them having passed close to Arthur unnerved him as it suddenly did her. She began to be afraid. Reality was starting to vaporize again. Arthur was here. She could feel it. What was he waiting for? She looked around. Was he waiting for her to leave?

Mike's words broke in on her thoughts. "Help me get over to that fenced area. There's a side spur off the gravel road. It leads to the fence. You can drive up to it. That's if you decide to come back for me." He gave her a weak smile. "I need something to protect my backside. That cliff. The fence. Get me over there."

They reached the place where the tall chain-link fence surrounded the deep pit where *cyprinodon diabolis*, the desert pupfish, lived. Only in that hard struggle across the slope did Melody realize how badly Mike was injured. Perhaps, because her thoughts were partly on Arthur's injuries, she hadn't seen what was happening to Mike. She'd seen Arthur crawl from the rocks beneath the hot sun, and her heart had twisted at the sight. He was hurt, too. *Where are you? Where are you, Arthur?*

As Mike tumbled to the ground by the fence because Melody was unable to bear his weight any longer, his shoulder barged against the lower edge of chain-link where it met the hard, shale-covered earth and forced it out of the soil. "Inside! Get me inside!"

Melody sat on the ground and used her feet to push the fence. The chain-link was new and strong and would not lift high enough to let him slide underneath. He had to use both hands to help her widen the gap. Finally he wriggled into the enclosure. He rested, then crawled the fifteen feet to the edge of the deep pit and studied the opposite side where the fence blocked the steep rain gully under the catwalk. The sand surface in the wash was smooth and showed no marks. The killer hadn't tried to come through there. Mike lowered his eyes and stared straight down. At the base of the sheer rock walls forming the three unbroken sides of the pit was water. He crawled back to the fence. "That wood, that branch. Give me that dead branch behind you."

Melody passed the thin, four-foot stick through the links. Mike dragged himself back to the edge of the pit. He sat up, took aim, and hurled the small lance down into the pool. It stuck in sand beneath water only inches deep. The branch slowly fell over, and the end that had stuck in the pool bottom floated up with a dollop of wet sand attached. The water was shallow, he decided, too shallow to hide a man.

Mike crawled back to the fence. He nodded at his rifle lying on her side of the chain-link barrier. "Maybe you should take it," he said.

She looked at him, then at the rifle, then back at him. She seemed to hesitate for a moment. The moment became a long moment. He watched her. Finally she spoke, "No. No way. Arthur won't do anything to me. I'll be okay. You keep it." She worked the PSG under the fence and he picked it up. "Please don't kill him, Mike. If he comes. Please don't."

He only looked at her as he sat and cradled the rifle. He stared at her through the pattern of steel mesh, looked into her eyes. "Why, Mel? Why? Do you love him?"

She used the back of her hand to rub dirt-streaked tear tracks from her face. She looked back at him. She didn't answer.

Melody got to her feet.

"Mel?"

"What?" A word sharp, impatient, unexpected.

"If something happens, if you can't make it back, don't worry about me. I'm safe in here. Even if I have to spend the night. He can't get through this chain-link without me hearing him. I'll be all right. Besides, I think he's out of rounds. There's nothing to worry about." He paused. "I mean it. I can rest here. If you think it's better that you go away, if you think it's best to get help or something, I understand."

She looked down into his eyes as he sat on the ground. Her eyes blazed, but she said nothing. She turned and walked toward the gravel road. When she reached it, she broke into a trot. Small puffs of dust from the heels of her jogging shoes rose in the sunlight and marked her progress up the grade.

She didn't look back.

High on the north crest the alpha animal watched the female run up the hill. The sight of something running by itself and away from the wolf fired a harsh sequence in his hindbrain. The beast imaged how he would take it down from behind. The images faded, but there remained twin streams of saliva loosed inside his mouth by the reactive process. He slowly swiveled his head back to look down upon the bleeding one inside the fence directly below him. The wolf's tongue, running fluids, extended and groomed each side of the sharp snout, bent whiskers, smoothed facial fur, and retreated. The mouth came open slightly, and a rhythmic panting began to flare the black lips in soft pulsations. The late noon sun was hot. The breeze had stopped.

Purple cores swirled in thick air and spaces opened, then closed in fading streaks of black. The other stopped ten feet away, and Arthur saw rage sparkle where eyes would be.

The other didn't wait, but spoke at once. "We are dying. Why are we dying?"

"I am hurt."

"You are always hurt. Where are we?"

"We are in water."

"Why?"

"You know why."

"The air is going. Why is the air going?"

"We are under the earth. The water of the pit is deep at one end. Very deep. We are in a cave. We breathe in a place between the water and the rock. It is a space of inches. I did not know this space was here, but I had no choice. Hurry. There is not much time."

"There never seems to be enough time."

"I have too much pain."

The other's head went back slightly as in a laugh, but no laugh sounded. "Too much pain? And you would give the pain to me?"

"Yes."

"You always give the pain to me."

"Please."

"This thing was ended."

"It is not ended," said Arthur.

The other waited silently. It turned and drifted away, then halted and came back. It stood in the rushing colors closer than before. More seconds passed.

And then it spoke. "Give me the body."

"Yes."

The water of the pool was flat and still. No breeze moved to corrugate the glassy surface. In the dark water tiny fish fed on algae strands. Silver-blue males and green-hued females swam courses eons old. The community of minnows moved mostly over the shallow shelf that defined 80 percent of the pool where the algae clumps were more abundant, but a few fish darted in the cold, deep upwelling that rose from the great depth below and from the limestone caverns that extended laterally into the rock.

Suddenly, like a single cloud, like a quick shadow, the small fish at the deep end migrated to the shallows.

The convex curve of a single eye and then a peak of nose rose above the smooth surface of the water in slow elevation. The parts stopped. With steel control the nostrils flared as the thing below gained oxygen from desert air. Silence as quiet as time kept counsel over the space. It took minutes before the flaring flesh seemed sated and a normal breathing pattern asserted itself. The single eye above the surface blinked once and took the measure of its world.

The tiny fish crowded desperately into the shallow end of the pool. Their universe was shared by something new.

33

Fences

The wolf's ears went up. He lifted onto his feet and looked down. His great wild heart beat faster, and he moved farther west by twenty yards. The alpha male picked his way carefully over the loose slate of the high ridge. A dislodged rock would fall into the place below and change what was happening there. Such a thing should not be. Pups and bitches did that.

He found a new place and settled onto the warm rock once more. He could see everything.

As good as his eye was for line, his eye for motion—no matter how small—was even better. It was the way of great hunters.

The other had risen halfway out of the water. His hands dug deep into and anchored him in the cool sand. He had held that position for two full minutes because of the sound. Beyond the steep wall rising vertically above him, somewhere near the top rim of the pit, he'd heard the sliding metallic action of a rifle receiver being worked. The clash of cams and the small click of a magazine being detached, then reseated, told him what he needed to know. The prey was there. Awake. Armed.

He rose completely clear of the water and, pressed against the bank, waited for the droplets to stop falling from his clothing. The falling drops would make noise on the pool surface. He removed his shirt. He needed quiet. As he looked down at the pants he wore, as he started to brush away the excess water, he noticed the ripped flesh and the curve of hipbone washed white by the soaking in the cave. He touched the collar of wrinkled tissue around the hard surface and pried one edge up to look beneath at the thin, cellophanelike membrane separating flesh from skeleton. He investigated the area objectively, then smiled and let the flap of tissue fall back.

He studied the rock wall that towered over him. The lower third of the pit was worn smooth by groundwater erosion. The first possible handhold was a narrow stone ledge that circled the crater at the twelve-foot level. With his heels he dug and built firm places for his feet.

He began to force his rate and depth of breathing. As he did so, he became aware of sharp irritations in the lower left side of his chest. Ribs. Broken ribs. But the lungs filled as they should have filled, and he knew the ribs had not punctured the lung space. All was well.

As he sucked in air, his mouth wide and his head tilted to one side to ease the breathing, he kept his eye on the rim above. His upper body wove a swaying figure-eight pattern, created a rhythm to key the explosive muscle release needed to reach the stone ledge. The lungs worked hard.

A cloud slid across the sun, and shadow moved over the pit. The sudden diminution of light lent an eerie patina to the space, and he felt a surge of chemicals in his blood. His lungs sucked one great piece of air. His chest closed on that air and crushed out the oxygen. Leg muscles exploded with extension, one great crack of energy, and he leaped up. His fingers, more claws than fingers, engaged the top curve of the stone ledge, began to slip, then held. Two fingernails on his left hand peeled off their nail beds. But he held on. His body seemed welded to the smooth vertical of the pit as though he were an obscene extension of the geology there.

He began to climb.

*   *   *

Melody jogged down the grade toward the cars. As the narcotic of physical release built, she experienced a fierce desire to keep running, to run past the cars, to run forever, a desire made more intense by what she was running from.

She came to the place where the cars were parked. She stopped and looked up at the twin rock upthrusts to the north. The images flooded her mind, and she stood for long, painful seconds while her body worked to resupply her blood with fuel, stood hypnotized by memory and burned by fatigue.

The gray beast stood. Below him he watched the two shapes, black forms against the gray, dry land. His heart pumped strongly, fired by the contagion of the hunt. The prey was busy with small things. The one that moved on the pit wall exuded killing purpose.

The smell of blood was back in the air.

It would not be long. He watched the stalking shape and hoped in his way that some of the kill would be left. He wanted the hard flesh behind the legs.

Mike cleaned the last of the desert grit from the top of the receiver. He picked two small grains of sand from the barrel mouth and lay back on the ground, the rifle across his chest, his feet toward the fencing, his head toward the pit. He looked up at the pastel sky. The agony in his foot had migrated to his groin, and a throbbing torment pounded his brain with every beat of his heart. He wanted to sleep. He felt safe within the chain-link confines, felt secure in his refuge. Whatever was out there could not reach him, not without noise, not without warning.

His eyes focused on the top of the fence and ran the length of the triple barbed-wire strands as he tried to forget the pain. He saw a flutter of fabric, or was it skin, in the middle wire above his head.

He stared at it.

He couldn't decide what it was.

Perhaps a feather snatched by the wire from a bird? Or the remains of a rabbit torn apart up there by a feeding falcon? The object stopped moving as the small wind pushing at it faded away.

The bit of material steadied in the sunlight. The thing hung motionless, and his vision was able to decipher color in the absence of movement.

Khaki color.

His world went from sun to ice. Foul acid rose from his gut into the back of his mouth. He held his breath. He was paralyzed. His limbs had turned to lead. Tons of sky pushed him against the earth. The flesh on the back of his neck contracted, and tight, cold shivers rippled across the skin behind each shoulder and down the backs of his upper arms. His fingers tightened around the hard length of the rifle resting across his chest.

No sound was in that place.

An overpowering desire to be on his feet and pressed back into a corner of the fencing swept over him.

But all he did was roll over slowly onto his stomach so he could face the pit edge.

Nothing.

There was nothing there. No thing there. He began to inch forward on his belly toward the rim. He felt the warm spill of blood start again from the stump of his torn ear. This time the tickling fluid trickled forward across his right cheek, and when it found the corner of his mouth, he tasted his own salt.

Melody couldn't find her keys. She went through both pockets, then got out of the car and searched under the seat. She hadn't had time to lock the car when she had driven up because of those sudden, first shots. She pushed her fingers into the joint between the seat and the seatback. No luck.

Where are they?

She began to look on the ground near the front of the car.

Mike neared the edge. Five feet more. Four feet. He froze. He could smell something hot in the air. He could smell fear, his own fear. The pain had gone away. More blood flowed into the corner of his mouth. He swallowed it.

He moved forward once more.

Three feet.

She found the keys. They were in the sand by the front wheel. She picked them up and brushed off the red dirt.

The car started on the first try.

*   *   *

A foot from the edge. Perhaps he was overdoing it. He'd lost a lot of blood and hadn't taken any water all that afternoon. He knew what dehydration could do to a man. It made one hallucinate and hear things that weren't there. He lowered his head to the ground and with his face against the earth, his eyes closed, he tried to gather himself. He lifted his head.

He stared into fierce, mad eyes inches from his own. An insane smile sliced through the face that floated disembodied before him. Mike's hands were still wrapped around the rifle when an arm of the thing raised in the air and came down on his back like a grappling hook. He felt the material of his shirtback seized in a vise of hand. He was pulled forward and he let go of the rifle and drove his fingers into earth he could not, in another time, have broken with a knife blade.

He must not go over the edge!

Hold the earth!

The thing seemed to rise like a flying beast before him and it blotted away the sun. He knew his own purchase in the hard dirt was the leverage the thing used to pull itself over the rim of the pit and onto his level. But he couldn't free his hands and allow himself to be yanked into space.

The thing was on its feet behind him, its hand still buried in his shirt. He was lifted up by an unreal force and thrown across fifteen feet of ground into the chain-link steel. The fencing gave somewhat, then, like a vertical trampoline, propelled him back toward the grinning shape that waited beneath a spinning sun. The thing stepped at him and took him by the throat with one hand as he rebounded off the fence and stumbled helplessly toward it.

The grip on his throat was powerful and professional, the fingers in front of the lateral neck muscles and curving around his windpipe.

Stars exploded in his brain. His world went black with shock and he almost passed out. But he didn't pass out. He made a fist of his right hand and slammed it with all his strength into the thing's left side. In all the confusion of the strike, Mike sensed something different in the way his fist sank into the chest wall. He'd fought many men, some in sport, most in earnest, and this was not the way a punch felt going into that area. It went deep. It plowed through ribs that were not held together.

The grip on his throat weakened in the instant, and Mike tore the strangling hand from his neck.

And stepped back.

The thing was down on one knee and bent over to its left side. It seemed to be trying to wrap itself around the impact point of Mike's single blow.

He took split seconds to look at it. It was the sniper. But it was not the sniper.

With a sound from hell the thing sprang at him. The top of its skull rammed into Mike's face and split it open from forehead to upper jaw. Front teeth fell like spilled Chiclets onto the red earth. His knees buckled and he fell backward, trapping his lower legs beneath his body. He was, in seconds, transformed into a sorry, helpless package.

But the thing was down again. On its knees. Again bent left. Again in deep distress, and this time pulling at the area where a broken rib speared through torn skin.

Mike rolled left and scrambled up. Red veils of hot blood cascaded around his eyes, and he knew he would be blinded. He drove balled fists into both sockets and twisted the blood away from the center of his face.

No time was left. One of his eyes lost its world to red almost immediately. No time was left.

Mike skipped forward with a stutter step and kicked his right boot into the hanging face of evil. The boot bounced off the front of the skull like it was rock, and that was good. That meant the blow was true and centered.

But the thing only shook its head and on its knees looked up.

A strange sound came from it. Words.

"You kill kids."

Mike stopped in disbelief.

"You kill kids with drugs."

Insanity. The thing wanted to talk. Mike moved forward and kicked again. This time the thing caught his shin with one hand, stood up, and tipped him over. His foot was held aloft. He tried to scrape the grip away with the edge of his other boot, but flat on his back he had no power. He tried again. The thing caught his other leg, spread both apart, and stepped hard on his testicles with the heel of one foot.

Mike's brain exploded in shimmering waves of physical grief so deep and distilled that he began to convulse. In the churning depths of a place beyond agony, a place he'd never known could exist, he became dimly aware of the world collapsing around him. Big shadows moved and the ground seemed to plow up and, despite the exquisite visit he was taking to hell, he felt himself pressed into the substance of the thing he fought.

Melody stood on the brakes and screamed. The van, its blunt snout wrapped in screeching, tearing chain-link, veered and skidded to a halt two feet from the edge of the pit. The pair of combatants, sent spinning on the ground by flailing coils of wire, still fought. Mike felt the other's jaws close down on the side of his neck, but he struggled up from the pain, and his right hand found the protruding rib and twisted it. The pressure on his neck went away.

A shot. Loud. Close. Melody pointed Mike's rifle at them.

"STOP IT! STOP!" Another shot. Very close. The thing's teeth were back on his neck once more. He twisted the rib again, then released it, found the shank of a thumb that plumbed his eye, and twisted the thumb back until it snapped with a loud click.

"STOP!"

They didn't stop.

"FOR GOD'S SAKE, IF YOU LOVE ME STOP!"

In slow increments, carefully, unbelieving but hearing, they stopped. They both stopped.

He watched them in the dying heat of the afternoon. The blood scent was heavy in the air. The first tendril of the waiting night's north wind ruffled his fur.

They lay apart on the earth like near-dead things. Limp. But each moved. The female had made mournful howls and clawed at the earth until one of the males had hit her to make her quiet, and he had nuzzled her, and she'd gone into a corner of the broken place where she stayed alone for a long time. Then they'd gone away, gone away together in the strong thing that had broken through the fence.

But that didn't interest him now.

Something else interested him.

When the fighting had stopped, while the three lay silent and separated down there, he'd caught the movement of something in the rocks far back to the east above the valley where the hunting had started. In the clear air he saw a fourth human, saw it move when the others passed beneath on the gravel road. The fourth human, a male, had one of the long sticks that killed, that made the land jump with noise, that put the smell of hot metal and blood in the air. With sharp eyes that could determine line, for that was the wolf's first skill, the powerful beast watched the fourth human move quickly along the distant ridge in the direction the others had taken.

The great wolf broke cover and raced east over the land.

34

The Feeding

Stay away from the open sand. Drive where the bushes are."
Mike gritted what was left of his teeth together after he spoke
the words. He lay next to Arthur. Melody had folded down the
rear seat so the two men could lie side by side, their feet toward the
rear of the van. She stared straight ahead as she steered off the road
past the boulders and drove slowly over raw basin land toward the
place where Mike had left the fifty-caliber weapon. Her eyes were
flat and empty, the eyes of one who'd survived searing violence. But
she did as she was told. The desert brush slapped and cracked
beneath the frame of the vehicle.

"Your car. What about your car?" she asked. Her sounds were
tiny, soft things.

"The hell with the car," growled Mike. "It's locked. We'll get it
later. It's the weapon I want. That won't last if we leave it. The
Bronco is insured. Get the weapon." The words came thick and rubbery out of damaged flesh.

The van bucked over the rutted terrain.

In wincing pain, Mike turned his head to look at Arthur. That one stared straight up at the overhead. "Kids. What was that about kids? Killing kids?" asked Mike.

There was no war left between them. Only deepening exhaustion. Slow rivers of red blood from each man met and merged on the vinyl surface of the folded-down seatback.

Arthur didn't reply.

"The casinos, right? They bought you to take me out."

Arthur twisted his neck and looked at Mike.

Mike rolled his head back and stared up at the dome light. "I should have figured it would happen," he said. As he formed the words, the terrible split that ran vertically from his forehead to his jaw pried open. Bright fluid welled out of the embrasure.

Arthur spoke. "They said you kill kids with drugs, with heroin and speed. In San Bernardino." But Arthur's words were lifeless.

"Who said?"

No reply.

"Christ! I got a kid of my own. No one with a kid would do that. No one! That kind of animal hasn't been invented!" Mike focused on the headliner. He spat out a white chip of tooth. It bounced off his chest. "What the fuck do you think I am?"

"I was told wrong, then. It wasn't for the money. It's never for the money. It has to be right."

"Well, you fucking son of a bitch . . . you didn't get it right this time."

No reply.

"They lied to your sorry ass!"

Arthur seemed to shrink, to deflate beneath his skin. The cracked ribs of his left side magnified the effect. "I'm sorry."

Despite what it did to him, Mike could not, absolutely could not suppress a grin. The red fluid turned to new blood. "Sorry? You're sorry? Jesus Christ on a stick! You're sorry?"

Arthur watched the blood. "If you keep talking, you'll bleed to death. You're white. Your breathing's flat. You're in shock."

"Sorry, Mel, he's sorry!" from Mike.

Melody's hands went white on the steering wheel. "You BOTH shut up! Just you SHUT UP! You're both INSANE! I hate you BOTH!" Her words wavered with a shrill intensity close to panic.

She stopped the car. "Where is it? We're here."

Mike closed his eyes. "It's behind the big rock. Where you took a leak last time. Get the case, too."

She was out of the car and back in a few moments. She set the weapon on the front passenger seat, and they started down toward the road. Melody tried to steer over the tracks the van had made on the way up to the shoot site.

Arthur spoke. "Stop the car. He needs liquids. We both need liquids. He's not going to make it."

Melody stopped. She reached under the hulking shape of the fifty-caliber weapon and retrieved a plastic gallon jug of water. "It's not cold. It's for the engine."

Mike couldn't control a sudden laugh. His face spread apart like sliced gelatin. "Cold? It's not cold? What kind of a trip is this? Not cold," he said.

Arthur tried to reach for the jug in Melody's hand, but his left side dissolved in pain, and he fell back.

Melody scrambled between the seats and poured water into Mike. Then she tore strips of muslin from the gun wrap and knotted the strips around his ashen, blood-crusted head to keep the laceration closed. Arthur managed to get into a sitting position and helped her tie the muslin. He took no water. "Better save it," he said. "We can keep him alive with the water."

Mike arched his eyebrows. "The water's not cold? I never heard of such a thing. Where's the manager?" Arthur wondered if the man was delirious or just a lot stronger than he appeared. Mike looked up at Arthur and squinted one eye. "That cornering shot. Where'd it get you? Stomach? Leg?"

"Hip. Got my left hip. Busted out all my loads. Only one was left in the chamber."

Mike forced a grotesque smile.

"Nice shot," from Arthur in thoughtful tones.

Melody looked from one to the other, an incredulous expression displacing one of fright.

Mike's eyes peered out from bands of muslin. "You got my toes with that slap shot. Couldn't have been more than a dime's worth of target." His words were muffled through the wrap. "That's pro stuff."

Arthur nodded. "Thanks."

Anger flared in Melody. "NO! THIS IS *NOT* HAPPENING!"

"It's okay, Melody. Maybe you could drive?"

"DRIVE, ARTHUR? I'LL DRIVE!"

The van moved onto the gravel road and accelerated. Pale yellow dust rose in a rolling train behind the vehicle.

After going a few hundred yards, Melody stood on the brakes. The van skidded to a stop in a boiling billow of dust and crunching rock.

Parked crosswise and blocking the road ahead was a white stretch limo with the Crystal Casino logo on its side.

The first round shattered the center of the van's windshield with a vicious crack that sent shards of glass all the way to the rear of the interior. Melody screamed. The skin in the center of her right cheek trickled a delicate tine of blood.

"Turn it, Mel. Turn it and stop." Arthur's words were calm and strong, and Melody obeyed in what seemed a slow-motion trance as more bullets pinged into the metal flank, then into the back of the van as it stopped in the center of the trailing dust cloud.

The rear window of the van turned into air as a fusillade of bullets from the limo dissolved the glass.

"On the floor, Melody. Get down on the floor." Arthur. Quiet words of command. Not urgent, but full of force.

As Melody tried to make herself part of the floormats, she was aware of the black shadow of the fifty-caliber body rising up beside her, then seeming to float over the seatback.

Through the fearsome splatter of impacting rounds, she heard Mike's words. "More bad people? That's nine-millimeter stuff, isn't it?" The words seemed far away. Melody shook with a violence born of terror and exhaustion and pressed her forehead into grains of sand on the floor beneath the glove box.

"It's nine-millimeter." Arthur's voice.

The heavy, purposeful clank of metal on metal came from the other side of the seat. The van rocked with movement.

"Who the hell do they think they are?" Mike's words. Words that sounded more amused than concerned. "You set?"

"Set." Arthur's voice. "Open it and cover up."

Melody heard someone move. Then she heard the familiar sound of the hatchback latch being thrown. The rear door squeaked as what was left of it was pushed up.

Immediately the inside of the van seemed part of a monstrous detonation, and Melody unleashed a scream that dressed the massive reverberation in icy filaments of female terror. The contrast was total and unique.

The sequence began to repeat: the muscular explosion of the fifty in a garland of ear-piercing female horror. Then again. And again. The scream perfectly anticipating each eardrum-crunching explosion by the fifth shot.

The annoying clink of the smaller rounds coming into the van disappeared like a nickel slot machine jamming in the middle of a payout. She heard Arthur and Mike quietly talking in clipped sentences between the soul-shattering thunderclaps of the big gun. But she could not control her screeching. She was a reflex in those moments, a mere soundmaking organism that lived a terrible, simple reality activated only by the chamber of the vicious weapon and what was happening there. The van interior was sour with powder residue from the big gun. Gray motes floated in the air and found Melody's nose. The floor beneath her jumped and rattled and bounced her forehead on the black rubber floormat with each hell clap. She felt sheets of gritty heat wash her skin after each blast. She was nothing. Only fear.

Boom! Scream!

Boom! Scream!

Boom! Scream!

Boom! Scream!

Scream! No boom.

It was over.

The two in the back of her van chatted. Though her brain wouldn't accept word strings, she knew they talked about guns and about bullets. She heard words she'd only heard spoken by these two. "Trajectory." "Boattail." "Copper jacket."

And she felt as though she were like something liquid on the floor of her car. Like she might flow through the tiniest opening down into the yellow dust of the road. *Please don't be an opening.*

When the shattering noise of the shootout between those in the van and those in the limo had erupted on the low plain, the big wolf had altered the direction of his furious run and angled south up a slope toward the high rocks. His charge, energized by hunger and his killing instinct, had been incautious. The sudden explosions, violent and deep, slowed him only momentarily, and the new direction brought him to a place where the scent of the fourth human painted the air and rock. The smell of the man was acid and repugnant, as it was from all humans, but the wolf followed the human's line of travel until he came to a place where the land began to fall away toward the roadbed below. The wolf stopped. From his new position he watched the dust rise above the vicious battle on the roadbed and he cringed at each sharp retort. Halfway between his position and the confusion on the road, he saw the fourth human. The man had stopped in a narrow rock rift, had crouched down, and was pointing his killing stick at something. The Timber wolf followed the sight line of the fourth human.

Crouched in the rock rift, Montana fought to control his body. His breathing came in searing, nauseating gasps. Sweat clouded his eyes with maddening mists. His limbs shook as much from his frantic run along the ridge as from the fear that held him in that moment. His brain boiled chunks of thought. The weight of what he'd done, the hell he'd sent Arthur into—that foul realization fought with images of Arthur when they'd hunted Charlie in that far time when friendship and loyalty had been the only things that mattered. For an instant the image of Karla's face came to him, her bright eyes cherishing—eyes that failed to see the flaws he'd come to see in himself.

Each image derailed the preceding and all seethed in disarray. He leaned his forehead against hot rock and closed his eyes and wished the corrosive horror would disappear—wished that he could breathe again, that he could be down on that roadbed standing between Arthur and the evil that was trying to kill him. He opened his eyes and watched the squat figure of a man back away from the limo into a shallow gully, watched the man move toward his own position in an attempt to flank those in the van. And the figure carried an ominous weapon, a short pipe that was tipped with a pineapple-shaped mass. Grenade launcher.

The figure with the grenade launcher scrambled along the gully toward Montana. It would be over. It would be ended. Ended in a crunching moment of eviscerating violence. And Arthur would be gone.

The man with the launcher knelt and sighted the weapon over the lip of the gully, drew down on the van. Montana tried to focus on the man, tried to aim but couldn't see. Salt rivulets stung his eyes. He couldn't clear them.

Montana's first shot missed low and tore the earth below the forward end of the grenade launcher. The figure rolled down into the shallow gully and looked in Montana's direction. Montana's second shot punched a hole in the bank behind the man. He'd missed high. The third shot exploded from Montana's rifle and shared an atom of time with the yellow flash of the grenade launcher. Through a veil of shimmering light, Montana saw the entire left half of the man's neck evaporate in a hanging blossom of red.

But a dark shadow came.

They made Melody drive. It took a while to get going. But she did it. She had to drive. They couldn't.

Melody had a vision of the big limo on fire and seeming only half as high as it was when she first saw it. She saw parts of men on the gravel. An arm ... detached and alone. The top half of a bald head. A cigar still trailing smoke as it lay in the dust. A long sausage-like tube that was strung out fifteen feet behind a dark suit that had a large hole in the back about where a waist would be. Off to one side, beneath a mesquite bush, a shiny black shoe with something that looked like a shin sticking out of it, a black sock still neatly up ... But that was ridiculous. *How could that be?*

She drove on.

Drove rather slowly through the twilight of that day.

Drove away from the place called Devils Hole.

And now an hour of silence had passed. The great gray wolf had waited long enough. He cleared the opening into the rift where the fourth human lay. The smell of blood was thick and sweet.

He circled the still form. The side of the human's skull was broken away, and small things fed beneath an early moon. The great hunter moved close and smelled the dried ear of one of his own kind that hung on a leather thong from the neck of the human.

With a forepaw, the alpha male nudged a white piece of brain out of the open skull. The piece was still warm. He settled onto his massive chest and pulled the pale fragment beneath his jaws.

He ate.

35

Words

Melody looked across the kitchen table at Arthur. "How many weeks has it been? Three? Four?"

"Twenty-four days."

"And nothing?" She pulled a rubber band off the morning edition of the Las Vegas newspaper. She put the rubber band in her pocket and unfolded the paper. She looked at him, not the paper.

"Nothing. I haven't heard a thing from him," he replied.

"He almost got you killed." She sipped her coffee.

"He did something worse than that. Montana lied to me. I could have killed Mike, a man who didn't deserve killing. There was no reason for that, no reason on earth. Montana and I were friends. More like brothers. I don't think I'll see him again. Not him. Not in this life."

"People aren't gods, they're people."

He stared at her. "How can you say that after what happened?"

"It's not easy to say. But I say it. I don't understand people like you. You have a chance to stop, but you don't stop. Why?"

"I don't know why."

She looked down at her lap. "Maybe I know why."

He looked at her.

"If you had killed Mike," and she hesitated, "I think I would have killed you."

He said nothing.

"It's like a disease, isn't it? Once it starts, it spreads like fire. That's what violence is about."

"Not for everyone. I don't think it's like that for everyone."

"You're wrong."

"I could be wrong."

"You're wrong and you know it. That's why you stopped me."

"Stopped you?"

"When you thought I was going to shoot Mike to protect you. You stopped me with your last round."

He got up from the table and went to the coffeemaker on the counter and refilled his cup. He walked over to the refrigerator and opened the door. "You want a banana?"

"I don't want a banana!"

He closed the refrigerator door. He went back to the sink and stood there drinking his coffee.

She turned her head and looked at him. "How's your chest?"

"It hurts. It hurts like hell."

"Good."

"I have to wear this damn corset for another month. How's your boyfriend's teeth?"

"Expensive."

"Sorry about that."

"He can afford it."

"Sorry about your van."

"What van?"

"And your rifle."

"I'll never be able to touch one again. Not now."

"That was a bad day." He studied the coffee he swirled in his cup as he stood there.

She looked at him, an amazed look on her face, and slowly shook her head. "It would have been a lot worse day if that damn cross-wind hadn't been blowing to beat hell, you bastard."

"You're upset."

She fought down a smile. It wasn't difficult.

"No hard feelings?" he offered.

"Of course there's hard feelings. I hate you." Matter-of-fact words. She pushed her coffee cup away. "I hate people who don't work right."

"That's not a nice thing to say."

Melody was silent for a long minute. "I loved him, you know."

"I'm happy for you. Does that mean you're going to cry? More coffee?"

"No more coffee." She rested her head in her hands.

He turned to look out the window over the sink. "You're lucky you don't love me." His words were soft. "You wouldn't last out the year." He waited. The moment was awkward, and she didn't look at him.

"You don't love anybody," she said. "You can't love anybody. You're sick."

"So I'm sick. Maybe your boyfriend's sick, too."

"Don't use that word. He's more than 'boyfriend,' one hell of a lot more."

"Sorry."

"You're a hell of a lot more too, Arthur. And you goddamn well know it." Her words were not loud, but they were intense words, almost furious words, and they cut the air in that small kitchen to ribbons. She got up from her chair. But she didn't go to him. Instead, she stood by the table and faced him with her arms at her sides. "Look at me!"

He turned from the window.

She took a deep breath. "I've spent the better part of two days talking to myself in the mirror. I've got better things to do, so listen up. I'm a woman, not a child. I've been hurt before, and I'll be hurt again. No big deal. I have my weak moments, but this isn't one of them."

He lowered his eyes to look at the table.

"Look at me!"

He did that.

"I love you, Arthur. I love you more than I love him. I know that with all my goddamn heart. I don't have time to do this like they do it in the movies, so here it comes. I've made my choice. I'll love you as hard as I can and I'll love you like you won't believe. Just you. But I won't martyr myself to that . . . that . . . that thing I saw trying to kill Mike. Not me. Not Melody. I'm too strong for that. Not too weak, Arthur, too strong! I won't waste my love on half a man. Not anymore. Not in this life. I'm too damn good a person."

He said nothing, only stood there.

"Whatever it is you do, you won't do it anymore and have me. I can get through tomorrow. My world's not that empty. A woman knows how to hope and she damn well knows how to hurt. It's what we do, and we're good at it."

Arthur could not take his eyes from hers.

She reached down and spun the newspaper around on the table-top so it faced him. "I think I know what *you* do. Do you think you can save the whole world? Look. Look!" She flattened the front page with the palm of one hand, then jabbed a finger at the headlines and pictures. "Three kids burned while their mother is out getting drugs. Two nuns raped in the back of a church. An old guy shot on his way to the library. Some guy who admits to a dozen rapes just released from prison. Are you going to fix all this? Are you? How much time do you think you have? Let it go! Let it go while you still have a chance to love someone like me!"

He looked where she pointed, stared at the newspaper. He didn't speak.

"Make up your mind, Arthur." Softer words. "Make up your mind." She stepped over to him and with the undefiled candor of a small child took his hand and kissed him on the cheek. He made a move to put his arms around her, but she stopped him and stepped back. "No," she said. "Not that, not today. You go somewhere and figure it out. Go somewhere and hurt like I hurt right now. Don't make me settle for second best."

He nodded.

She walked straight through the living room to the front door. He rinsed his cup, placed it upside down on the sink board, and followed.

She held the door open.

He stepped past her into the hall. He halted and, with his back to her, he said, "Better get that phone off the toaster."

"I'll get around to it."

When he turned to face her, she saw tears in his eyes, and her spirit ached like it had never ached before. "I love you, Arthur," she said quietly. But she didn't move.

She watched as he touched the broken ribs on his left side. Or did he touch his heart?

"Go get an honest job, Arthur. I'll be here. But I won't be here forever. Not me. Go decide."

"I'll go," he said. "Maybe I *will* get an honest job." Then he almost smiled. "Maybe I'll open a fix-it shop."

She saw the almost. And wondered. "What can *you* fix?"

"Tomorrows."

"What do you mean by that?"

"It beats fixing yesterdays. Give me a chance and I'll show you." He turned and went down the stairs.

He was gone.

She closed the door.

She headed for the kitchen and brushed against the end table. The Hummel figurine, the boy holding the green umbrella, toppled off onto the thin fringe of the secondhand rug and shattered. Because Melody was crying, she didn't hear it fall. And she didn't hear it break.

Epilogue

The two stood on red sand beneath a sky of yellow oil. They were shadows.

Ten feet apart they were, and the child-shape threw a ball to the man-shape. Far behind them, near a black rock that sat beneath a black tree that grew beside a pool of silver water, a small black dog ran and made red dust swirl. The dog barked at a hawk that soared high above the red sand, that soared higher than the yellow sky . . . that soared up near the edge of things. On the left horizon towered a shale pile, a heaped stack of heavy slate that cracked and clicked and snapped inside itself, with no outside thing to act upon it. The brittle sounds came across red sand and through all that place, but did not come loudly.

"You see?" said the man-shadow. "I told you."

The black ball curved through yellow air. The boy-shape caught the ball with its glove. "Yes, you told me."

The ball was thrown back. The man-shape caught it with both hands and tossed it again. The boy-shadow caught the ball and stopped the sequence. It held the ball and looked at the man-shape and asked a question: "Have you seen her?"

"Yes."

"What is she like?"

The man-shadow shifted its feet and looked away.

"Did you do something to her?" asked the boy-shadow.

"One night. Yes." The man-shadow did not seem to want to say more. Instead, it receded at great speed over the sand and disappeared into the deep distance. But its words sounded for the boy-shadow as if the distance were not real . . . "I think we can be left alone now. I will catch the ball with you later."

The boy-shape walked across red sand and came to a place where a black man with silver hair sat at a blue table and dealt cards to a fat man wearing a white shirt and tan pants. The black man wore a blue-gray uniform, a bus driver's short-peaked cap. From the fat man's neck hung a lavender necktie . . . next to his elbow a pocketknife rested on the table with its blade opened. The flesh of the fat man's face and arms was charred black . . . a mismatched image of burnt flesh and unburnt fabric . . . a child's nightmare construction. But the fat man showed no pain.

In the center of the table, beside the stack of discards, a single long-stemmed rose extended from a delicate crystal vase. The boy-shape looked at the rose and touched it with one finger, then smiled, turned, and walked away. The small black dog scampered out of time and followed.

The fat man called out, "Hey, Red!"

The boy-shadow stopped and looked back. A friendly grin split the face beneath the fat man's tiny eyes.

The fat man spoke once more:

"So long, kid!"

THE END